Julie Ellis is the author of, among other books, *The Only Sin*, *Rich Is Best* and *East Wind*. She lives in New York City.

£2·00

By the same author

Rich Is Best
Maison Jennie
East Wind
The Only Sin

JULIE ELLIS

Glorious Morning

GRAFTON BOOKS

A Division of the Collins Publishing Group

LONDON GLASGOW
TORONTO SYDNEY AUCKLAND

Grafton Books
A Division of the Collins Publishing Group
8 Grafton Street, London W1X 3LA

A Grafton UK Paperback Original 1989

Copyright © Julie Ellis 1982

ISBN 0-586-20369-9

Printed and bound in Great Britain by
Collins, Glasgow

Set in Sabon

All rights reserved. No part of this publication may
be reproduced, stored in a retrieval system, or
transmitted, in any form, or by any means, electronic,
mechanical, photocopying, recording or otherwise,
without the prior permission of the publishers.

This book is sold subject to the condition that it
shall not, by way of trade or otherwise, be lent,
re-sold, hired out or otherwise circulated
without the publisher's prior consent in any
form of binding or cover other than that in
which it is published and without a similar
condition including this condition being imposed
on the subsequent purchaser.

For Bessie Satlof and Esther and Sam Meyers – three
very special people.

1

Fourteen-year-old Rissa Lindowska swept her long, dark hair away from her face as her eyes sought to penetrate the cellar darkness. She leaned forward to collect potatoes from the near-empty barrel, and tried to find pleasure rather than fear in the realization that tonight was the seventh eve of Passover.

On the seventh eve of Passover three years before – in 1903 – the Jews of Kishinev were massacred with a brutality that stunned the world. Grandpa said it would never happen to them in their small *dorf* – too few houses to be called a *shtetl* – sixty kilometers from Warsaw. God would not allow it to happen to them. Grandpa was on special terms with God.

But this morning, like everyone of an age to understand, Rissa had been terrified when a man from the Christian village rode into the *dorf* with the accusation that a young Christian girl had been raped by a Jewish boy, David Pinski, the son of Abraham Pinski.

The girl said that David had sneaked into the village early in the morning and accosted her as she drew water from the well.

Despite her fear she had been proud when grandpa, the *dorf*'s rabbi, said that he would return to the village with the man and talk to the peasants.

Grandpa was respected even by those in the Christian village. They knew he was a man of honor.

Grandpa told the villagers he knew it could not have been a boy from his *dorf*. At that hour of the morning every male over the age of thirteen had been in his presence reciting the morning prayers. He swore this before God. He came home convinced that all was well.

'Rissa, my heart – ' her mother called from the kitchen of the two-room thatch-roofed cottage, 'bring up extra potatoes.' Mama had forced herself to forget what happened this morning. Had not grandpa said that everything was well? For mama that was enough. 'Grandpa has invited two *luftmenshen* for supper.'

'Mama, again?' Rissa protested. Each year papa and mama struggled to have enough for the Passover table, and each year grandpa brought *luftmenshen*. Those with no real trade, who 'lived on air.' As the rabbi, grandpa felt it was his obligation.

'Rissa, we must have *rachmones*,' mama chided. To grandpa, *rachmones* – compassion – was the mark of a true Jew. 'And stop dreaming. We have work to do.'

'I'm looking for potatoes without eyes,' Rissa alibied.

Mama thought she was dreaming about the evening a month ago, when she was Queen Esther in the Purim play. And mama knew she dreamed about going to America, though papa said that could never be. Such stories came back about the country across the ocean! Her face lighted in recall. Tekla, the wise woman of their *dorf*, said that someday she – Rissa

8

Lindowska – would go to America. She would become rich and important. In America this could happen even to a woman.

Papa said that to go to America was to cease to be a Jew. In America the ones who dared call themselves Jews ate *trayf*. To them the Sabbath was just another day in the week. Twice a year – on Rosh Hashanah and on Yom Kippur – they remembered they were Jews and went to *shul*. Some didn't even fast on Yom Kippur.

But grandpa, the rabbi, closed his eyes to tradition and taught her to read Hebrew and Polish, even though she was a girl. From him she had learned to be as fluent in Polish as in Yiddish when no one else in their *dorf* spoke more than a few words of Polish.

When a stranger passing through left behind a Yiddish newspaper from Warsaw, grandpa secretly devoured it even though it was three months old. Even though the strictest Jews said the newspapers were full of heresy. And grandpa managed to leave it around so that she, Rissa, could read it, too.

Papa worried that the others in the *dorf* might come to recognize that grandpa was less strict than the Talmud demanded. Though he never talked about it, grandpa had lived for a while in the big city of Warsaw.

Rissa straightened her small, slight frame and frowned, shaken from the reveries that made life endurable by a surge of unfamiliar sounds above her.

'Mama?' she called uneasily.

The trapdoor had dropped into place without a sound. The meager light provided by the opening in the cellar was gone. In total blackness Rissa clutched at the edge of the barrel.

Terror descended upon her. Something terrible was happening upstairs. Since she was old enough to understand, she had lived – like every Jew in Poland and Russia – in fear of pogroms.

Above her she heard a rush of heavy feet. Shouts. Her mother screamed.

'Mama!' she cried out without a sound. 'Mama – '

A chorus of screams rent the air, rising above the clamor. She heard the sounds of women shrieking epithets, and she knew the intruders were the peasants from the Christian village. They had not believed grandpa this morning.

Rissa gritted her teeth to stifle the anguish that threatened to pour forth as she listened to the rampage above her. She flinched at the smashing of furniture. The frightened cries of her brother Joseph, not yet a year old.

And then the cries stopped abruptly.

Rissa was immobilized. A statue of ice. What was happening upstairs to mama and papa, grandpa and the children? Her four brothers and sisters? She clutched at the barrel for support. Her mouth was dry. Her heart pounded. She knew she must stay here. She could not help her family by going up into the kitchen. Mama had told her what the peasants did to young girls in a pogrom.

Why didn't they go? *'God, why don't You stop them? Why do You let this happen?'* she railed in ineffectual pain and rage.

Why didn't the soldiers come? She grasped at the

10

dim hope. She knew they wouldn't come until tomorrow or the next day. Grandpa had told the family that this was the way it always was. In Kishinev the soldiers and the police could have stopped the pogrom. They chose not to.

With startling suddenness every sound in the two rooms above the cellar ceased. Rissa listened tensely. No sound. Not even a whimper. Nothing. She groped for the stairs. But instinct laid a heavy hand on her as she set one foot on the bottom step.

'You must not go upstairs yet, Rissa!'

It was as though mama's voice spoke to her. She must wait for a sign that it was safe. A drunken peasant might still linger in the cottage. A shiver darted through her. On those rare times when she went to the Christian village with mama to sell beets, she had seen the way the men looked at her.

She started up the insecure wooden planks that served as stairs. Halted again. Her mother's voice in her ear.

'Rissa, wait until it is safe.' The peasants could be at the house next door. They might return.

So many times she had listened to the stories of how young girls like herself were mistreated by peasants and soldiers alike. When a pogrom came upon a *dorf* or *shtetl*, young girls were hidden in feather quilts or barrels or in cellars as she herself had.

Wait, mama's voice commanded. Only when every peasant had returned to his village could she help her family.

Trembling, Rissa sat on the bottom step. Subconsciously she rocked to and fro in the eternal movement of anguish. The dirt beneath her bare feet was winter-cold, though it was late April. The air was musty and damp with the trapdoor shut. The horror that she had feared all her life had come to pass.

Rissa strained to hear some sounds of life in the cottage. She sat until she could sit no more. At last she hurried up the stairs and pushed the trapdoor upward. It opened partially, encountered an impediment. For a moment panic gripped her. Then she understood. Mama must have pulled the table above the opening to the cellar. Hoping the peasants would not see the trapdoor. Though she was a woman, mama was wise.

Rissa contrived to push the table aside, climbed up on hands and knees and emerged from beneath the table. The candles had burned low. They lent a meager illumination. But there was sufficient light for her to see the devastation wrought by the intruders.

Every piece of furniture in the two rooms had been hacked into pieces and thrown into a heap at one side of the kitchen. Then, at the edge of the rubble, she spied a figure on the floor.

'Mama!' Her voice rose into a high, thin wail. 'Oh, mama, mama!'

Rissa dropped to her knees before the body of her mother. Mama lay on her back. Her eyes stared upward in death. Her dark cotton dress had been thrust high above her thighs, her undergarments ripped away. Sick at her mother's shame, Rissa pulled down the dress, then buried her face upon her mother's breast.

'Mama, mama – ' How could she go on living without mama?

Fresh fear brought her to her feet. Where was papa? Grandpa? The younger children? She stumbled across the kitchen to the doorway of the other room of the cottage. She stopped there, her mind refusing to accept what met her eyes.

Bodies lay strewn about the small room. Grandpa. Still wrapped in his *tallith*, a hand clutching Katie's small hand. Papa, holding Joseph in his arms. Hannah and Chaim – who was to have been bar mitzvahed next month – clinging together in death.

The room moved before her. The bodies on the floor swayed in a macabre dance. Mercifully, she slid to the floor in oblivion.

Rissa stirred into consciousness. Moaning as she returned to ugly reality. Only one candle remained lighted. Dark shadows shrouded the still-warm bodies. With an effort Rissa pulled herself to her feet. Her family was gone. She was alone.

What about the Kaminskys next door? The Epsteins on the other side? She dragged herself into the ominous silence of the night. Absurdly a near-full moon lent eerie brilliance to the earth below.

Not a house was lighted, yet doors were flung wide open. She spied the figure of a woman lying face down in a muddy puddle between the Epstein cottage and her own. Her breathing labored, fearful of what she would find, Rissa crossed to stoop beside the woman. Her wig had been ripped off and lay beside her.

Gently Rissa turned her over. An involuntary scream rose in her throat and pierced the night. One breast had been cut off. Her stomach ripped open. Rissa turned away from the desecrated body, a hand at her mouth as she battled against nausea.

Now she summoned a strength of which she had not thought herself capable. She walked from house to house to see if anyone other than herself remained alive. But as she had known in her heart, she was alone.

She mustn't stay here. She must run lest the peasants decide to return to burn the houses to the ground. Even as she moved quickly back to her own cottage, she resolved *she* would survive. As Tekla, the wise woman, had prophesied, she would live to make the name of Lindowska honored before the world. A memorial for her family, for whom she could not even sit *shivah*. Could not bury.

With a deep breath, she forced herself to go inside. She dropped to her knees for one final embrace of each family member. Over each beloved body she whispered:

'*Yisgadal v'yisgadash shmei raboh. Amen.*'

'Magnified and sanctified by His great name in the world that He has created according to His will.'

Though it was not for a woman to say Kaddish, Rissa was sure that God would understand.

Tenderly she removed from her grandfather the embroidered white silk *tallith* that was his pride. Grandpa's prayer shawl was all that she would take with her from this house of death. At thirteen a boy became a man. Today, at fourteen, she became a woman.

She sped on bare feet from the house and out into the night that would forever remain etched in her memory. Her vow to survive gave her courage and strength. She – Rissa Lindowska, who had never been more than six kilometers from her home – would go to Warsaw.

2

By night, her grandfather's *tallith* protecting her against the chill, Rissa walked as though pursued across the undulating fields of rye, oats and beets.

A constant inner dialogue plagued her. How could she wish to live when mama and papa, grandpa and the children lay dead? But mama wished her to live. Only because of mama's quickness of wit was she alive. Wasn't that a sign she was to go on? God had spared her for some larger purpose. She was to make something important of her life as Tekla, the wise woman, had prophesied.

Rissa walked until her body rebelled. By day she concealed herself in the woods, thick with pine and spruce, tensing at every woodland sound. Small animals darting about the earth. A pine cone falling to the ground. An unexpected burst of song from a bird on a bough above her. She searched the brush for early berries and mushrooms to assuage her hunger, drank from springs or brooks.

Rissa kept count of the days as each drew to a frightening, lonely close. At intervals her hands stroked the soft silk of her grandfather's *tallith*, folded across her breasts. She envisioned grandpa at the Passover table, in their tiny *shul* on Rosh Hashanah and Yom Kippur. She visualized her family seated around the Friday-night supper where mama

16

had blessed the candles. For a poignant moment she could believe they were alive.

On the fourth day of her journey a young peasant girl coming into the woods for a tryst with her lover compassionately gave Rissa bread and milk and told her which road to follow to Warsaw. In the city, Rissa sought to convince herself, there would be other Jews to help her. She would no longer be alone. She would find work.

On the seventh night of her flight, while the first pink streaks of dawn warned that she must take cover, Rissa heard a wagon rumbling close by. She spun about in alarm. She stood in the midst of fields hung with fog. The nearest refuge – the woods – stretched at an ominous distance.

Then she heard the sounds of their voices in song. Excitement brought color to her face. They were singing *Rozhinkes mit Mandeln*. 'Raisins and Almonds.' They were Jews. Impulsively Rissa darted forward into their path.

'Please – ' She spoke to them in Yiddish. 'Do you have room for one more in your wagon?'

A middle-aged man with a warm smile and a slight paunch jumped down. A small, spare, elderly woman sat on the board while three others – the man's wife and two daughters, Rissa assumed – were in the back.

'We're on our way to Warsaw,' the man told her.

'I, too.' She was breathless with relief.

'I am Yankel Paulowski. This is my wife, Feigele, her mother – Bubbi,' he bowed to the elderly woman with a flourish that told Rissa there was real affection

17

between them, 'and my two daughters, Esther and Manya.' Yankel's wife was a big-bosomed woman with strong, pleasant features. Esther and Manya seemed to be in their late teens, Manya the younger.

'I'm Rissa Lindowska.' All at once she was shy.

'What is a young and pretty girl like you doing away from her *shtetl?*' Bubbi clucked. But her sharp, dark eyes, which showed the sadness of one who has seen much pain, were gentle.

In tortured gasps, reliving the horror so close behind her, Rissa told them of the pogrom. The kind of horror Jews had known for thousands of years. The atmosphere was pungent with their sympathy. Their rage. Bubbi rocked back and forth in an anguish that had become her own.

'Word came to us on the farm that a pogrom had hit a nearby village. When will it stop?' Yankel reached to help Rissa into the wagon. 'You will stay with us in Warsaw.'

'Yankel,' Feigele fretted, looking nervously behind them, 'come. Let's be on our way.'

'Rissa will help in the house,' Yankel decided while he prodded the horses into movement. 'Manya's bed is big enough for two.

'And Bubbi can stop complaining about how hard she works. When we have to go off and play on tour in the hot months, Bubbi will not be alone. Rissa will be with her.' Yankel chuckled at Rissa's air of bewilderment. 'We are an acting family. Not so fine as the Kaminska family. We don't act in a grand theater like the Elysium on Karova Street or the

Jardin d'Hiver on Chmielna Street, but we perform well,' he said with relish.

Manya looked at Rissa with friendly curiosity. 'A fire broke out in our theater,' she explained. 'While they fixed the damages, we went to visit cousins on a farm nearby. But we have to be in Warsaw tonight because we are appearing in Goldfaden's *Shulamith*.'

'When there's no business for us in Warsaw – like in the summer – we play the "railroad station theaters." That means,' Yankel continued, 'that we must play, because of the police, on the platform of the railroad station. There the police cannot touch us. We take the money, get on the next train out, and pouf, we're off to play the next "railroad station theater."'

Rissa's feelings were in a torment of confusion. The joy and relief at being once again with people she could talk to, people who would help her – even take care of her – gave way to mistrust. She was upset to discover the people in the wagon were an acting family. Papa thought actors were not respectable; the theater, he said, was an abomination. But grandpa had confessed to her in secret that, years ago in Warsaw, he had seen a performance of *Shulamith*.

'We play "German theater."' Feigele's face was eloquent with sarcasm. 'We say the lines in *daytshmerish* – a Yiddish that sounds like German, because in 'eighty-three the czar – ' she spit into the brightening dawn, 'the czar prohibited Yiddish theater. But most times we talk Yiddish unless we think a spy from the czar is in the theater.'

Rissa stared from one member of the Paulowskis

19

to another. They had accepted her so quickly – a total stranger – an orphan. Who was she to make judgments?

'I'll work hard for you,' Rissa stammered. 'I can cook. Mama taught me. I'll clean and wash and sew.'

'And before long you'll be looking to the theater.' Bubbi nodded knowingly. 'And wanting a part in the play.'

The wagon rumbled over the narrow cobblestoned streets of Warsaw. Only a sprinkling of people hurried through the early morning, en route to work or church or synagogue. Rissa strove to see everything at once. Yet simultaneously she was frightened by so much that was new.

Manya appointed herself Rissa's guide. She pointed out the fourteenth-century Gothic cathedral of St John, and further on the royal castle that overlooked the Vistula. In Castle Square Rissa saw the monument to King Sigismund III Vasa, erected in 1643, then a street – Krakow Boulevard, Manya identified it – lined with palaces and churches built as early as the fifteenth century.

Soon they were traveling along less elegant streets. Here many of the men and boys wore *yarmulkes*. She saw wooden synagogues and prayer houses. Esther told her that this was the district where most of the Warsaw Jews lived. The tension that had brought an ache to Rissa's shoulder blades seemed to retreat. She felt a little less alone.

Rissa sniffed at the aromas of fresh bread baking in a shop, realizing her hunger. She craned her head

20

to follow the actions of a man hanging long sausages from the ceiling of another store. Everywhere were signs that announced kosher food.

'Our flat is on Krochmalna Street,' Manya told her. 'Near the square.'

'And you can't wait to get back,' Esther giggled, 'because next door lives Meir, who sits in the coffee house all night and talks about Zionism.'

'Better Meir the Zionist than Esther's friend the Socialist,' her mother said drily. 'What good does a strike bring to the Jew when nobody wants him in the factories that pay better? And if he works in a small shop and demands more wages, what is his master to do but close up? You can't get blood from a turnip.'

'Mama, the Socialists are fighting for our rights.' Esther was zealous. 'Jacob says that a new soul has entered him since he started to study with a Socialist teacher.'

'So what was wrong with the old soul?' Yankel demanded. 'All of a sudden what was all right for the mama and papa is no good for the children.'

Rissa listened in astonishment to the talk that rippled so freely between the members of Yankel's family. Manya's Bubbi wore the traditional wig, but everything else about this Jewish family was strange to her.

Rissa soon learned that in Warsaw, Jews went to museums and theaters and libraries. They read the kind of books that papa had said were blasphemous. To read them was to burn in hell or to come back to the world as an animal.

Grandpa had always nodded his head in agreement. Did not all the rabbis believe the same? Yet Rissa knew grandpa secretly read the Yiddish newspapers, and once she caught him with a book about scientific knowledge. An evil book that contradicted the holy books. He said he had taken it away from a boy in his class.

But in Warsaw even the women of the Paulowski family read the Yiddish newspapers and argued about what was said. Rissa was entering a frightening yet fascinating new world. She tried not to feel herself a traitor to grandpa and papa and mama; for so long unasked questions had plagued her. Now she would ask, and she would receive answers.

The flat on Krochmalna Street, though it was in the Warsaw slums, seemed fine to Rissa, fresh from a *dorf*. In bed that first night Manya whispered that in certain houses near the square were brothels, where young girls like her could be pushed into prostitution.

'A pretty young girl must be careful in the city,' Manya warned, and Rissa trembled with pleasure that Manya thought her pretty. Manya herself was beautiful. Tall, with huge dark eyes and midnight hair. 'Here there are men looking for girls like us. They drag them off in their carriages, and the next thing they know they're on a ship for Buenos Aires, in South America. To work in houses like the ones on Krochmalna Square.'

'I'll be careful,' Rissa promised. Shivering at the prospect of being snatched away by such men. 'It won't happen to me.'

* * *

After her initial excitement, Rissa was once again overwhelmed by sadness. She sought to ease her grief by work. Yet at unguarded moments her mind was assaulted by sounds best hidden away. By torturous images. By unanswerable questions. Why was she here in the flat on Krochmalna Street? She should have died with mama and papa and grandpa and the children. Little Joseph, who had not yet learned to walk, and Chaim, who should have been bar mitzvahed by now. Tiny Katie and Hannah, who had been mama's Hanukkah present.

With painful regularity she awoke with a scream rising in her throat, in a cold sweat, because once again she saw herself climbing out from the table above the trapdoor in the kitchen.

But all her anguish lay locked within her, too terrible to be paraded even before the compassionate Paulowski family. Work, she ordered herself. Keep busy every waking moment. Go to bed at night too tired to do more than listen to Manya's prattle about what had happened in the theater that day.

The flat shone in cleanliness. Rissa helped Bubbi with the meals. She washed and ironed. She sewed costumes. And she held the *bikhl* – the script – while Manya strove to learn the lines of the newest play in the company's repertory.

Manya and Esther teased her about clinging to the house. She refused to venture forth into the streets. Bubbi scolded them. Bubbi understood.

'When Rissa is ready to go into the streets, then she will go,' Bubbi said with regal authority. Bubbi knew what it was to endure a pogrom. She had lived a long time. She told Rissa about Prince Czartoryski, who hunted Jews because there was not enough game left in the province to make him happy.

At intervals during the day and in the evening when only Bubbi and she remained in the flat, Rissa hung out the front window, watching the procession of people that marched along Krochmalna Street from morning till late at night.

She was astonished at the girls and women who dared to carry purses on the Sabbath, and at the mothers with children who defied the Talmud to show their bare heads in the streets. The boys laughed and talked with the girls. Once Manya confided that Meir had kissed her in the dark hall that led up to their flat.

If Manya wished to marry Meir, she could do this. Marriages were not arranged as they were in the *shtetl*. Sometimes she heard the sounds that came from the kitchen, where Yankel slept with Feigele. When they came home from the theater and the performance had gone well, Yankel would slap Feigele across the rump and tell her she drove him wild.

Rissa had never thought about how it would be to marry. The purpose of marriage was to have children because that made God happy. But in the Paulowski household Rissa learned something new and startling about the relationship between a man and a woman. She had seen farm animals mate. She knew what happened when the peasants or soldiers grabbed a young girl. But this was different.

Feigele worried that Esther was so in love with Jacob that she would go off with him to Palestine.

24

And Yankel talked with reverence about a Yiddish writer in Warsaw named Peretz. He was a lawyer forbidden to practice law because he had taught unionism to groups of workers. Esther idealized him because he taught respect for women. To his house came earnest young writers, who talked with him far into the night about the new Yiddish culture that was springing up all over Europe.

'It began more than a hundred years ago,' Yankel said in a rare serious mood, 'when Moses Mendelssohn in Germany began the movement to make the Jews expand their lives. Oh, the rabbis moaned and carried on; but the Jew has a thirst for knowledge. The young men — and the young women,' he added with an air of great revelation, 'they all want to know about the rest of the world.'

She wanted to know, Rissa acknowledged. Just reading the Yiddish newspaper each day made her realize how much she wanted to learn, and once again she yearned to go to America. The papers were full of stories about that great country. Someday she would go to America, she vowed. But as Bubbi would say, this was not the time. She did not yet know enough. But the time would come, and she would go.

The hot Warsaw summer gave way to autumn. Rissa and Bubbi, left behind when the troupe traveled, rejoiced in their return. Again the flat was filled with the sounds of laughter and good-humored argument. But Rissa dreaded the approach of Rosh Hashanah. The New Year. The first Rosh Hashanah she would not share with mama and papa, grandpa and the children.

25

She helped Bubbi with the heavy cleaning that was part of the holiday preparations. She climbed up to bring down the special dishes for the holidays. She polished the candlesticks – with tears spilling over as she visualized mama polishing the candlesticks in their thatch-roofed cottage. On the morning before Rosh Hashanah eve she helped Bubbi with the two round *hallah* that were part of the New Year tradition – round so that there should be no end of good things.

Well before sunset, as tradition demanded, the family sat down to partake of the holiday supper. Rissa fought against fresh tears as she remembered other Rosh Hashanahs, when grandpa sat at the head of the table. She watched Yankel take knife in hand and begin the *brokha* as he sliced a large chunk of *hallah*.

She clenched her teeth to push back the sobs that threatened to emerge. Yankel tore the chunk of *hallah* into six pieces so that there would be one piece for each of those at the table. He took each piece and dipped it into honey before he passed it down to the others – honey so that it would be a sweet and good year.

When at last the holiday supper was over, Rissa helped Bubbi and Feigele clear away the dishes and wash them. Tonight she would leave the flat to go to *shul* with the family. Out of respect for her family she must do this. She would sit with the other women behind the curtain that separated them from the men.

But except for venturing to *shul* on Rosh Hashanah and again on Yom Kippur, Rissa clung to the house.

* * *

'Rissa, go to the library,' Bubbi said grandly one afternoon, and produced a groschen from a box that held her personal belongings. 'For money you can even bring a book home for a month. Go,' she commanded. 'You have been long enough in the house.'

The prize was too enticing to reject. Groschen in hand Rissa set out to find the library on Novelinki Street.

Despite her shyness and fear Rissa breathed in the excitement of the city, guilty that she could feel such exhilaration. She walked slowly, staring into the window of a coffee shop where patrons ate rolls with herring or enjoyed slabs of cheesecake. She passed shops where salt pretzels and bagels were sold.

She walked past bakeries and grocery stores and taverns, intrigued by the differences between people in the streets. The Orthodox men wore long black coats and forelocks flanking their beards, and the young men without beards dressed in a fashion she had come to recognize as modern. She saw Orthodox women like mama, with wigs covering their shaven heads, and lively young matrons who wore their own hair – sometimes long, sometimes even cut short.

Rissa found the library, walked into the huge, high-ceilinged room where more books were on display than she ever imagined could exist. The books were printed in both Hebrew and Yiddish and even girls were allowed to read, though Manya told her that not even Christian girls could go to the university in Warsaw. The library became Rissa's obsession. Each week Rissa went to borrow more books. No more did the man there ask her for money. He gave her the books for free.

On a late February afternoon, the sky laden with fresh snow, Bubbi stopped her at the door with instructions to hurry to the theater instead of the library. She must take a freshly pressed costume for Manya. It was the first night of a new play; Manya must look her best. She would have no time to come home between rehearsal and performance.

'How will I get to the theater?' Panic overwhelmed her.

'On your feet,' Bubbi said drily.

The theater was Manya's other life that Rissa and she whispered about at night in bed. A new young man had come into the company; Manya thought perhaps he was more handsome than Meir. The leading woman was a pig, who kept putting in things that were not in the script.

'Bubbi, nobody knows me at the theater,' Rissa hedged.

'You will say that you bring the costume for Manya Paulowski to wear tonight. You will be admitted,' Bubbi insisted. 'Go, Rissa.'

Rissa hurried through the streets with the feeling that her life would never be quite the same after today. She had been invited often to attend a performance. She had demurred; she was in mourning. It would not be right to give herself such pleasure. Besides, she still wasn't quite sure it was respectable.

In truth she remembered the terrible stories whispered in the *dorf* about actors and actresses and was afraid to dishonor the memory of her family by going

28

to a performance, even though grandpa himself had gone to a performance in a weak moment. But now she must go. She had no choice.

She was breathless with anticipation as she approached the tiny theater. She knew that it was only a long, narrow store with a stage up front and about two hundred seats, but every night magic was offered on that stage. She paused to inspect the colorful posters plastered across the front. A proprietary pride filled her at the sight of the names she knew.

She explained her mission to the man who sold tickets and was ushered into the darkened theater. Only the stage was illuminated. Onstage the company was rehearsing. Enthralled she slid into a rear seat to watch for a few moments.

Each time Manya delivered her lines, Rissa said them with her, without sound, her lips framing the words. She knew the part as well as Manya. Better, because Manya made many mistakes.

When at last the rehearsal was over, Rissa rose to her feet and impulsively applauded. Color stained her high cheekbones as the short, balding man seated in the front row rose and swung about to confront her. But Yankel was smiling.

'Who is there?' the man's voice was imperious. He couldn't see her in the darkened theater. 'Come here.'

Rissa hurried down the aisle with her package.

'I have brought a costume for Manya Paulowski,' she explained, breathless in this fascinating new environment.

'Bring it to me, Rissa,' Manya called. 'And hurry

home before it grows dark,' she warned, leaning down from the stage to take the package.

'I will,' Rissa promised, shy before the penetrating stare of the director.

Every night in this theater Manya and Esther performed on the stage. How could it be wrong to bring pleasure to people who had so little? How wonderful to be an actress in the theater!

Rissa had already been up for three hours and busy in the kitchen with Bubbi when they heard Manya coughing in the next room. All night Manya had twisted and turned in the bed she shared with Rissa, sitting up at intervals in little fits of coughing.

'Feigele, do you hear Manya?' Yankel was worried.

'I'll take her a glass of hot tea,' Rissa offered. 'With honey for the cough.' That was what mama always gave them, Rissa remembered; and her grief was as fresh as yesterday.

'She won't be able to play tonight.' Feigele walked to the door, drowning in anxiety. 'What will we do?'

'Who'll play for her tonight?' Yankel spread his hands in a gesture of despair. 'At the theater already three actors are sick. All over Warsaw people have terrible colds. Mendele will be mad enough to kill.'

'I know Manya's part,' Rissa said softly. Her heart pounded at her daring. Yet the prospect of appearing on the stage with the company was too enticing to abandon. 'I could play it tonight. I know every line.' Her eyes darted pleadingly from Yankel to Feigele.

'Ooh!' Manya's wail rose to an outraged crescendo. 'Such *hutzpah*! I rehearsed for four whole days!'

After an hour of running through the scenes where Manya appeared, the cast retired to the two dressing rooms. Tea and black bread was served along with optimism from Mendele.

'Rissa, you will be fine,' he promised. 'The audience will love you. I guarantee it.'

When they had eaten, Esther applied the makeup Rissa was to wear onstage. She sat immobile, trying to brush from her mind the accusations she imagined papa would have heaped upon her for becoming part of the theater. But she could not believe it was wrong. The way she had lived at home was different from the way she was living now; but this way wasn't wrong.

'Rissa, you're beautiful,' Esther murmured, surveying her artistic efforts. 'How is it I never noticed?'

'Esther, what happens if I forget my lines?' Rissa clasped her hands together in alarm.

'Somebody else will talk,' Esther soothed. 'Don't worry. Talk loud,' she admonished. 'They get mad if they can't hear.'

When the curtain opened and she heard the voices of the audience, Rissa fought an impulse to flee. But she waited for her turn to walk out onto the stage. Soon she would no longer be Rissa. She would be the girl in Abraham Goldfaden's play.

Rissa moved through the performance in an aura of unreality. When the audience laughed not once, but three times, at what she said in the first act, she was exuberant. She was not a failure. The people in the seats out there, who had paid money to come into the theater, liked her.

'Rissa,' Mendele strode toward her as she started for the dressing room at the end of the performance. 'Tell Manya to give you the *bikhl* for tomorrow night's play.'

Rissa started in consternation.

'I don't know that one.'

'By tomorrow you'll know enough.' Mendele was philosophical. 'You'll play till Manya is well.' His eyes were smug. 'And when Manya comes back, we'll find other parts for you.'

At first the family was pleased that she had become part of the acting company. Rissa was ecstatic at appearing on the stage six nights a week. On Friday night, of course, they gave no performances in deference to the Orthodox Jews. Only Bubbi warned her that success would cause trouble.

Rissa was bewildered. But she knew that Manya was aggrieved that Rissa, who had never appeared on a real stage before, had replaced her for three nights.

When she received her 'mark' – her share of the receipts – from Mendele, she took it to Yankel.

'You give what Esther and Manya give,' he stipulated, handing part of the cherished wages back to her. 'Your share of what it takes to pay for the flat and buy the food.'

But as weeks sped past, Rissa emerged from the euphoria of being an actress. She was conscious of new tensions in the household. At night when they went to bed, Manya turned her back to Rissa and pretended to fall asleep immediately.

'Bubbi, what did I do wrong?' Rissa yearned to feel the affection she had received in her first months in the flat. 'Manya doesn't like me any more.'

'*An auleh – di kalle iz tsu sheyn*,' Bubbi dismissed this. A fault, the bride is too pretty. 'Now it's Rissa who is Mendele's little darling. Rissa who gets the best parts. Yankel says the audiences like you. Who can say why?' Bubbi was philosophical. 'God has blessed you.'

On a night when the theater had to be closed again because of a leaking roof, Rissa took herself to the fine Elysium Theater on Karova Street to see Esther Rachel Kaminska in *The Kreutzer Sonata*. Rissa knew she was in the presence of a great actress. She recognized that Kaminska played in a style of acting that was different and exciting. Tears of pleasure filled her eyes. Someday she would play like Esther Rachel Kaminska.

Rissa loved being part of the theater. It was her refuge from reality. From ugly, hurtful memories. But she knew she must soon leave the flat on Krochmalna Street, and this terrified her.

On a late spring evening, two nights after she had lit the *yortsayt* candles for her family killed in the pogrom, Rissa was astonished to be brought a bouquet of fresh violets. Among the heart-shaped leaves and five-petaled flowers was a small card.

'It's written in Polish,' Esther recognized with respect, though she couldn't read it. 'What does it say?'

'I hope you will do me the honor of having supper with me after the performance,' Rissa read. 'It's

35

signed "Phillip Cambridge."' She stumbled over the unfamiliar name.

'What kind of a name is that?' Manya was contemptuous. 'Not Polish.'

'Will you have supper with him?' Esther's eyes held a romantic glow. 'Make him take you to Dovidl's café,' she urged. 'It's expensive, but all the students go there for special occasions.'

'I can't,' Rissa said, shocked at the prospect. 'I mean, a man I don't know.' With a strange name such as she had never heard. She had never been alone with a man. Not even with a boy. She had listened in dismay to the stories Manya used to whisper to her beneath the blankets on their bed. To Manya it was delightful to be kissed by a man. Once, she confided, Meir — who considered himself a man though he was only eighteen — had dared to touch her breasts. 'No,' Rissa said resolutely. 'If he's waiting after the performance, then I'll walk right past him.'

Why was a man with a name like Phillip Cambridge attending a performance of Yiddish theater. Why was he sending violets to her? An excitement that was unnerving stirred in Rissa.

Tonight, at traitorous moments when she was not onstage, Rissa thought about Phillip Cambridge. Was he watching the performance? Would he be at the stage door when she left the theater? No! It was a mistake. The flowers were meant for somebody else, at another theater. No one would be there at the door waiting for her.

That she had been singled out for this attention —

if it could, by some miracle, be true – was exhilarating. She *would* go to supper with him. She *wouldn't* go. But instead of changing into the skirt and shirtwaist that she usually wore home, she changed into the flower-printed cotton she wore in the second act of tonight's performance.

Beset by exquisite anticipation and agonizing uncertainty, Rissa dawdled. The violets were in a glass of water on the makeup table. Manya and Esther had each rushed off to a rendezvous. Now Yankel and Feigele announced they were going to a café with some of the others.

'Come with us for cheesecake and tea?' Yankel asked.

'No, not this time,' Rissa refused with an awkward smile.

At last Rissa knew she must leave the theater. Her shawl draped about her shoulders and violets clutched in one hand, she moved self-consciously through the door to the street. A figure emerged from the shadows. A tall young man, dressed in the fashion of students. He had curling blond hair and handsome features. Instinctively Rissa knew the young man had come from a home where there was wealth. Her eyes discerned the fine materials, the expensive cut of his clothes.

'You're as beautiful offstage as on,' he said in satisfaction. His Polish was adequate but little more. 'I'm Phillip Cambridge.' His eyes bathed her in admiration.

'I can't have supper with you,' Rissa stammered. Yet she knew she would. 'I don't know you.'

37

'I've just told you who I am,' he laughed. 'I'm Phillip Cambridge from London. And I want desperately to paint you.'

'Are you an artist?' she asked, trying to cover her confusion.

'I want to paint more than anything in the world,' he admitted. Rissa saw rebellion and rage and frustration in his eyes, in the tautness of his mouth. Emotions she knew so well. 'My father demands that I join him in his business. That's why I'm here in Warsaw. To handle problems in a factory he owns here.'

'Are you a good artist?' She blushed at her temerity.

'I could be with the proper subject.' Phillip pulled her arm over his. 'But we'll talk about it over supper. Where shall we go?'

'Dovidl's,' she blurted out, lightheaded as she told him its location. She had never been to so fine a restaurant. She had been to a café with the Paulowski family and others from the theater. But to walk into Dovidl's with Phillip Cambridge was beyond her imagination.

They strolled in the soft night air of late spring. Two young people who captured the eyes of passersby because the glow about them set them apart. This was not happening to her, Rissa Lindowska. She was playing a part in a beautiful new play.

Phillip talked to her about his father, who was outraged at his decision to become an artist. As punishment his father had banished him to Warsaw for a month. Rissa listened with sympathy. Would her own father have been different?

Phillip talked about painters of hundreds of years ago. Leonardo da Vinci. Michelangelo. Rembrandt, who painted portraits of the Jewish rabbis who lived on his street. Was it because of Rembrandt that Phillip Cambridge was here in the Jewish quarters of Warsaw?

'Have you been to the National Museum?' Phillip asked eagerly. 'They have some magnificent paintings.'

'No.' Her voice was low and sweet. Her heart pounded with the pleasure of standing beside Phillip Cambridge. She dared not let herself think what papa and mama would have said about her being alone with a man. A *goy*. But here in Warsaw girls were more free. Yet she knew even in Warsaw there were girls who lived as she had lived in the *dorf*. Who would never dare to walk in the streets with a boy. 'I know little of Warsaw. I've been here only a year.' The Warsaw he knew would not be her Warsaw.

'Have you been to the Saxony Garden?' he pursued, his smile dazzling.

'No,' she confessed.

'Rissa, we have so much to see!' He was jubilant.

Her eyes incandescent, she walked with Phillip into Dovidl's, the exotic haunt of students, in a celebratory mood. Most of the patrons were young. The sounds convivial, the scents savory. White tablecloths and candles on each table.

For a moment, when Phillip stopped talking, Rissa trembled. What could she talk about to someone so

39

educated and fine? But the waiter came, and Phillip conversed with him easily about their supper. Rissa tried not to laugh at his awkward Polish.

Then they were alone again. Her heart raced while she searched her mind for something to say.

'Why did you come to the Yiddish theater?' she asked at last, color flooding her face.

'A friend in London told me that the most beautiful girls in Europe were on the Yiddish stage. When I saw you, I knew he was right.' He leaned forward, absorbing every feature of her delicately chiseled face. 'I must paint you.'

The next two hours were an ecstatic haze. When Phillip deposited her at the flat on Krochmalna Street, he lifted her hand to his lips and told her they would go tomorrow to Saxony Garden during her hours away from the theater.

'It's the perfect time of year, people tell me,' he said. 'When may I come for you?'

The days swept into one another as Phillip Cambridge showed Rissa a Warsaw she had never experienced. They visited museums, walked through Saxony Garden – where, Esther told her, men in the long gaberdines and married women in the wigs of the Orthodox Jews were not allowed. They strolled through Lazienki Park, inspected the fine old palaces and churches. And all the while Phillip pleaded with her to pose for him.

Rissa knew that the Paulowskis disapproved of her seeing Phillip. Each for a different reason. Bubbi was outraged that Rissa was spending hours each day with a foreigner. A *goy*. Yankel reproached in silence, with long looks and shakes of the head. Feigele declared Rissa was giving herself airs. Only Esther approved. Rissa was like a character in one of the novels serialized in the Yiddish newspapers, which she read with religious fervor.

Manya warned her she would find only unhappiness with Phillip.

'He'll go back to London, and what'll you have left? The fancy presents he gives you? He'll never marry you.'

Each night at supper Phillip would present her with some small gift. A piece of jewelry, a miniature, a fine handkerchief. And each night he pleaded with her to come to the house on Stare Miasto Square, in the old quarter of Warsaw, where he was staying. The house had been loaned to him by a family friend.

'There are a dozen servants in the house,' he pleaded. 'We'll not be alone.' One evening he pressed her more fervently than usual. 'How can I go back to London without having painted you?'

Rissa was stricken. Three weeks had fled by. She had refused to see reality, to remember he was only a visitor to Warsaw. Now Phillip talked of going back to London. How could she go back to a life without Phillip? She had so quickly accustomed herself to his presence in her life. She awoke each day with instant realization that in two hours, or three or four, she would see Phillip. He dominated every waking moment.

'I should leave this week,' Phillip admitted. 'I can push for a week beyond. Rissa, love – ' He reached for her hand and pressed it to his lips. 'Come to the house tonight.'

She could no longer refuse.

She would pose for Phillip in that house full of servants. And afterwards he would bring her home to Krochmalna Street and kiss her in the darkness of the hall.

The feelings that surged through her when Phillip held her in his arms and kissed her were frightening and wonderful. But Phillip knew she was not one of those girls Manya had whispered about, who did the things with men that a girl did only with her husband – and then only to produce the children God wanted of them.

Phillip found a droshky to take them to the house. Rissa was trembling. In the droshky Phillip tried to entertain her with stories of his travels in Italy, where he had gone for a summer and secretly studied with an artist; but Rissa thought only of the end of her idyll with Phillip. He would go to London, and she'd never see him again.

The droshky deposited them before a house with a white sloping roof and a gray front with ornate sculptured adornments. They were admitted by a servant and walked into the elegantly furnished foyer.

'Frederic, we're famished. Will you please ask Hela to send supper up to my rooms?'

Rissa allowed Phillip to take her hand and lead her up the wide curving staircase to the pair of rooms that were his private quarters. She had never been inside so magnificent a house.

'There's a balcony off this room,' Phillip said,

crossing the beautiful old rug to push aside gold brocade drapes that masked a tall narrow window. 'Come, look.'

Rissa stood beside Phillip on the balcony and gazed out upon a small courtyard bathed in moonlight. She felt the touch of his lips at her throat as his arms moved from behind her to encircle her waist. She trembled at his nearness.

'Oh, Rissa love – ' He turned her about to face him. Towering above her. 'How can I go back to London without you?'

His lips reached hungrily for hers. His arms held her tightly against him. The whole world ebbed away before the intensity of her emotions.

'How wonderful it would be if the two of us could go to Italy together,' he whispered. 'I'd paint all day while you posed for me. And all night we'd make love.'

Still clinging together, they heard a faint knock at the door. Phillip cursed under his breath at the swiftness of Frederic's arrival, but he stepped decorously away from Rissa as he received the servant.

Frederic brought in a silver tray and placed it on a small mahogany dining table which he proceeded to move in front of the sofa covered in needlepoint. Rissa was awed by the beauty of the translucent gold-rimmed white plates, the matching cups and saucers, the gleaming silver.

'Shall I pour, sir?' Frederic asked, a hand at the silver teapot.

Phillip dismissed him with a wave of his hand.

Rissa sat beside Phillip on the sofa. They were

43

alone. She ate, aware that the food on the plates before them was such as she had never tasted, yet too uneasy at being alone with Phillip to enjoy the delicacies.

'More tea, Rissa?' Phillip tried to put her at ease.

'Please.' Her voice was unsteady. She fought against an urge to flee. Her eyes darted about the small sitting room. 'Where are your paints?'

'In my studio through the door there,' he said. 'When you've finished with your tea, I'll show you.'

Her heart pounded before the ardor she saw in his eyes. Phillip was neither a Jew nor a Pole; but he, too, was in rebellion. The young Jews rebelled against the rules of the old. The Polish rebelled against Russian rule. And Phillip rebelled against his father.

Her hand in his, Rissa walked with Phillip into the room that had been set aside as his studio. Most of the furniture had been removed. At one side was an empty canvas, sitting on an easel flanked by a special arrangement of lamps. Opposite was a Grecian scroll-ended couch covered in lustrous ivory velvet.

'I'll paint you sitting there,' he told Rissa. 'Your hair loose about your shoulders.' He tugged at the pins, and her dark hair billowed into freedom. 'You look like Rebecca in *Ivanhoe* – '

With one fluid movement their lips met. She had no will, she wanted to be here with Phillip. She made no protest when he lifted her from her feet and carried her into the bedroom that lay beyond yet another door. He carried her to the four-poster canopied bed in the shadows and deposited her upon the silken coverlet.

'My beautiful Rissa,' he murmured, lying beside her. 'Nobody will keep us apart. Not even my father.'

Trembling, cold though the night was warm, Rissa waited for Phillip to teach her how to love. Tonight Manya would sleep alone in the flat on Krochmalna Street.

4

Rissa moved between ecstasy and remorse. Reaching the heights of happiness in Phillip's company, pained by the unspoken recriminations she felt in each member of the household on Krochmalna Street. Phillip pleaded with her to go with him to London when he must leave. From there they would travel soon to Italy.

'Phillip, I'm afraid,' she whispered each night in his arms. Though after that first night in the fine house on Stare Miasto Square, she insisted on returning to the flat at a suitable hour, to lie beside Manya, huddled at the edge of the bed. 'Give me time. Please.'

And each night Phillip reproached her with the reminder that their time was growing short.

Three nights before Phillip was scheduled to leave, Mendele announced that he had found himself a young genius who was writing a play especially for Rissa. Rissa recoiled from the shock and anger on the faces of the three Paulowski women.

Rissa is a child,' Yankel sputtered. 'Fifteen years old!'

Mendele shrugged. 'Fifteen is a woman. Fifteen marries.'

'What about Manya?' Yankel was incensed. 'Four years she's sweated for you.'

'Manya will play Rissa's friend.' Mendele avoided Yankel's eyes. 'She'll have enough lines.'

46

'You promised you'd have a play written for me!' Manya stormed. For one overwrought instant her eyes wished Rissa every misfortune. 'Papa, tell him!'

Yankel's eyes sought those of his wife. Paternal pride battled with the fear of insecurity. Feigele was about to cry. Though the theater paid meager wages, the Paulowskis needed their jobs for survival. Mendele drew himself up to his utmost stature, infuriated that his power was being challenged.

'I won't be here.' Rissa shattered the ominous atmosphere. She could not remain here at the theater; she could not stay at the flat. 'I'm leaving in three days for London.'

Mendele broke into a tirade. Rissa fled while the voices of the others rose in a clamor of insults and recriminations. Simultaneously exhilarated by her declaration and terrified of what lay ahead, Rissa roamed about the streets until it was time to return to the theater for the night's performance. When Phillip came for her, she would tell him she would go with him to London.

Only when Phillip and she lay together in the four-poster bed in the house on Stare Miasto Square did Rissa face the obstacle that stood before her.

'Phillip, I have no passport.' Rissa had heard the stories about Polish Jews who tried to cross the border illegally. Peasants made promises for a sum of money, then demanded even more money. Many were robbed of what little they managed to save without escaping across the border. 'How can I leave Warsaw?'

'We'll buy you a passport,' Phillip soothed.

For a man like Phillip an expensive Russian passport was nothing. For an instant she was mollified.

'But sometimes even with a passport they stop a Jew.' Panic was closing in about her. 'You don't know these men who carry out the Czar's orders. Sometimes even in Hamburg or Antwerp they send back people.'

'Rissa, we'll buy you a passport,' Phillip repeated. 'One the authorities must respect. For money these things can be arranged. You'll be my English cousin who is a mute,' he decided exuberantly. 'If you don't speak, who is to know?' Though Phillip took pride in the amount of English he had taught her, she was clearly Polish. 'We'll buy you a beautiful dress to wear on the trip. Everybody will be enchanted by you. No one will ask questions. No one,' he emphasized, 'will try to send back my beautiful young English cousin. My father is a British lord; they wouldn't dare ask questions.'

Awe and trepidation filled her heart. Phillip's father was a lord. She, Rissa Lindowska, was loved by the son of a lord. Wouldn't Esther be excited if she knew! But she would never tell Esther. She had brought her few belongings here to Phillip's house. Choosing a moment when only Bubbi would be in the flat – and Bubbi was napping.

She would see Esther only at the theater tomorrow and the next night. They would talk only onstage. She was leaving Warsaw forever behind her. Now she understood how those who left Poland for America must feel. To leave behind everything that was familiar. To have to learn to speak a strange language.

Time sped with astonishing swiftness. Phillip bought her not one but three new dresses, and a fashionable cape such as the fine ladies in Saxony Garden wore. They boarded a train in Warsaw that provided them with a private compartment. No one questioned her presence.

In the compartment to Berlin and yet another from Berlin to Hamburg, Phillip made love to her. In Hamburg, mute and white with fear lest her passport be challenged, Rissa clung to Phillip's arm while he led her through customs and onto the small boat that was to take them to London. He had chosen one of the less luxurious vessels, which carried mostly immigrants, so that Rissa could avoid socializing with English travelers. Except for an elderly couple in the cabin next to their own they were the only first-class passengers.

Rissa forgot her fear of the sea in Phillip's arms. With him she stood on the deck the following morning in her ecru silk shirtwaist suit and black wool cape and watched the shoreline as the boat sailed up the Thames. She watched fascinated by the city that rose through the mists on either side of the river, absorbed in Phillip's story of the Tower of London, which lay just ahead of them.

Rissa's eyes strayed at intervals to the cluster of men, women and children in the stern of the boat. Most of the men wore the garments of the Hasidic Jew, the women in peasant garb, shawls over their heads. Polish and Russian Jews carried their worldly goods in baskets or bundles tied in kerchiefs.

Rissa stiffened in silent anger when she saw a German soldier shove his way through them with coarse oaths. A woman snatched a toddler to her bosom, murmuring reassurances. The men moved aside without a word, their faces etched with the memory of three thousand years of wandering. The other women clutched their bundles, eyes downcast as they made way for the intruder. But for Phillip she would be one of them.

'The customhouse officers will come aboard in a moment,' Phillip told her, a hand at her waist as the boat came to rest among a forest of masts.

Her heart pounded. She must remember to remain silent. Phillip would take her through this ordeal.

In her fine attire, with Phillip at her side, Rissa left the boat for the landing stage. Phillip tried to divert her from the painful confusion they encountered there. Some lucky immigrants were met by relatives, and the greetings were poignant. But most were being accosted by what Phillip referred to as 'East London parasites.' These slimy individuals pushed forward to grab the bundles or baskets of the new arrivals with offers of tickets — nonexistent, Phillip whispered in compassion — for those who wanted to proceed to America, and offers of free lodgings to the others.

While Phillip prodded her forward, Rissa looked over her shoulder at a small man with a badge that read Hebrew Ladies Protective Society and who instructed bewildered families in Yiddish to go to the Poor Jews' Temporary Shelter in Leman Street. Rissa flinched at the ribald laughter of the loungers about the dock, who ridiculed the clothes and the language of the new arrivals.

Phillip found a carriage to take them to their lodgings. Rissa gazed avidly out the window, trying to see everything at once. She was in London. With Phillip. God had wrought a miracle for her.

They left the carriage at a narrow street off Rose Mary Lane, before a modest, five-story tenement. An area, Phillip told her, where many Irish lived. Phillip carried their belongings up the four flights of dark stairs, Rissa close behind him. This was Phillip's London studio.

He unlocked a door, threw it wide, and ushered her in with a courtly bow.

'Welcome to my studio.' He freed one hand to draw her to him. 'Our studio.'

For one urgent moment their mouths clung. Then he released her to inspect her new home. A one-room flat. All their own, Rissa rejoiced. And she was impressed that they would not have to do with a tap on the landing; in an alcove off the room were a sink and a toilet. In the *dorf* she had to walk half a kilometer each day for water.

A bed with a rumpled coverlet dominated one side of the room. Opposite, between two small chests, were three canvases in varying stages of completion. Instantly Rissa was hostile toward the girl in the paintings.

'A model I hired,' Phillip told her, amused by her wary inspection of the paintings. 'I won't need a model anymore. I'll paint only you, Rissa. You'll

51

pose for me every day while the light is good.' He crossed to a window to push aside the red damask curtains that seemed oddly grand for the modest furnishings of the room.

'I'll cook for you,' Rissa said impetuously. 'And clean and sew.'

'And make love with me,' he stipulated.

She burrowed her face against his chest, her arms clasped about him.

'Rissa, how did I live without you?' She felt his rising passion and rejoiced. It could not be wrong to love as they loved.

'Lock the door and close the curtains,' she whispered because already his fingers were fumbling with the buttons on her shirtwaist.

She was impatient with the slowness of her undressing. She wanted to lie on the bed in their first real home and be filled with Phillip. She was cold, but Phillip would warm her.

'Beautiful little Rissa,' he murmured, standing beside the bed. His clothes in a heap at his feet. 'I'll paint you like that.' His eyes swept over her high, provocative breasts, the slender waist and hips.

'Oh, Phillip, you couldn't.' She was shocked.

'It'll be a masterpiece,' he chortled. 'With you to inspire me, how could it be otherwise?'

Phillip lifted her onto the bed and lowered himself above her. His hands moved about the familiar contours of her body. His mouth at her throat, in the valley between her breasts.

'Oh, Phillip, I love you,' she cried out as he entered her. This was her world – Phillip.

* * *

She wasn't like one of those girls from the houses around Krochmalna Square, Rissa told herself guiltily when at last they lay quiescent. Phillip and she loved each other. God had made man and woman to love.

Yet Manya's small taunt punctured her rapture. 'Rissa, he'll never marry you.'

5

On their third night in London Phillip announced that he had reserved seats for them at the new Gaiety Theatre at Aldwych and the Strand. They were to see a performance of the new play *The Girls of Gottenberg* that had just opened. The theater was a short distance from their flat on the fringe of the East End, yet to Rissa this was another new world with which she must cope.

Neighbors gaped at Phillip in his opera cloak and opera hat and at Rissa in her beautiful blue silk gown, bought only that afternoon in a store so elegant she had been abashed to enter. She had gasped when she saw the money that passed from Phillip to the saleswoman in payment. Her quick mind computed what the sum of English money meant in Polish zlotys. More than the entire Paulowski family earned in a year.

'We'll have to walk to Rose Mary Lane for a hansom cab.' Phillip was irritated by the catcalls of a pair of young boys lounging on the steps next door. Were they laughing at her? Rissa agonized.

They found a cab at last. En route to the theater Phillip told her about an art exhibition they would attend next week. He was eager for her to learn about paintings. Her heart thumped as they drove through the night-darkening street to the theater. She had so much to learn.

The hansom cab deposited them before a gray stone structure banded with strips of green marble and topped by a green dome. Above the dome was a golden female figure blowing a trumpet – this was the new Gaiety Theatre.

As he helped her from the cab, he pointed out the royal entrance.

'When the theater opened four years ago, King Edward and Queen Alexandra were here for the first performance,' Phillip told her. 'A great honor for the company.'

Phillip pulled her arm through his and guided her into the sumptuous auditorium. The decor was delightfully gay, in rich golds and yellows and browns. The ceiling was beautifully painted, the lights soft, the carpet beneath their feet lush.

They walked to their seats in the dress circle. Rissa admired the gowns of the ladies in the stalls and boxes at each side of the theater, fearful that she might make a move that would disgrace Phillip. She spoke in whispers, lest those around them should scoff at her accented English. She knew that immigrants were ridiculed as 'greeners.'

Rissa focused her attention now on the act drop, on which was depicted the figure of a lovely girl draped in gossamer clothes, a jeweled girdle about her waist. Above her head the girl held a lamp that glowed mysteriously. Phillip leaned to whisper that an electric light was behind it.

Don't look so awestruck,' Phillip chided after a moment. 'There isn't a woman here that can touch you for looks. Not a girl on that stage tonight you can't match.'

Rissa reached for Phillip's hand as the drop rose and the performance began. This was not the Yiddish theater in Warsaw. This was lavish beyond anything she had ever dreamed. She struggled to follow the dialogue and the lyrics, difficult with her meager command of English; but the costumes of the Gaiety Girls required no knowledge of language.

'The hats that the girls in the chorus are wearing cost sixty guineas each,' Phillip whispered in her ear.

Rissa remembered what Yankel and Feigele had said about the productions of the more affluent Yiddish theaters in Warsaw. But not even the plays with Esther Rachel, the queen of the Yiddish theater, offered the opulence Rissa saw onstage tonight.

She was stricken when Phillip admired one of the Gaiety Girls.

'Her name is Gladys Cooper,' Phillip told her. Sensing her sudden despair, he reached for her hand. 'She's almost as beautiful as you.'

Between acts Phillip took her into the Dutch bar of the theater for a glass of wine. She was conscious of the admiring glances of other men. Phillip was pleased. She smiled with fresh confidence as they returned to their seats in the dress circle.

The audience here behaved with a decorum that enchanted Rissa, though at the end of the performance they applauded enthusiastically. This was not the kind of entertainment Rissa knew, full of pain and tears. Nobody sobbed aloud at tonight's performance, though when the act drop rose on the first

56

Rissa debated with herself. Her natural instinct was to withdraw rather than upset Manya. Yet logic overrode instinct. Mendele, the producer-director, would blame Yankel for Manya's absence. Manya talked about Mendele's petty vindictiveness; he would make life miserable for the Paulowskis for weeks to come. She knew the part. She wanted to play it.

'I know every line,' Rissa reiterated with a stubbornness that was new to her. 'If there's no one else to play, I know I can do it.'

She spoke with deliberate calm. The only calm voice in the flat this morning. Yankel weighed her offer in his mind. There were never enough young girls to play parts. Too many fathers refused to allow their daughters to appear on the stage.

'You'll come to the theater,' Yankel decided. 'Mendele will bring the company together.' He ignored Manya's outcry of betrayal. 'We'll see if you know the part.'

Rissa stood on the dimly lit stage, avoiding the skeptical eyes of the other members of the cast. Manya was right; she had *hutzpah* to say she could play Manya's part tonight. Playing Esther in the Purim play for those in the *dorf* was not the same as playing before a theater full of strangers who had paid money to see a performance.

Mendele hovered in the pit, feet wide apart, his smile encouraging as he spoke; but to Rissa he was a small, vindictive god who would bring unspeakable havoc upon the Paulowskis if she failed. Panic tightened her throat. Did she know the lines?

'Rissa, remember. Talk loud. If everybody stops talking, then you know it's time for you.' Mendele gestured eloquently, 'We'll go through just the scenes where Manya plays.'

Rissa heard her voice saying the lines. The others on the stage propelled her to where she was to stand. Later there would be a prompter, she remembered. But so many times the other actors didn't say what was in the *bikhl*; they made up their own words. That was because they had to learn so many plays. Each night a different one was played.

Tonight those empty seats out there in the darkness would be filled with people. She would forget every line. She would ruin the play. The people would ask for their money back!

scene and she saw the Blue Hussars march onstage, she was for a moment terrified.

'You're tired,' Phillip said tenderly when they moved out of the theater onto the pavement. 'We won't go to supper.'

'I'll make tea at home,' Rissa said. She was, in truth, exhausted by the evening's experience.

Phillip found a hansom cab for them and gave the driver directions.

Rissa sat with her head on Phillip's shoulder, enjoying his nearness, fighting off slumber. How envious Manya would be if she knew about this evening!

'Rissa,' Phillip prodded her into wakefulness as they stopped before their flat.

Phillip helped her down from the cab and told the driver to wait. Rissa loked at him in bewilderment.

'Tonight I must go home to my parents,' he apologized. 'But I'll be back tomorrow afternoon. Early enough to paint for a while.' Rissa looked at him in stunned silence. 'Rissa, you know I have to spend time with my family,' he soothed.

'Yes,' she whispered. Not knowing at all.

Though she was exhausted, Rissa lay awake until dawn. She was afraid, alone in the strange city, in a strange bed. Each sound in the hallway upset her.

Rissa shivered in the dank morning chill. It seemed to her that the sun never shone in London before noon. She was never truly warm. She longed to go to Italy where she and Phillip would be together always.

Rissa entered into a world of wonderful days and nights, when Phillip took her to the theater, art exhibitions and horse races. He even took her on brief trips into the English countryside, where they spent the night in quaint English inns.

Together they went to the Savoy Theatre where D'Oyly Carte was presenting Gilbert and Sullivan, to the St James and the Lyceum and the Empire. She sat enthralled at a play by Bernard Shaw called *Doctor's Dilemma*. When Phillip took her to see a play by a man named Pinero, and told her that he was Jewish, Rissa was overwhelmed with pride.

She recognized the difference between Pinero's plays and the melodramas presented in Mendele's theater and wondered why the Yiddish theater couldn't present such plays?

'It's rumored that within another year or two King Edward will knight Pinero.' Phillip smiled indulgently at her delight. 'He'll be Sir Arthur Pinero.'

What a wonderful country England was, Rissa thought, where Jews could acquire royal titles. At the theater one night Phillip had pointed out Lord Rothschild to her; and he had told her about Benjamin Disraeli, who rose to become Queen Victoria's prime minister with the title of Earl of Beaconsfield.

But Rissa dreaded the nights when she lay alone, remembering the horror in the *dorf* she had left behind her. Fighting shame because she knew the words papa would spit at her if he knew how she lived. But she knew she couldn't have stayed in the theater in Warsaw. She could not have gone on living with the Paulowskis. And she *loved* Phillip. That made everything all right.

Yet she worried that Phillip made so little progress

with his paintings. Each night that he left her alone, she was a prisoner of panic. What would she do if Phillip did not return tomorrow? How would she survive?

She knew no one in the house where she lived. Her meager English embarrassed her, though she spent hours each day fighting to learn the language. She hung on every word Phillip uttered, making him explain each new word that she did not understand.

She sensed a certain hostility among those she encountered in their neighborhood. Phillip told her that the other tenants were Irish laborers. If sometimes they got a bit loud from too many beers, she was not to worry. But the women looked at her, and knew she was not Phillip's wife. They looked at Phillip and knew he was from a class above their own. She was conscious of their resentment.

Late in the summer Phillip told her he must go away to his family's country house for a week.

'I'll hate every minute of it,' he said passionately. 'Garden parties and tennis parties and dinner parties day after day. And father telling me constantly that I must prepare myself for taking over the business one day.'

'A whole week, Phillip?' Rissa was desolate.

'I want you to go shopping for some pretty things,' he cajoled. 'You'll have money to buy something special each day. And when I return,' he promised with an audacious smile, 'I'll take you to a buffet supper after King Edward holds "court." I'll present you to the King of England.'

Rissa stared in disbelief.

'Phillip, you wouldn't dare!'

'I'll dare,' he promised, fishing in his purse for bills. 'You're to enjoy yourself while I'm away. We'll celebrate on my return.'

For the first two days of Phillip's absence Rissa clung to the flat, as she had clung to the flat on Krochmalna Street when she first arrived in Warsaw. Then restlessness seized hold of her. Phillip had given her an enormous amount of money. She would do as he said; she would shop for something special tomorrow. Not for herself; for the flat.

Rissa left the flat the following morning with a heartening sense of adventure. She had never had so much money in her purse. She smiled at a little girl who sat on the steps of the house as she emerged. Seemingly emboldened by Rissa's friendliness, the little girl spoke to her.

'Are you a kike?'

Rissa stared with incomprehension.

'A Hebrew,' the little girl said impatiently. 'A Jew.'

The color drained from Rissa's face. This was England. Not Poland. No pogroms here.

'Yes.' Involuntarily she lifted her head in defiant pride.

'Then why don't you live in the East End with the rest of 'em, like my mum says?' The little girl giggled and ran down the street.

Rissa stood immobile. Her mind racing. 'Why don't you live in the East End with the rest of 'em?' There must be a Jewish section here in London. Nostalgia for all that was familiar to her, for her heritage, enveloped her like a tidal wave.

Rissa began to walk, determined to find the East End. As she walked in the direction pointed out, Rissa became aware of the change in the neighborhood. Here the row houses were decayed and paint-hungry. Broken windows had not been repaired. The streets gradually became more crowded. She saw Orthodox men in long coats and forelocks, young boys scurrying about with *yarmulkes* on their heads. Here and there she saw prosperous-appearing men with heavy gold watch chains and girls in flashy hats, a sharp contrast to the pallid-faced immigrants that predominated.

Excitement brought color to Rissa's face. This was the East End. The Jewish district. Already she felt herself less alone.

She turned off into a crowded alley. The air was moist from last night's downpour. Steam was rising from the streets. She smelled the aroma of *hallah* baking in an oven and realized this was Friday.

Tears welled in her eyes and spilled over without her being aware of them. She visualized the Sabbath supper table in the *dorf*. Mama leaning over the candles. The *hallah* warm in the oven. Or fish that she and Chaim had managed to catch that morning in the river. She saw matzoth in a shop window, and she remembered Passover with mama and papa, grandpa and the younger children. Joseph too young yet to ask the four questions. Gone. They were all gone.

Rissa smelled the heavy scent of fried fish, of herring in a barrel before a tiny shop. Hawkers urged her to buy vegetables and fruit and items of clothing.

Only now did she realize that she appeared an outsider here.

From every corner, it seemed to Rissa, came the whir of sewing machines. The muffled noise of the pressers' irons. She stopped to read a sign on a door. The sign was written in Yiddish, Polish and what she recognized as Russian and German. The notice said that the man who lived within wrote letters for one penny a page for those who could not write and wanted to communicate with their families in Poland or Russia.

A tiny store selling religious matter captured her attention. She went inside and bought a *mezuzah* to put on the door of the flat. It would protect them. But rebellion broke through. Where were You, God, when the peasants came to kill us?

She hurried out of the shop, unnerved by the sight of the fine *tallithim* to be bought here. Would papa and grandpa be ashamed of her for loving Phillip and putting aside much of the old ways?

A vendor reached out to touch her arm, holding up a salted, golden pretzel. She reached into her purse for a coin, on impulse speaking to him in Yiddish. She had not spoken her own language for weeks.

'Do you have in London a Yiddish theater?' she asked.

'Of course we have a Yiddish theater.' He shrugged in pride. 'The Pavilion, where last year came Jacob Adler back from America, and on Commercial Road the Grand Palais. And from Russia comes troupes of players who try to make a living. We have even a Russian Jewish Opera Company.'

Eagerly Rissa questioned him about the theater and was startled to learn that on Saturday afternoons there were performances. Matinees. Here, too, were Jews who had moved away from the old ways. Tomorrow, Rissa decided in a surge of anticipation, she would go to the matinee at the Yiddish theater.

When she was exhausted from shoving her way through the crowds, Rissa shopped for black bread to take to the flat with her. She cradled her still warm bread in her arm as she retraced her steps.

The black bread was mama and papa, grandpa and the children. When there was no fish or potatoes, black bread and tea had been their supper. Tonight the family would surround her while she sat down alone to her supper.

6

Rissa bought her gallery ticket for the matinee performance at the Yiddish theater on Mile End Road. She was glad that she wore the shirtwaist suit she had made for herself in Warsaw rather than any of the fancy clothes Phillip had bought for her.

The atmosphere inside was convivial. The audience had come to the theater with special delicacies for the occasion. Oranges, unknown to Rissa until Phillip had introduced her to them, monkey-nuts, chocolates, even chicken legs and wings emerged from purses and parcels.

A symphony of Yiddish swelled about her while the audience waited.

The music in the pit began. Rissa discovered herself viewing the performance with critical attention. Except for the time she had come to the theater with a dress for Manya, she had always been part of the performance. She had developed a sense of what pleased their audiences. Mendele repeated what Bubbi said. *Gott hut dir gebentcht.*

But here in London she had been exposed to superb theater. She wished that the actors this afternoon would shout less. Would keep their gestures less exaggerated. The actors should be real.

Yet even with her new critical perspective Rissa enjoyed the performance. She moved with regret out into the street again. Nearby was a small kosher restaurant. She decided to treat herself.

She found a table in the restaurant and ordered hot apple strudel and tea. A pleasant-faced young woman took the seat opposite. In moments they were talking. Rissa realized with delight that the young woman had been in the chorus of the company she had just seen. When Rissa explained she too had acted in the Yiddish theater, the woman quickly became friendly and told Rissa her story.

Olga was from a *shtetl* near Warsaw. Her husband had been conscripted into the Russian army. When word came that he was dead, twenty-two-year-old Olga gathered together her mother-in-law and her small son, and they made their way to London. They had been here four years, during which time Olga had worked in the Yiddish theater.

'It's not as good here in London as it was a few years ago,' Olga shrugged. 'At one time the East End was full of Yiddish theaters, but so many actors have run off to America. So many Jews run off to America,' she emphasized. 'But last August Jacob Adler came for two weeks at the Pavilion. I saw him twice,' Olga said in triumph. 'In *Uriel Acosta* and *The Jewish King Lear*.'

It was arranged that Rissa would see a performance without payment the following evening; all she had to do was sit at one side of the stage as an extra. Rissa was enthralled. After the performance, Olga introduced her to the producer, who himself had visions of going to America and starting a theater company there.

'In New York the Yiddish theater lives,' he said with ecstatic gestures. 'The word comes back to us. In New York Jacob Adler plays. Thomashefsky, Kessler. They are treated like gods. They are rich.' His eyes glistened with pride. 'When Adler played *Uriel Acosta* in London, the great Jews of the city came to see him.' Olga nodded reminiscently. 'Even Rabbi Adler himself and one of the Rothschilds came.'

The producer invited Olga and Rissa to the restaurant across the way for tea. Rissa listened avidly to his stories of Yiddish theater in New York.

'But enough talking about America,' he reproached himself at last. 'I have to go back to the theater.' Now he looked closely at Rissa. 'Olga says to me that you played with a Yiddish theater in Warsaw. How do I know this is true?'

'Give me a part and you'll see,' Rissa shot back. Startled by what she had said, she turned to Olga for reassurance. Olga beamed.

'My soubrette leaves next week. Learn her parts. You'll play,' he said grandly.

Rissa was overwhelmed by her acceptance into the Yiddish company so quickly. While the theater offered none of the grandeur of the English-speaking theaters to which Phillip had taken her, it was palatial compared to the modest structure in Warsaw where Mendele presented his plays. She threw herself into memorizing the parts, though Olga reminded her that here, too, much improvisation took place onstage.

The days were occupied, but the nights in the tiny flat were long and empty. On the day on which

Phillip was scheduled to return to London, she stayed at home. She sat by a window watching for him, listening to every sound in the hallway. Twice she changed her dress. Which would Phillip like best? Was her hair all right? Did she look too pale?

'Rissa!'

She leapt to her feet and darted to the door at the sound of his approach. She pulled the door wide just as he arrived at their landing.

'Phillip!' She threw herself into his arms. 'Oh, Phillip, I've missed you so much.'

'I hated every minute I was away from you,' he whispered when he released her mouth. 'Every night I wished you were lying there beside me.'

'Would you like me to make you tea?' She stammered in her excitement. 'Are you hungry?'

'Only for you.' He lifted her slight figure in his arms and carried her to the bed. He sat beside her, kissed her eyelids, her lips, her throat. 'We'll make up for every miserable night we were apart,' he promised.

Exhilarated by their lovemaking Rissa lay in Phillip's arms while he debated about plans for the evening.

'Phillip, I have not told you my news,' she bubbled effusively when he paused. 'I have a part in a play.'

She felt him tense, saw the anger on his face.

'What theater?' he demanded. 'How did it happen?'

'The Yiddish theater on Mile End Road –' She had expected him to share her pleasure.

'I won't allow it.' Phillip pulled his arm away from

her. 'In a Yiddish theater on Mile End Road?' She flinched before his contempt.

'You found me in a Yiddish theater in Warsaw,' she reminded him softly.

'No,' he reiterated and swung his legs over the edge of the bed. 'We won't ever talk about it again.' He crossed to the chair where he had thrown his clothes and began to dress. 'Wear the pink silk frock tonight. We're going to see Herbert Tree and Constance Collier in *Anthony and Cleopatra*.'

Rissa was desolate at having to give up her part in the Yiddish theater. But she clung to Olga's friendship. With Olga she was able to pass some of the long hours when Phillip was away. She tried to tell herself that it was sufficient that Phillip loved her.

With the approach of Rosh Hashanah and Yom Kippur she was especially conscious of the loss of her family. Each holiday throughout the year was a bitter reminder that she was alone. Olga shared this recurrence of grief with her.

With Olga she would attend the Rosh Hashanah services at a nearby *chevras*, founded by Jewish immigrants in a long wooden building with a skylight that resembled a 'sweater's' workshop. She would sit with Olga behind the trellis in the woman's section.

Rissa knew about the strange ways of the English Jews, whose fine synagogues with their lofty ceilings, their stained glass windows, appeared more like a cathedral than a *shul*. She knew that the English Jews had their United Synagogue with a chief rabbi, since 1890 Dr Hermann Adler. Dr Adler wore the insignia of the Royal Victorian Order. Olga said – with awe – that it was rumored that Edward VII had once referred to him as 'my chief rabbi.'

In Poland and Russia one rabbi might be praised above another for his knowledge, his wisdom, his piety; but who in Poland or Russia knew of a chief rabbi? And the English rabbis were called 'Reverend.' They dressed in the manner of the British clergy, in black coat, broad-brimmed hat, and the English dog collar. And the British synagogues were open only at certain hours of the day!

On a pleasant afternoon when Olga was free from the theater, she took Rissa to the Great Synagogue at Duke's Place, at the edge of the East End. Both knew they would not be able to afford to join the congregation, but they were curious about what seemed to be an institution among English Jews.

'In the flat above me lives a very old man,' Olga told Rissa as they walked through the crowded streets in the direction of the Great Synagogue. 'He's one who knows much about the Jews in England. Did you know that in 1272 – in the English calendar,' she emphasized, so new in comparison to the Hebrew calendar, 'King Edward ordered every Jew to leave England within four months?'

'Why?' Rissa stopped dead. Could such terrible things happen in England?

Olga shrugged.

'Since when did anybody need a reason to tell Jews to leave a country? But then there was a "resettlement" in 1657, and the Jews came back.' Olga's face lighted. 'There. Just ahead. The Great Synagogue.'

Olga pointed to an elegant brick building constructed in the most simple of Grecian architecture. The roof supported by massive stone pillars.

'In the front over the porch is a large hall where poor Jews are allowed to have their weddings,' Olga pursued. 'It's an honor to be able to say "I was married at Duke's Place." And the synagogue provides, also, fifty free seats for the poor.'

'We can pray in the *chevras*,' Rissa declared, recoiling from the prospect of being a subject of charity. 'God will hear us there.'

While she herself was plagued by fresh grief at this second Rosh Hashanah without mama and papa, grandpa and the children, Rissa was aware of a new unrest in Phillip since his return from the country. His lapses into irritability at odd moments disturbed her. He spent little time on the portrait of her. Day after day his paintbrush lay untouched. He was away from the flat more nights than he was there.

On an early September night as they lay in bed together, Phillip told her he must go away the following morning for the remainder of the month. His father had ordered him to accompany his mother to the baths in Wiesbaden. It was the 'season.'

'That's almost three weeks,' Rissa whispered, forlorn at the prospect.

'Invite your friend from the theater to visit with you,' he encouraged. Phillip had encountered Olga in the flat one afternoon. 'Take her to an English theater.'

Rissa lay sleepless until dawn. To be alone in London without Phillip for almost three weeks was a devastating prospect. If she were working in the theater, she would not feel so alone. But Phillip had forbidden it.

She tried to be cheerful when Phillip kissed her good-bye in the morning. He reiterated his distaste for the trip with his mother.

'It's something I have to do, Rissa. I'll make it up to you,' he promised. But he had not taken her to the buffet supper following King Edward's evening 'court,' as he had promised when he left for a week at his family's country house.

In the afternoon Rissa walked over to Whitechapel. Here was a whisper of home. The sounds of Yiddish, familiar aromas, faces that reminded her of her family. A bearded elderly Jew with a twinkle in his eye, holding the hand of a small girl, brought tears to her eyes.

Rissa turned off onto the narrow, crooked lane where Olga lived with her mother-in-law and son. She climbed the four flights to their two-room flat. Olga was alone, busy sewing a costume, a cup of tea at hand. She seemed startled by Rissa's appearance.

'Have I come at a time when you're busy?' Rissa was apologetic.

'Rissa, no. I leave soon for the theater.' Olga pulled her into the room. Her face was somber. Her eyes angry. 'I wanted to see you today.' Since the accidental encounter with Phillip, Olga avoided the flat.

'I was lonely.' Rissa's smile was wry. 'Last night Phillip told me he must leave for Wiesbaden with his mother this morning. Already I'm lonely,' she reiterated.

'Rissa, it breaks my heart to tell you – ' Olga paused, her eyes filling.

'Olga, has something happened to your little boy?' Rissa was anxious.

'No, he's fine. Mama is fine. Rissa, sit down. I have to show you something.' Olga went to the table by the window and picked up a folded-over newspaper. The *Morning Star*. She turned around to face Rissa. 'I don't know any other way to tell you than to show you this.'

Rissa took the newspaper Olga extended to her. Totally unprepared for the photograph of Phillip that stared back at her.

'That is your Phillip, isn't it?' Olga asked.

'It's Phillip.' Even with her inadequate English she could read the message. Tomorrow afternoon Phillip would be married to Lady Diane Venable. The wedding was to be held at the home of the groom's parents, Lord and Lady Cambridge, in Mayfair. The words performed a macabre dance in her mind.

'He told you nothing?' Olga's voice trembled with impotent rage.

'Nothing.' It was as though she had heard that Phillip had died. He was not going to Wiesbaden today; he was preparing for his wedding. 'He told me he would be away with his mother until the end of the month. I was not to worry. He would be back before we must pay the money for the flat.' Not with his mother, her mind taunted. With his bride.

'Then he will keep on being with you,' Olga consoled.

'I don't want him back!' Pride made her voice

72

harsh. For a moment washed away the anguish in her eyes. 'I don't want him when he's married to somebody else.'

'Rissa, what will you do?' Olga was concerned; all over the East End people were crying about the heartless landlords who incessantly raised the rents. 'You'll stay with us,' Olga decided. 'Somehow we'll manage.'

'I'll find work. I don't need Phillip. I'll take care of myself. From this day on I will always take care of myself.' Her small passionate mouth was set. She would not be hurt this way again.

'Come with me to the theater,' Olga coaxed. 'I don't want to leave you alone. There's always a seat onstage for extras. We never have enough.'

'I need to be alone, Olga. Tomorrow night I'll come to the theater.'

Her heart beat quickly in passionate resolve.

Tomorrow morning she would call on Phillip at his fine Mayfair house. How dare he treat her this way!

Despite Olga's insistence that she stay at the flat on Philpot Street, Rissa returned to her own quarters. She walked inside, lit a lamp and stared about at the drab walls that had seemed so beautiful only this morning. She looked at the painting of her on which Phillip had worked with such enthusiasm in their early weeks together and then all but abandoned. In her purse was the scrap of paper that had reduced her to despair.

Tomorrow Phillip was being married. *'He'll never*

marry you.' Manya's taunt ricocheted in her brain. Her eyes fell on a pair of trousers Phillip had left behind. She picked them up and hung them on a hook in the alcove, beside his dressing gown – and then withdrew her hand as though it had been burned. Phillip intended to come back to her, but he'd be married to that other girl.

No. She wanted no part of Phillip Cambridge. Only to tell him to his face her contempt for his lies. Tomorrow she would go to his house on St James's Square, and she would tell him not to expect to find her in the flat when he returned.

Through most of the night Rissa lay sleepless. At dawn she rose from the bed she had shared with Phillip but would never share again. She washed her face and fixed herself a pot of tea. She must wait until a respectable hour to go to Phillip's house. She would wear the dark suit from Harrods that Phillip had told her was right for visiting Kensington Museum or Kew Gardens.

Shortly before 10:00 A.M., pale and wan in the dark blue suit, Rissa left the flat. The morning was gray and damp. In her mind she went over the directions she had acquired that would take her to St James's Square, all the way over in central London. She must take two buses.

As she walked, she tried to frame the words she must say to Phillip. At odd moments her mind insisted this was a terrible nightmare. But the scrap of paper in her purse attested to reality.

She caught a reflection of herself in a shop window, and found meager reassurance. She was properly dressed. Her dark blue suit was fashionable. The jacket tailored, with a short flare. The skirt draped fully about the hips and very narrow at the hem. Phillip had bought her the white chiffon shirtwaist with a cascade of lace at the throat especially to wear with this suit.

On first one bus and then another Rissa rode without seeing. She struggled to gear herself for the confrontation with Phillip. She must have the courage to walk into the house on St James's Square and tell him of her rage. Pride demanded this. Yet her awareness of her limited English was an ever-present humiliation.

Rissa left the bus and walked through the gray coolness of the morning to St James's Square. Subconsciously she admired the gardens, the beautiful plane trees, as she sought the great town house of Lord Cambridge. Now her steps were slow. Her throat constricted.

Then she stood before the tall, elegant eighteenth-century house that Phillip had described to her. This was where Phillip lived. Not with her in the flat on Rose Mary Lane. Her eyes swept over the brick-and-stone mansion, its porticoed central block flanked by an east and west wing. A wrought-iron fence surrounded the house. This morning a gate had been left carelessly ajar.

Rissa girded herself to walk up to the entrance and ask for Phillip, trying not to be intimidated by the grandeur of the town house. Waiting at the door for someone to reply to her summons, she inspected the motor car that sat on a strip of road before the house. A driver sat at the wheel.

A liveried footman opened the door and looked inquiringly at her.

'I'd like to speak to Mr Phillip Cambridge.' Rissa managed an air of confidence. Her suit and her hat were from Harrods, were they not? Still, her accent appeared to disturb the footman.

'Will you please wait, ma'am?' The footman was uneasy. He left the door only inches ajar. Rissa could hear much activity within the house.

She waited. Her fragile poise shaken. But she would not leave here without confronting Phillip.

In a few moments another manservant appeared at the door. He loomed tall and forbidding over Rissa.

'What is it you wish, miss?'

'I wish to speak with Mr Phillip Cambridge.' Rissa's voice was astonishingly commanding. It belied the confusion that welled in her.

'I'm sorry, miss.' The manservant frowned in reproach. 'Mr Phillip can see no one this morning. He's being married this afternoon.'

'I will not leave until I speak to him.' Color stained Rissa's cheekbones. 'Tell him, please, that Rissa Lindow – '

'Hugh, what is going on here?' an irritated, imperious masculine voice interrupted.

'There's a young woman asking for Mr Phillip, your lordship,' Hugh explained. *Phillip's father.* All at once Rissa's heart was pounding. She had not expected to encounter Lord Cambridge. 'I've told her he can't be seen this morning.'

'And I've told him,' Rissa raised her voice loudly enough to reach the man in the foyer, 'that I will not leave this house until I speak with Phillip.'

'Show her into my study, Hugh,' Lord Cambridge instructed.

Reluctantly Hugh opened the door wide enough for her to enter the great hall. Phillip's father disappeared into a room to the left.

'Follow me, please,' Hugh ordered, his face indicating his disapproval of such permissiveness.

Rissa followed the manservant down the hall with a vague consciousness of the grandeur of the furnishings, the fine paintings that adorned the walls. Then he led her into a large, high-ceilinged room, its windows masked by heavy, wine red brocade draperies. He bowed slightly to the tall, graying man who sat behind an ornate writing table, and left them alone. Discreetly he closed the door behind him.

Phillip's father, bearing little resemblance to his son, scrutinized her for an instant before he spoke.

'Phillip is being married today. Whatever you have to say to him you can say to me.'

'I will say it to Phillip.' Rissa refused to lower her eyes before the disdain in his. 'This is a matter that concerns Phillip and me.'

'Phillip is being married in six hours. He can see no one.' Lord Cambridge was wary. 'What do you want?'

'Phillip lied to me!' Her voice soared in fresh hurt and indignation. When he left our flat yesterday morning – ' She saw Lord Cambridge wince in comprehension, 'he told me he must go with his mother to Wiesbaden. He said he would be home at the end of the month. Then I read the *Morning Star*.' Despite her efforts her voice broke. 'Phillip said nothing of a wedding.'

'We can handle this matter ourselves.' Lord Cambridge appeared serene and businesslike, but Rissa felt his nervousness. Now she understood. He was afraid she would make a terrible scene. He was terrified that she might burst into the house in the midst of the wedding. *He was afraid of her.* 'What do you want?'

His eyes held hers. Arrogant yet conciliatory. For a moment silence hung like an ominous shadow between them. Rissa's quick mind recognized the situation she had unwittingly created. She had not come here to demand; she had come to pour her anger on Phillip's head. But suddenly, with dizzying clarity, she recognized her bargaining position. Phillip's father wished her out of his life. He needed assurance that Phillip would not return to her arms.

'I cannot remain in London and not see Phillip,' she said with quiet strength. 'I require a ticket to the United States.' She would never forgive Phillip, but his father would be permitted to make partial restitution. 'Not steerage,' she stipulated. 'First class. And ten pounds.'

Rissa trembled at her daring and watched in wary excitement while Lord Cambridge debated within himself.

'You'll need no passport for travel in the United States,' he said after an agonizing wait.

'I'll need papers to stay there,' Rissa pointed out.

Olga had talked about the month-long wait her cousin Shirley endured, running between the British offices and the American consulate before she knew she would be permitted to stay in America.

'That can be arranged,' Lord Cambridge said tersely. 'I'll post the funds required in this situation. Tell me where you live. The ticket, the money and the papers will be delivered to you within three hours. A man will conduct you to the train for Liverpool. Be ready to leave with him.'

'I'll be ready.' Rissa's voice was strong.

All at once the fog had lifted. It had turned into a glorious morning. America! As Tekla, the wise woman in the *dorf* had predicted, she was going to America!

7

Rissa left Phillip's house in Mayfair to go to Olga's flat. Her head whirled from the happenings of the last half hour. She knew that her whole future had been shaped by a look on the face of Phillip's father and her instant comprehension of her position. *God had showed her the way.*

She could never take up with Phillip again; he chose to marry a girl of his own class. His father was relieved to know she would be gone from London. The cost meant nothing to him.

Within three hours, he said, the man would be at her door to take her to the Liverpool train. To make sure there would be no ugly scene at Phillip's wedding. Lord Cambridge had no way of knowing she would never shame herself in such a fashion.

Olga was simultaneously joyous and sad. She gave Rissa an address of a cousin who lived on Essex Street in New York.

'Go to Shirley. She'll help you,' Olga assured. 'Shirley Levine.'

Rissa hurried to her own flat to pack. Phillip had left, in the alcove where they hung their clothes, a small suitcase which he used during the summer for their short trips into the country. For a moment memory of those beautiful days assaulted her. How could she have been so stupid? So trusting! Rage took the edge off her pain. Enough. Phillip was gone from her life.

Rissa packed only the few clothes that Phillip had bought for her and her grandfather's *tallith*. The clothes she had brought from Warsaw would remain behind. She hesitated, then rolled up the canvas of the discarded portrait of her Phillip had begun.

She was snapping shut the valise that lay across the bed when a peremptory knock on the door shattered the silence. So soon? With a final look about the flat where she had been so happy with Phillip, Rissa went to admit Lord Cambridge's emissary.

'Rissa Lindowska?' he asked. A tall, spare man in his forties with a bristling moustache.

'Yes.' She stood small and proud before him.

'I am to escort you to the Liverpool train,' he told her.

'My ticket to the United States?' Rissa refused to be intimidated.

'I will give you a first-class ticket on the *Campania* plus ten pounds when you are on board the train,' he said bluntly. 'That is your luggage?' His gaze settled on her valise.

'Yes.' So his lordship didn't trust her to leave London. He didn't know how pleased she would be to put this city behind her. To be rid of Phillip, who had lied to her from the moment they arrived here.

The brown leather traveler's bag that Phillip had bought for their country trips across her lap, Rissa sat in silence beside Lord Cambridge's man while they rode in the family carriage to Euston Station. She stood beside him in silence while he bought her ticket. A train for Liverpool would leave Euston Station in twelve minutes. In twelve minutes she would be on her way to America.

There would be a day's wait before her ship, the Cunard Line's *Campania* would leave Liverpool. She was told where to find a suitable night's lodging. Not until they stood at the entrance to the train, minutes before departure, did Lord Cambridge's man give her the ticket and the ten pounds she had demanded.

On the train ride to Liverpool Rissa tried to fight the surge of apprehension that now replaced her earlier euphoria. She was about to put the Atlantic Ocean between herself and everything she had ever known!

Rissa clung to the hope that she would find Olga's friend Shirley Levine at the address she had been given on Essex Street in New York. In that city were many Yiddish theaters, Olga said. Far more than in London. She would find a job. She would live.

Now she was shamed by the memory of the months with Phillip. Of being dependent upon him. Never again would it happen that way. Never again would she not be able to care for herself.

In Liverpool she went to the street where cheap lodgings were to be found. She left the tiny, dreary room only when hunger demanded it. Next morning she went to the nearby dock. Impatient for the moment to board the *Campania*.

She stood on the dock and inspected with awe the floating palace with two huge funnels that was to transport her to America. She waited with hordes of other passengers, clutching the small suitcase that held all her worldly possessions.

At last the eager passengers were permitted to board the ship. Rissa was directed to a small stateroom. She stood inside, admiring its furnishings, when the woman who was to share it with her arrived.

'I'm Stella Dimon from Atlanta, Georgia,' the middle-aged lady introduced herself in an English that was only slightly reminiscent of the London English with which Rissa was familiar. 'I came over on steerage because my nephew, who is nineteen and hardy, insisted it was a grand adventure.' She rolled her eyes expressively. 'If sitting cramped up in a filthy, foul-smelling compartment with twenty other people, half of whom are sick, is an adventure, he can have it.'

'I'm Rissa Lindowska,' Rissa wished her English was purer. 'I'm going to live in the United States.'

'Then you must be terribly excited.' Stella Dimon radiated friendliness. 'If you ever come down to Atlanta, you must look me up. I have a big old house, with only mama and me rattling around in it.'

Rissa was pleased with Stella Dimon's companionship. Together they explored the *Campania*. They visited the ladies' salon, where men were admitted only with a special permit, observed the blooming geraniums and sweet mignonette, the lovely carpets and comfortable lounges. At Stella's insistence they took morning and evening constitutionals about the first-class deck, collapsing afterwards into deck chairs to enjoy the exhilarating salt air.

Rissa was glad she did not have to face the huge, crystal-domed dining room alone. It sat four hundred and thirty passengers in revolving armchairs that bore the imprint of the Cunard lion on the back of each. Stella had confided to her with relief that it was not necessary to dress for dinner.

But when Stella suggested they visit the steerage deck, Rissa demurred. In Warsaw she had heard the horrors of traveling steerage. To see for herself would only inflict her with guilt. But she was pleased one evening to hear the sounds of voices singing to the music of a fiddle from the steerage deck far below. First the rebellious *Funia Ganev*, that spoke of the Jews' contempt for the Czar. Then the romantic words of *Oifn Oivn Zitst A Maidel*. 'A Girl Sits on the Stove.'

Rissa flinched. She had no wish to hear a love song.

On board ship it seemed to Rissa that time had ceased to be. Not until the final night did excitement overtake her. She found it impossible to sleep. At dawn she left her bunk and went on deck. She watched with a mixture of emotions – joy, fear, nostalgia for home, grief for her lost ones – while the huge ship approached New York harbor.

A heavy fog lay over the water. But as the *Campania* moved closer, Rissa spied the tall statue of a woman holding a torch. A shiver went through her. The Statue of Liberty. She was truly coming to America.

Papa had been afraid to come to America, where 'Jews become *goyim*.' Yet now she felt as though she were about to be reborn. In New York she would be

Rissa Lindowska, independent, free. Never would she allow herself to love a man as she had loved Phillip.

Tears filled her eyes, temporarily obscuring the dramatic sweep of skyscrapers rising above the mists against a blue sky. She had loved Phillip with all of her being. He must have known from the moment he sent her the violets in Warsaw that they were meant to part. Only she had believed in their love.

For Rissa, a first-class passenger with papers, there was no agony of Ellis Island. In London Lord Cambridge had arranged to post funds to allow her entry into the United States. She said good-bye to Stella Dimon, took her address in Atlanta and promised to look her up if she was ever in that part of the country. She watched while a porter carried Stella's luggage to a waiting hansom cab, then with valise in hand inquired for directions to Essex Street. She could not afford the luxury of a cab.

Clutching her small valise and traveling bag, she made the circuitous trip down to Essex Street on the lower East Side via a trolley car and a raucous monster called the Elevated that rolled frighteningly above the crowded city streets. Simultaneously intrigued and alarmed by the hordes of people, each seeming in a desperate rush to arrive at a destination, Rissa left the Second Avenue Elevated, uneasy on the stairs where everyone seemed intent on traveling in the opposite direction. Another inquiry sent her toward Essex Street. In relief she realized it was very much like the East End. She walked along the noisy crowded street.

It mattered not at all to her that the endless rows

of drab houses hinted at accommodations as cramped and squalid as those in the East End. She was in America, where the Yiddish theater lived.

Hungrily she took in the sights – bearded men in skullcaps and long coats, women in the traditional Orthodox wigs were everywhere. The windows of the tiny shops, much of their merchandise thrust out upon the sidewalk, bore signs in Yiddish. Pushcarts loaded with fruits and vegetables, old and new clothes, shoes, eyeglasses crowded the streets. The pushcart merchants coaxed potential customers to buy with the drama of a Jacob Adler. The sounds of Yiddish that ricocheted from every side were a symphony to Rissa's ears.

She paused, pulled out the scrap of paper with Shirley Levine's address, inspected the number on the door before her. This was the house. She walked up the low stoop to the door and into a dark, dirty hallway that smelled of urine, rendered fat and herring.

Shirley lived on the fifth floor. Slowed down by the weight of her valise Rissa climbed the murky staircase.

'Morris, stop loafing and practice your violin!' a woman screeched on the third floor. 'For what do I pay the man every week if you don't practice?'

Breathlessly Rissa arrived on the fifth-floor landing. From behind the door marked Shirley Levine came the clatter of sewing machines. Rissa knocked. Suddenly she felt shy and self-conscious. Olga had not heard from Shirley in over a year. How would she be received?

The door opened. A small, full-bosomed woman with striking blue eyes and a Roman nose stared in wariness at Rissa.

'You come from a shop?' The woman's voice was guarded.

'No. I'm a friend of your cousin Olga in London.' The words poured out. 'Olga said you would help me to find a place to live – '

'Olga's friend from London!' Beaming, Shirley drew her inside the small square room where two girls sat at sewing machines at one side. A third machine, idle now, sat between the other two. Half-sewn garments were strewn about the floor. The hands and faces of those in the room were stained with the blue dye of the material on which they worked. 'Girls, she knows my cousin Olga, the actress!'

The girls smiled, nodded, but continued to work.

Shirley insisted that Rissa stay with her. She had the whole room to herself, she explained proudly. Of course, during the day it became 'the shop.' At first Shirley had worked for others. Then she had learned that she could 'rent from Mr Singer' and be in business for herself. When she had sufficient capital, she bought three used sewing machines.

'It's not easy,' Shirley shrugged. 'The slow season comes. The schlemiels begin to drop their prices. A lot of us go under.'

Shirley was enthralled when she heard that Rissa had been an actress in Warsaw. Shirley was devoted to the Yiddish theater.

'I'll take you tonight to see Boris Thomashefsky in

Yeshiva Bocher at the People's Theater. And afterwards we'll go to a café for noodle soup and a glass of tea.'

Rissa's face was incandescent. In London she had heard about the great Thomashefsky. And now – on her first night in America – she would see him onstage. While Shirley returned to the sewing machine, Rissa unpacked her few belongings, aware of the wistful glances of the two seamstresses. Clearly, the finely dressed Rissa Lindowska was a somebody.

Shirley prodded Rissa through the animated crowds that clogged the streets, toward the People's Theater on the Bowery. They had walked up from Essex Street; who wasted money for a trolley car or the Elevated when it was possible to walk?

'We'll be there by the time the doors open,' Shirley promised.

Others had the same idea. The sidewalk before the large, pretentious theater was jammed with people eager to see Boris Thomashefsky. Rissa avidly read the signs in Yiddish on display across the front of the theater, feeling a rush of excitement that eliminated the fatigue of the day's adventures.

In minutes the doors were opened. Shirley pulled Rissa along with her, up the steep staircase to their gallery seats.

'My two girls come here twice a week, like clockwork,' Shirley confided while they took their seats. 'It costs them maybe half a week's wages, but they still have enough to eat on. In New York a poor working girl can eat *and* go to the theater.'

When Thomashefsky appeared onstage, the audience went wild. The performance was received with an excitement that surpassed anything Rissa had encountered in Warsaw or London. By the end of the evening she was exhausted, vowing to find a place for herself in this blossoming Yiddish theater.

'Did I tell you wrong?' Shirley asked complacently while she guided Rissa around the corner from the theater toward Second Avenue. 'Nowhere is there an actor like Thomashefsky. He's rich. Even if he wasn't, he'd have a harem to support him.' Shirley sighed. 'You can't imagine the women he has in his bed. All ages. Young girls dying for love of him, middle-aged women who would pay to spend a night with the great Thomashefsky. Even grandmothers.'

'How many Yiddish theaters are there in New York?' Rissa shared the convivial mood of the theatergoers who thronged the streets.

'A dozen at least,' Shirley told her. 'What Jew doesn't love the theater?'

They went into a small café on Second Avenue for bowls of golden noodle soup and glasses of tea sweetened with gobs of strawberry preserves. Rissa was fascinated by the ebullient faces at the tables around them. This was America, where a Jew was free to rise in the world. Yet Shirley's stories often described the fate of young Jewish girls whose lives ended in suicide.

'They come here thinking to find money growing on trees. They want to send money home to their families. Maybe to bring them over here. You don't earn this sewing shirts,' Shirley said bluntly. 'They go to live in the houses on Allen or Forsythe, and they sell their bodies.' Shirley gestured with the sadness of a Keni Liptzin. 'Then they look at themselves in the mirror, and it's too much. They drink carbolic acid, or they turn on the gas.'

Such stories amazed Rissa. Life was a precious gift from God. How could anyone throw it away? In America there were no pogroms. There were jobs to be had for those who were willing to work. Life here was full of hope.

Tonight Rissa harbored no doubts of her future in the New World. She would find herself a job in the theater. Were there not at least a dozen Yiddish theaters in this wonderful city where everyone seemed to be Jewish?

The next morning, while Shirley and her girls worked at the sewing machines, Rissa prepared herself to go job hunting. Her blue serge dress with a touch of white lace at the collar would be just right, she decided. Already she longed to be performing in one of the theaters where Yiddish plays flourished. The theater was her refuge. The place she felt most safe and happy.

But three hours later, after having been summarily dismissed by half a dozen managers, Rissa became alarmed. Nowhere, it seemed, was there a job for a young actress. Three of the managers had shocked her with crude invitations to their beds. Nothing like this had occurred in Warsaw. Olga had spoken of no such troubles in London.

An elderly woman coming out of a stage door behind Rissa smiled sympathetically when Rissa paused on the sidewalk in uncertainty.

'Did that old fool try to take you to bed?' she asked bluntly.

'I only want a job.' Color stained Rissa's cheekbones. She was unaccustomed to such candid talk.

'Feldman never misses a chance if the girl is young and pretty. And there are others just like him,' the actress warned Rissa. 'Like Thomashefsky.' Her face softened. 'But from a man like that it's a favor already. Who can blame him if he has a girl with her skirts up in his dressing room before every performance? He's a god,' she sighed.

'I wouldn't consider it a favor.' Rissa was regal in her rejection.

The woman chuckled. 'Here in the Yiddish theater we're free of the old life the Torah ordered. The young ones are drunk with freedom.' Her smile was whimsical. 'It should only have happened thirty years ago when I was young enough to enjoy it.'

'I came to New York to be an actress,' Rissa said with a lift of her head. 'I've worked in Warsaw and in London. I thought it would be easy.'

'Come, I'll buy you a glass of tea,' the woman consoled. 'Let Bertha explain to you what goes on now in our theater.'

In a small nearby café Rissa listened to Bertha Finklestein, who had acted in Yiddish theater in Rumania, London and New York.

'It has always been hard to be an actor.' Bertha was philosophical. 'The managers – the *mamzerim* – persecute us. So finally a few years ago we got together and formed a union. We saw hardly enough money to eat. Is that right for actors and actresses who play kings and queens? But with the union came other problems. For young people like you it is hard. The union won't let anybody in until somebody already in the union dies. And it's a shame when an actress – a bubbi already – plays a fifteen-year-old on the stage.'

'But how can they keep us out?' Rissa stared in disbelief.

'They make the rules. First you have to play for years in theaters out of New York. That's Local Number Two. Then you do a *probe* before the judges. If they think you're good enough, you can join Local Number One and work here.'

'I won't leave New York!' Rissa was indignant.

'You can be a variety artist in New York,' Bertha soothed. 'You can work in the music halls. For that you can join Local Number Five.'

'What about three and four?' Rissa asked. What was this craziness? She was an actress.

Bertha shrugged.

'Nobody knows what's Number Three and Number Four. That's a secret even to the union. But a pretty girl like you can sing and dance a little and make a living here in the city.'

'I'm an actress, not a singer,' Rissa said stubbornly. She had sung in Mendele's company when it was necessary but her voice was not her real talent.

'Later you'll be an actress,' Bertha said. 'You're hitting your head against the wall to try to get into Local Number One. In wheelchairs already the actresses insist they can play young lovers.' Bertha reached a hand across the table to Rissa. 'Stars will come from the variety theaters yet. There's a young singer – her name is Sophia Tucker – I saw her myself in a variety house. You'll see, someday she'll be a big star. And look at Anna Held, already a big star uptown. Do you know where she came from?' Bertha's face was bright in triumph.

'No,' Rissa admitted. She didn't know who Anna Held was.

'Mr Ziegfeld's big star with the French accent, who's supposed to have been the toast of Paris – ' Bertha leaned forward in glee. 'She was in the chorus line in the Yiddish theater in London. She improved herself; she played *Shulamith*. Then she went to Paris and became French. That's where Ziegfeld found her.'

Rissa returned to Shirley's flat in despair. How could she be a singer in the music halls? For Mendele's little theater in Warsaw, her singing was all right. But she would not leave New York. She would stay here even if she must learn to sew shirts on those machines, like Shirley. She would succeed. Resolutely, she lifted her chin.

She, Rissa Lindowska, would become an actress in New York.

8

Max Miller tried to adjust his tall, slender frame to the clumsy, horsehair chair in Yetta Bernstein's ugly Victorian parlor. He had been summoned to the West Eighties brownstone, bequeathed to Yetta at her husband's death four years ago, for a 'business talk.' The music hall on the Bowery, which he managed for Yetta, was one of the investments she inherited.

Twice before Yetta had summoned him to her house. Both times she had been waiting in the cluttered parlor when he arrived. But now the maid told him that Yetta would 'receive' him shortly. That meant she wasn't coming downstairs, Max interpreted. Fat, fifty-plus Yetta would make yet another try to bring him into her bed.

Though the room was not overwarm, Max felt rivulets of perspiration form on his forehead. He ran a hand through his dark, unruly hair. His handsome, almost aristocratic features betrayed his discomfort. Twenty years of growing up in Georgia had not prepared him for the Yetta Bernsteins of the world.

The wages Yetta paid him were not impressive, but he needed the job. He needed the experience. It was theater, where he had vowed to spend his life. It didn't matter that this was the bottom of the ladder. He would rise.

Now Yetta hinted strongly that she might be

persuaded to back him in his own theater company. Not a storefront music hall. A real theater to present plays. Not the *shund* that everybody insisted was all you could show to Yiddish audiences. Max dreamed instead of Yiddish translations of Shakespeare and Ibsen.

'Mrs Bernstein will see you now.' The maid, immigrant Irish, hovered in the doorway. Her face conveyed her disgust at Yetta's sexual longings. 'In her bedroom on the third floor.'

His shoulders hunched in tension, Max hurried from the parlor into the narrow, dark, carpeted hallway and up the stairs.

'Maxila?' Yetta's East European accented voice came coyly through an open door. 'What takes you so long? At your age it's hard to climb the stairs?'

'I'm coming, Yetta.'

Yetta sat up in a massive mahogany bed, ensconced against a mound of pillows. Her heavy breasts were encased in a white satin, lace-trimmed negligee. Her cheeks rouged like a stagebound soubrette. Her eyes blackened with kohl. Hair hennaed. The newest edition of *Town Topics,* the gossip sheet about New York society that enthralled endless readers, lay at the foot of the bed.

'I'm so exhausted from my morning phone calls I couldn't bring myself to get up from bed, even though it's after nine. You forgive me, Maxila?' she crooned.

'Of course.' Max hovered in the open doorway. Yetta couldn't keep him here long. Now that he had added the one-reelers to their schedule, they opened at eleven in the morning. He had to be at the place by ten-thirty to set up.

'Darling, close the door,' Yetta ordered with a wave of one bediamonded hand. 'The maid has to hear our business?'

With a strained smile Max closed the door behind him.

'You're so tall and handsome.' Yetta was coquettish. 'Like a star in a play uptown. But to me you don't look Jewish.' Her eyes glittered. Did she expect him to open his pants and show her he was circumcised?

'I'm Jewish,' Max assured her. His father came from a small town near Riga. His mother from Kishinev.

'Herschel, may he rest in peace, always said Southern Jews were *goyim*. But what kind of name for a Jew is Miller?' Yetta clucked.

'In Europe it was Mueller,' Max explained. Though papa's family lived near Riga, German had been the language spoken. 'At Ellis Island they changed it to Miller.'

Yetta nodded.

'My cousin was named Rumshinsky. At Ellis Island all of a sudden he was Ryan.' Yetta patted an area of silken sheet. 'Come sit by me, Max. We'll talk business.'

'You're not too tired?' But he knew there was no escape this time. If he could just close his eyes and pretend she was that pretty girl that walked out of the music hall last night, saying she'd earn more as a whore on Chrystie Street than what Yetta Bernstein paid her.

'I'm never too tired to talk business. Herschel, may he rest in peace, always bragged about my business head. You're sure that thief at the door isn't robbing me blind?' Yetta's eyes narrowed in suspicion.

'I count the house,' Max soothed. 'Now with the one-reelers I have plenty of time to check up.' Bringing in the one-reelers with Ben Turpin and Mary Miles Minter to alternate with the acts in the evening had been his idea. He was intrigued by the new form of entertainment. Also, making the music hall into a nickelodeon by day increased their revenue.

'Max, you figured out how much it would cost to put up a theater?' Yetta leaned forward, allowing the negligee to part, displaying blue-veined pendulous breasts. God, she's older than mama, Max thought in revulsion. 'My lawyer tells me I'm *meshugah*, but I trust you.'

'I've got the finances all worked out.' He reached into his jacket pocket to bring forth the piece of paper over which he had labored with high hopes. He was convinced Yetta had more than enough money to handle the operation of a theater. 'We can bring something new into the Yiddish theater,' Max said enthusiastically. 'Audiences will love it.'

'Maybe I'll be less lonely with a new business.' Yetta sighed and reached for his free hand. Ignoring the paper he held in the other. 'You know I'm devoted to the theater.'

'It'll be exciting, Yetta.'

'You're exciting, Max. Like a young Thomashefsky. I'm jealous of those women in the music hall. All of them pulling up their skirts for you.'

'No time for that.' Max tried to sound like a tired roué. He was perspiring again.

'I'm a woman who needs a man in her bed.' Yetta was blunt in her heat. Max saw the rapid rise and fall of her breasts, heard her noisy breathing.

'Plenty of men must be chasing after you.' He managed an admiring smile.

'Old men after my money.' She brought his hand to her breast. 'Max, fuck me.'

Yetta lay back against the pillows, eyes closed, mouth parted in passion. Max forced himself to bring his mouth to hers. One hand fondled the white breast he coaxed from beneath her nightgown.

While Yetta moaned in appreciation, Max threw off the sheet with his unoccupied hand and pulled the white satin nightgown above her fleshy thighs.

'Oh, Maxila, good. Good,' she crooned while his hands fondled her.

He lifted himself above her and fumbled with the flap of his trousers. Yetta was a head shorter and sixty pounds heavier than he, Max speculated while he sought to arouse himself.

'Max, now,' Yetta implored, pulling him to her. 'Do it already!'

With his eyes shut, thrusting himself into Yetta, Max was astonished to find himself able to perform. She moaned in vocal approval. Yetta's husband must have had a hard time satisfying her. Everybody said older women were hot.

* * *

98

Max stood beside the bed, shaking in rage. This overheated bitch was using him.

'Max, you come to me and show me you've got a Thomashefsky or an Adler, and I go right to the bank for the money,' she said dramatically. 'But without a star, what's the use?'

'I have to go down to the music hall.' He tried to keep anger out of his voice. 'I have to hire a new singer. Lottie walked out last night.'

'That *kurve*. That whore,' Yetta said in contempt. 'Better she's gone.'

All the way downtown Max cursed himself for allowing Yetta to drag him into her bed. She never meant to open up a real theater; she just wanted to be screwed. As soon as he could find another job, he'd leave.

Arriving downtown Max stopped in a delicatessen for a corned beef sandwich. The same delicatessen where he had worked behind the counter little more than a year ago. Now people knew him. Actors who couldn't get into the union came to him and asked for jobs.

'Max, so when you're gonna be a big producer?' his ex-boss jibed good-humoredly.

'When I find somebody with money to back me. What about you, Izzy? You're rich.'

'Sure, I go out every morning into my backyard in Brownsville, and I pick the money from the trees.' Izzy piled the corned beef into a staggering heap on a slice of rye. 'What's the matter with Yetta Bernstein?'

'She's a horny old bag,' Max said. Now his face

was serious. 'Izzy, if you hear of somebody who wants a new manager, let me know.'

Max ate his sandwich with gusto; he knew it would be close to midnight before he could leave the music hall to eat again. When he got there this morning, he would find performers waiting to see him. He had put a sign on the window that he needed a young female singer.

When Max arrived at the store plastered with posters offering the delights of the new one-reelers by day plus 'variety acts' by night, he found the cashier waiting for him to open up.

'I sent six women away,' Seligman reported with an air of importance. 'All dogs.'

'You should have let me see them,' Max reprimanded, slipping a key into the padlock on the door.

'Max, you asked for a young girl singer,' Seligman protested. 'The youngest was forty-five.'

'So we should be different from the other theaters?' Max laughed.

'Hey, Max. That girl coming toward us,' Seligman whispered. 'She's been walking back and forth three times already. Always reading the sign. A beauty,' he clucked in appreciation.

Max turned to inspect the small, slight, dark-haired girl walking toward them. Sixteen or seventeen, he guessed. With those looks she shouldn't have to be able to sing.

Max opened the door and walked inside. He watched her approach. If she didn't come in, he thought on impulse, he'd go out and talk to her. She was new to the lower East Side; she was scared to come in and ask for the job. Yet he saw the hunger on her face.

The little dark-haired beauty lifted her head with an air of confidence that stirred him unexpectedly. She opened the door and walked inside, hesitated a moment before she spoke to him.

'You're looking for a singer?' Her voice told him she was not long in this country. But it was not the typical 'greenhorn' accent. From England, he guessed. She had learned her first English over there. Upper-class English, he noted with approval. Not cockney.

'You sing?' He couldn't hire her without some byplay. She'd have no respect for him.

'I sing a little.' She was honest. 'I was an actress in the Yiddish theater in Warsaw and London. Sometimes I sang.' She seemed disconcerted by the intensity of his gaze. 'I don't want to go out of town,' she filled in the silence that hung over them. 'The union says I can work only at a music hall.' She tried for a wry smile.

'Sing for me,' Max ordered. ' "Raisins and Almonds." ' Every singer knew it.

'Without music?' She was frightened. She didn't know that Max had already decided to hire her.

'Seligman,' Max called to the cashier who doubled as a musician when he was needed. 'Play for her.' He turned back to his new singer. 'I'm Max Miller. The manager.'

'I'm Rissa Lindowska,' she said and went to stand beside the piano.

Max settled himself on a chair at one of the front tables. He felt her anxiety. Her eagerness to please him. She was right; she sang a little. But it was enough. He recognized instinctively a quality in her that would reach out to audiences. All at once he was excited about Rissa Lindowska's talent. If she handled herself right, that one would be another Keni Liptzin.

'You'll go on tonight,' he said, and her eyes widened in relief. 'You'll sing "Raisins and Almonds" and play in four skits.' Without moving his eyes from Rissa, he gestured to Seligman to go set up the one-reelers because the projectionist hadn't arrived yet. 'I'll run through the skits with you.' Lottie had sung four raunchy songs. He recoiled from the prospect of hearing such lyrics emerge from Rissa Lindowska. He'd give them to the character woman, he decided recklessly.

'You have a prompter?' All at once Rissa was nervous.

'For skits who needs them?' Max smiled reassuringly.

'Max,' Seligman called. 'Hymie's late again. I'll have to be piano player today.' Seligman was pleased.

'Where's Jake?' It was Jake's job to run the projector.

'Snoozing at the door,' Seligman said. 'Jake,' he yelled, 'bring your ass inside.'

'I'll have to be at the door to collect money until the piano player gets in,' Max apologized. 'Come stay with me at the cash box, and we'll go over the skits.'

* * *

Lightheaded with satisfaction Rissa walked across Second Avenue and downtown to Essex Street. Max had told her that here was no different from anywhere else; the actors made up lines, put in their own little bits. But she would know every word to be prepared, she promised herself. Tonight she would be on the stage again. She would be home.

She let herself into Shirley's flat, where the sewing machines would whir until it was time for her to go to the theater. She told Shirley she had a job.

'I'll come to the theater tonight!' Shirley was awed at sharing her flat with an actress.

'Wait till Saturday,' Rissa pleaded. 'When I'm not so scared.'

Relief welled up in her. After twelve days of frenzied searching she had a job. Each time she took money from the stake provided by Lord Cambridge, she was nervous. That money was her only protection against the world.

Earlier than necessary Rissa headed back to the music hall. She felt an exhilarating sense of adventure as she passed the brilliantly lighted theater marquees proclaiming the names of Thomashefsky, Adler, David Kessler, Keni Liptzin. Magic names.

Rissa stared into the procession of cafés and the coffee-and-cake parlors that seemed to explode with life. This was a Yiddish theater new and exciting to her. Warsaw and London seemed weak replicas of New York.

She would not stay at the music hall, Rissa promised herself. She would discover a way to play in the theaters that the Hebrew Actors Union claimed were barred to her until she had performed for years in cities with strange names like Boston, Philadelphia, Chicago and Cleveland.

She felt a familiar shyness when Max Miller introduced her to the other members of the company. Still, the backstage atmosphere was warm and friendly, though she didn't understand some of the things that were said and made everybody laugh. Only a statuesque woman in her forties, who proclaimed herself the company prima donna, inspected Rissa with hostility.

Rissa sweated through the evening's performance. She was letter-perfect; the others in the skits roamed off into private soliloquies, injected unexpected bits. She was conscious of a competitiveness that had not been apparent in Mendele's theater until her collision with Manya.

Changing from her costume for the final skit, Rissa worried that Max Miller might have been displeased with her, though after her song the audience applauded loudly. Max was young — perhaps as young as Phillip — but he seemed so sure of himself. If he wasn't satisfied with her, he'd tell her to go.

Max closed up the cash box for the night and locked it away. Watching for Rissa to emerge from the rear. He'd take her out for tea and cake. They had to talk about what else she could do in the company.

'Rissa – ' He saw her stop short at the sound of his voice. What a beautiful smile she had! 'Rissa, I thought we ought to talk about another song for you. We'll go over to Marcus's for cake and tea.'

Max saw the wariness that crept into her eyes. Already she'd heard the stories about the wild life on Second Avenue, he thought. She knew about all the little shopgirls and sewing-machine operators who sprawled on the couch in Thomashefsky's dressing room. She was afraid he was going to try to throw her on her back.

While he guided her through the heavy after-theater crowds that made walking an obstacle course, Max told Rissa about the cafés. Oases for actors, writers, musicians, intellectuals. Most of the immigrant workers on the East Side came into the cafés only on special occasions.

At Marcus's he led her to a table in the bright, cheerful room, hazed over with cigarette smoke and tea steam. He told himself that it was insane to feel as though his whole world had changed because he met a little dark-haired girl named Rissa Lindowska. Mama could stop worrying that he would fall in love with a *shiksa*.

'I was born and raised in a little town midway between Atlanta and Columbus, down in Georgia. So small you could spit across it.' He chuckled at her incomprehension. 'Georgia is a state down south. We didn't have Yiddish theater down there. I spent all my time reading plays I took out of the school library. Shakespeare, Ibsen, Shaw.'

'I saw a play by Shaw in London,' Rissa volunteered. '*Doctor's Dilemma*. It was wonderful.' Curiosity pushed aside shyness. 'Did you come to New York to be in the Yiddish theater?'

'I came to New York to be part of the theater,' Max said softly. 'I don't think I really understood that I was a Jew until just before I left the South. There were three Jewish families in town. On Rosh Hashanah and Yom Kippur my father went to Columbus to attend services at their *shul*. On Friday nights my mother lit candles. Beyond that – ' Max shrugged expressively, 'I was a *goy*.'

'But you speak Yiddish.' Rissa seemed perplexed. 'I've heard you.'

'When I came to New York, I knew a few words. The only Yiddish spoken in the house was by my grandmother. She died when I was seven. We were Georgians except on special occasions. Until 1903.' Max's face tensed in recall. 'My parents had saved for twenty-two years to have enough money to bring over my three aunts and their families in Kishinev.'

Max was too caught up in memory to see Rissa's face go pale. 'The tickets had been sent already. All at once the whole world – even Belleville, Georgia – knew about the massacre at Kishinev.'

'Please,' Rissa whispered, and he was stricken by the desolation in her eyes. 'May I go home?'

'Rissa, did I say something wrong?' he stammered.

'The massacre at Kishinev.' Tears filled her eyes and spilled over. 'Three years later, on the seventh night of Passover, the peasants came to my *dorf*. They killed my mother and father, my grandfather, my two sisters and my two brothers. Only I escaped.'

'Rissa, I didn't know.' He reached a hand across the table to cover hers.

'I'm sorry.' She tried to brush away the tears.

106

Max felt a protectiveness toward her that he had never experienced. He shouldn't even think about how it would be to make love to Rissa, he reproached himself. She was sweet and untouched and beautiful. Rissa was marriage and children and the tomorrow about which he dreamed.

'I'll take you home, Rissa,' he said tenderly.

9

Rissa's joy at being again on the Yiddish stage after all the fallow months in London was clouded by a growing comprehension of the bawdiness of the presentations at the music hall. While Shirley and she sat in a café near the music hall between Sunday matinee and evening performances, she confessed that the dirty jokes, the vulgar songs, the suggestive gestures disturbed her.

'*Bubele*, it's no different in the theatres,' Shirley soothed. 'Sure, the theaters think they're so much better than the music halls, but what's the difference? Music halls, theaters – they all got to give Moishe what Moishe wants. So Abraham Cahan wrote a letter in the *Forward* to Jewish actresses, asking them as "honored ladies of the Yiddish stage, decent women and mothers," to stop using dirty language, to stop singing dirty songs.'

'What happened?' Rissa found little comfort in Shirley's wisdom.

'What could happen?' Shirley suggested. 'Jewish actresses want to eat, too.'

'I feel bad just standing there on the stage when they say those things.' Rissa knew that her presence was interwoven with the raunchy humor that brought bursts of laughter from the audience. So far Max had given her nothing to do that she could not have done in Mendele's theater. So far. 'I remember what papa said about actors. To him they were dirt. I'd told myself being an actress wasn't bad. It wasn't wrong; it was different. But now I worry. Mama and papa would spit at me for working at the music hall.' She had vowed to bring respect to the Lindowska name. Now she shamed it.

'Rissa, stop worrying,' Shirley ordered while her brilliant blue eyes moved about the café in search of stage faces she knew. Rissa brought her in touch with a world she had worshipped from afar. 'People come into the music halls and the theaters because they need to forget their *tsores*, their problems. They need to laugh, Rissa.' Shirley's face took on a solemnity rarely in evidence. 'They come to America from pogroms. From being kicked and starved. Every ship from Europe brings more of them. And what do they find here? Streets of gold like we heard in the Old Country?'

'No,' Rissa admitted. For the rich there were houses on Fifth Avenue. Immigrants lived crowded together in small dark rooms.

'Here they sweat fourteen, sixteen, even eighteen hours a day. Making shirts and pants and button-holes. But they can do this, Rissa, because once or twice a week they run to the theater or the music hall. They can laugh. For a few hours they forget the sweatshops.'

'Max told me he wanted to do fine one-act plays at the music hall. Between the songs and the dancing. His boss says no.' She would have tea with Max after tonight's performance. He was giving her a part in another sketch. He kept giving her more to do. She was pleased, but remembering Manya, she worried that the other actresses would be angry and cause trouble.

'Max is smart. He knows his boss wants to make money. The music hall is not the Ladies Fuel and Aid Society. He has to give people what they want to see,' Shirley reiterated. 'And everybody says now business is not so good. Only last week my contractor cut what he pays me for each piece we finish. He talks to me about the Standard Oil scandal and the trouble on Wall Street. What do I know about these things? I know only that I'm making less money.'

'Shirley, go to the talks at Cooper Union,' Rissa urged. 'There you'll learn.' She knew that Shirley, orphaned at eleven and without brothers and sisters, was sensitive about her lack of education.

'For three years I went to night school,' Shirley reminded. 'So for a while let me go to the theater instead.'

'I'll be home late tonight,' Rissa warned. 'I'm going to Shulem's for tea with Max after the performance. To talk about another sketch.'

'One month at the music hall, and seven times already Max takes you out for tea,' Shirley teased.

'Shirley, it's business,' Rissa said. 'It's the only time Max has.'

Max was pleased with her work. He told her their audiences liked her. But sometimes he looked at her in a way that made her uncomfortable. She saw in Max's eyes, in unguarded moments, the same look she had seen in Phillip's eyes.

She wanted no more of love. Even now, when she had told herself her love for Phillip was dead, she lay awake nights remembering the agony of seeing his face staring at her from the *Morning Star*. She seethed with the realization that Phillip had meant to come back to her after his honeymoon. To go on lying to her. Never would she allow another man to use her that way again.

'If you weren't young and pretty, Max Miller wouldn't talk business over tea,' Shirley said. 'He takes his horse-faced prima donna out for tea? That fat cow who sings dirty songs and wiggles her ass and hates you because you're thirty-five years younger than she is?'

Rissa was distressed.

'Don't tell anybody I told she she's nasty to me.' She was a member of the union now, though she could only work as a variety artist in New York; she didn't depend on marks at the end of the week. She had a regular salary. For that, she admitted, she had to thank the union. She didn't want to lose her job. Not when everybody was crying about how terrible business was.

'The great prima donna would be less nasty if her husband, the great comic, wasn't always trying for a feel.' Shirley was blunt.

'I have to go back for the evening performance,' Rissa apologized. She knew Shirley would like to stay as long as they could stretch a piece of cake and a glass of tea. 'I have to sew a button on my costume. The neck's too low.'

'The audience would be happier if you left it off,'

Shirley laughed. 'The men especially would be happier.'

Rissa hurried back to the music hall. She was discomfited as much by the hostility of the prima donna as by the lecherous efforts of the lady's husband. Onstage he took liberties; he used the excuse that the audience loved it. His wife hurled insults at Rissa; Rissa tried to ignore them. She must keep this job.

Max was at the cashier's booth, stifling yawns as he sold tickets between performances. Tonight, instead of going himself, he had sent the cashier up to Yetta Bernstein's house with the sealed cash receipts for the week. For the second week he had used the excuse that he had a bad cold.

For two weeks before his 'bad cold,' he had delivered the receipts to her lawyer. Yetta had been out in Chicago to supervise the *bris* of her newest grandson. He had been spared a rerun in her bedroom.

His eyes brightened as he spied Rissa returning for the evening's performance. He had always fallen asleep each night the minute his head hit the pillow, until he encountered this small, dark-haired beauty whose face made him think of the Bible.

Max cursed the pogrom that had left Rissa orphaned. He would remember forever the anguish on Rissa's face when he told her how his mother's family was wiped out in the massacre at Kishinev.

Rissa trusted no one, he warned himself. Damn that son-of-a-bitch comic, trying for a cheap feel every chance he got. Onstage and off. He'd warned the bastard to leave Rissa alone. Why didn't his wife slap him down?

He must be careful the way he approached Rissa. If he showed a romantic interest, she'd run. But the right time would come, he consoled himself. No girl had ever rejected him. But he had never been serious about any girl until Rissa walked into his life. This was not a girl to take to his room for a night. This was his little Jewish nun who would someday be his wife.

'Max – ' The cashier intruded. 'Mrs Bernstein wants you should come up to her house tomorrow morning. If,' he stipulated, 'your cold is better.' He grinned. 'I know. It's gonna be worse tomorrow. If you don't go, call her. She'll have to look for somebody else to give her a *shtup*.'

Max waited for the performance to be over. All the while making notes to pass on to the company. Rissa must be given more to do onstage. The audience knew she was special. Rissa would bring customers.

She had perfect timing, he thought with pleasure. With no training Rissa knew the value of a special look, a special smile at the right moment. Instinct, he thought in proprietary pride. No training could teach an actress what Rissa knew.

Where the hell would he find comedy material good enough to show her off? She could make an audience cry, and she could make them laugh. But the Hebrew Actors Union said she couldn't play in a Yiddish theater in New York. Only in a music hall.

At last Max was able to close up for the night and

go with Rissa to Shulem's. Earlier he had nodded in a show of sympathy to the prima donna's string of complaints about Rissa. Let her complain if it made her happy.

Tonight over tea Max confided to Rissa that he yearned to direct in Yiddish theater.

'But not *shund*,' he said scornfully. 'Why must Yiddish plays all be trash?'

'There are good plays,' Rissa protested, her eyes aglow with a zeal that evoked passion from Max. 'Aren't there?'

'Yes,' Max smiled wryly. 'Keni Liptzin loses money every time she presents a Gordin play, but she has a husband who can pay the bills. Even Adler has to give in and play *shund*.' His eyes grew luminous. 'I wish I had been in New York when Adler played Shylock. People from uptown came down in droves to see him. Two years later he played Shylock on Broadway. God, what an actor!'

Rissa was struggling to assimilate what he had said. Sometimes he forgot she was so new to America.

'Broadway is uptown theater? The Gentile theater?' Rissa was puzzled. 'But how could Jacob Adler play in the theater where they speak American?'

'English,' Max corrected her. 'They speak English. Adler played Shylock in Yiddish; the rest of the company played in English. Last year Bertha Kalisch played *Kreutzer Sonata* in English on Broadway.'

'Gordin's *Kreutzer Sonata*?'

Max chuckled.

'A translation of Gordin's play from the Tolstoy novel,' Max explained. Enjoying the current of excitement that suffused Rissa each time they talked about theater. 'Of course, today everybody insists Gordin is old-fashioned. They don't understand that he sees theater as more than entertainment,' Max leaned forward in his eagerness to make Rissa understand. 'Gordin expects a play to bring knowledge to an audience. To stimulate their minds.' This was the kind of theater that obsessed him. Broadway had fine actors, yet no new playwrights worthy of their talents. Where were the new playwrights? It was difficult for a new director with ambition to break through uptown. Downtown the opportunities were better. 'Rissa, the audiences need to be educated to enjoy fine plays.'

'Shirley says that Gordin's play *Elisha ben Avuya* played only a few times,' Rissa remembered. 'Even with Adler in it.' She shook her head in astonishment.

'It's out of its time,' Max reiterated. He stirred his tea with unnecessary vigor. 'Someday it'll be presented again and be a sensation,' he predicted. 'But Gordin, too, has had to "bake" a few plays in his times.'

'Bake?' Rissa was bewildered.

'That means he had to write plays that were just like the others, made from the same batch of dough. Over and over, the same old junk. It's an expression everybody in the Yiddish theater uses.'

He could make a star of Rissa Lindowska, and in doing so prove himself as a director. Seeing her in their rotten skits he knew this. So she didn't have a great singing voice. Was Adler a singer?

But he must move slowly. Rissa was scared by

what she saw on Second Avenue. The obscenity on-stage. The stories that circulated all over the East Side about Thomashefsky's women and Adler's women. She was shocked by the way actresses and sewing-machine girls alike were ready to lie down for any actor who was good-looking. They were all drunk on the new freedom they discovered on the lower East Side.

'Max, you're an American. Why do you want to be in the Yiddish theater?'

Rissa had forgotten what he had told her that first night he took her out for tea, Max thought. How he had discovered he was a Jew when mama's family died in Kishinev. His grandmother, aunts, uncles, cousins had been brutally murdered. It could have been papa and mama and himself. He was no longer just an American. He was an American and a Jew. He'd looked at his neighbors in Belleville and he knew that this was the difference between them. It wasn't a question of what God each respected. It was a whole different culture. Now it meant something special when mama lit the candles each Friday night. The holidays held a special meaning.

'Max?' Rissa probed uneasily.

'I'm sorry,' he apologized. 'I was thinking about being a Jew in Georgia. But even though my Yiddish is sometimes ridiculous,' he chuckled, 'I want to be part of the Yiddish theater. With all my complaints I still love the special excitement down here. I make fun of the audience's taste but I admire their passion.'

'But here everybody talks about going uptown to Broadway,' Rissa reminded wistfully.

'Bertha Kalisch divides her time between uptown and downtown,' he pointed out. Damn Yetta for not putting up the money for his own company. In three years, with his own company, he'd make a star of Rissa. He'd comb the city for new plays for her. Surround her with fine actors. The critics would rave about her. 'Jacob Adler was satisfied to do just Shylock uptown,' Max admitted. 'Anyway, uptown they're doing only stupid plays with no substance. No real value. In the Yiddish theater I have a chance to become somebody important.'

It had shocked mama when he confessed he was determined to become part of the New York theater. It had shocked her more to find out he was intrigued with Yiddish theater. She had tried since she was a little girl to become as Americanized as their neighbors in Belleville, Georgia.

'In Warsaw we did plays by Goldfaden, or whatever Mendele bought for us to do.' Rissa was wistful. 'Just before I left Warsaw, he said he would have a play written for me.'

Someone else saw in Rissa what he saw, Max thought with satisfaction. She had a marvelous ear. In a year or two her English should be flawless. He lay awake nights now, too keyed up to sleep. Thinking of parts that Rissa could play as soon as her accent disappeared. Cordelia in *King Lear*, Anya in *The Cherry Orchard*, Nora in *Riders to the Sea*.

'What kind of plays did you do in London? The same old *shund*?'

Rissa lowered her eyes. Her fingers toyed with the glass of tea.

'I did little in London.' Color highlighted her cheekbones. 'It was a waste of time.'

She had been unhappy in London. He didn't dare probe.

'We'll go over the new skit when I walk you home,' he said. He was reluctant to part from Rissa. His cheap hall-bedroom, which he preferred to call a studio, offered no incentive to go home. When he first rented it, he had gloried in having a place of his own. He had pasted the walls with theater posters, bought a painting to hang over his cot from a neighbor who was studying at the Art Students League. He hesitated. 'Have you ever seen Central Park?'

'No.' The sharpness in her voice startled him. For an instant he retreated.

'It's beautiful,' he cajoled. 'I thought you might like to walk through the park one afternoon.' He'd manage for somebody to cover for him for a couple of hours. He worked seven days a week; Yetta couldn't complain if she found out. 'The leaves are beginning to turn red and gold and brown. When I get homesick, I go to Central Park.' His smile was charismatic.

'I think I'd like that,' Rissa agreed after a moment.

'Tomorrow?' Max was exhilarated by this success.

'Tomorrow,' Rissa said.

10

On her cot in the kitchen Rissa tried to sleep despite the whirring of the sewing machines in the next room. This morning she found it difficult. In another hour she must rise and dress for her trip to Central Park with Max. She had not traveled above Eighth Street except on the day of her arrival.

Why had she said she would go to Central Park with Max? Already she heard whispers backstage about Max and her. Because he tried to help her, she thought defensively. He knew how anxious she was to hold her place in the company.

The curtain between the 'shop' room and the kitchen parted. Shirley came into the kitchen to fix another pot of tea.

'Rissa, you're awake so early?' Her eyes, which Rissa thought the most beautiful she had ever seen, were compassionate. 'The machines woke you.'

'No,' Rissa denied. 'I came home early last night.' Shirley was always asleep when she arrived home from the music hall; she rose at five in the morning.

'I know,' Shirley jeered. 'You're rushing up to the Astor Library again. Soon they'll run out of books for you to read,' she laughed.

'This morning Max is taking me to Central Park,' Rissa explained.

'Ah-hah,' Shirley said with delight.

'No "ah-hah,"' Rissa reprimanded. 'Max is home-sick. When he's homesick, he goes to Central Park. Because I remind him of his little sister, he asked me to go with him,' she improvised. Max had no little sister; he told her he was an only child.

'He didn't ask the prima donna to go with him,' Shirley pointed out.

'Max wasn't looking for a grandmother to go with him to the park,' Rissa shot back.

'Never mind,' Shirley soothed. 'Someday you'll be playing with Thomashefsky and Adler and Kessler. You'll have your own *patriotn*.' Rissa knew about the special fans of stars, who provided ovations at every appearance onstage, showered the stars with gifts, were eager to run their errands. 'And I'll talk about how you lived with me on Essex Street.'

To Rissa the trip uptown with Max on the Elevated was a great adventure. Even Shirley admitted she had been uptown only twice since her arrival in New York. To most East Side immigrants, uptown was a foreign country.

With Phillip she had seen much of London, but that had been a transitory period. New York was where she meant to spend the rest of her life. She was greedy, as was Max, to see every inch of this fantastic, sometimes exciting, sometimes frightening city.

From the Elevated, still a daring journey to Rissa, she saw the slums of the city that followed the lines of the Elevated trains.

'Look at the windows in the tenements,' Max said with a rare bitterness. 'Behind every one of them are

120

men and women breaking their backs sewing, pressing. From six in the morning till midnight. I've taken the Elevated at night. Not just the Jews. Every nationality from Europe goes through the same hardships. Three-quarters of the city lives in tenements, works unbelievable hours.' He smiled faintly. 'Down in Belleville my father opens the store at six in the morning to catch the millworkers' business. Mama complains that he doesn't get home again till after six in the evening. But when papa is tired, he sits down. What profit comes in is his. If he has something special he wants to do, he leaves mama in the store. But here they come from Europe to live like slaves.'

'Still, in New York it is better,' Rissa said with the wisdom of one who had seen life in the Old Country. 'No pogroms here. Freedom. *Hope*, Max. Someday it can be better.'

Max prodded her from her seat as they pulled into a station. He guided her out onto the platform and down the stairs to the street. They walked west toward Central Park. Rissa was entranced by this New York that was new to her.

'Oh, Max!' She paused at intervals to drink in the sights that assaulted her from every side.

She was awed by the brown sandstone palaces that rose majestically along Fifth Avenue. She stared at the elegant carriages with liveried coachmen that rolled along the avenue, at the occasional automobile that attracted the attention of pedestrians.

'That car there,' Max pointed out. 'It's a taximeter cab, run by electricity. A bunch of them were imported from Paris in May.'

'The people who live in those houses must be very rich,' Rissa said softly. Like Phillip's parents.

'This is Millionaires' Row,' Max said. His face wore the intensity of a religious zealot. 'Some day, Rissa, we'll live like that.'

At the entrance to Central Park, Max pointed out the newly completed Plaza. He showed her the fourteen-story, columned Hotel Savoy whose interior was said to be decorated with Oriental opulence. The Romanesque New Netherlands Hotel.

'We'll go to the zoo,' Max decided. 'You'll enjoy that.'

Rissa felt a surge of pleasure as they walked into the park. She had forgotten there could be such vast expanses of open land. She remembered the undulating fields in Poland, the beauty of rye swaying in the breeze. In London, and now on the lower East Side, she lived in a dark little area where every inch of land seemed to be weighed down with tenements.

She was conscious of Max's hand at her elbow as he guided her along the path to the zoo. Max made her feel cherished and protected. But she distrusted these emotions. She had felt cherished and protected with Phillip, but it had been a terrible lie.

He was lonely, she told herself. Wasn't it natural for him to want someone close to his own age to share this trip to Central Park? Besides, Max was her boss; how could she have refused?

They deserted the zoo after a pleasant interval and settled themselves on a swathe of still-green grass beneath the autumn-touched trees. Rissa drew in a deep breath. Even the air seemed different here.

Max pulled a small book from his jacket pocket to read to her. It was a play. A translation of Strindberg's *Miss Julie*. Rissa sat with her back resting against a tree and listened while Max read. To their far left a group of boys played ball. To their right a carriage rolled over the road.

'Do you like the play?' Max asked when he had finished.

'It's beautiful,' Rissa said. She must look for it at the Astor Library. Max had read words she didn't understand. It was a compulsion with her to learn.

'The park is beautiful. It's a joy.' Max squinted reflectively. 'I wonder if I could survive in New York without the park? Sometimes the lower East Side is so depressing I feel an urge to run. Of course, I write my mother that everything here is wonderful,' he laughed. 'But sometimes I miss the wide streets, the lawns, the quietness back home.' His eyes softened with nostalgia.

'But you wouldn't want to go back?' All at once she was fearful of losing Max.

'Never,' he assured her. 'Except to visit my folks when I can afford it. It's been over three years since I've seen mama and papa. I'd never been away from them for a day until I came here. But each time I think I have the train fare, I lose my job and the money disappears for food and rent. Someday I'd like you to meet mama and papa,' he said quietly.

Rissa tensed. She stared at her hands in discomfort. *Please, Max, don't say anything.* Let everything stay just as it was. She wasn't ready for anything more.

'But I love this crazy city.' Max deliberately shifted

123

moods. 'I crave the excitement the city provides. The theaters, the cafés, the people. What kind of intellectual stimulus would I find in Belleville? I love the lectures at Cooper Union. The visits to the Metropolitan Museum of Art. We must go to the Metropolitan,' he said ebulliently, and paused at her sudden look of discomfiture.

'Shouldn't we be going back downtown?' Rissa rose to her feet in such haste she stumbled and would have fallen if Max had not reached out to catch her. She didn't want to think about museums of art. Paintings. She had visited too many museums and art exhibitions with Phillip.

'Max, I miss you here behind the counter,' his former boss at the delicatessen admitted while he sliced the pastrami with the abandon Max appreciated. 'The women still ask about you. God knows why, but to them you were another Mogulesko.'

'And you paid me like a bit player,' Max reprimanded, enjoying the exchange of verbal insults with the delicatessen owner. 'When are you going to back a theater company for me?'

'How come Yetta Bernstein isn't doing it?'

'Fuck Yetta Bernstein,' Max grimaced.

'That's what she's asking for.' With a wide grin Max's former employer handed over a pastrami sandwich where meat was thicker than bread. 'Put a paper bag over her face, and who's to know the difference?'

Max finished his sandwich and tea at the delicatessen and sauntered back to the music hall. The afternoon with Rissa had been good, he thought, though he was still conscious that she held him at a distance. But there were moments when she relaxed with him. She loved the theater the way he loved it.

The evening was crisp and cold, a harbinger of winter. His first winter in New York he had suffered from the cold; now he was used to it. Rissa would love Central Park in the winter, with snow blanketing the earth.

The cashier beckoned frantically to Max as he approached.

'What's the problem?' Max hovered before the cashier's booth.

'She's here,' Seligman said in an exaggerated whisper, gesturing inside. 'Yetta Bernstein.'

'Damn!' In the seven months that he had been working at the music hall, Yetta had come down twice. Each time half the company had walked out because of the way she talked to them. Her lawyer tried to keep her away.

Max hurried inside and strode toward the backstage area. Already he could hear his prima donna's outraged tones as she blasted Yetta with complaints.

'Yetta, how do you expect me to perform with that little nothing – that Rissa – making faces every time I have a good line?' She was complaining about Rissa's appealing way of listening to another actor. 'She thinks every man sitting out there is dying to stuff himself into her! On my best laughs she leans over so her *tsitskes* are almost hanging out!'

'Sweetheart, keep calm,' Yetta soothed. The prima donna and she were old friends. 'With your talent

125

what's to worry about? Who's gonna look at her *tsitskes* when you're onstage?'

'She's lying!' Rissa charged from the dressing room as Max arrived backstage. Her face was scarlet. 'I don't try any funny business on her lines. And I would never be so vulgar as to display myself for the audience.' Subconsciously one hand rose to the neckline of her modest shirtwaist.

'Rissa's right,' Max said to Yetta, her corpulence barely contained in a red satin dress that matched her rouged cheeks. 'Rissa has never made one move to steal anybody's scene. She's — '

'Sure, Max is going to defend her,' the prima donna interrupted. Her voice was shrill and vindictive. 'Why shouldn't he? She's giving him what he wants every night. Yetta, thick as thieves they are.'

Yetta gasped. Her eyes swung to Max. She saw herself as the betrayed lover. Rissa had stolen Max from her.

'I run a music hall here, Max. Not a whorehouse!' Her face worked in rage. 'No monkey business!' She turned to Rissa. 'You're fired. Get out.' She waved one heavy hand in dismissal.

Stricken, Rissa turned to Max in mute appeal.

'Yetta, calm down,' Max coaxed. 'Rissa is becoming our star. People come back to see her. You don't want us to lose our biggest attraction.'

'She's fired!' Yetta shrieked, a hand at her bosom. 'She don't play tonight. I don't give money to a whore.'

'Shut up, Yetta!' Max abandoned cajolery. How dare the old bitch talk like that about Rissa.

'Don't tell me what to do, Max. I could fire you, too,' Yetta warned.

'Don't bother!' he yelled. 'I quit.' He turned to Rissa. 'Get your things, Rissa. We're through with this place.'

'You can't quit!' Yetta screamed. 'You're fired! I'll tell every music hall operator in New York how you both stole from me. You won't work in another music hall as long as you live.' She stood there, churning in impotent fury while Max helped Rissa gather her things.

11

Feeling herself in the midst of a fresh nightmare, Rissa walked with Max into the cold night. The roaring of an Elevated train charging above the Bowery brought an involuntary flinch of protest. Tonight the noise was an ugly intrusion.

'Rissa, don't look like that,' Max implored. 'Everything will work out all right.'

Rissa lifted her eyes to Max. Despite his show of optimism he was worried. She had been so concerned about herself she had forgotten that Max, too, was out of work. *Max had quit his job because of her.*

'Max, you should not have talked back to Mrs Bernstein.' But a warmth suffused her despite the sharp drop in temperature. Phillip would never have made such a noble gesture. 'Because of me you don't have a job.'

'It doesn't matter,' Max insisted. 'I couldn't stay there without you.' He put a protective hand at her arm as they were jostled by the early evening hordes along the Bowery. 'Let's walk uptown a piece. We'll talk.'

Rissa listened to Max with only part of her mind. She was stunned that, in brief moments, she could have moved from popular actress to unemployed immigrant. Shirley had said she would teach her to use the sewing machine if she ever found herself without a job. Shirley's 'cockroach contractor' would be glad to send in more work. Rissa frowned. No. She was an actress. She would work only on a stage.

At Fourteenth Street Max led her into the Automat, a strange kind of self-service café that had opened four years ago, he explained. Here they dropped coins into a slot; a door opened and they pulled out their choice of the food available. But despite Max's efforts to dispel her despair, Rissa was haunted by the knowledge that she was without a job.

'Mrs Bernstein meant what she said?' Rissa sought Max's denial of the threat. 'She'll lie? She'll tell people we stole from her?'

Max's hand reached across the small white table to cover hers in consolation.

'Yetta will tell them,' he admitted. 'She's a vindictive old witch. But that's not to say they'll believe her. We'll find jobs, Rissa.'

But in the weeks that followed Rissa grew increasingly alarmed. Business was bad everywhere. In the music halls, in the stores, in the cafés. Max conceded that Yetta had made it hard for them in the music halls, but even without her everybody was cutting back.

New Yorkers had been shocked when the Knickerbocker Trust Company closed its doors to depositors. Now other banks in New York, and all over the country, were closing. Businesses were failing.

Each dollar that Rissa withdrew from her small stake was a wrench. She was frightened at what would happen if she didn't find work before her money ran out, though Shirley insisted that Rissa could continue to share the flat without pay.

Together Max and she searched for work. In between, Max took her about New York, with Rissa protesting the wasted nickels he spent on carefare. He showed her Washington Square, though he never invited her to come up to his studio in a rooming house on the south side of the square.

The once fine houses on the south side of Washington Square had been turned into cheap lodgings because of the six- and seven-story railroad flats rising behind them to house the Italians swarming into the area. The red brick houses on the north side of the park remained elegant private homes.

At 21 Fifth Avenue Max showed her the house where Mark Twain lived, and then clutched her arm in excitement when a man with white flowing hair, wearing a white serge suit, emerged.

'That's Mark Twain,' he whispered.

'Is he an actor?' Rissa whispered back while Max prodded her along the avenue.

'He's a writer,' Max explained.

Max took her uptown to see the Broadway theaters. At each theater they paused to inspect the photographs of the actors and actresses on display out front. Max was interested in the David Belasco production of William C. DeMille's *The Warrens of Virginia*. Rissa remarked that the little blonde in the company, named Mary Pickford, had a sweet face.

Max took her to one of the Child's restaurants in the neighborhood for coffee and pastry. Tea, he chuckled, was part of their downtown life. They sat in the white-tile floored restaurant with its white marble tabletops and waitresses in crisp white uniforms and talked about theater.

'Broadway is controlled by the "theatrical trust."' Max's face showed his contempt. 'Six of the most influential managers in the business. Charles Frohman, Marc Klaw, Abraham Erlanger, William Harris, Al Hayman and Frederick Zimmerman. They have a monopoly on the theaters. They've bought or leased all the best houses. David Belasco won't have anything to do with the trust. Harrison Fiske, Minnie Maddern Fiske's husband, called them "the octopuses" in an editorial in his magazine. They even control the road,' Max said bitterly. 'Sarah Bernhardt and Mrs Fiske have had to play out west in circus tents. Of course,' Max grinned, 'they created a sensation.'

With the approach of Hanukkah, Rissa's depression increased. Hannah's birthday had been on Hanukkah. Her own birthday was on Sukkoth. Each year she ignored it.

In an effort to cheer her up, Max wangled free seats for the opening night performance of *Ben Ami*, a new play by Goldfaden. Rissa took pride in the way that people responded to Max. He was having trouble finding a job, but everybody seemed eager to be helpful.

Rissa was enthralled by the prospect of attending the opening performance – on Christmas night – of the new Goldfaden play presented by Thomashefsky. The playwright who had written *Shulamith, Shmendrick, The Witch!* She was shocked that Max was

131

not an admirer of Goldfaden plays. To Max, Goldfaden – the father of Yiddish theater – wrote plays that were old-fashioned.

But Max's lack of appreciation for Goldfaden's plays detracted not at all from her joy at being in the theater where Goldfaden himself sat in a box during the performance. In Warsaw she had played a part in *Shulamith*. At the music hall she sang Goldfaden's song 'Raisins and Almonds.'

Rissa experienced new heights of ecstasy when the curtain fell and the audience broke into tumultuous applause, calling for the stars, for the author. Goldfaden was brought from his box onto the stage and presented with laurel wreaths. There were elaborate curtain speeches, tears, toasts, laughter. When it was at last over, Rissa was reluctant to leave the theater.

Early in January Rissa was relieved to find a job in a music hall just under the bridge in Brooklyn. In celebration she stopped at a bakery for *rogelach* to take home for Shirley and herself.

'You see,' Shirley pointed out. 'I told you, God will provide. And if He doesn't,' she added philosophically, 'Shirley Levine will.'

At least a half hour earlier than necessary next afternoon, Rissa set out for Brooklyn. The sky was gray. The weather cold. She would rehearse the songs she had to do, and the two skits. She brushed from her mind the realization that the lyrics to the songs would bring blushes to her face. But like Shirley said, actresses needed to eat.

She sought out the store on Brooklyn's Henry Street that had been transformed into a music hall, uncomfortable as she walked along the unfamiliar street. She was relieved when at last the music hall came into sight. But what was this? Perplexed she stared at the sign plastered across the door: 'Closed.' She was too early, she chided herself. Soon the music hall would open.

She turned away from the door in mental debate about how to pass the time in the dreary cold until someone arrived. As she hesitated, a wagon pulled up at the curb. Two men jumped down. One held a key in his hand. Neither of these was the man who had hired her.

The men brushed past her. The one with the key unlocked the door. They went inside, slamming the door behind to shut out the sharp wind from the river. Rissa was reluctant to follow them. Instinctively she knew they were not part of the company. She'd wait here until somebody else showed up.

A few minutes later the door flew open. This time the younger of the two men propped it wide with a chair. He carried a table to the wagon. The other man followed with another table.

Immobilized by disappointment she watched while they loaded the tables on the wagon and went back to bring out more of the furnishings. She understood now. The music hall was out of business. But why had the man hired her yesterday when he knew the music hall was closing up?

Walking to the trolley stop Rissa was oblivious of the awesome beauty of the Brooklyn Bridge, hanging high above the East River. Its myriad cables edged with a filigree of snow. Cables and two granite towers imposed against the gray sky like a magnificent modern painting. She was impatient to tell Max about this newest indignity. Eager to be comforted by him.

Back on the lower East Side she sought him out. She found him in a favorite candy store, engaged in an intense discussion. At the sight of Rissa he withdrew from the cluster of avid listeners.

'Rissa, what happened?' Max took her arm and led her out into the snow again.

'The music hall closed up.' Why couldn't something good happen? 'I'll have to start to work for Shirley,' she said, sick with defeat. It would mean working through the night, when a sewing machine would not be in use by the others.

'Let's talk,' Max soothed. To Max there was no problem that talking couldn't solve.

Max took her to the delicatessen where Izzy, his former employer, always offered a sympathetic ear as well as oversized corned beef sandwiches.

Max exchanged the requisite number of good-humored insults with Izzy, who had an admiring eye for Rissa. Tonight Izzy's humor lacked its normal sharpness.

'I'm depressed,' Izzy confided while he sliced corned beef. 'You saw? The store next door closed up. A woman would go in there and buy a dress for herself, a shirt for her husband, a pair of shoes for a child. She'd feel good – she'd decide to come in here for a sandwich. At least, for a glass of tea and cake. Now, with money so tight, they forget about *oysesn*. Who has money to eat out?'

'Izzy, you need an angle,' Max said.

'I need rent money from my tenant,' Izzy said bluntly. 'That's my store that's empty next door.'

Izzy handed over their sandwiches and turned his attention to arriving customers. His man behind the counter was slow. Max propelled Rissa to a table at the rear of the store.

'Izzy owns property?' Rissa asked with awe.

'Izzy looks everywhere to make a dollar,' Max confided. 'He's a moneylender, too.'

'Max, why did the manager at the music hall say I could have a job when they were closing up today?' Rissa returned to her own problem. Anger routed out despair for a moment.

'They hoped for a miracle,' Max's voice was gentle. 'Even the theaters are doing bad business. They play to empty houses except on Saturdays. They can't drop their prices to encourage business – their expenses are too high.' He shook his head in frustration.

'They pay the actors so much?' Rissa was impressed.

'No, Rissa. The union is strangling the theater. Uptown they don't have a union. But down here the Hebrew Actors Union says each manager must employ fourteen actors who are members of the union, fourteen chorus people, all union members, nine musicians belonging to the Musical Club, ten union ushers, four union bill posters and three union dressers with two union assistants. All of them for the whole season of thirty-eight weeks.'

'But if it's a play with only five actors?' Rissa could not understand such manipulations.

'The union doesn't want to hear. They tell the manager he must take the whole package. Even if he doesn't use chorus people, he has to hire them. Do you wonder we have so many music halls? The union can't tell the music halls they have to take these packages.' All at once Max's face was incandescent. 'Rissa, that's the answer! We can put on a play in a music hall. We'll sandwich it in between two musical turns. That makes us a music hall instead of a theater. The union can't strangle us!'

'But to do a play on such a small stage?' Rissa protested.

'It's a matter of choosing the right plays. We can't do what Thomashefsky does at the People's Theater. But a play with a small cast, yes.' Max pushed back his chair and turned away from Rissa. 'Izzy, come over here. We have to talk.'

'Max, I don't run a dance hall,' Izzy called back. 'This isn't a social organization.' But business at the counter was slow. He poured himself a glass of tea and joined Max and Rissa at their table.

'Izzy, what's the odds of your renting the store next door?' Max probed.

Izzy flinched.

'Who's opening up a new store with business like this? But I can't tell the tax man the store ain't bringing in money.'

'You're complaining you don't have enough people coming into the delicatessen,' Max said with spurious calm. 'Right?'

'Right.' Izzy was listening.

'Then you should use the store to bring more people into the delicatessen. Izzy, let's open a music hall in the store.'

'Max, the music halls are dying,' Izzy protested.

'I mean a new kind of music hall. Not just variety turns and skits. A full-length play sandwiched between two variety acts to satisfy the union.'

'The union wouldn't let you get away with it,' Izzy objected.

'You put in enough tables to serve maybe a hundred people. No more. The union won't bother with such small potatoes. But Izzy, you'll sell a lot of corned beef sandwiches and tea.'

'They won't come,' Izzy said after a pregnant moment. 'For a nickel they can go to a movie house.'

'Izzy, they'll come for a live show if the price is low,' Max insisted. 'You'll make your money on the food you sell. It won't take much investment.'

'How much?' Izzy made a show of skepticism. 'A stage is gonna grow by itself? Tables and chairs are gonna just walk in? Actors are gonna work for nothing?'

'Izzy, we can handle it.' Rissa was fascinated by Max's cool approach. She could feel his inner excitement. 'We'll need a small, simple stage. We can build it ourselves. I'll provide the curtain,' he promised. Rissa interpreted that to mean that Shirley's sewing machine would be drafted for the task. 'Give me a piece of paper, Izzy. Let me show you how little it'll cost. Everything secondhand.'

'The actors, too?' Izzy chuckled.

Rissa sat on the edge of her chair, watching Max convert Izzy into a producer. They would do fine plays that would enrapture the critics. Everybody would flock to the music hall. Izzy would need half a dozen waiters to serve the customers. Now Max gave him the figures. To Rissa the sum of money involved seemed terrifyingly large. Izzy groaned, but he continued to listen.

'Izzy, don't you understand?' Max cajoled. 'You'll be a *macher* around here. "Izzy who produces plays." Like Adler and Thomashefsky.'

'Max, I don't know.' Izzy hedged, but his eyes glowed. 'You're talking about a lotta corned beef sandwiches.'

'Izzy, from what one hit play earns you can buy a dozen delicatessens!'

The atmosphere was supercharged. Rissa's throat tightened with tension while Izzy mentally debated. She saw the pulse hammering at Max's temple.

'We'll try it. For a month,' Izzy stipulated. Rissa was exultant. *She'd be seen in a real play. Maybe a critic would come down and write about her.* Max was wonderful! 'How soon can we open?' Izzy asked.

Max made a swift mental calculation.

'In three weeks. In three weeks Izzy Weinberg's Music Hall will be in operation.'

'Weinberg's Music Hall,' Izzy corrected in mild reproof. 'That sounds more dignified.'

Hand in hand, wrapped in dreams, Rissa and Max walked out into a snowfall that threatened to develop into a blizzard. Twilight had fallen on the city.

Streetlights lent an eerie glow through the white curtain that was the snow. People hurried along the street in an effort to reach their homes before the city became impassable. Only Rissa and Max walked as though this were a beautiful, sunlit afternoon.

At a recessed doorway halfway down the block, Max suddenly pulled Rissa into the protective shadows and drew her to him. His mouth sought hers with a hunger that touched off sparks in both of them. Then quickly he released her. His eyes were dark with apology.

'Rissa, excuse me. I have no right.' Max's humility evoked a surge of tenderness in her. 'Not until I know I can support a wife can I ask you to marry me.' He hesitated. 'Rissa, will you? When I can take care of you? Will you wait for me?'

'Max, I – ' Conflicting emotions battled within her. She was not prepared for a marriage proposal. After Phillip she had convinced herself that no man would wish to marry her. She told herself she needed no man in her life. She had a mission: to make the world respect and honor the name of Lindowska. She had vowed this over mama's body. But standing there in the semiprotection of the doorway, with snowflakes the size of silver dollars assaulting them, she knew she wanted Max to be forever a part of her life. 'Oh, Max, yes! Yes!'

'I won't push myself on you. I'll remember my place. Rissa, I just want to be near you. My little Jewish nun.' He lifted her hand to his mouth, and she felt like one of those girls who screeched with joy each time Boris Thomashefsky walked onto the stage

139

in tights. 'By next summer,' he said with fresh enthusiasm, 'the music hall will be a success. We won't play for the summer months, of course. Who can play in the heat? I'll take you down to Georgia to mama and papa. They'll give us a wedding.' In his excitement his speech reverted to the liquid Southern tones of his childhood. 'You'll have a family again, Rissa.'

Now fresh doubts assailed her. Marriage brought limitations into a woman's life. She could not be the kind of wife Max's mother had been. Could Max accept that?

'Max, I have to tell you.' Her voice was unsteady. 'I can't be the kind of wife who'll be satisfied to keep house and raise children. I have to be an actress.'

'You will be,' Max said tenderly. 'The two of us together in the theater.'

'I don't want to have children until I'm older,' she faltered.

'Sweetheart, there are ways to avoid having children,' Max soothed. 'Trust me. When the time is right, we'll have children. Not before.'

In a private world of their own they emerged from the recessed doorway into the stinging sheet of snow. Max took her hand in his. Her mind raced as they walked toward the flat on Essex. With both of them out of work Max came home with her for tea and conversation more often than they went into cafés. The cafés were for actors and writers and musicians with jobs.

But as Max and she forged ahead through the snow, Rissa felt her earlier joy ebbing away. He had called her his 'little Jewish nun.' Max didn't know about Phillip. He was sure no man had ever touched her. How could she go on letting him believe that? But how could she risk losing Max by telling him about Phillip?

Tonight she must talk to Shirley.

Rissa tried to contain her restlessness while Max and Shirley talked with passionate enthusiasm about the deal he had wangled with Izzy. Both Max and Shirley spoke loudly, in order to be heard above the victrola music in the next flat and the violin on the floor below.

'It'll be the same as a theater,' Max insisted. 'Only we won't have two thousand seats and the union to worry about. It's a chance to bring good plays to the East Side. Not a play for an hour. A whole evening. A play that'll make everybody know that Rissa Lindowska is an actress to watch.' Max's face was incandescent. Despite her anxiety about confessing to Max that he would not be marrying a virgin, Rissa was drawn into the spell he wove. 'We'll have the critics from the *Forward* and the *Tageblatt* and the *Morning Journal* down to the opening. Rissa, in two years you'll be a star.'

'Max, it's late. Shirley has to be up at five.' Her head was pounding with such extravagance. She would be in a play. The critics would come to see her. Max was so smart. He knew so much about acting. He'd help her. *But would he want to help her when he found out about Phillip?*

Even in Shirley's presence Max reached for her

141

hand and kissed it. Shirley, a complex blend of wild romanticism and stern reality, sighed with pleasure. Rissa led Max to the door while her eyes told him she loved him.

'Good night, Max,' she whispered, wishing she were going with him to his studio on Washington Square, guilty because all at once she wanted Max to hold her in his arms and make love to her.

Rissa closed the door, listening to Max's footsteps in descent.

'So why have you got *shpilkes in hint'n*?' Shirley demanded, her eyes tender.

'Max asked me to marry him.' For a few moments it was enough to glory in this knowledge. 'In the summer if everything is all right with our jobs.'

'*Maz'l tov*, darling!' Shirley swept Rissa to her ample bosom.

'But I have to tell him about Phillip,' Rissa said.

Instantly Shirley released her.

'Are you *meshugah*?' Shirley was aghast. 'You're going to tell him his little Jewish nun is Mary Magdalene?'

'Who's she?'

Shirley shrugged.

'I think she was a prostitute.'

'I'm not a prostitute!' Rissa was indignant. 'There was only Phillip.'

'One man, a hundred men – you think that makes any difference to a nice Jewish boy like Max? From Georgia? Is Phillip coming to America from London to tell him, "I lived with Rissa"? No, darling.' Shirley was emphatic. 'What Max doesn't know won't hurt him.'

'He'll know,' Rissa said pointedly. 'After the wedding he'll know.' How many times had Shirley mourned that her own young indiscretions would stand in the way of her marriage? Already twenty-two, Shirley wouldn't even go to the dance halls to look, the way most girls were doing now.

'Max doesn't have to know,' Shirley dismissed this. 'There are ways to make a man believe he got there first.'

'No,' Rissa rejected. 'I have to tell Max. I have to be honest with him.'

'But why, Rissa, why?' Shirley was plaintive.

'I'll never love any man in my life but Max,' Rissa said softly. 'But I can't marry him without telling him about Phillip. Because I love him I have to be honest,' she said with stern resolution. 'I'll tell Max, and he'll make his decision.'

But how could she live if Max didn't want to marry her? How would she survive?

12

Rissa and Max plunged into the project of bringing together a theater company prepared to perform within the three-week deadline guaranteed Izzy. The major problem was to locate a play.

No *shund*, Max declared. A quality play, of which there was little either in the Yiddish theater or Broadway. He disappeared for hours each day, saying only that he was on the trail of a script. He couldn't hire actors without a play.

Max sent Rissa scouting for cheap tables and chairs, Izzy would then go down to the prospective seller, haggle, moan and buy. When her workday was over, Shirley labored over the curtain. Her working hours were becoming shorter than normal. In order to keep both girls with her, she divided the incoming work among the three of them. She was equally concerned about the survival of all of them.

Rissa and Max agonized over the reports in the New York *Herald* about the soaring unemployment in New York, the increasing number of destitute families. They walked past the lines of listless or frightened men at the Bowery Mission, who waited each morning for free coffee-and-roll breakfasts that might be their only meal of the day.

Though the lower East Side was rich in charitable agencies – and there was much unorganized but ready help for the needy — the depression had struck with such intensity that even this collective aid was inadequate. The people who in other years could be depended upon to help were themselves destitute.

Max ranted about the greed of corporate organizations, which — President Roosevelt said — were responsible for the recession. Though himself a traditional Georgia Democrat, Max admired the Republican president for his fight against corruption and fraud.

In the evenings Rissa and Max saw the homeless men sleeping in doorways despite the bitter cold. This was a vision of America that was new and frightening. The deprivation extended beyond the lower East Side. It encompassed the nation.

Coming home from rehearsal one evening Rissa was startled to discover Shirley depositing a small, sleeping boy on the bed in the workroom.

'Don't talk loud,' Shirley whispered, pulling a blanket over the small sleeping form. 'It's Dora's child. You know, the woman across the hall. He'll sleep here while his mother entertains her customers,' Shirley explained delicately. Rissa's eyes widened. 'Dora has no job. She has a child to feed. So for a few hours a night she supplies a service, and Dora and the child survive.' Shirley was a realist.

'But to become a prostitute?' Rissa recoiled from such degradation. 'I'd starve first.'

'Would you let your child starve?' Shirley countered. 'Rissa, where you have men without women, you have prostitutes. The men come over from Europe to find work and save money to bring their families here. Sometimes it takes years. But they don't stop being men. They have needs.' And because of this, Rissa thought with pain, Dora and her little boy would eat.

With an air of anticipation, Shirley settled down now with the day's *Forward*, turning first – as always – to the 'Bintel Brief.' The letters, mostly from women readers, to the editor, and his responses.

Rissa shivered as she thought about Dora, who lived across the hall. She knew the stories about the girls who committed suicide when they could no longer endure that way of life. She read the suicide notices in the *Forward*. *Where was God in times like these?*

'My contractor keeps telling me we're in a depression,' Shirley sighed as Rissa and she left the flat shortly before noon because no work was available. 'And Max expects people to come to Weinberg's Music Hall and spend money?' She shook her head in skepticism.

'They'll come,' Rissa promised, but she worried.

She knew about the Hebrew Free Loan Society, the day nursery on Montgomery Street for women working in factories and all the other associations. But what was happening now was like a plague.

Shirley remembered that she needed to buy needles for the machines. They took a circuitous route to the Bowery. As they attempted to cross the street they were almost knocked down in the rush of children.

'What's happening?' Shirley demanded of an eager little boy of about nine, detaining him with one hand.

146

'Lemme go!' he yelled. 'They're givin' free lunches to schoolchildren at Lorber's!'

'I'll buy the needles tomorrow,' Shirley said, and she and Rissa crossed to the other side of the street, unnerved by the hordes of children battling to get into the restaurant for the free lunches. Youngsters of seven, eight, nine were fighting each other for entrance. Rissa spied a pale little boy with huge, dark eyes and a triumphant smile; he had managed to grab several rolls and was running home to present them to his hungry family.

'At least in Europe we ate,' Rissa whispered unhappily.

'Sometimes we ate.' Shirley's face was taut in recall. 'I remember nights when I went to bed hungry.'

Rissa hesitated.

'Sometimes we had no more than black bread and tea,' Rissa admitted. 'And mama and papa ate little so there would be enough for the children. Shirley, when will this – this depression be over?'

'You think I'm the president of the United States?' Shirley laughed. 'But it'll be over soon,' she soothed. Rissa and she took turns encouraging each other.

'It would help if I could get a job for a week or two until the play opens.' Only after the opening would they be paid. Rissa knew Max was pressed for money. Her own small stake was shrinking.

'Who can get a job now?' Shirley dismissed the idea. She turned to Rissa as they walked. 'Did you tell Max yet?'

'Not yet,' Rissa confessed. 'I don't want to upset him right now. I figured it would be better to wait.'

'Keep waiting,' Shirley urged. 'Wait forever.'

Max was at the music hall when they arrived. He held Izzy a captive, while he read to him in shaky Yiddish from typed sheets of paper.

'The play!' Rissa was ecstatic. Now they could start rehearsing.

'The play,' Max nodded. 'I had to have it translated into Yiddish. Without spending money,' he chuckled.

The play had been written by one of Max's neighbors in the rooming house on Washington Square South. It had been rejected by a dozen Broadway producers, but Max was awed by the playwright's talents. In a late night session in the café on Mac-Dougal Street, Max had persuaded the playwright to 'lend' the manuscript. Max had been struggling with the help of two elderly Jewish men amused by his efforts to translate the play into Yiddish.

Max's landlady, who considered herself a patron of the arts because thirty years earlier she had sung in the chorus of Gilbert and Sullivan operettas, introduced him to one of her roomers. This older woman – Max made a point of emphasizing her age – was a typist with access to a Yiddish typewriter. She had agreed to take on that task of typing the play for them. There were even copies for the actors. A supreme luxury.

'Out of the goodness of her heart she typed?' Shirley was dubious.

'I told her I'd pay her later, when the play was a success.' Max good-humoredly ignored Shirley's insinuations.

Now Max concentrated on assembling a cast. To

Izzy's pleasure they required only five performers, including Rissa.

Almost from the first day of rehearsals Max ran into difficulties with the cast. Rissa accepted his decree that they be letter-perfect. The others resented this.

'Max, you've got to be crazy!' their leading man protested. 'Who has time to learn every line like the playwright wrote it down? You'll have a prompter.'

'We'll have a prompter for emergencies,' Max said quietly. Rissa knew he loathed being dependent on a prompter, who sat in the pit and sometimes read the entire play in a voice that could be heard throughout the theater. 'On Broadway, actors can learn their lines. Downtown you can learn them, too.'

'Who's got time to learn all these pages?' the character woman demanded.

'We've got time.' Max was insistent. Rissa sensed the impatience bottled up within him. The director, Max said, must be calm. He must be in command. 'You're not going on with one rehearsal. We've got two whole weeks to rehearse just this one play. We don't start rehearsing another until we're playing this one. Let people see that Yiddish actors can memorize lines, too.'

Rissa listened to Max like a neophyte at the foot of the master. Instinctively she realized that Max, despite his youth and inexperience, knew what was right. He insisted the cast cut down the broad gestures, the melodramatic readings with which they were familiar.

Max hammered at the cast to give him what he

wanted. With her memory of London Theater Rissa understood what Max was trying to do. But Shirley, who had free time to be at rehearsals because work was so light, was uneasy.

'Rissa, what does he think he'll have sitting out front watching the play?' Shirley's eyes were somber, belying the levity of her voice. '*Intelligentn?* Working people he'll have, who never saw anything but Yiddish theater. What Thomashefsky gives them they want.'

'But Shirley, this is much better.'

'Maybe better they don't want,' Shirley warned. On one evening Max cut rehearsals short to take Rissa to Broadway to see a rising young actress named Ethel Barrymore. One of his Washington Square friends had provided him with passes. They sat, not in the gallery, but in tenth row seats. Rissa was enthralled with the performances of these American actors whose speech was so beautiful. Would she ever learn to speak like that?

It was an unseasonably warm evening. Rissa and Max walked all the way home from the theater to the flat on Essex Street. Rissa told herself this was the time to tell Max about Phillip. She tried to gear herself up for it.

'Rissa, you saw Ethel Barrymore tonight. You know what I'm trying to get from the company.'

'I know, Max.' Tenderness filled her for his dedication, his love for the theater.

'The others don't matter to me.' He was candid. 'I'm thinking only of how to show you off. You're a shining light up there on that stage, Rissa. You are special. And I'm your personal manager.'

'Max, do you think the critics will come?' She longed for a sign that she wasn't wrong about her talent. That Max wasn't wrong. She needed to be recognized as an actress by those who knew.

'I'm trying, sugar.' In moments of tension Max lapsed into a Southern tenderness that Rissa found appealing. 'I've tried to arrange for us to open on a night when nothing big is scheduled. I don't know,' he admitted. 'But one way or another we'll make it, Rissa. Nobody will be able to stop us. I'm fighting now with Izzy about running ads. I knew he'd balk at spending the money.'

'Do we need ads, Max?'

'We have to let people know we're running. Ads are important. I wrote mama about the music hall and about us.' His eyes caressed her. 'I told her about you. She sent me money to buy you a ring. Not much, but mama always has a few dollars hidden away somewhere for something special.' He hesitated. 'Rissa, would you be upset if I borrow that money to run some ads? I'll buy you a ring before we go home for the wedding.'

'I don't mind,' she consented readily. She suspected that his mother was upset that Max was marrying an actress, and a 'greenhorn' at that. But it was what Max wanted, and she had sent him money for a ring.

'I'll go to the *Forward* office tomorrow.' Max was happy. 'You'll see your name in the newspaper ad.' He grinned. 'With so small a cast I'll list everybody. Let them be happy. And nobody will start a battle.'

But tonight Rissa was not thinking about her name in print. Max was buying her a ring. It was true; she would be Max's wife. *When would she tell him about Phillip?*

As their opening date approached, Max slaved over his actors. Why couldn't the others understand him? Rissa asked herself. They didn't want to understand him, her mind taunted. Behind his back they mimicked his flawed Yiddish. Even his Southern-tinged English evoked mockery.

They were indignant that he insisted they stick to the script, that they were not allowed to perform in the familiar mold. They didn't see the beauty of the play, Rissa mourned, thinking of the playwright who never appeared at the rehearsals.

At their dress rehearsal Shirley sat in the darkened music hall and watched. For their set she had cajoled neighbors into loaning furniture in exchange for free tickets. Izzy wailed that opening night would be crowded with patrons content to buy only a 'glass of tea and a piece of cheescake.' He wanted to sell sandwiches. Meals.

After the run-through Rissa and Max came to sit beside Shirley. Questions in their eyes.

'I felt sorry for the people,' Shirley acknowledged. 'Rissa made me cry.' She was trying to be optimistic. She didn't think the people who came would like the play, Rissa interpreted. 'But couldn't the music before the play and after be happy?' she coaxed.

'It would destroy the mood,' Max rejected. 'If we get even one reviewer and he likes it, we'll be a success,' he predicted with shaky optimism. 'Audiences will love Rissa. They'll recognize she's not like the others. Rissa should be playing at the Thalia or the People's Theater or the Windsor,' he said passionately. 'Her talent shines through.'

'What you need is money shining through the cash box,' Shirley shot back. 'Make the music happy.'

Knowing that Rissa and Max would want to be alone this night before the opening, Shirley hurried home on the pretext that she must be up early in the morning. Rissa and Max lingered in the deserted store turned music hall. Exhausted, fearful, yet exultant that they had brought the play this far.

Max changed the position of a chair onstage, a table, then ordered Rissa to walk through the movement of her big scene to see if this was an improvement. Tomorrow night Max would prove himself a producer-director. Rissa would be appearing in a play in the Yiddish Rialto.

'The people will see what we're giving them,' Max said. 'They'll appreciate the difference. They'll talk about it to their friends.' They had no more money for advertising. Word of mouth was their sole means of drawing business. 'We'll start rehearsing the new play in two days. We'll be able to play repertory by the end of March.' Rissa saw the nervous perspiration on his forehead.

'Max, I have to tell you something.' All at once she could not be silent about Phillip. There would always be something to stand in her way; she must tell Max now. 'I've tried so many times. I – I don't know how to say it.' Panic gripped her. Was Shirley right? Should she be silent?

'What, Rissa?' Max's voice was tender. His eyes searched her face. Then all at once he was anxious. 'You've decided you don't want to be an actress?'

'Oh, Max, don't even say that.' It was blasphemy. 'I'll never not want to be an actress. But I have to be honest with you.' Her face grew hot. 'You asked me once about London. I couldn't talk about it then. I was hurting too much.' The compassion with which he listened to her brought a tightness to her throat. 'Max, I met someone in Warsaw – when everything was bad. When I knew I must leave the company, but I didn't know where to go. Phillip was sweet to me. He said he loved me. I – I thought I loved him.' Her eyes implored compassion. 'When Phillip went back to London, he took me with him.'

Despair gripped Rissa in a vise as she saw Max come to grips with what she had confided. Shirley had been right. Max didn't understand.

'You lived with him.' Max stared down at her in disbelief and reproach. 'I called you my little Jewish nun. I never touched you.' Slowly he shook his head as if to deny what he now knew to be true. 'You lived with a man.'

All at once Max's reaction – normal, she knew – seemed absurd.

'Why is that so important?' Phillip was gone from her life. She loved Max.

'A man expects to be the first with his wife. It's his right.' Max gazed at her as though he had never truly seen her before.

'Have you never made love to a girl?' Now Rissa abandoned defensiveness. Even as a six-year-old she had resented that a young Jewish boy was supposed to thank God each morning that he had been born a male. 'Can you say to me that you've never made love to a girl?'

'Of course not.' Max frowned in irritation. 'But that's different.'

'Why is it different?' Rissa hovered before him. A small avenging angel. 'Do you think a woman doesn't wish that she's the first love of her husband? Why is it all right for a man to have as many women as he likes; but if a girl has one man in her life before him, she's a whore.'

'I didn't say that!'

'You're thinking it,' Rissa challenged.

'I wanted to marry you, Rissa.' His voice was a whisper. 'To me there was something holy about you. So small and sweet and beautiful. I wanted to love you and take care of you.'

'And now you don't want to marry me.' The words were wrung from her. 'Because I was scared and alone, and I let Phillip take care of me. I thought someday we'd be married – '

'He walked out on you?' Max was fighting an inner battle.

'I left him.' Rissa lifted her head in pride. 'When I found out he was being married, I knew I wouldn't be at our flat when he came back to me. I went to his fine house to tell him my contempt, but I saw his father instead. A fine English lord. That's how I came to America. When Phillip's father asked me what I wanted of Phillip, I told him I wanted a ticket to America. First class.'

'I'll take you home, Rissa.' Max wavered. 'I have to think.'

'I'll take myself home,' Rissa said. 'Good night, Max.'

She walked out into a light snowfall that threatened to become more serious. Already the flakes were beginning to stick. She walked with aching swiftness. Seeing nothing. Hearing nothing. Sure that she had lost Max forever.

Rissa lay sleepless on her cot in the dank cold kitchen. The fire in the stove had long ago been allowed to go out. The price of a bag of coal made each lump a luxury. Penetrating drafts seeped into the flat. Rissa huddled under the pile of blankets, augmented tonight by her winter coat. Her knees were drawn up to her breasts, not only in reproach to the weather but in an instinctive protectiveness against the agony of losing Max.

Clutching the blankets about her she shifted slightly to inspect the clock. It was almost three in the morning. In two hours Shirley would be getting up. Shirley had been right. It had been a mistake to be honest with Max. Yet how could she spend the rest of her life with him without telling him the truth?

She started in faint alarm at the light knock on the door of the other room. Who could it be? It was too early for the girls to arrive for work. Was her clock not working? Then she heard a second cautious knock. In sudden comprehension she tossed aside the

156

covers and darted into the other room and to the door. Shirley was asleep.

'Max?' she whispered.

'Who else?' he whispered back.

Rissa pulled the door wide. Max stood there, his coat laden with snow. His dark hair capped in white.

'Rissa, I want you to marry me,' he said without preliminaries. 'Please.' He was poignant in his humility. 'Tell me you'll forget what I said.'

'Yes, Max – oh, yes!' Rissa flung herself into his arms. They kissed with a passion that seemed bottomless. 'Oh, Max, I love you.'

'You were a baby,' he whispered when their mouths at last parted. 'I'd like to kill the son-of-a-bitch.'

'Max, it's all right now.' She made a move to draw him into the room. Shirley was a heavy sleeper. They had joked about that to Max.

'No,' Max rejected her silent invitation. 'Not until we're married. I respect my wife-to-be.' He hesitated. 'Does Shirley know? About London,' he added awkwardly.

'No,' Rissa lied. Why make Max unhappy? Why make him feel less of a man?

'So nobody knows but you and me.' Max was relieved. He bent to kiss her lightly. 'Sleep late,' he ordered. 'You have an important performance tomorrow night.' He grinned and corrected himself. 'You have an important performance tonight.' Unexpectedly he chuckled. 'You really asked a British lord for a ticket to America, first class?'

'First class,' she confirmed.

'That's the way we're going to travel from here on.' His face was taut with determination. 'First class.'

13

Although she would not appear until the first eight minutes of the play had been performed, Rissa stood in the wings when the red velvet curtain parted. She was engulfed in the faint uncertainties that besiege an actress before each appearance onstage, no matter how much experience is behind her. Did she remember her lines? Would the audience like the play? Was her hair – in the fashionable new Psyche knot – secured by enough hairpins?

'Hannale, look!' a feminine voice shrieked in the audience. 'Your table on the stage!'

'Sssh!' The familiar remonstrance that inevitably evoked yet another 'sssh,' and then another.

Every seat was taken tonight. Most of them 'paper' – free seats distributed in return for the loan of furniture, to Izzy's special customers, to friends of the cast. Max admitted that no critic had accepted his invitation, but he had hopes for later in the week.

Subconsciously, as she thrust herself into the role she loved, Rissa became aware of the sounds out front. The raucous rattle of spoons stirring in glasses of tea. Overloud verbal comments at intervals. But for the most part this was an unfamiliarly quiet audience. They were listening to the play, Rissa decided with pleasure at the end of the first act.

At the conclusion there was much applause. As

coached by Max, Shirley called out, 'Author, author!'
The company knew that the depressed author, who
had sat through one rehearsal of his play in Yiddish
in bewilderment, had fled the country on the Cunard
Line's *Mauretania*, which offered 'special low saloon
rates to Europe' at seventy-two dollars and fifty cents.
But it was the mark of a successful opening that
someone in the audience call 'Author, author!'

When the audience and cast had departed, Izzy
invited Max, Rissa and Shirley to stay for cheesecake
and tea. He was elated by his new image as a
producer. Tomorrow night his wife and five children
would make the trek from Brownsville to be at the
performance. He was less sanguine about the future
of Weinberg's Music Hall.

'So what did they buy?' Izzy complained. 'Like I
told you, cheesecake and tea. I can make a living
from that?'

On the second evening, Max warned, they were
facing their real test. This was not a 'friends of the
cast' audience. Rissa peeked through a slit in the
curtain at intervals before the performance. Most of
the seats were filled before the curtain parted for the
singing act that introduced the play. The advertise-
ment in the *Forward* had brought in customers. But
minutes after the play began, Rissa knew they were
in trouble.

Conversation in the audience started as isolated
whispers grew in number and volume until by the
end of the first act the actors were shouting to be
heard. Max gave no indication that he was disturbed.
Tomorrow night, he promised, a critic would be out

front. After that they would have a different kind of audience. Intellectuals who recognized good theater.

By the time the curtain closed on the last act, two-thirds of the audience had left. Izzy was wringing his hands.

'They had the *hutzpah* to order only tea,' he wailed. 'And they asked for jam in it yet.'

'Izzy, tomorrow night will be better,' Max soothed.

Rissa felt a simmering disrespect for the play among the cast; they knew their jobs were shaky. She was fearful that they would look around for other jobs, though Max was unconcerned about this. They talked somberly as he walked her home.

'With business even in the theaters so bad, where are our actors going to find jobs?' he asked with contempt for their talents. 'I heard this afternoon that Jacob Adler may not renew his lease on the Grand.'

'Oh, Max.' Rissa was shocked.

'But Rissa, we're giving them something fine.' A vein throbbing in his forehead betrayed his show of calm. 'If we only had the money to advertise!'

'Izzy won't spend any more,' Rissa guessed.

'Tomorrow night the critic is coming. Not a man from one of the big papers, but I respect his judgement,' Max said conscientiously. 'We'll see.'

Shirley was blunt with Rissa. Max's play was beyond his audience. They weren't ready for what he had to give them. Max came from a whole different world. He couldn't understand their needs, Shirley pointed out while she poured tea for them despite the lateness of the hour.

'Max works so hard,' Rissa protested. 'He has no

money. He knows what it is to fight for every little thing.'

'But if things are bad, Max can go home to his parents in Georgia. That's the difference, Rissa. We can't go home.'

'Max won't go home,' Rissa said quickly. She didn't want to visualize a life without him. Max was forever.

'Thomashefsky is the smart one,' Shirley pinpointed with the shrewdness that Rissa had come to admire. 'He knows what the people want. He gives it to them. Make Max put together a new play. Fast.'

The third performance was received with no more approval than the second. But the next day's paper carried a glowing report of the play itself, of Max's direction and of Rissa's performance:

'Last evening I saw the arrival of a new star on the Yiddish theater horizon,' the critic rhapsodized. 'Rissa Lindowska is beautiful, young, talented. She will go far.' He was less kind to the others in the company.

In exultation Max posted copies of the review in front of the music hall. Rissa moved in an aura of disbelief. A critic liked her. But the rest of the cast was in revolt. One of the actors threatened to castrate the critic.

The next night only a handful of people attended the performance. The newspaper that carried the review had little circulation. Before the curtain was entirely closed at the end of the last act, Izzy was arguing with Max.

'Max, you're ruining me! Max, do something! Change the bill fast. Make them sing and dance, do skits – I don't care what as long as you get rid of the play!'

'We got great reviews!' Max was indignant. 'We have to give the play a chance!' Rissa came to stand beside him while the others hurried off to the dressing room to talk among themselves.

'A good review,' Izzy acknowledged, 'but how many people read that *farshtunkener* little paper? Max, how many times do I have to tell you? On the lower East Side they want what Thomashefsky gives them. What your fine critic says about the play won't pay my bills. I can't take his review to the bank!'

'We have to give the play at least another week.' Max was adamant. Izzy grunted in rejection. Rissa was unnerved. Why was Max arguing with Izzy? Without Izzy they would have no music hall. Let Max pull together some songs and skits. They could change over by tomorrow night. But she died a little inside at the prospect of abandoning the play. 'Izzy, word has to get around,' Max pursued.

'Word from where?' Izzy was triumphant. 'From the six people out front tonight?'

'Izzy, the reviews. If we throw some real ads in the *Forward* and the *Tageblatt*, we'll be turning away customers. You'll have to squeeze in more tables. You've got a new Yiddish theater star on your hands.' He pulled Rissa to him. 'Rissa is money in the bank for us. She'll be another Bertha Kalisch. And everybody will say, "Izzy Weinberg discovered her."' Rissa saw Izzy waver. 'One week, Izzy,' Max pressed.

163

'If we had money to advertise, maybe,' Izzy said grudgingly. But his mind was involved in rapid speculation. Now he smiled. Rissa saw what Max referred to as Izzy's horse-trader look come over his face. 'You know who came in this afternoon for corned beef sandwiches? Your old friend Yetta and two *yentas* she was treating.'

'Yetta's no friend of mine,' Max shot back. Rissa winced, remembering their last ugly encounter.

'She asked about you. Yetta's always had a soft spot for you, Max.' Izzy's voice was kitten soft, yet Rissa was conscious of an undercurrent between Max and him that she didn't yet understand.

'The last thing Yetta said to me,' Max grinned in recall, 'was "I hope you die with a hard-on."' He glanced apologetically toward Rissa, but her command of the English language – despite the vulgarity she encountered backstage – did not extend to obscenities.

'Yetta asked about you,' Izzy reiterated. 'She said to me, "How's that good-looking Max Miller? Such a nice boy." She forgot already about the argument.' Now Rissa intercepted the eye exchange between Izzy and Max. A coldness came over her.

'I hear she closed up her music hall.' Max appeared casual, but Rissa knew from the set of his jaw that his mind was grappling with the message Izzy was transmitting.

'She closed it three months ago. She said they were stealing her blind. Max – ' Izzy's smile was indulgent, 'I'll bet if you asked her, Yetta would put up some money for advertising for a piece of the profits. On a short-term basis,' he emphasized. Rissa gazed from Izzy to Max in dismay. Would Max even consider asking Yetta Bernstein to invest? 'You know Yetta's always anxious to make a buck. She's got a phone. Call her. Make an appointment to go up and talk to her. What's to lose?'

'Yetta can be a problem,' Max said pointedly. Rissa comprehended the problem, though she was sure Max was unaware that she did. She didn't want her future husband to go up to Yetta Bernstein's house to talk about money. She'd heard backstage about Yetta's habit of discussing money deals in her bedroom. 'Izzy, let me think about it,' Max hedged.

'Without advertising we don't keep the play running.' Izzy's tone was ominous. 'Better I should try again to rent the place.'

Max sighed. Rissa watched while he deliberated.

'I'll phone Yetta in the morning,' he capitulated.

While Max walked with her to the flat on Essex Street, he talked enthusiastically about what advertising – plus some handbills and posters – would do for the company.

'Rissa,' he said zealously, 'advertising will put us on the map.' Yet Rissa knew he was unhappy about approaching Yetta. *She* was unhappy about it. How could she marry Max if she knew he was in Yetta Bernstein's bed? She felt sick at the prospect of life without Max.

'Max, it's wrong to be begging Yetta to invest in the company after what she said to us.' Rissa was desperate to abort this campaign. Didn't Max understand what this would do to them?

'She asked about us.' Max was defensive. He held her arm, but he kept his eyes straight ahead.

'She asked about you.' Rissa was blunt. 'She said terrible things about me, Max.' Rissa's face was hot as she visualized that last encounter.

All at once the atmosphere between them was tense.

'Rissa, sometimes in business people have to be practical. We have to do things we don't like. We've come this far. I won't lose this play. It's too important.' *More important than she?*

'Talk to Izzy again,' she pleaded. If he went ahead with the deal with Yetta, he would lose her.

'Izzy won't spend another cent. He's scared when the whole country is in such bad financial shape. There's nobody to get money from except Yetta,' he said flatly. 'And we don't know that she'll want to invest.'

'When will you see her?' For Max in her bed Yetta would invest. At this moment Max and she were two strangers. With a few minutes' conversation Max was destroying their whole lives.

'Like I told Izzy, I'll phone her in the morning. I'll go up whenever she says.'

When Max kissed her good night, Rissa sensed his distraction. But he would phone Yetta in the morning. He'd go up to her house to talk to her. If he decided the money was important enough to sleep with Yetta Bernstein, then everything they had between them was over. No matter how much she loved Max, she would not share him.

On her cot in the kitchen of the flat, Rissa lay

sleepless until dawn. She knew how desperate Max was to keep the play running. Was he desperate enough to gamble on their marriage? How could he believe that she could marry him if had so little respect for their love?

Max stood before Yetta Bernstein's brownstone in the West Eighties and tried to swallow his distaste. Everything in life came with a price tag. If he wanted to keep the play running, he'd have to make some compromises.

He walked up the stoop to the door and pushed the bell. He pulled out his watch. When he talked to Yetta on the phone, he'd agreed to be here in an hour. He was ten minutes early. But the maid opened the door and ushered him in.

Again he was ushered into the cluttered Victorian parlor and told to wait. Sitting at the edge of the bilious green horseshoe-backed chair, Max thought about Rissa's face when they had talked about his coming to see Yetta. She didn't *know* that anything had happened between Yetta and him. She was just letting her imagination run wild. She knew how people talked.

'You can go up to see Mrs Bernstein now,' the maid interrupted his introspection. 'She ain't feelin' well. She's in her bedroom. It's on the third floor. The door's open.'

'Thank you.'

Max hurried up the stairs to Yetta's room. Get this over with, he exhorted himself. But don't be a *shmuck* like last time. First a deal.

167

'Max, darling,' Yetta called to him as he appeared in view. 'Every time I see you, you're looking more handsome. Come sit here by me, and tell me what you're up to these days.'

Max pushed himself to sit at the side of the bed as Yetta indicated. In the flowery language that Yetta would understand, he told her about their activities at the music hall.

'We've got a potential big money-maker,' he summed up. 'Lots of money, Yetta. The critics raved. But you know how it is. Without advertising who knows what we have? Izzy and I talked about the situation. We're willing to cut you in for twenty percent of the profits each week if you put up money for the necessary advertising.'

'Wait, Max. Let me figure this out. How much will you need for advertising? How many seats you got? What're you paying the actors? And it's Izzy's store,' she pointed out. 'You can't charge for rent.'

Carefully Max went over each item with her. Damn it, Yetta could make a bundle each week with them. He saw the recognition of this in her eyes as one fat bediamonded hand scribbled figures on a notepad.

'Maybe we can do business, Maxila,' she crooned. She was all heated up already, he realized in revulsion.

'I'll have the papers drawn up right away.' He rose to his feet. If Yetta thought she was getting him into her bed before she signed, she was crazy. 'I'll have them back this afternoon. Let's make it for a minimum of six weeks,' he improvised.

'A month,' Yetta substituted and reached a hand to fondle his thigh. 'And twice a week we have a business conference here. At nine in the morning, when I'm feeling my best.' Her eyes glittered in anticipation. 'I want that in the paper.'

Max stared at her in shock. All at once he felt like a gladiator in an arena. Worse. Like one of the whores on Chrystie Street. Would he be any better than they if he went along with what Yetta demanded?

'No,' Max said in cold deliberation. 'This is a business deal, Yetta. You come down to the office twice a week, if you like. Izzy and I will go over all the figures with you.'

'I should drag myself downtown? Get out!' Yetta was outraged. 'Who needs your kind of business? I gotta go down to the East Side to see how you're wasting my money? Get outta my house!'

Walking over to Broadway Max was conscious of a deep relief. God knows, he was hungry for that advertising money. But he couldn't put himself through what Yetta demanded. They'd lose the play, but they'd survive. He remembered Rissa's stricken face when he was fighting with Izzy. She was always worried about survival. But she'd be relieved that he wouldn't do business with Yetta.

They wouldn't lose the music hall. They'd pull together a typical music-hall revue. But at the same time they'd rehearse another play. He wouldn't bury Rissa and himself in *shund*.

They presented the play that evening to another

near-empty house. After the performance Max assembled the cast onstage.

'Everybody back here at ten in the morning,' he ordered crisply. 'We're changing over to a revue. I'll stay up tonight and work out a program. But it's temporary. At the end of the week we start rehearsing another play.'

'Max, a real play?' the character man coaxed warily. 'Something we can get our teeth into? Something the audience will like? Stop worrying about *beser teyater*!'

Rissa rejoiced that Max had rejected Yetta. And she suffered with Max over the loss of the play. She knew the intensity of his disappointment. She, too, was sad to abandon the play, which held much appeal for her. It was a wrenching loss to relinquish a role that had won her a critic's approval. His approval echoed in her mind at intervals, giving her fresh strength and determination.

She remembered what Tekla, the wise woman of their *dorf* in Poland had said: '*Someday, Rissa, you will go to America. You will become rich and important.*' When would that day come? When would the name of Lindowska be known by all who loved theater? A perpetual candle to the memory of mama and papa.

Like the others in the company Rissa threw herself into the new routine. She felt their satisfaction that the play had been dismissed and sensed their malice toward her because she had been singled out by the reviewer.

Max was recurrently angry. How could so fine a play be a failure?

'I remind myself, Rissa,' he said with a new bitterness, 'that just a year ago two wonderful plays by Sholom Aleichem – one presented by Thomashefsky and another by Adler – opened on the same night and closed two weeks later.'

'It's the wrong time, Max. A time will come for good plays.'

The music hall played to near-empty houses during the week. On Saturday evening every seat was taken. Izzy was philosophical; he wasn't making the big profits Max had envisioned, but he wasn't losing money. Music halls elsewhere were closing. All over the city – the nation – businesses were failing.

Max was rehearsing the company in a Lateiner play, though Rissa knew he was sick at heart at resorting to *shund*. Now Izzy was a producer. He exhorted Max to listen to the actors when they protested direction to cut down their broad style.

'Max, look what's happening at the Windsor.' Izzy pantomimed his admiration. 'For weeks already Kessler is playing in *The Jewish Heart*. It'll run a year,' he predicted. In Yiddish theater a steady run was a miracle. Often a different play was presented every night in the week. 'So we've got a Lateiner play, too,' he said with pride. 'We'll run a year – if you'll let the actors act.'

Rissa was pulled in opposite directions. She yearned to do the fine plays that Max was determined to bring to the Yiddish theater. But there was no point in playing to empty houses. She dreamed of audiences that laughed and cried with her.

The new melodrama did well on weekends, which was as much as anybody could expect in a depression year, and a second was in rehearsals. Izzy was jubilant at this much success, but Max was upset that Yiddish audiences craved *shund*.

It had hurt Max that Gordin's last play, *Dementia Americana*, had been a failure while Lateiner's melodrama was bringing in customers even in the midst of a depression. Now Thomashefsky was packing in the huge People's Theater with *Minke the Servant Girl*. More *shund*.

Rissa was restless, impatient to move ahead. She knew she ought to be grateful that she was working when so many Americans were fighting hunger, but she wanted more. Playing in a tiny music hall was like being back in the Warsaw ghetto. She was making no progress.

The nickelodeons were hurting the Yiddish theaters and music halls. For five cents audiences could see anything from slapstick to Shakespeare. On Avenue B next month they would see *Romeo and Juliet* and *Rip Van Winkle* with Joseph Jefferson. The shows ran half an hour; and if there were empty seats, those who wished could see the film over and over again. Audiences were mesmerized by this new diversion.

Nickelodeons were operating all over the country, Rissa discovered. They were not merely a New York phenomenon. Max told her about the studio that Edison had built in the Bronx. Vitagraph was filming in Flatbush. Selig and Essanay in Chicago. Rissa was troubled that Max was becoming so fascinated by the new moving pictures.

On a sunny spring afternoon Max, ever a compulsive walker, took Rissa for a stroll across East Fourteenth Street. He paused before an old brownstone house that had clearly once been a mansion.

'That's the Biograph studio,' Max told Rissa. 'They're putting out two films a week in there.' His face betrayed a wistful intensity, an obsession for this strange new form of entertainment that disturbed her. 'Someday films will be far bigger than the theater.'

'Max, no.' Rissa was shocked at such wanton prophecy. 'How can something you see on a white piece of cloth compare to live actors?'

'It'll take time,' Max admitted, 'but moving pictures will become the biggest form of entertainment the world has ever seen. Give it ten years, at the most. And when pictures are big, Rissa, you'll be a star in them.' His voice deepened with conviction.

'Never, Max!' She hurried past the old brownstone house as though demons might burst out and claim her. 'I'll never play anywhere except in the Yiddish theater.'

'Rissa, of course you'll do moving pictures.' Max moved to catch up with her. 'And you'll play in the uptown theater. On Broadway. It'll all be yours.'

'No,' Rissa said with painful certainty. 'I can never play uptown. I could never speak the lines in English.'

'You think in English,' Max pinpointed.

'Most of the time,' she conceded. 'Except when I'm excited or upset. But when Jacob Adler played uptown, he played in Yiddish.' She clutched at this. *Could* she play uptown someday in Yiddish?

'Rissa, you're young and improving your English each day,' Max told her, but Rissa resolutely shook her head. 'Bertha Kalisch plays downtown in Yiddish and uptown in English,' Max reminded in triumph. 'You'll do the same.'

'I'll never do it,' Rissa said with fatalistic calm.

'All right, let's not talk about Broadway,' Max soothed. 'But you don't have to talk in pictures. The audiences don't hear voices – they read captions.'

'My home is in the Yiddish theater.' Rissa was emphatic. Now she managed a wry smile. 'Someday I'll play in a real theater.'

'You won't stay in the music hall, Rissa.' Max's eyes held hers. 'You'll play in a real theater. As your personal manager I guarantee that.'

As much as she loved Max and longed for the day when she would be his wife, Rissa yearned to take her place beside the new generation of young Yiddish theater stars.

Max was contemplative.

'There are ways to get around the union rules. The "walking delegates" of the union have to approve the cast of every play. Sometimes a delegate insists a manager hires a girl he – likes.' Max broke off. 'No, that's not for you.'

'Max, how long can the union keep me out?' Despair made her voice sharp.

'If a manager has already hired the amount of actors the union demands, then he can hire another

174

of his own choosing.' Max reached for her hand. 'Rissa, we'll find a way.'

'It seems so unfair.'

'Yesterday I was talking with a man I met in the square.' Rissa marveled at the way Max drew people to him. He talked to everybody. Everybody liked him. 'He works for Biograph. I could ask him to introduce you to the man who hires for the films. It's a business with a big future,' he tried again.

'Please, Max. No.' She was upset. 'They wouldn't want me with my accent.'

'They don't hear you in the movies,' he reminded her.

'But I'd have to talk with the people who make them. I don't want to work anywhere but in the Yiddish theater.' Here she felt safe. Each time Max took her beyond the boundaries of the East Side, she was convinced everyone knew she was a 'greenhorn.'

Max couldn't understand how she felt when she was with people who spoke English with no accent. With them she felt one inch tall. The way she had felt whenever Phillip and she had met his friends at a theater or restaurant or museum. Phillip had taught her to smile and be silent. He had been ashamed of the way she spoke, for all he praised her for learning English so fast.

'Max, we won't play on the eve of the first seder?' Why had she asked him that? She didn't want to think about the agony of Passover until it was here and there was no way to avoid it. She trembled, turned cold in recall.

'We won't play,' Max said quietly. He understood.

'I thought we'd go to a seder together. Twice in my life I've been to a seder,' he reminisced. 'When the Feinbergs in Columbus, whom papa knew from the *shul*, invited us to share with them. This year we'll go to this family Izzy told me about near Prospect Park. For twenty-five cents each stranger can share their seder with them. Izzy will tell them to expect us.'

Rissa's face lighted. Passover would be less painful with Max. Then she remembered Shirley.

'Max, I can't leave Shirley alone – '

'Shirley will come with us.' Max smiled. 'I took that for granted.' He reached for her hand.

Last Passover she was with the Paulowskis on Krochmalna Street. The whole eight days had been a time of agony. This year she would be with Max and Shirley. Her family now. Thank God.

14

The afternoon before the seder Rissa went with Max and Shirley to Prospect Park.

They had decided to arrive long before sundown in order to have time to walk about the park. Last year Rissa had been affronted by the arrival of spring. Caught up in grief she had recoiled from the promise that spring brought to the earth.

Though her grief had not lessened, this year she could look at the tiny green buds on the trees with pleasure. Tonight she forced herself to lock away the agony of Passover two years ago.

'This reminds me of home,' Max said softly. 'Trees and grass and flowers.'

Crocuses had burst through to emblazon the earth. Daffodils promised a sea of golden splendor at any moment. Like the spring flowers, her life was blossoming anew. She had Max and Shirley. For now she could face the Passover holidays.

As the sun retreated, the three left the park and went in search of the nearby Park Slope house where they were to attend the seder. They walked past the homes of the well-to-do along the park frontage to a more modest address on Union Street. Their hosts lived in a brownstone with three-sided bay windows facing the street and a tiny front yard. A couple whose children had scattered, they had divided their house into three apartments. Each year, with their children too distant to attend, they brought strangers into the house for the first seder.

In the dining room two tables had been pushed together to accommodate the guests. White table-cloths were draped to make the tables seem one. Eighteen places had been set. As they settled about the table, the conversation shifted from Yiddish to English. The others showed amused indulgence toward Max's Southern brand of Yiddish.

Despite the joy in the holiday an aura of sadness glowed in the eyes of those gathered about the table. Memories of Kishinev – only five years behind them – of the failed 1905 revolution against the czar, of pogroms through the years, infiltrated the convivial atmosphere.

Rissa tried to focus on the beauty of the table at which she sat. The tall candles, the fine silver Elijah cup used only on this occasion, the special china and wine glasses.

She looked at the covered plate that concealed the three unbroken pieces of matzoth, at the center plate with its greens, its hard-boiled egg, the shank bone, freshly peeled horseradish, and the *haroseth*, at the lettuce that would later be dipped into the dishes of salt water, which symbolized the tears shed by the Jews when they were slaves in Egypt.

The head of the household began the service. With hands that were suddenly perspiring Rissa opened the book at her place. She was the youngest; she would ask the four questions. She clenched her teeth to keep back the sounds of anguish. If Joseph had lived, tonight it would have been he who asked the questions.

As the service proceeded, she visualized papa and grandpa wrapped in their *tallithim* at their last seder. Mama flushed from the heat of the stove, pleased that they had managed to have enough to celebrate the feast, even with the *luftmenshen* at the table. Katie, so serious and sweet, asking the four questions.

Rissa's voice was a tremulous whisper as she asked the questions. Max reached to hold her hand in his, pressed it in encouragement. He knew where her mind was tonight. Could it be otherwise?

At last they arrived at the point in the service where they were instructed to eat. Rissa was awed by the abundance of food that appeared. First the fish, then chicken soup with matzo balls, chicken with vegetables, stewed prunes.

Now the seder service was resumed. They sang the seder songs while the woman of the house began to remove the dishes. Rissa and Shirley arose to help her.

Over tea and sponge cake the conversation became lively. Rissa felt lightheaded from the wine. She was proud that everybody seemed to be drawn to Max. Every woman at the table envied her.

On the trolley to Essex Street, with Rissa's head on his shoulder, Max talked about his parents. He was eager for them to meet Rissa. In her last letter mama had asked for a snapshot.

'Then we'll find someone with a camera to take a picture,' Shirley contributed, her smile warm and sentimental.

As they approached the tenement on Essex Street, Rissa sensed Max's reluctance to part.

'Max, would you like to walk for a while?' she asked.

'Yes.' His face radiated pleasure. 'Good night, Shirley, Happy Passover.'

Max took Rissa's hand in his, and they walked off into the night. He knew that Rissa and he had no worries about encountering hostile Italians when they crossed the line between Yiddish and Italian territory. He with a touch of the South still in his voice and Rissa with her beautiful London dresses, which set her apart from the typical immigrant girl, traveled safely through the city.

Max talked about his parents in Georgia while he strolled with Rissa in the direction of Washington Square. On holidays he felt a special loneliness. With Rissa's hand in his he was slightly less alone. He fought against a compulsion to take her up to his room and make love to her. They were going to be married, his mind teased, why shouldn't they make love?

'Max, isn't the moon beautiful?' Rissa pulled him to a stop.

'Beautiful.' On the near-deserted street he paused to draw her into his arms. 'Like you.'

He kissed her with a passion that left them both shaken.

'Max?' Her eyes questioned him. She wanted him to take her up to his room. She wanted him to make love to her as desperately as he wanted it.

'It's getting chilly.' He reached for her hand again. 'We'll walk.' This was Rissa, his wife-to-be. When he took her home to mama, he wanted to know that he had never touched her.

They strolled across the square, past the red brick Georgian houses on Washington Square North. Rissa shivered in her black wool cape that had been adequate in the springlike afternoon.

'We'll go somewhere and get warm,' he comforted.

Max led her toward a late-night café on Mac-Dougal Street, where they could warm up over cake and coffee.

In the cozy, small café, its windows pleasantly steamed over, they were drawn into volatile discussions with a cluster of writers and actors willing to talk till dawn about the problems of the world – Roosevelt's fight on behalf of conservation, the efforts of the Zionists, the rise of Socialism in America, the tyranny of the czar, the outburst of strikes in the trades.

Max relished the verbal battles, enjoyed the companionship of creative people like himself.

'Rissa, are you tired?' he asked solicitously, close to midnight.

'No,' she assured him. 'Let's stay.'

At last the café owner announced he was closing. With good-humored insults the patrons took their leave. Max was glad that he had brought Rissa here tonight. She must learn that there was a world beyond the Yiddish East Side. She must realize she could be part of that world.

'I've kept you up so late.' Max smiled down at her

while they walked in the first light of dawn. 'You'll have five hours' sleep, with luck, before rehearsals.' Though there would be no performance on the night of the second seder, they were rehearsing another play during the day.

'It'll be enough,' she said blithely. They were young – they could miss a few hours' sleep.

'I won't go home,' Max decided. 'I'll nap at the music hall until rehearsal time.'

He left Rissa at her door and headed for the Bowery. What had promised to be a sunny day had dissipated into a foggy early morning. The streets were already busy. Small boys, laden down with garments over one arm, hurried to make deliveries for parents who did piecework at home. Pushcarts, rented at ten cents a day, were being set up along Hester, Ludlow and Suffolk streets. A horse trotted, unattended, back to his stables at Grand and Garrick.

Nostalgia brushed Max as he spied a woman walking tall and proud with a bag of rags atop her head. The way colored women walked down the wide-lawned residential streets back home, hawking fresh vegetables, fruit and butter.

At the music hall Max fell into a drugged sleep until the clatter of dishes at the delicatessen awoke him. He splashed water over his face, settled at a table with coffee and a bagel. This morning Izzy was oddly somber.

'Izzy, what's bothering you?' Max asked after a while.

'I've got a problem,' Izzy admitted. 'I don't know how to tell you.'

'Tell me,' Max said with foreboding.

'You know how my taxes keep going up on the stores. Tax people got no heart,' Izzy railed. 'But yesterday a man comes to me. He wants to buy the building. He says he'll rent me the one store at a rent that ain't so bad. Not good,' Izzy pinpointed, 'but I can live with it. And he'll give me a ten-year lease.'

'You mean no more music hall,' Max interpreted.

'The season's almost over, Max.' Izzy was uncomfortable. 'But to come back in the fall, no.'

'All right.' Between now and September he'd have to figure out something else. 'We're not married, Izzy,' he said because Izzy seemed disconsolate. 'So you found a good buyer for the property. Congratulations.' He hesitated. 'Izzy, don't say anything to the others. Not even Rissa.'

'Not a word, Max.'

Throughout the rehearsal that day Max's mind wandered away to grapple with the future. Yiddish theaters and music halls closed for the summer. He'd have to try to book Rissa and a couple of the others into the hotels up in Catskills. Put together a tiny revue. That would carry Rissa and him through the summer.

Izzy came to sit beside Max when things got slow behind the counter of the delicatessen. He listened avidly, with the air of a connoisseur.

'They'll love this one,' Izzy predicted. Reveling in his role of producer. 'We play it tomorrow night?'

'Tomorrow night,' Max concurred. He masked his distaste for the play. How could he learn to reeducate their audiences? How could he make them see what was good and what was bad? 'All right, everybody,' he called out as the run-through was finished. 'We play it tomorrow night.'

Izzy returned to his place behind the counter. Rissa came over to sit beside Max. She knew how miserable he was with this rotten play.

'I'm going home to change clothes,' Max said. He felt like one of the bums who slept in doorways at night. 'Walk over with me? You can wait in the park.'

'My feet still hurt,' Rissa apologized. 'I'll stay here. I have to sew the hem of a dress, anyway.'

Max hurried across to Washington Square. Maybe Rissa and he would take advantage of the night off to go up to Fourteenth Street to see a moving picture at Keith and Proctor's. The new medium was raw and untamed, but he visualized its potential. It would have an audience of millions. At the music hall he catered to a hundred twenty-five people a night.

Climbing the stairs to his hall-bedroom Max was engrossed in the world that would one day be Rissa's and his.

Max unlocked his door and walked inside. He fumbled for the chain that would bring light into the small, narrow, meagerly furnished room. He stared at the small yellow envelope his landlady had propped against a book on the table in the center of the room. A telegram.

Warning signals zigzagged across his brain. Mama always said that telegrams were reserved for terrible news. He reached for the envelope and ripped it open. Pulled out the sheaf of yellow paper and read the words:

YOUR PARENTS DIED TODAY. STOP. TWO DAY HOLDUP OF FUNERAL ALLOWED.

The sender was one of the two Jewish men in Belleville other than his father.

Max tried to grapple with reality. Mama and papa dead? Both? How could that be? All at once he saw his round dark-haired little mother, who had once been beautiful. His lean, spare father who loved to argue politics with his pharmacist friend. *Dead?* Papa was fifty-two, mama forty-nine.

Numb with shock he reread the words strung across the paper with the economy demanded in telegrams. How had they died? What happened? The telegram said so little.

He checked the time; the telegram had been sent at just before midnight. It must have been delivered early this morning. While he prowled about the city with Rissa. Why hadn't he come home last night?

At last he moved into action. He had to go home. How much was the fare? Could he get home in time for the funeral? His hands shaking he gathered together his funds, trying to remember what it cost for a railroad ticket to Belleville. Why had he waited so long to go home?

He threw a few essentials into the valise that he had brought with him to New York three years ago. He'd have to check the train schedules. Borrow a few dollars from Izzy. Instead of going home in June for a wedding, he was going home to a double funeral.

Rissa felt Max's grief almost as deeply as he. She refused to allow him to borrow money from Izzy; she gave him what little remained of her own stake. With Izzy's support she would manage to keep the company together until he returned. At sixteen she felt herself a woman.

The new play was set; surely they could run it a week. In her mind she promised herself that Max would return within a week. She found a new strength in Max's need. He clung to her, numb and disbelieving. Later he would cry.

In dismay Max discovered he could not take a train to Belleville until the following afternoon.

'Rissa, I'll be there too late for the funeral,' he said in despair while they walked hand in hand through the deserted night streets, knowing that Orthodox Jews must be buried within twenty-four hours of death. 'Why didn't I go home last night? I could have been on this afternoon's train.'

'You'll be there as soon as you can,' Rissa consoled, remembering that she had suggested they walk after their return from the seder.

Rissa and Max stayed together in the empty music hall talking through the night. The next afternoon Rissa went with him on the ferry from West Twenty-third Street to the Exchange Place terminal in Jersey City. She saw him aboard the Southern Railway train that would take him to Atlanta, where he would change for another train for the brief ride to Belleville.

Tears spilled over as she watched the train pull out of the terminal. Only now did she admit to the fear that gripped her. *Once back home in Georgia, would Max ever come back to New York? Would she ever see him again?*

15

Max sat in his day-coach seat and stared out into the darkness as the train sped through the night. He had dreamed of going home with success in his hand. To say lovingly, 'Mama, this is for you.' He would never have the chance now.

Mama had taken such pride in him. Sometimes he was embarrassed the way she had bragged about his grades in school. He remembered a neighbor's daughter who had accompanied him from 1-A straight through high school. When he was chosen as graduation speaker, she said to him, 'Max, don't you know? Smart people are never happy.'

Her mother, mama's friend, said it was no wonder he graduated first in his class. He was such a hard worker, always studying. But he wasn't always studying. He was always reading. Looking, even then, for a world beyond Belleville, Georgia.

Nobody understood – not even mama – that he could not be content to spend the rest of his life in Belleville, to take over the store someday from papa. He knew an exciting world existed beyond Belleville, and he was determined to be part of it.

At four the following afternoon the train pulled into Union Depot in Atlanta. Max looked at his pocket watch. By now mama and papa had been laid to rest. He fondled the nickel-plated watch with its silver chain; his present at high school graduation.

At Union Depot Max waited two hours for the train that would carry him the short distance to Belleville.

In Belleville he descended from the train into a dreary night drizzle and walked the few quiet blocks from the depot to the small white frame house where his parents had been tenants for the past fourteen years, always hoping to be owners.

In June mama and papa were to be at the depot to welcome him home along with their daughter-in-law. They would have been full of talk about the wedding. Mama would have been cooking and baking for at least two days. *Why hadn't he come home soon enough to see them alive just once more?*

The man who had sent him the telegram was waiting with his wife at the house.

'We came so you shouldn't walk in alone,' he said with awkward compassion.

Max listened to the report of his parents' last hours. Papa had suffered bad business reverses. That day he had declared bankruptcy. But mama had said nothing of this in her last letter, Max thought in bewilderment. Papa and mama had not wanted him to worry. *He should have been here with them. He should have helped.*

After the seder, upset at losing the business he had spent a lifetime acquiring and building up, papa left the house to talk with his friend the pharmacist.

'It was dark,' papa's friend explained. 'He didn't see the car speeding toward him at twenty miles an hour. The driver didn't see him. He was killed instantly, Max. The doctor said he didn't suffer. As soon as your mother heard, she collapsed. It was a heart attack. Within an hour she, too, was dead.'

The store was gone to the creditors. With a sickness churning in his stomach Max walked past the padlocked store. Visualizing papa trying to 'pull in' customers, even as they did on the lower East Side. Papa's store had catered to the millworkers and the 'colored' trade. On the next block were the stores with the fancy windows and the nice manners.

He called in a used-furniture dealer and sold him everything in the house, too distraught to argue price, though he knew he was being robbed. How much could he take back with him to New York? Only mama's wedding ring, the tiny diamond papa had given her for their silver anniversary last year, and mama's pair of brass candlesticks. Now they would be Rissa's. Those things and a box of family pictures he took with him on the train to New York two days later.

Papa's friend reminded him he was not to sit *shivah* for his parents. They had died on Passover eve. They were blessed.

Rissa felt her own loss anew in Max's bereavement. She cried when he gave her his mother's diamond as her engagement ring, though she knew he could not think about a wedding now. She watched in helplessness while she saw his grief tear him apart inside. Not even work seemed to assuage his loss. Night after night he sat with Rissa over glasses of tea and talked about his mother and father.

'Rissa, I should have been home to receive the

190

telegram,' he berated himself. 'I shouldn't have sat in that café until it closed. I slept in the music hall while the telegram waited on the table in my room. I could have been in Belleville in time for the funeral.'

'Max, you couldn't have known,' she consoled.

But as the days went past, Rissa felt Max moving away from her. Waking from restless sleep one night she suddenly understood.

Max blamed her because he had not gone home to find the telegram.

Knowing she would not sleep again tonight, Rissa left her bed. Though warm weather had descended upon the city, an unseasonable chill seeped into the room at dawn. She reached for a shawl to wrap about her and walked to look out into the gray morning.

'Why aren't you sleeping?' Shirley scolded from the doorway.

Rissa whirled about to face her.

'I woke you.' She was contrite.

'Walking from the bed to the window you woke me?' Shirley clucked. 'I woke because I was cold. Last night I was hot. I kicked off the blankets. This morning the weather forgets it's May already. I'll put up water for tea.' Pulling on her bathrobe Shirley crossed to the stove. 'Darling, what bothers you?'

'I worry about Max,' Rissa admitted. 'It's like – like he's moving away from me. I talk to him sometimes, and he doesn't even hear me.'

'Rissa, you know what it's like to go through what he's been through.' Shirley was gentle. 'Give him time.'

'It scares me.' She hesitated. 'I think he blames me for not getting home in time for the funeral.'

'What did you do?' Shirley put up the water and turned to face her. 'You grabbed him by the arm and told him not to go home? It's nobody's fault Max couldn't be there. It was *bashert*.'

Two nights later, when Max and she remained alone in the music hall after the performance, Rissa determined to confront him. She could not endure this breach between them another night.

'How much longer will you be?' she asked Max self-consciously while he fiddled with a lock that was a prop in the play.

'I'm finished,' he said. 'It just needed oiling.'

Rissa rose to her feet. She was trembling.

'Max, you're angry with me – '

Max stared at her, seeming startled by her accusation.

'Why should I be angry with you?'

'You blame me because you got to Belleville too late for your parents' funeral.' Tears filled her eyes. 'Max, I couldn't have known about the telegram.'

'No, Rissa.' His voice cracked. 'I blame myself. I should have been there to see them once more. I'm all they had in the world. I should have been there!'

'Stop blaming anyone,' Rissa pleaded. 'If they could know, they'd understand. Max, be grateful. You remember them alive. That's a blessing, Max.' Forever her mind would be stamped with the memory of her family in death.

'Rissa – ' Max reached for her.

Rissa held him in her arms while the tears that had

been held back so long gushed forward. She rocked him as though he were a small boy. It was better to cry. Now Max and she could begin to live again.

Max pulled himself out of his despondency. The hot weather was almost upon them. He loathed summers in New York. People hung from every window, slept on fire escapes and on stoops. Tempers were short. Babies cried. Crime rose.

With the season over Max enlisted two members of the company to work with Rissa and him for the summer in the Catskills.

'I'll work up a short revue,' he explained. 'We can change the routines each night. We'll take the revue to the mountains. We won't need an agent – I'll go up to the hotels myself and set up the bookings.' The money might be minimal, but they would have room and board plus fresh air and sunshine for ten weeks.

The Yiddish newspapers carried enticing advertisements about the hotels in the Catskills, where for as little as eight dollars a week, room and board could be had. The fancier places – those with electric lights, telephone, bowling, dancing and entertainment, could run as high as fifteen dollars a week, with children half-price. The railroads offered special 'vacation fares' to encourage travelers. Every immigrant family dreamed of a week in 'the mountains,' though few could afford this luxury.

Max took a train to the mountains, hired a horse and buggy and went out to sell. He offered hotel owners stars straight from 'success in the Bowery theaters.' He guaranteed them replicas of Bertha

Kalisch, Boris Thomashefsky and Anna Held, who — after all — was a poor little girl from Poland who married the great Ziegfeld.

At the end of June Max traveled with his revue to the first resort hotel where they were to play. The air was sweet. The grass, the trees, the flowers reminded him of home. The small room assigned to him in the attic of the converted farmhouse was filled with four cots. He shared the bedroom with the male member of his revue, a waiter, plus an impecunious boarder who could afford nothing better. Rissa and their prima donna shared a somewhat larger room with three daughters of the family.

Max was upset to discover the proprietors expected him to attend the hotel dances and hayrides, providing male companionship for the young girls and women. He insisted on exemption on the grounds that he was in mourning.

He knew Rissa was upset that the women — and girls — were in constant pursuit despite his protestation of being in mourning. The only men present at the hotels during the week were employees or an occasional more prosperous husband. Most husbands arrived only for the weekends.

Max managed to remain unentangled through the ensuing weeks, though not without effort. Then they moved for the final two weeks of the summer to Hershman's Happy Acres. At dinner before the first performance he became aware of eyes focused on him from a table across the room. They belonged to a well-endowed, flashily dressed young matron of considerable attractions. Later she managed to have herself introduced to him.

'I'll bet you're a real good dancer.' She smiled in unabashed invitation, and Max knew the invitation went beyond the dance floor.

'I'm in mourning,' he said politely and made a fast retreat.

For the next four days Lita Abramowitz made every effort to become familiar with Max. He congratulated himself on avoiding her, though the efforts were becoming more painful. Since he had asked Rissa to marry him, he had not slept with a woman.

On a cloudy afternoon just before the weekend, Max left the hotel – which had formerly been a dairy farm – and went for a walk. He enjoyed the stretches of grass and trees on every side. He walked well away from the hotel, toward the cluster of outbuildings.

'Max,' a feminine voice called out. He turned around to see from where it came. 'Over here,' the voice beckoned provocatively. 'In the barn.'

The barn door flew open. Lita stood there. Shoulders thrust back to emphasize her curvaceous bosom, white peekaboo blouse unbuttoned indecorously low.

'It was drizzling for a minute,' Lita said. 'I popped in here. Don't you love the smell of new-mown hay?'

'Not particularly,' he shrugged, moving cautiously toward her.

'I'm so tired of being stuck up here in the country with the kids and mama,' she sighed.

'Your husband will be up tonight or tomorrow morning,' he guessed. What the hell was he doing here in the barn with Lita Abramowitz?

'Big deal.' Her eyes trailed over Max. 'He'll sit out on the porch and play pinochle all day. That's what gives him a thrill.' She moved in closer to Max. He could see her nipples hardening beneath her blouse. 'Max, it must be awful exciting to be an actor.'

'I'm not an actor. I'm a company manager.' He tried not to stare at her breasts, but the long nights of celibacy mocked him.

Lita's hand darted out to touch him. Her face lighted with triumph.

'You're hot as a pistol.' She reached to unbutton her blouse the rest of the way.

With a strangled grunt Max pulled her to him. How could he walk out now? Her mouth reached up to his. Her hands roamed about his back as they swayed together.

'Max,' she whispered when they broke for air, 'go close the door. Quick.' Her eyes were full of promise.

When he came back from closing the door, Lita had already stripped to skin. With no preliminaries he prodded her onto a bed of hay and thrust himself within her.

'Max, hurry,' she whimpered. 'Now, honey, now!'

'Lita, shut up,' he ordered in alarm. 'You want the whole hotel to hear?'

Later, when Lita and he lay motionless, his body limp above hers but reluctant to separate, Max told himself that it was time Rissa and he got married. He wouldn't go looking outside if he had what he needed at home. Yet how could he marry, his mind rebuked, until he was able to support a wife? He was alone in the world. He had no parents to turn to in an emergency. He couldn't go back to Belleville.

'Lita, let's get the hell out of here,' he said abruptly, pulling himself away from her. 'Before somebody walks in on us.'

Moments after Rissa joined Max in the dining room for dinner, she sensed something had happened between Lita Abramowitz and him. The scent of a pungent perfume lingered about him.

Her heart pounded as she evaluated the situation. She searched Max's face for some inkling that she was right. There was a guarded, guilty look in his eyes. Across the room Lita sat with her family. Her gaze moved at regular intervals to Max. Rissa flinched. Something had happened between Lita and Max this afternoon. Everything that could happen between a man and a woman happened – and Lita had found it good.

Rissa barely touched the food on the plate before her. She had been upset when she thought Max would sleep with Yetta Bernstein for money to keep the play running. She had told herself she would not marry him if he did this. Now she felt differently. Lita was young and pretty, and she had thrown herself at Max. Max was young and healthy – with the needs of a man which so far she had not satisfied.

She wished that it were time to go back to the city. How could she stand by for another week and watch Lita throw herself at Max?

Now every time Max was out of her sight, she was sure he was with Lita. Max couldn't know how desperately she wanted him to make love to her. The nights she couldn't sleep for thinking about this. But to Max – who had forgiven her for Phillip – his future wife must remain untouched. She was the girl he had meant to take home to his mother.

She wrote an impassioned letter to Shirley, pouring out her anguish. Did Max feel he had the right to play with Lita because she had lived with Phillip? Not until they married would she feel secure.

Back in New York, Rissa and Max discovered that Weinberg's Music Hall was now a saloon. An avid gatherer of theater gossip, Shirley reported that Jacob Adler had sailed for Germany two weeks ago. He was going to tour the world.

Hearing that the great Adler had forsaken New York theater, two of Max's company of three defected to jobs in Chicago, where the union allowed them to work. If Adler went elsewhere, what was there in New York for them? Rissa worried that she had been able to save so little over the summer.

On their second night back in New York Shirley took Rissa and Max to supper at Ratner's on Pitt Street.

'My big celebration,' she confided to them over the sumptuous twenty-five-cent meal provided by Ratner's. 'Today I told my cockroach contractor, "Pay more for each piece or we don't work." With all the strikes I could be brave.' Shirley grinned. 'He gave me a raise.'

Rissa suspected that Shirley harbored other

motives. Not until the hot apple strudel arrived did this surface.

'So when's the wedding?' Shirley inquired sweetly. 'If I'm going to make a wedding gown, I need time to prepare.'

Rissa stared at her in consternation, her face hot with shame; but Shirley displayed no remorse. A forkful of strudel frozen midway between plate and mouth, Max seemed incapable of speech.

'Shirley, I'm in mourning,' he mumbled at last.

'Your parents, may they rest in peace, have been gone over three months. You can marry after three months if there's no music at the wedding. Do you have to have music?' Shirley smiled indulgently.

'As soon as I'm set in a job,' Max said. He accepted Shirley in the role of 'mother of the bride.' 'Then Rissa and I will be married.' He turned to Rissa. 'You know I'll never try to earn a living working in a store or behind a pushcart. I mean to work only in the theater. Or in the movie business,' he added after an instant's reflection.

'I wouldn't want you to do anything else,' Rissa said softly. She brushed aside his mention of the moving pictures. 'You belong in the theater.'

'I know about running a theater,' Max said, his smile wry. 'I know nothing about running a wedding.'

'I'll help, Max.' Shirley was effervescent at the prospect of a wedding. 'You don't need a lot of money. You can be married without a hall and a hundred people. At the rabbi's flat is good enough.

I'll start looking on Division Street for material for the veil – '

'First,' Rissa halted her, touched by Shirley's happiness, 'Max and I must find work.'

16

Every day Rissa and Max traipsed the East Side in search of jobs. Only a sprinkling of music halls remained opened. Some became annoyed at Rissa and Max's persistent efforts.

'We'll hold out,' Max vowed after he had rejected an offer from Izzy to return to a job behind the counter of the delicatessen.

'We can't hold out much longer,' Rissa worried. If nothing happened in the next week or two, she would have to try to sew for Shirley's contractor.

'I'll work out something,' Max insisted, his face resolute. 'What future would we have if I'm a clerk in a delicatessen? Life has to do better for us, Rissa.' He made a sudden decision. 'Rissa, Friday night I'm taking you to the Café Royale.'

'It's expensive!' Rissa protested.

'It's an investment,' Max pointed out. 'We have to have an angle. Something to start us moving.'

'We'll find that at the Café Royale?' Rissa was skeptical. She knew about the fine café that had opened on Second Avenue at Twelfth Street last year. Here, especially on Friday nights, gathered everybody who was anybody in the Yiddish theater.

'We'll look,' Max said, and grinned. 'I hear their chicken *paprikash* is the best to be had in New York. I know a waiter who works there. If the bill is too high, he'll give me credit.' Rissa frowned; she was terrified of credit. 'Rissa, relax,' Max coaxed. 'Better times are coming. This is an election year. Business always improves when a new president comes in.'

'Who will you vote for, Max?' Rissa was fascinated by the democratic system of voting for officials. When Max and she were married, she would become a citizen. But she rebelled, like Shirley, against the law that said women could not vote.

'I'm a Georgia Democrat.' Max smiled. 'Who would I vote for but William Jennings Bryan? But the gamblers are saying Taft will succeed Roosevelt.' Rissa knew that Roosevelt had refused to run again; he said no president should run for a third term.

'What shall I wear to the Café Royale?' All at once she was insecure.

'You'll wear one of your beautiful dresses,' Max said tenderly. One of her London dresses. 'And you'll be the loveliest sight in the café.'

Shortly before eleven on Friday night Max escorted Rissa, wearing a Merry Widow hat especially concocted by Shirley for tonight's excursion and a lilac gray silk frock, into the Café Royale. The restaurant was uncrowded because performances were still in progress. Rissa's eyes moved with pleasure about the mahogany-walled, oblong room. About fifty tables were provided for diners. At the rear Rissa spied other tables set up for pinochle players.

'We'll sit there,' Max pointed. Rissa wished he had chosen a less conspicuous table. Already she was conscious of admiring inspections.

'Max, what do you expect to find here?' Rissa asked worriedly when the waiter had taken their orders and bustled off to the kitchen.

'I'll know when I see it.' Max radiated confidence. Everyone here seemed gay and confident.

Rissa tried to enjoy the superb chicken *paprikash*.

'Everybody's saying that the theaters will move soon to Second Avenue,' Max said, playing the successful theatrical entrepreneur. 'The Bowery's become loaded with saloons and derelicts. Second Avenue is a clean, wide street with no Elevated trains running overhead. It's ideal.'

'The performances are over,' Rissa whispered. 'There's Boris Thomashefsky!' The actor and his entourage were being conducted to hastily pushed-together tables by an effusive waiter.

Within minutes the Café Royale was filled with laughter, ebullient conversation and cigarette smoke. At a table next to Rissa and Max, a man and a woman were performing a scene from a new play for the verdict of their companions.

'Max, there's Leo Gunsburg!' Rissa said in astonishment.

'Who's Leo Gunsburg?' Max's gaze followed Rissa's to a man seated across the room, tall and handsome with prematurely gray hair and a presence that Max instantly respected.

'He was the star in a theater in the East End. In London,' Rissa explained. 'I was offered a place in the company – '

'What's he doing here?' Rissa knew Max's inquiry was not casual curiosity.

'Things are bad in London,' Rissa said. 'Years ago there were a dozen Yiddish theaters. Now there are only three. Actors leave the country.'

'We'll go over and talk to him.' Max was decisive. Rissa felt the excitement in him and it made her uncomfortable. 'About what?'

'Tell him you saw him play in London,' Max instructed. 'That you had been invited to join the company. You said you knew someone at the theater?'

'Olga Cohen. She played small parts.' Rissa's eyes moved across the room to Leo Gunsburg. She knew this meeting was important to Max. She must do as he said.

Rissa and Max made their way through the maze of tables to where Leo Gunsburg sat alone.

'Mr Gunsburg?' Rissa questioned softly and the actor's face brightened. 'Leo Gunsburg from London?'

'Yes.' His smile was dazzling. She sensed his relief that someone knew him.

'I saw you at the theater on Mile End Road. My friend, Olga Cohen, was in the company.' Rissa smiled warmly. 'I was invited to play soubrettes, but I had already made plans to come to America.' She felt the faint pressure of Max's hand on her arm. 'May I introduce Max Miller?' She was faintly unnerved by Leo Gunsburg's lingering stare.

'An actor?' Leo asked with mild condescension.

'No.' Max oozed self-confidence. 'A manager.'

'Handsome enough to be a matinee idol.' Gunsburg was alert to possibilities. He had no job in New

York, Rissa interpreted. 'Would you have a glass of tea with me?'

Rissa listened with a show of interest to the rapid-fire conversation that bounced between Max and Leo Gunsburg. Leo was lyrical about his success in London, though he conceded that Yiddish theater was dying in that city. Max talked about his music hall company and the company he 'took on tour.'

Rissa struggled to hide her alarm when Max leaned forward to confide in low tones that would not carry to neighboring tables. 'Mr Gunsburg, if I talk to my partner about forming the company around you, I must have your word that you will not discuss working for another manager in New York.'

'I give you my word, Max.' Leo extended a hand. 'My word is my bond. When can we meet to discuss the terms?'

'Monday evening,' Max said with split-second hesitation. 'Ten o'clock. Here.'

'My pleasure.' Leo's eyes returned to linger on Rissa's curvaceous bosom. 'You'll be in the company, of course?'

'Of course,' Max concurred before Rissa could reply. 'Rissa and I are to be married shortly.'

'Ah, *maz'l tov*! A long life to you both.' He lifted his glass of tea as in a toast. His smile was meant to be paternal but managed only to be lecherous.

Max and Rissa walked out into the balmy late September night. He reached for Rissa's hand as they started down Second Avenue.

'The old bastard,' he fumed. 'How dare he look at you like that!'

205

Rissa laughed. Max's jealousy was precious to her.

'What were you trying to do in the café?' She was suddenly serious. 'He thinks you have a job for him.'

'I mean to.' Max was calm. 'I've got to push Izzy into investing. He still has the cash from the sale of the building.'

'Izzy isn't going to put up that kind of money.' Rissa stared at Max in disbelief. 'You know what the union makes a manager take on. It's a fortune.'

'It's a lot of money. Izzy has it. And if the full amount of actors are hired that the union demands, then I can hire one more of my own choosing. You.' His smile was triumphant. 'You'll be Leo Gunsburg's leading lady.'

'Max, you're dreaming.'

'I'll do it,' Max swore. 'Izzy is itching to invest. He can never resist a bargain. We'll get Leo Gunsburg, a star of the London stage, for nothing. He'll play for anything we offer, to be able to appear in the New York theater. Rissa, he's scared to death.'

'Everybody in London talks about how much Yiddish theater stars earn in New York,' Rissa warned. 'They hear about Adler and Kessler and Thomashefsky.'

'They hear, too, how bad conditions are here now. They know that Adler didn't resign his lease on the Grand. That he's touring Europe. Rissa, I can put this deal across.' Max's face was incandescent. 'Watch me!'

Rissa tried to enjoy the luxury of lox and bagel for breakfast at Ratner's. It was difficult to concentrate on this epicurean delight while Max and Izzy argued about Max's proposed theater company. Max had brought Izzy further downtown to meet him on equal ground.

'Izzy, can't you see what I'm giving you?' When he was excited, a vein pounded in Max's forehead. 'A star from the London Yiddish theater who'll work for you for twelve dollars a week. Nobody knows he's here yet.'

'He's at the Café Royale and nobody knows?' Izzy scoffed, but Rissa saw a gleam of interest in his eyes.

'Nobody there recognized him – they don't know London actors by sight. Adler would know, but he's in Europe. Kessler wasn't there. Thomashefsky was busy with his *patriotn*. Izzy, it's the chance of a lifetime. Rissa saw him play. He's marvelous.'

'In what kind of plays?' Izzy turned to Rissa, and she saw the warning Max beamed at her. Izzy scoffed at what he referred to as fancy-schmancy plays.

'He played for the people,' Rissa said. 'Like the plays Thomashefsky gives at the People's Theater.'

Izzy's face lighted. He knew the fortune Thomashefsky was making. With *shund*. But then he frowned.

'It's too much of a gamble, Max. How do I know we can fill a theater? Where do we find a theater?'

'We'll have no trouble finding an empty house with business so bad,' Max pounced. 'We won't start with a big place like the Grand. We'll get advance bookings for midweek performances. You know everybody in all the lodges, the *landsmanshaftn* societies. Leo Gunsburg is as handsome as a Greek god. The women will love him. Izzy, we'll pack the house!'

Rissa was enthralled by Max's rhetoric. Even before Izzy voiced agreement, she knew Max had acquired a partner. The theater would open with Leo Gunsburg as its star, and she would be his leading lady.

The next three weeks passed in dizzying activity. Leo Gunsburg was at first insulted when Max made an offer. Then he was philosophical. He signed the contract with Izzy and Max on their terms. The company was hired according to union demands, though Max complained bitterly at buying actors 'by the yard.'

Rissa was relieved that Max ignored his better instincts. He directed as though this was a Thomashefsky play. Privately he promised Rissa that there would be midweek nights when the plays – and the acting – would be more to his liking.

The Sunday before their opening Max and Rissa were to be married. Rissa alternated between joy that she would at last become Max's wife and grief that her family would not be with her to share the occasion.

Max's landlady was able to provide a larger room with a corner kitchen. Rissa was startled by the amount of the rent, but Max insisted they could afford it. He was determined to remain on Washington Square.

'I couldn't live on the East Side,' he confessed. 'Those dark, ugly rooms stifle me.'

Shirley took charge of the wedding preparations. Since the parents of both bride and groom were dead and the graves too distant to visit, they must go to the synagogue to offer a prayer inviting the spirits of their parents to the ceremony. Shirley arranged for the wedding to take place in the home of a rabbi on Jefferson Street. Shirley and Izzy would be the witnesses.

Shirley was making the bridal gown. With Rissa she haunted Grand Street to make sure the gown would be in the latest fashion, as brought to Grand Street from Fifth Avenue. White satin with a long veil, Shirley decreed.

'You're being married like an American, not a greenhorn,' Shirley chortled. 'Without a *shadkh'n*. In America, who needs a marriage broker?' But Shirley dismissed the prospect of marriage for herself.

Only the night before the wedding, while Rissa stood before her in the wedding gown so Shirley could make the final adjustments, did Shirley explain her conviction that she must remain single. Alone in New York, not long after her arrival from London, Shirley had loved a man. He talked about a wedding 'someday.'

'Then his wife and children came over from Russia, and it was over.' Shirley's face was desolate in recall. 'For him it was over. He left a little present in my belly.'

'Oh, Shirley – ' Rissa reached out a hand in sympathy. 'What did you do?'

'I went to a woman on Rivington Street. For two dollars she took away the baby. And then, for punishment, I had to go to Bellevue Hospital and stay there for three weeks. I almost died. Before I left, the doctors told me I'd never have another baby.

God's punishment. But enough already.' Shirley banished morbid conversation with a wave of one hand. 'We have to get ready for a wedding.'

At five the next afternoon Rissa and Max signed the *k'sube* – the marriage contract – in the sitting room of the rabbi's railroad flat, where the handful of guests gathered together. Shirley, Izzy and his wife Ida, Max's landlady, his typist neighbor – twenty years younger than Rissa expected – and two young male friends from Max's non-Jewish world of Greenwich Village.

Max's friends, Rissa suspected, were slightly uncomfortable in these strange surroundings. Though the typist was Jewish, she was quick to point out that her family lived uptown.

Looking handsome yet strained, Max took his place beneath the tiny red velvet *hupah* set up for the occasion. The canopy represented the wedding couple's future home. Unfamiliarly solemn, Shirley escorted Rissa, exquisite in her white satin gown with veil over her face as tradition demanded, to her place beside Max. Izzy, accompanied by his wife, stood by to represent Max's family.

Tears filled Rissa's eyes while the rabbi offered the prayer that welcomed the spirits of the deceased to the wedding. Her eyes moved with tenderness to Max while the rabbi began the ceremony. She saw the tears he tried to conceal. For Max and her this was a happy time, yet grief was fresh today for those who could not be with them.

At the proper moment Rissa walked seven times

around her groom. Max and she drank from the same glass of wine to show they would be partners in joy. He placed his mother's wedding ring upon her finger. The rabbi intoned the final words: 'I hereby declare you man and wife according to the laws of Moses and Israel and by the power vested in me by the state of New York.'

The rabbi reached for the paper bag that contained the glass that was a symbol of the destruction of the second temple. Max dropped the bag to the floor and stamped on it. The rabbi explained that the glass is broken to remind the Jew that the glory of the Jewish nation has been broken, and to remind the young that all must ultimately return to dust.

Max lifted the veil to kiss his bride. The others rushed forward with congratulations.

'Ida, stop crying,' Izzy exhorted his wife. 'A wedding is a happy occasion. We have supper waiting for us at the delicatessen. Everybody's invited.'

Seated beside Max while Izzy poured the wine at the festive wedding table, Rissa was suffused with joy. Max was her husband. On Wednesday evening she would play her first performance in New York theater. Max, Izzy, even Leo Gunsburg were convinced the audiences would love her.

On Friday night before the performance she would light the candles in the candlesticks that had once belonged to Max's mother and were now hers. She would say a special thanks to God. What could go wrong in her life when Max was her husband?

17

For Rissa and Max their wedding night was a precious oasis in the midst of a terrifying obstacle course. They awoke on Monday morning in each other's arms at the callous intrusion of the alarm clock. They had slept at exhausted intervals between lovemaking.

'Max,' Rissa's eyes were soft with pleasure while she reached to silence the intruder, 'we have to get up.'

'Later,' he resisted, manipulating one leg across her slender thighs. The nightgown Shirley had made with delicate hand-stitching had been discarded a dozen hours ago.

'The rehearsal,' Rissa reminded. But already her body responded to his.

'To the devil with the rehearsal.'

For a while they gave themselves over to morning passion. The small room overlooking Washington Square was silent except for the sounds of their lovemaking. Rissa's hands fondled Max's shoulders while he rested within her. She was glad she had come to Max knowing about love. How many brides enjoyed their wedding night as she had enjoyed hers?

'Max, we have to go to rehearsal. The manager-director can't be late,' she said firmly.

'It says so in the Torah?' Max laughed.

'Max, they'll like the play?' Fresh misgivings closed in about her.

'They'll like it.'

They dressed now with an awareness to what lay ahead in the next few days. Tomorrow they went into the dress rehearsal. Wednesday night they opened. The following Monday they must start rehearsing the second play in their repertory.

The union allowed her to appear because Izzy had signed for the full amount of required actors. Leo and she were 'extra' actors. She would perform without payment. Max had made this agreement with Izzy. But Max and she could survive on his salary. Her first play in a real theater in New York!

'Where the hell is a clean shirt?' At rehearsals Max was calm. Always in control. Alone with her he dared to show his anxieties.

'I put your shirts in this drawer.' Rissa went to the battered chest provided by their landlady. 'I'll put up the tea. We won't be late,' she soothed. In truth, it was she who was obsessive about punctuality.

When they left the apartment that morning, Rissa felt she emerged as a new person. She was Max's wife, living with him in Greenwich Village. She was Leo Gunsburg's leading lady. Everything seemed possible.

Rissa was nervous before every performance. Tonight, with their opening barely two hours away, she was impatient with her fears. Max had insisted she come home to rest. She lay on the bed, rehearsing in her mind a difficult scene.

'I've fixed a little something for you.' Max sat on

the edge of the bed and deposited a plate with a buttered bagel plus a cup of tea on the table.

'I can't eat before a performance.' Rissa shuddered.

'You'll eat a bagel and drink a cup of tea,' Max insisted. 'How would it look if the leading lady keeled over from hunger?'

'We'll have a critic tonight?' She simultaneously prayed for this and dreaded it.

'I guarantee it.' Max's smile betrayed no doubt about the outcome.

'Will he like the play?' Rissa forced herself to bite into the bagel.

'He'll like Leo, and he'll like you.' Max was blunt. 'The others the union pushed on us. They'll get by,' he conceded. 'We don't have an audience of people who understand fine theater. The play is *shund*,' he said with familiar contempt.

Rissa hesitated. Rarely did she allow herself to disagree with Max. But honesty propelled her into candor.

'Max, I think you're too far away from the audiences to understand how they feel. You grew up in Georgia, in a world so different from theirs.' So different from her own.

'I understand that even Kessler and Adler have to present *shund*.' Max shook his head in frustration. 'I understand that only for *shund* – and Leo Gunsburg – would Izzy have put up the money for the company.'

'There's more for you to understand.' Over a plate of noodle soup in Ratner's one day when Max was involved in placing their ads, Shirley had made her see what Yiddish theater meant to the people who flocked religiously into the playhouse every week. 'Max, *shund* has something special to say to immigrants. It goes straight to their hearts, Max, forgive me – but you don't know how homeless the Jews have been through the years. You've heard about it,' she said quickly before he could interrupt. 'But immigrants – we know. You grew up in a small town in Georgia, living like everybody else. You didn't come from a *dorf* or a *shtetl* or a ghetto. You discovered you were a Jew with Kishinev. The people who sit out front in the theaters look at the play on the stage, and it's their lives they see up there.'

'What about Yiddish culture?' Max protested. 'Why can't the immigrants see Gordin and Andreyev and Tolstoy and understand how this relates to their lives? Why is an actress like Keni Liptzin playing in a theater that seats hardly three hundred people?'

'They're not ready for culture on the lower East Side,' Rissa said flatly. 'And what's the good of playing to empty houses? Who'll pay to produce plays that don't bring in customers?'

'Eat,' Max ordered. His face was somber. 'Even on Broadway they're not presenting art except for short runs. Mrs Minnie Maddern Fiske plays in *Salvation Nell*,' he said in derision. 'Marie Dressler in *The Boy and Girl*. Anna Held in *Miss Innocence*. The talent is there, damn it. Where are the plays?'

'That will come.' Rissa was firm in her belief. 'We're young. We can wait.'

'I hate the disrespect even the stars show toward the Yiddish theater,' Max railed. Rissa knew he harangued from nervousness tonight. 'You know the story about Thomashefsky, Adler and Kessler – when they were appearing together in a play? Three big stars of the Yiddish theater, and onstage they begin to horse around. Thomashefsky breaks not the one plate the script calls for, but two. Kessler decides to break a few. And Adler – he was playing a quiet rabbi – joins in, too. They deliver their lines and keep breaking plates. When the dishes are gone, they break up the furniture. Of course, the audience loved it,' Max said bitterly.

'Let's go to the theater.' Rissa was restless.

'When you finish the bagel and tea,' Max stipulated. 'To be an actress in the Yiddish theater requires a lot of energy.'

While they walked to the theater, Max gave Rissa final instructions. She must not allow Leo to upstage her. Even at rehearsals he tried this. Leo Gunsburg was forty-eight years old and acting for years. Rissa was not long past her seventeenth birthday. But Max fought to provide her with every possible advantage.

'Rissa, hold it down a bit tonight,' Max pleaded. 'Remember that fine line between the strong and the melodramatic. The audience won't know the difference. The critic will.'

Backstage was bedlam. Shirley had hoped to be Rissa's dresser for opening night. Union regulations forbade this. But Shirley pushed her way backstage with Max's help on the pretense of bringing Rissa a cup of tea. 'For good luck' she sewed on a button for Rissa before a dresser's assistant became belligerent.

Izzy came to the women's dressing room to wish her luck. Tonight he was a producer; the delicatessen was deserted. His wife sat in her fine new directoire dress, bought at Lord and Taylor in honor of the occasion, and waited for him to join her before the play began.

'Rissa, talk loud,' Izzy pleaded.

'I will,' Rissa promised.

'If Ida knew how much money I had in this company, she'd kill me.' Izzy pulled out a handkerchief and wiped his forehead. 'The union should drop dead. For the play we need seven actors. So why do I have to hire fourteen? Nobody sings, but I have to hire fourteen chorus people and nine musicians.

'Rissa, do you know how much we have to take in each week just to break even?' Izzy sighed. 'I can't believe it myself. Almost two thousand dollars. That's a lotta corned beef sandwiches.'

'Izzy, it's going to be a big hit,' Rissa comforted. Not daring to think otherwise. 'You'll make a lot of money.'

Without realizing it, Rissa stood on tiptoe in the wings while the orchestra struck up the brassy music that told the audience the play was about to begin. She could hear people rushing down the aisles to their seats, exchanging noisy greetings. The house-lights went down. The prompter switched on the light in his box. The curtain opened.

By the end of the first act Rissa was sure the audience liked the play. Those out front were talking excitedly about what was to come – when the play moved from Russia to America. They had seen the same plot endless times with different actors under different titles. They sat waiting to see their own lives played before them.

During the lengthy intermission Rissa geared herself for her big scene in the second act. She sat in a corner of the dressing room, talking to no one. Max had worked with her on this scene for endless hours away from the theater. *She would play it exactly as he wished.*

Max was mesmerized by what he heard about Konstantin Stanislavski's work at the Moscow Art Theater, which came into being in 1898. He read every word translated into English about Stanislavski and the Moscow Art Theater, bought endless cups of tea for Mischa, the elderly character man in the company who had worked with Stanislavski for four years in Moscow before fleeing Russia.

Mischa had told Max and Rissa how Stanislavski had dared to banish the custom in fashionable Moscow theaters to leave the houselights on during performances. Heretofore, Moscow theater audiences expected to drink, talk and inspect the wardrobes of the ladies while the actors performed.

Stanislavski demanded a vivid, realistic style of acting from his company. He taught that they must draw these emotions out of their own experience. The actors must work together as a unit. As long as they were on the stage, they must be part of the scene. Listening, reacting, playing together. In English, Max told Rissa, it was translated as 'ensemble playing.'

'Rissa, do it this way, and the audience must

believe,' Max had reiterated with zeal. 'Don't listen to what Leo is always saying!'

Leo insisted that life onstage had to be far bigger than on the street. Why should people come to hear actors if they talked just like themselves, he scoffed. People came to the theater every week – sometimes twice a week – to escape their own lives.

Rissa tensed as she stood waiting for her entrance in the second act. She wasn't Rissa Lindowska now. She was a young Jewish girl in Russia, betrayed by her lover. She walked onstage, paused. Instinctively knowing the impact of that moment of silence as she gazed about the room where she had once been so happy.

When the audience sobbed aloud, Rissa hardly heard them. She was reliving her own desolation at her betrayal by Phillip. In the end, when the girl in the play found happiness in her marriage to the dashing hero, Rissa walked around her groom – in this case Leo Gunsburg – with the same ecstasy she had walked around Max at their wedding.

At the curtain call the audience applauded enthusiastically. But when Leo Gunsburg brought forward his young leading lady, they went wild. They stamped their feet, whistled, called out their admiration.

Rissa knew that Leo was furious. He had expected the heaviest applause to be for himself. Wasn't he the star? Rissa was aware that she was not molded in the form most pleasing to Yiddish theater audiences. She was too slender, almost fragile. Max teased and said that only her bosom made them aware she was onstage. But while she wasn't *zaftik*, Rissa had a presence onstage that Max recognized and nurtured.

Max waited in the wings for her as she came offstage.

'Rissa, they loved you!' He pulled her into his arms. 'We'll all go to the Café Royale to celebrate!'

'Max, that's so expensive.' But she shivered with pleasure at the prospect of walking into the Café Royale after the triumph she had experienced.

'Who worries about money tonight?' Max laughed. 'Besides,' he patted her on the rump, 'Izzy's paying. He's the money part of this team.'

Rissa knew when they walked into the café that some of their audience had preceded them and spread the word that Miller and Weinberg had opened a hit play tonight. The waiters knew.

Three of the waiters rushed forward to pull together tables, adjusting tablecloths, rearranging silverware. With remarkable speed a banquet-size arrangement materialized in the center of the room.

Izzy beamed.

'They couldn't do better for Adler,' he said with relish. 'Everybody sit.'

With unexpected tact Izzy gestured to Leo to sit at the head of the table. With his wife, Izzy sat at Leo's right. Rissa and Max at Leo's left. Rissa pulled Shirley beside her. Other members of the cast settled in the unoccupied chairs. Everybody was excited.

Rissa was lightheaded with exhilaration. Everybody at the Café Royale seemed interested in their presence. Tonight was the most important night of her life. Next to her wedding night.

Leo pretended the furor was all for him. After all, in London he had been a star. He paid extravagant attention to Izzy's wife, talked with Shirley about her cousin Olga Cohen who had been part of the company on Mile End Road. He ignored Rissa, for which she was grateful.

A critic who had been at the performance came to the table to congratulate the company. His gaze settled on Rissa.

'The theater is richer for your presence,' he told her with an elaborate bow while Rissa gazed at him in ecstatic disbelief. 'I hope we'll see much more of you, Miss Lindowska.'

'Thank you.' Her smile was dazzling.

Leo Gunsburg glared at her. Furious that she had been singled out for this attention. But she would allow nothing to spoil the joy of this night.

'We'll keep this play running four weeks without a break,' Izzy predicted exuberantly. 'You start rehearsing the next one tomorrow?'

'Not till Monday,' Max told him. 'Let's give the cast a break.'

'Max, think of the organizations,' Izzy warned. 'Sure, we'll fill the houses on Saturdays and Sundays with this play for months yet, but what about bookings for the rest of the week?' All at once Izzy was an authority. 'They're used to having the pick of a hundred plays. What have we got to offer?'

'Izzy, you stick to corned beef and pastrami,' Ida told him. 'Let Max take care of the plays.' Izzy's wife beamed at her husband's producing partner.

'You have nothing to worry about,' Leo said

221

grandly, 'I've played in hundreds of productions. They'll have a choice to match any theater. I'll sit down with Max and work out a repertory.'

The first shadow of the evening fell across Rissa's happiness. Max was agreeable to playing *shund* on weekends because this was necessary to keep money coming in, but he had vowed they would do good plays the rest of the week. Plays chosen to show off Rissa's talents. She suspected that the organizations – peopled by immigrants – would reject Max's efforts to uplift their theatrical tastes.

'We won't have to offer a hundred plays.' Max was firm. 'The lodges and the societies will choose from a select list.'

'I'm prepared to play on an hour's notice in as many plays as Thomashefsky or Kessler,' Leo boasted. 'In London women flocked to see me in any role.'

Shirley leaned forward to whisper in Rissa's ear.

'He wants to dance across the stage naked to the waist in tights like Thomashefsky.'

'Max – ' Leo's smile said he considered Max a young upstart. 'We'll talk tomorrow about the schedule.' He turned to Izzy. 'You're a businessman. You understand that the customer is always right.'

'Rissa, they're all looking at you,' Shirley whispered in pride. 'Already they know how wonderful you are in the play. And the men,' she clucked. 'Oy, is Max in for competition!'

Rissa was disconcerted for a moment when she realized that the pretty young blonde at a table adjacent to theirs was openly flirting with Max. Now

222

she placed her hand over Max's, her wedding ring, with the tiny diamond that had been worn by Max's mother, in prominent display.

Let every woman in the Café Royale know that Max Miller was Rissa Lindowska's husband.

18

Leo received lavish praise in the Yiddish newspapers. Max extracted every ounce of publicity available from Leo's London reputation. The critics were lyrical about Rissa's talents and beauty. Word of mouth spread the news across the lower East Side. They played to packed houses on weekends. Organizations bargained for midweek bookings.

Almost immediately Rissa was conscious that the company was split in its loyalties. Half were on Leo's side, half for Max and her. Izzy was concerned only about the weekly grosses. They were better than breaking even, he admitted. Still, he worried that the union held him responsible for a thirty-eight-week season.

'In any other business you don't make money, you cut down on the help,' he wailed at regular intervals. 'But in the Yiddish theater the union says "fuck you."'

Rissa was pleased with their success but unhappy about the backstage bickering.

Leo was the seasoned performer, whose successes in London were talked about at Zeilten's and Marcus's and Shulem's, and at the Café Royale where Leo held court nightly after performances and bemoaned the shabby treatment being accorded him by Miller and Weinberg. He had forgotten that Max was the first to offer him a place in New York's Yiddish theater.

Half of the company resented Rissa's youth and talent, her fast rise. But she was grateful for those in the company who were charmed by her, respectful of her ability.

While the theater dominated their lives, Rissa treasured her personal life with Max. She enjoyed cooking for him. Spoiling him. Here in New York was an abundance of food that never ceased to astonish her. Even though their income was modest, it seemed to Rissa that they ate like a king and queen.

'Rissa, I remember mama making this!' Max's face would light with pleasure as he tasted a dish. 'Not too often,' he acknowledged. 'But sometimes on Friday nights or on special holidays.'

She would make *tsimes*, *cholent*, *halipses*, *grivines*, all the things her mother had taught her. More prosaic meals included *loksh'n* and cheese, *potatonic*, *kasha varnishkes*, *lotkes*, blintzes. On Friday nights there was usually matzo ball soup and chicken.

On Friday nights at sunset Rissa lighted the candles in the candlesticks that Max's mother had used before her. When they sat down to supper, she insisted he wear grandpa's *tallith* about his shoulders, though she knew that – at first – Max felt uncomfortable in this Orthodox touch. On Friday nights Rissa felt that her parents and Max's parents hovered over the supper table and blessed them.

Shirley came to the apartment and baked for them. Sponge cake, honey cake. On Purim, *hamantashen*. Her eyes would light at Max's rhapsodic approval.

Rissa and Max ate with sensual enjoyment, made love with abandon but with conscientious awareness that Rissa must not become pregnant. At every possible opportunity Max coaxed Rissa into going up to Fourteenth Street to see a movie.

Max was fascinated by the new Griffith film, *A Corner of Wheat*. He pointed out Griffith's clever use of lighting, his respectful treatment of the subject. The opening and closing sequences were modeled after Millet, which Max clutched at as an indication of the artistic qualities that films could offer. The cast included Henry B. Walthal, James Kirkwood and an extra named Max Sennett. But Rissa harbored no enthusiasm for this new medium.

The months raced past despite the constant strife in the theater, the battles over which plays to present. Here Izzy sided with Leo.

'Keni Liptzin can be artistic,' Izzy argued. 'She's got a rich husband to pay the bills.' Michael Mintz, Liptzin's husband, owned the Yiddish *Herald*.

Max was frustrated at being pushed into presenting *shund* and more *shund*.

'Max, the time will come when we can do better plays,' Rissa encouraged. 'Didn't you tell me that Rachel Kaminska will appear with Kessler next season? In Warsaw I saw her play in *The Kreutzer Sonata*. Watching her was like watching a fine English actress. People will come to see her in New York, and they'll begin to understand what you want us to do.'

Max squinted in thought. 'Rissa, tonight play more softly. I want the audience to know what you feel

226

inside. You don't have to throw it at them. Ethel Barrymore is a powerful young actress, but she doesn't shout.'

'Max, I don't shout!' For an instant Rissa was hurt. Yet she knew that Max was right. Sometimes she disregarded Max's directions.

'Rissa, you're trying to please both the audience and me. Trust me. Play it my way tonight.'

With infinite caution Rissa began to adjust her style to what Max wished of her. It was a painful learning period. But she had a strong instinct for what was right.

When they lay in each other's arms after making love, Max would dissect a scene in the night's performance. Searching for a different reading of a line, or a fresh interpretation. Theater was woven into the tapestry of their lives.

With the season drawing to a close Leo announced that he had better offers. Max had expected this. Izzy and he were prepared to negotiate. They knew that together Leo and Rissa were a strong combination to bring in customers.

Even while they fought to work out a contract with Leo, Max and Izzy faced a new crisis. They had rented the theater for a season. Now they discovered they could not extend their lease. The theater had been sold to a movie company.

Max insisted they had an option to renew their lease. He fought with Izzy to go to court and demand their rights. Izzy was terrified of lawyers, fearful of court costs. He remembered the terrible experiences of Adler in holding onto the Grand.

'Max, you want us to be beat up by Italian and Irish gangs?' Izzy was upset. 'I'm too old to go through that craziness. I got my family to think about. Sophia Karp, may she rest in peace, died because it looked like the Grand might become a movie palace.' Izzy closed his eyes in ecstasy. 'Oy, when Sophia Karp sang "Eli Eli," you thought you were in heaven.'

'Why did she die because of the theater?' Rissa was perplexed.

'It was that madness about who owned the Grand.' Izzy gestured his incomprehension. 'Sophia was afraid to leave the theater – she had been one of the original owners. She slept in a cold dressing room until she came down with pneumonia. She died from it. Her funeral was something the East Side will never forget.'

'Izzy, we have to fight for the theater,' Max tried again.

'No,' Izzy rejected.

Max sought in frenzy to acquire another playhouse. But the country was pulling out of the depression. Other theaters were being rented and at higher rates than Izzy could face. Adler was returning from a triumphant European tour to reopen at the Grand.

In the midst of Max's campaign to move their company to another house, Izzy's wife suffered a heart attack. She survived, but the doctor warned of a lengthy convalescence.

Izzy decided to move to Florida for her health.

'He said I shouldn't say nothing to you,' Ida sighed, when Rissa visited her in the hospital. 'He's trying to get up the nerve to tell Max. He's selling the delicatessen. He'll open a store down in Miami.'

Now Rissa must tell Max there would be no money for a Miller and Weinberg company next season. She left the hospital and hurried down to the delicatessen. How was she to tell Max it was all over? Where would they find somebody else to put up the money for next season? Izzy knew Max; he believed in him. Izzy had been another of Max's miracles.

Max was waiting for her at a rear table. A glass of tea in one hand. His face seemed tense.

'I've got some news that's not so good,' he said as Rissa slid into the chair opposite him. 'Leo, the son-of-a-bitch, has signed with somebody else. He'll be with Jack Fain next season.'

'There's more trouble, Max.' She reached out a hand to cover his. 'I had a talk with Ida. The doctor told Izzy she should live in a warm place. He's selling the delicatessen.' She flinched at Max's instant comprehension of their own disaster. 'They're moving to Florida.'

'Izzy won't reinvest. We're right back where we started.' Max clenched his free hand into a ball and slammed it onto the table.

'No,' Rissa denied. 'You've managed a company for a whole season. I've got good reviews.'

'We can't sit around and waste time. Companies for the new season are being set up already. They start rehearsing next month!'

'Can we find another Izzy?' Rissa tried to sound hopeful.

'No,' Max admitted. 'Izzy was a gambler. Even if we could find somebody, it'd be too late for this season.'

'We have some money saved. We'll manage for a while.'

'Everybody knows that Leo and you bring in customers. I'll talk to Jack Fain about hiring you for the company, and about letting me direct. But first,' he stipulated, 'I'll look around quick for a possible investor. Just to make sure we're not missing out on something. If nothing happens in two weeks, I'll talk to Fain.' His face settled into stubborn determination. 'Rissa, nobody will stop us. We'll have it all before we're thirty!'

Max made desperate, futile efforts to raise capital for another season. Then he went to Jack Fain. He presented himself as the director for last season's Miller and Weinberg company and as Rissa Lindowska's personal manager.

He sat in a chair across the desk from Jack Fain in a tiny, bare office at the rear of the Fain Theater and talked about the past season's successes.

'Leo was a big draw,' Fain said, his eyes watchful for Max's reaction.

'Leo and Rissa together were a big draw,' Max emphasized, stimulated by the realization that Fain was ready to talk business. Play this right, he exhorted himself. Rissa needed to be seen. She had to follow up her last season's success with another. A

230

career didn't happen; it was constructed. Leo would make it tough for her, yet it was to both Leo's advantage and hers for them to appear together again. 'How often do you find an actress of Rissa's talents who's so young and beautiful?'

Fain smiled with a show of indulgence.

'You're both so young, Max; it scares me.'

'That's what the theater needs,' Max pounced. 'Fresh young talent. Every producer knows this. The Yiddish theater is worn down by actors who refuse to give way to time. And the theater is changing,' he pushed on. 'People are changing. They expect more.'

'Leo will never accept you as a director,' Fain told him, watching again for Max's reaction. 'He said he had trouble with you all last season.' So Jack Fain and Leo had talked about Rissa and him.

'Leo had his nose out of joint because Rissa was received so well.' Max decided on candor. 'But that kind of competition pushed both of them into giving their best. Leo without Rissa won't be half the draw he was last season. She's available,' he said with a show of guilelessness. 'For family reasons Izzy Weinberg is withdrawing as a producer. I don't have the financing to go ahead on my own. You and I both know that Rissa will be one of the biggest stars in the Yiddish theater within five years.'

'She's not in the union,' Jack pointed out.

'Leo's not in the union,' Max reminded. 'So you'll have to hire her as an extra person.' Max shrugged. He acted confident; almost arrogant. 'Rissa Lindowska doesn't work for union minimum. Deduct the minimum from her salary,' he said with a show

231

of generosity. 'To cover the actress you have to hire in her place. I came to you first because I think it's good for Rissa to work with Leo again. But if you're not interested, I can go to – '

'Maybe we can work out a way to use Rissa.' Jack snapped at the bait.

They settled down to haggle. Max ended up with a salary that, he knew, would bring delighted astonishment from Rissa. But the best he could wangle for himself was a job as stage manager for the company. At least he would be there to work with Rissa. He would make Rissa the star she deserved to be.

Walking home from the Fain Theater, Max thought about the movie he had taken Rissa to see three nights ago. *The Lonely Villa* was a Biograph picture. While most Broadway actors – and Yiddish theater actors – looked down on picture making, Max was aware that two of those in the cast had legitimate theater backgrounds. James Kirkwood, who played the villain, had toured in the road company of *The Great Divide*. And the girl – Mary Pickford – had appeared on Broadway in David Belasco's *The Warrens of Virginia*.

Damn, why was Rissa so against working in pictures? This was the entertainment of the future. His blood pounded as he considered its potential.

He'd work the season as stage manager, Max coddled his injured pride. After that he'd hold out for directing. And when he wasn't busy he'd look into what was happening in pictures.

19

Rissa was astonished and exhilarated, as Max had anticipated, when she heard the salary he had wangled for her from Jack Fain. To her it seemed a fortune, though it was minuscule compared to the earnings of the stars of the Yiddish Rialto. Thomashefsky and Adler were living like millionaires, Shirley told her. The depression was over.

But Rissa was unnerved that Max would not be directing.

'I'll be with the company.' Max fought to hide his disappointment. 'Privately I'll direct you.' They both knew little other directing would be provided. With the scanty rehearsals, the rush to vary their repertoire, the director would have time for only basic stage business.

'Without you, I'll be afraid,' Rissa confessed.

'You'll be fine,' he insisted. 'Away from the theater we'll work on your part. I've told you. Nobody will stop us. You'll be a star. Then you can insist I be your director. Three years, Rissa,' he advanced his schedule. 'In three years your name will be in electric lights. You'll demand that Max Miller direct the company.'

Not until the first rehearsal did Rissa and Max realize that Leo had been promoted to star-director status. For Max this was a painful humiliation. Nor did Max realize that, out of his presence, Leo was prone to overplay the amorous scenes between Rissa and himself.

Rissa dared not mention Leo's behavior to Max. With all the theaters already in rehearsal, where would they find jobs now?

Max made it clear that he was Rissa's personal manager. He battled with Jack Fain to have Rissa's name included in the advertising, and he threatened to withdraw Rissa from the company when Fain had second thoughts about the money he was paying a nonunion actress. Both times, Max won.

But Leo laughed at Rissa's warnings to keep his hands to himself.

'Rissa, this is a theater. Not a convent!'

'You're old enough to be my father,' she threw at him under her breath in the midst of a rehearsal when he pulled her into an embrace that wasn't in the script. 'You could almost be my grandfather!'

'I'm more of a man than Max,' he boasted, stung by her accusation. 'I could show you what it is to be a woman.'

Her eyes blazed. Max was the only man she would ever want in her life. 'Stop being crazy, or I'll tell Max.'

Max was fascinated by the spread of the movie houses. Over a hundred had sprung up in New York already, many of them on the lower East Side. He sought to kindle his own enthusiasm in Rissa. On a sweltering late August night when rehearsals were over, Max walked her up to Fourteenth Street to see the spectacle of hundreds of people standing in line to get in to see a movie.

'Rissa, look at that line. For a nickel they can go in and see a picture and forget about their troubles. We can get into the business right at the beginning. Do you know what that means?'

'I can't, Max.' Rissa recoiled from acting in pictures. 'I wouldn't feel safe.'

'But why?'

'The people. Max, you know.' But he didn't know. He couldn't understand that to her the Yiddish theater was home.

Max took her to cafés in Greenwich Village, where she never felt comfortable. At Coney Island last month she had felt comfortable only with people who spoke with an accent.

At the Greenwich Village cafés she listened to the others. She talked only in moments when she forgot herself. Beyond the lower East Side she felt like a greenhorn.

The new season was launched with Keni Liptzin appearing in *Mirale Efros* at the Old London. The Gordin play that was always a hit, though Gordin was dubbed too old-fashioned for the modern audience.

Two nights later the Fain company opened. Again Rissa was singled out by the critics with high praise. Catty comments circulated backstage. Rissa fought to insulate herself from the barbs of the others. She knew her performance drew people to the theater.

Rissa was rescued from Leo's advances when he

began a liaison with a woman in the company, Sara Moscowitz. Twice Rissa's age, Sara was jealous of her. She connived with Leo to make life in the company difficult for Rissa.

Despite Rissa's shyness, she now became emotionally involved in a situation that involved Shirley and the entire lower East Side. With the end of the depression Shirley faced a shortage of workers. The girls were attracted to the shirtwaist factories that paid more than Shirley could afford.

Shirley herself soon gave up being a 'boss' and went to work for the Triangle Shirtwaist Company. But she wasn't happy.

'The shirtwaist shops pay more than the others,' she admitted. 'They're cleaner and newer. But because we're women, they cheat us, Rissa. We have to pay for needles, electric power, supplies at a profit – I *know* – of twenty percent! They charge us for lockers. For rent of the chairs we sit on!'

'Shirley, what will happen?' Rissa surged with sympathy for these girls, most of them Jewish, though some were Italian.

'Rissa, we must have a union.' Shirley could conceive of no alternative. 'If nothing happens, we'll have to strike.' Her smile was wry. 'Don't think that every union is like the Hebrew Actors Union. This will be a good one. This union will make sure we're not treated like dogs.'

On 22 November a meeting was called at Cooper Union. Shirley was among the thousands who attended. At that meeting a young firebrand named

236

Clara Lemlich brought the crowd to its feet in a screaming demand for a strike.

The strike went on week after week. Most of the shops closed down. A few made an effort to operate with scabs. The striking Jewish and Italian girls were supported by suffrage workers of all classes. This was truly a women's movement. Lillian Wald and Mary Simkhovitch came forward to handle publicity. Bail money for arrested strikers was put up by Mrs Oliver Belmont and Anne Morgan. Students at Wellesley College sent a thousand dollars to the strike fund. Rissa reveled in the strength of the new woman.

Rissa shared Shirley's jubilation when the strike was settled in the middle of February. While some workers considered it a defeat because the union had not won official recognition, Shirley – like many others – was pleased that their working conditions had been improved. Local 25 of the ILGWU, which had hardly a hundred members in November, now boasted a roster of ten thousand members. Rissa declared the shirtwaist workers were heroines.

Rissa's first fight with Max came in March. They had just opened the final play in their repertoire. Because of Leo's influence, it was a play that provided only a small role for Rissa. But under Max's guidance she had created a gem. The audience had applauded her with such enthusiasm that the performance was delayed for almost five minutes.

Rissa and Max left the theater alone while the rest of the cast dawdled backstage. As they emerged from the door, Rissa was greeted by members of the audience with extravagant cries of praise. Rissa Lindowska had created her first *patriot*. Fans.

One small, maternal woman turned her attention to Max.

'You're Mr Lindowska?' she asked affectionately.

Rissa flinched. She saw Max turn pale.

'I'm Max Miller,' he told Rissa's *patriot*. 'She's Mrs Max Miller.'

Rissa walked silently beside Max, one small hand in his, while they headed up Second Avenue to the Café Royale. It was a tradition now for them to go to the Café Royale after the opening of each new play. She was distraught at his unhappiness.

Not until they were seated and had ordered their usual *palatchinken* – Hungarian crêpes suzettes – and tea did Max discuss what was on his mind.

'Rissa, it's time for you to become Rissa Miller in the theater.' His face was stern.

Rissa stared in disbelief.

'Max, you know,' she stammered, 'in the theater I must always be Lindowska. I swore before God that the world would someday know my family's name.' And her grief, though four years old, was as fresh as the day she climbed out of the cellar in the *dorf* in Poland.

'But your name is Miller.'

'In the theater it is Rissa Lindowska.' She struggled not to fall apart at this first real clash with Max. Max and Shirley – they were her family now. 'You'll honor your family as a director one day. Max Miller.' She made it sound like a benediction. It upset Max to be a stage manager who pushed around furniture and scenery. His soul rebelled. 'I must do this for my family.' Rissa paused, searching his eyes for some sign of capitulation. 'Max, look at Keni Liptzin and Michael Mintz. Keni didn't change her name to Mintz.'

'Since when are you on such friendly terms with Keni Liptzin?' he mocked. 'You, who don't even want to see her play in *Mirale Efros* after Rachel Kaminska played it at the Old London?' He knew how she worshipped Kaminska, whom many called the Yiddish Duse. Unexpectedly Max smiled in capitulation. 'All right. In the theater you're Rissa Lindowska. In our bed you're Rissa Miller.'

In the summer Rissa and Max went on tour with a hastily organized company. Rissa as leading lady 'from triumphant successes in the New York theater,' and Max as company manager. Rissa was fascinated by the new cities they visited, yet conscious again of what had faded from her mind in the excitement of the last year. Women of all ages seemed to find Max fascinating. They were not reticent about showing their admiration.

Max made it clear, Rissa acknowledged, that he was devoted to his wife. He never left her side during the hot, uncomfortable months that they moved from one large city to another. But the stream of women eager to throw themselves at Max unnerved her.

Rissa was relieved when they returned to New York and the familiar small apartment overlooking Washington Square. Again she rejected Max's pleas that they move into larger quarters.

'Max,' she reproached, pleased that they had a sunlit place of their own when most of those they knew lived in dark, people-crowded quarters, 'It's nice here.' And each week she sent Max to the bank with a deposit. Imagine! Rissa Lindowska with money in the bank.

But Max was impatient with their standard of living, refusing to hear Rissa's exhortations that they had accomplished much in an astonishingly short time. He was intrigued by the stories he heard about Thomashefsky's growing wealth. About Jacob Adler's four-story brownstone on East Seventy-second Street, with its fountain and elevator and fine furnishings.

'Every spring now Sara Adler goes to Paris to have her gowns made by Worth,' he ranted. Rissa's costumes were made with loving care and meager talent by Shirley. 'On the road Adler earns a thousand dollars a performance!' Max earned fifteen dollars a week. 'Thomashefsky has a twelve-room house in Brooklyn, a cottage by the sea, a country house with twenty acres in Hunter, New York.'

'Thomashefsky and Adler have been part of the Yiddish theater for twenty-five years. More,' Rissa pinned down. 'You want too much too soon.'

'I mean to have it.' Max's face was set. Rissa knew he hated living in a one-room-and-kitchenette apartment, even though sun poured in and they could see trees from their windows. Max remembered the spacious houses in Georgia. In memory, Rissa suspected, his own house – grand compared to what she had known – had acquired even more grandeur.

240

'Rissa, next season Jack will have to pay you five times what he's paying this season.' Max was irritated by the salary he had negotiated, though it doubled her earnings for the previous year.

Rissa would appear again as Leo's leading lady. Max and she had known it was useless to try to persuade Jack Fain to hire Max as director. Max was returning as the stage manager. Leo had married Sara in the course of the summer. He sulked because Jack had refused to promote her to leading lady.

The company was almost the same as last season. A character woman had been replaced by a statuesque redhead in her twenties. Jack admitted to Rissa and Max in a moment of rare confidentiality that a union delegate had forced Celia Kamenstein upon him.

'What could I do?' He was philosophical. 'Argue with a union delegate?'

As in the past Max worked with Rissa with a religious fervor. Yet Rissa sensed his restlessness as fall merged into winter. She sympathized in silence with his position as stage manager.

Irritated by Celia's poor performances, Leo appointed Max assistant director. It was Max's duty to work with Celia and a character actor whose brother-in-law had contrived to elevate him from pants presser to actor by way of union connections. Rissa was disturbed by Celia's overt attentions to Max.

Meanwhile, worn down by Leo's alternative pleas and threats, his tireless attempts to push his wife forward, Jack decreed that henceforth Sara and Rissa would share leading roles.

On an early March night Sara played a role previously portrayed by Rissa. Leo had cast Rissa in a bit part in the first act. Moments after her entrance Rissa was aware of an upheaval in the audience. They had assumed that Rissa would appear as the leading lady.

Sara walked onstage for her first scene. Rissa hovered in the wings.

Suddenly outraged voices interrupted the performance.

'Rissa! We want Rissa! Rissa! Rissa!'

Max closed the curtains. In Jack Fain's absence he acquired the authority of producer. He ordered Leo to tell the yelling audience that the performance would be resumed immediately, with Rissa playing her usual role. It was decided that Sara would star in other plays.

Though the night was one of triumph for Rissa, it made backstage life even more difficult.

On a Friday evening late in March Rissa played despite a burgeoning case of laryngitis. Jack Fain was upset. The Friday evening performance and the two on Saturday were the most heavily attended in the theater.

'Rissa, go home. Drink tea,' he ordered. 'Tonight they could hardly hear you. Tea with honey. Max, look after her!'

'I'll be all right by tomorrow,' Rissa promised, though her throat was raw and her head groggy. How could she get sick when she had a performance to give?

But when she awoke in the morning, Rissa knew

that she would not be able to play the Saturday performances. Her voice was totally gone. Jack would have to schedule another play. One with Sara as leading woman.

Max exhorted her to stay in bed. He left her with a pot of tea on the table beside the bed. Blankets piled high. His concern brought tears of pleasure to her eyes.

'You don't play until you're well,' he insisted.

'But Jack – ' Rissa began.

'Fuck Jack. It's you I worry about.' He bent to kiss her. 'You don't play today or tomorrow.'

Max left for the theater. Rissa slept again. She awoke two hours later feeling infinitely better. But her voice would not carry six feet.

By half-past four Rissa was consumed by restlessness. She would go out to the store to buy a box of tea, she told herself, inventing an excuse. Shirley would be getting out of work at the Triangle Shirtwaist Company any minute. Maybe she would meet Shirley.

She left the house and turned east. Horse-drawn fire engines were rushing toward Greene Street. Looking up into the sky she saw smoke billowing into the air. Alarm hastened her steps. Where was the fire? Shirley's factory was at Greene and Washington Place.

Now Rissa ran in soaring fear. *The fire was at the factory where Shirley worked.* Others, too, raced toward the factory. Smoke poured from the windows of the three top floors. Screams rent the air.

Firemen were raising ladders now. But they

reached only to the sixth floor. The fire was on the eighth, ninth and tenth floors. In horror those on the ground watched while a cluster of girls tried to use the fire escapes, only to find them break beneath their weight.

'Blankets!' a woman screamed. 'Bring blankets so they can jump!'

Firemen rushed forward with fire nets. But three or four young girls leaped together, and their bodies broke through the nets, crashing onto the industrial glass sidewalk and falling to the cellar below.

Rissa's gaze was riveted on the burning inferno. Tears spilling over unheeded, she prayed. Those on the high floors – girls and men – were jumping. *Oh, God, where was Shirley?*

From every ledge, it seemed, girls and men were poised to jump. Rissa saw a man kiss a woman, then push her off the ledge. Seconds later, his clothes aflame, he jumped. Now the sidewalk was littered with bodies.

'Look up there!' a man shouted. 'On the roof of the college!'

Like the others Rissa stared upward. Students from the NYU law school were helping girls up a ladder from the roof of the factory. Shirley worked on the top floor, Rissa remembered in a flurry of hope.

The elevators had stopped working, someone in the crowd reported. Those on the three top floors were trapped unless they could reach the roof. The wails of the onlookers blended with the outcries of those unable to escape.

'Rissa!'

Rissa whirled around to face Shirley.

'I was afraid you were up there,' Rissa whispered. 'Shirley, I was so scared.'

Tears rolling down their faces, they clung together.

'The foreman sent me on an errand,' Shirley explained. 'I should have been in there with the others.' She trembled with anguish.

'No, Shirley. God meant for you to live,' Rissa insisted. The way He had meant for her to live when the rest of her family died in the pogrom. 'We can do nothing here – ' Her voice broke. 'Come home with me.'

Max and Shirley were her family. How could she survive without them? For the first time since her marriage Rissa thought about having a child. With Max for a father and Shirley for an aunt, her child would have a lovely family.

The tragedy of the Triangle Shirtwaist fire hung over the lower East Side. But within five days the owners of the factory had started up production in another building. Shirley bitterly reported that in this new building, machines blocked the way to the fire escapes. The deaths of one hundred forty-five workers – most of them girls and women – meant little to the men who owned the Triangle Shirtwaist factory.

New word came from Europe that on the very day of the Triangle fire another tragedy occurred. At the end of March every Jewish immigrant in America was catapulted into shock by the news that leaked from Russia. Each knew it could have happened to him if he had not been lucky enough to have escaped from Russia. To Rissa, the news was especially terrifying.

A Jewish laborer in a Russian brick factory in Kiev had been arrested for what the Czar's government called a ritual murder. Mendel Beilis was accused of inflicting forty-seven stab wounds on a twelve-year-old Christian boy, so that the 'blood of a Christian child could be used to make matzoth for the approaching Passover holidays.'

The plight of Mendel Beilis was a personal tragedy to Rissa. In addition, Rissa was tormented by the idea that Celia Kamenstein was throwing herself at Max at every possible opportunity. She was always underfoot. Only to Shirley did Rissa confess her unhappiness.

'It's terrible for me to worry about such a small thing when Mendel Beilis lies in a Russian prison,' Rissa said with guilt. 'And it's not Max's fault about Celia. She can't keep her hands off him. She keeps begging him to help her with her part.'

Shirley's eyes were wise. 'She's tall and with a pair of *tsitskes* that every man in the audience wants to grab. An actress she's not. But she'll do for window dressing.'

'Max hasn't touched her,' Rissa vowed. 'He looks,' she conceded. 'What man in the company doesn't look when she throws herself around the way she does?'

'Maybe it's better you should look the other way,' Shirley said. 'No man's an angel. Who doesn't know about Thomashefsky's women? Adler's women? The divorces, the remarriages among the actors and actresses? To everybody it's natural that men like them should be chased by women. Rissa, whatever makes women chase after Adler and Thomashefsky, Max has, too. If he wanted to be an actor, he'd be rich.'

'I won't share Max with other women.' Rissa's eyes smoldered in rebellion. Her body tensed, as though prepared to fend them off physically. She thought about Phillip, who had plotted to divide himself between his wife and her. 'Max is my husband. I'm his wife. We should be enough for each other.'

'How many times did Sara Adler – his third wife,' Shirley emphasized, 'leave Adler because of his women? But she always comes back. If Max plays a little, it's the end of the marriage?'

'Max won't play.' All at once Rissa trembled with new confidence. 'We'll have a baby.' A child of Max and herself would be special. A child with theater in his blood. She remembered the awe with which Max talked about the Drews and the Barrymores. John Drew and his wife played in theaters all over the country. All over the world. Their son was a famous actor. His niece was Ethel Barrymore, whose brothers were actors. What did Max call it? *A dynasty of actors.* Max and she would begin their own dynasty. 'Shirley – ' Rissa reached out to clutch her arm in emphasis. 'It's time Max and I had a child.'

'But you're an actress – ' Doubts began to assail Shirley. 'How can you take time out now?'

'I'll give Max a baby.' Subconsciously her hands closed across her small, flat belly. 'He won't look anymore at Celia Kamenstein's *tsitskes*. He won't look at any woman. All he'll think of will be his child. I'll be away from the theater for only a few months.' She paused as Shirley snorted. Her mind plotting. 'Shirley, I can play until I'm six months' pregnant. I can come back when the baby is a few weeks old.'

'You'll bring the baby to the theater with you?' Shirley was indignant. 'Your child deserves better.'

'He'll have better.' Her eyes were luminescent. Her voice soft. 'Max will get more money for me next season. We know that already. Maybe, instead of working at the Triangle Shirtwaist Company, you'll come to stay with the baby when I have to be at the theater. We'll be able to pay more than you earn at the sewing machine. Shirley, will you help take care of the baby?'

'Rissa, you trust me?'

'Only you will I trust,' Rissa told her with love.

'So hurry up already and have this baby.' Shirley pulled Rissa into her arms. 'But don't tell Max we talked this way. Men don't have to know everything.'

'As soon as I can, I'll get pregnant,' Rissa promised. 'And you'll know before Max.' Her laugh was tremulous. 'Because Max I won't tell until I'm positive. You I'll tell the first day I'm suspicious.'

Max and she with a family. Like the Drews and the Barrymores. Like all the Adlers. Another *theater dynasty*. That would be the finest gift in the world for her husband. Max would never again look at another woman.

20

To Rissa's astonishment she found it difficult to talk with Max about having a baby. Why did she feel this way? God created man and woman to reproduce themselves. Did she feel guilty before God because she enjoyed what happened between Max and her in their bed?

Shirley admitted that she, too, found pleasure with the man she had hoped to marry. Shirley looked with scorn on those women who complained about submitting to their husbands' needs. Rissa smiled as she considered this. She had never refused Max. Sometimes it was she who made the first move. She rejoiced that he found special pleasure in this.

But to wish for a baby was not something to talk about, Rissa justified her discomfort. It should happen because Max and she loved each other. Making a baby was an act of love. Everything surrounding it should be beautiful. It should not be *planned*.

All at once she walked through each day wrapped in sentiment. The sight of a pregnant woman on the street filled her with wistful envy. At unwary moments she envisioned herself taking Max's hand and bringing it to her heart.

'Max, darling, you're going to be a father.'

She imagined herself with their newborn son in her

arms. A tiny mouth tugging at a nipple for the nourishment of her body. Their child. Max's and hers. But for her to become pregnant without Max's knowledge would be difficult.

This morning, sentiment gave way to strategy as she moved about cleaning their tiny apartment. She would set the stage. That was the woman's way. It would still be beautiful and natural.

Max kept their 'protection' in a drawer of a table beside their bed. She would rearrange the few pieces of furniture in the room. To go for their protection Max would have to leave the bed. A passionate man like Max could be detained beyond the point of safety. When they arrived home tonight, he wouldn't even notice she had moved his table. His head would be too full of the movie business.

This evening before the performance a *patriot* brought her daffodils. A golden promise of spring that she carried home with her. While she put up their nightly pot of tea that would accompany their after-theater meal, Max reported the gossip he had picked up at the Automat this afternoon.

'Griffith had taken a huge step forward for the whole industry.' Max spoke with the excitement of a real convert. 'Imagine, Rissa. A movie in two cans. To run almost thirty minutes! One of the Biograph crew told me the company plans to present it in two installments, but I'll bet that the public will want to see it all at one sitting.'

'Max, to listen to you this man Griffith is some kind of genius,' Rissa teased. What actor from the Yiddish theater or Broadway would work in movies?

Nobody wished to work for pictures that were shown on a sheet! And Max himself admitted they paid their performers only five dollars a day for short-term work. In the Yiddish theater a union actor was guaranteed thirty-eight weeks of work. 'I expect you would drop to your knees if you could meet this Mr Griffith.' Her eyes were indulgent.

'I'd give five years of my life to work with Griffith,' Max said reverently. 'The man sees the future in what will become the biggest entertainment industry this world has ever seen. And he knows how to present it. Only Griffith has the *hutzpah* to bring a camera in close enough to make an audience understand what a character is thinking. He shows only the face when nobody dares to do this. He knows how to shorten shots to make the suspense stronger. His technique, Rissa, is genius.'

'This summer you'll work in the movies.' Rissa was stoic. When the summer was over, Max would be with her at the theater again. Even now she was nervous if Max was not close enough to come if she called. Max was her strength. Her confidence. Every day she learned from him.

'I have to talk to Jack about the contract for next season.' Max was somber. 'It's a disgrace what he pays you. The bastard knows it.'

'Max, don't make him angry.' Despite success Rissa was fearful of losing her place in the company. She wasn't a union member.

'Honey, I want you to have what you deserve. Sure, Jack will battle and curse and carry on. But he'll give you the contract I demand.'

251

'We're doing so well.' His eyes were anxious. It was so hard for her to make demands. 'We go every week to put money into the bank.' Another miracle in her eyes.

'Rissa, we have worlds to conquer.' She tensed. Sometimes Max frightened her with the extravagance of his dreams. Yet her intuition told her to let Max talk. She could be strong when it was necessary. 'The future for actors is in pictures. Someday there'll be sound. Actors will be heard. Someday there'll be color. Every little town will have its movie house. People will flock to see the pictures.' Max reached to take her hand in his. 'Rissa, if you would only let me go out and talk to Griffith about using you in a movie. We can grow with the industry!'

'No.' Terror made her voice harsh. 'Max, you promised me. No more talk about such foolishness for me.'

'We'll be in New York this summer. It wouldn't interfere with the plays. Rissa, try it.'

'No. I can't, Max. Please, let's don't talk about it anymore.'

'Some day you'll see I'm right.'

'Let's have our supper. That's what is right, Max.' Her eyes were tender. Max was unaware that she had rearranged the furniture. For that she could thank the movies. 'You want to send my husband to bed without food?'

'With you in my bed I can do without food.' Already in his mind he was in her bed, Rissa thought with pleasure. It took so little to make him feel that way.

Rissa brought food and tea to the table. Max put the daffodils in a vase and placed them next to her plate.

'We won't go on tour this summer,' he reminded her. 'In June I'll be directing the two-reelers.'

'So we won't go on tour.' Rissa shrugged this aside. In June, with luck, she would be pregnant. 'Eat, Max.' Her eyes told him that she was eager to be lying in his arms in the darkness.

They ate quickly. While Rissa washed the dishes, Max prepared for the night. When she turned off the lights and joined him in the bed, she realized he was naked beneath the blankets.

'Still my little Jewish nun,' he clucked. 'Why bother to come to bed in your nightgown when it's coming right off?'

'Because you enjoy taking it off,' she laughed.

She was never too tired to make love while Max and she touched and kissed and finally moved together. Her arms tightened about his shoulders as she drew him within her.

'Wait,' he whispered, and made a move to withdraw.

'Max, no.' She held him to her, moving in fresh insistence.

He forgot their protection. The sounds of passion blended with those of her own. For a few moments he lay above her. Quiescent. Still caught up in the satisfaction they had shared.

'Rissa, I'm sorry – ' He was abject at his negligence. 'I'm always careful.'

'It doesn't matter,' Rissa soothed. 'This is the time of the month when nothing can happen.'

Max slid over to lie beside her.

'And when did you become an authority?' A hand rested on her breast.

'The wise woman in our *dorf* taught this to the married women. I heard them talking. Not every wife believed it was a blessing to have another baby every year.'

'And how long does this safe time last?' he asked. Seemingly amused. Yet Rissa sensed that he had enjoyed making love to her with nothing between them.

'Two weeks,' she fabricated.

'You believe this?' His smile was indulgent.

'I believe.'

Had Max given her a baby tonight? She prayed that he had.

When two months swept by and she knew she had not conceived, Rissa was upset. She remembered that she had not conceived with Phillip, though there were nights when he was careless. Was it that she could never have a child? Was that God's punishment for having defamed her parents by living with Phillip?

Max wanted to have children someday. How would he feel when he discovered she could not give him a family? Would he leave her for another woman who was not barren? Despair turned her cold. She could not bear to envision a life without Max.

The theater season was over. This year Max and she would remain in the city. He was waiting eagerly to direct the two-reelers to be produced by Clark Mattox, a new independent producer.

Mattox was working in secret in the top floor studio of a brownstone on East Fifteenth Street. In secret because the nine main manufacturers of films – including Biograph, Essanay, Pathé and Selig – had banded together in a Trust which owned most of the patents. Their intent was to keep out independents like Mattox. If a Trust detective showed up, they'd have to pack up and run. Mattox's work was illegal.

First Max was scheduled to begin work the first week in June. Then it was the end of June. Then July. In the meantime he was battling with Jack Fain over Rissa's contract for the new season.

The city in the summer was a new experience for Rissa. She loathed the oppressive heat, felt new compassion for those trapped in the tenements. Max and she, at least, lived on Washington Square. They made frequent trips to Coney Island and Central Park. They took boat rides up the Hudson. On the rare pleasant nights they walked downtown to the new Yonah Shimmel Knish Bakery for knishes and sour milk. Rissa was fascinated by the caricature of Caruso, made by the great Caruso himself, that hung on the wall.

On a sultry July afternoon Rissa sat with Shirley, just off from her job at the Triangle Shirtwaist Company, on a bench in Washington Square. She had waited with strained patience for Shirley to meet her. She knew it was too early to tell Max, but she would burst if she could not confide in Shirley.

'Shirley, I have to tell you – ' She laid a hand on Shirley's arm. Her eyes were luminous. 'I think I'm pregnant.'

'How late?' Shirley's joy lit up her face.

'Just five days,' Rissa admitted. 'But I'm never late. Never more than a day. Oh, Shirley, pray that I'm pregnant. I want Max's baby. I want it more than anything else in the world.'

'When are you going to tell him?'

'When I'm three weeks late,' Rissa stipulated. 'When there can be no mistake.'

Max stood in the improvised studio and listened to Clark Mattox. His face was white with rage.

'But you told me the job was mine! I was to direct a dozen two-reelers for you. I didn't look for any other job.' Because of his chance to direct the two-reelers Rissa and he were staying in New York this summer. They were losing money!

'Max, I planned to have you direct,' Mattox apologized. 'I like your ideas. They're new. But my wife put the pressure on me. Hire her nephew to direct or her father won't put up the money. What else can I do? She's got me over a barrel. I haven't got a pot to piss in myself. I need the old man's capital.'

'Where's the business headed with that kind of direction?' Max demanded. 'Movies have to move ahead. They can't stand still.'

'Maybe in six months,' Mattox placated. But Max was already stalking out of the studio.

Max headed downtown. The day was humid. He

256

took off his blue serge jacket and dropped it over one arm. The sweatband of his stiff straw hat was soaked.

At Fourteenth Street he hesitated. It was early for his appointment with Jack. Maybe he ought to kill some time in the Automat over a glass of iced tea. No, he decided. Go straight to the theater. Jack had a way of showing up ahead of time. Today they had to stop playing games and work out Rissa's contract.

Jack knew that Rissa was a bigger draw than Leo now. The plays to be scheduled had to show off Rissa. She was at a point in her career where they could make demands. Leo might threaten to quit out of jealousy, but he'd change his mind. Jack Fain's company would be a gold mine next season. And who else would allow Leo to act and direct? Again Max churned in frustration. Why wouldn't Jack let him direct? Jack knew how Rissa depended on him. He was good enough to work with Celia and the ex-pants presser. Why couldn't he share directing with Leo?

Walking down Second Avenue Max pondered over the changes in his thinking. When he came to New York he was fascinated by Yiddish theater. Spilling over with enthusiasm and dreams about what he would accomplish. Now he was moving away from the Yiddish theater. Movies filled his thoughts.

He felt stifled now in the small world south of Fourteenth Street. He visualized an exciting place for himself in the movie industry. It was new. Everybody involved was a pioneer. Every time he talked to somebody, there was some new development in the field. It was the place for a *young* man with ideas and ambitions.

A lot of the movie producers were moving out to California. Particularly the independents, who wanted to get away from the Trust. The climate around Los Angeles was perfect for making pictures. If he went there, he'd have a chance at directing. But how could he take Rissa away from the Fain company?

He pulled out his watch as he approached the theater. He was fifteen minutes early. But the doors were open. A workman was replacing a segment of worn flooring in the lobby. Jack liked everything just right.

Max walked over to the side door that led to Jack's office and knocked.

'Come in.' The voice belonged to Celia Kamenstein.

Max opened the door and walked into the small wood-paneled office. It was furnished with a desk, one chair, phonograph and a couch. Gossip said that the phonograph was used for mood music for Jack's sexual exercises on the couch. Young and attractive Celia was his favorite partner of the moment. Right now she sat behind his desk.

'Where's Jack?' Max was anxious to settle Rissa's contract. He'd permitted the haggling to drag out too long.

'He got tied up in some business deal up in the Bronx. He telephoned to say he'd be about an hour late for his meeting with you and asked me to stay here to take messages. Hang around.' Celia's eyes were a sultry invitation.

'I'll be back in an hour,' Max hedged.

'Max, I want to talk to you.' Celia leaned over the desk. Her white dimity shirtwaist was indecorously opened to display cleavage. Max cleared his throat as he tried to move his eyes away. Every man on Second Avenue had looked long at Celia Kamenstein's breasts. 'Jack's no help at all,' she pouted.

'What's the problem?' Max reached for a handkerchief to brush away the perspiration that edged the top of his high uncomfortable collar like an edging of filigreed lace.

'Jack gives me such tiny parts.' Celia left her chair to sit on the brown leather couch. 'He's always making promises, but that's all. He just keeps telling me to work with you on the parts he gives me, and the next one will be better.'

'We'll work again.' Max avoided meeting her gaze. Celia's talents were meager. The most she had to offer was her body. In pictures she'd do fine, he considered.

'Max, sit down,' Celia ordered. 'I'll go out of my mind if I stay on doing these awful bit parts.'

Reluctantly Max sat on the couch. Making a point not to lean back. In this heat his shirt would stick to the leather.

'You give any thought to making movies?' Male customers would flock to see that gorgeous body. They wouldn't bother to ask themselves if Celia Kamenstein could act.

'Max,' Celia reproached. 'I want to be an actress. I know what you've done for Rissa.' Her smile was wise. 'She'd be nobody without you.'

'That's not true,' Max contradicted. Sure, he worked hard with Rissa. But it was just a matter of showing her how to use her talent. It gave him joy to dissect a role with her. To show her how to point up a speech to make it more effective. Rissa took what he had to give and made it part of herself. 'Rissa would be a fine actress even if we'd never met.'

'Max, everybody knows how Rissa depends on you. Leo always complains that Rissa has two directors.'

'Leo has no time to do more than to block each play,' Max reminded. That was the routine up and down Second Avenue.

'Jack ought to let you do the directing.' Celia was sliding over the hot leather of the couch to lay a hand on his arm. 'Max, how can you bear the way they use you? Jack, Leo, even Rissa. You're the talent that nobody recognizes. All that applause every night for Rissa. All that money Jack pays her. While you get dreck. Max, it's not fair.' Celia oozed sympathy.

Max felt his face flush.

'Rissa and I have a partnership. I'm her personal manager. The stage managing is so I can be at the theater with her.' He'd never forgot the night the woman at the stage door asked him if he was Mr Lindowska.

'Why doesn't Rissa insist on you being the director? Why can't Leo be satisfied with acting? I'll bet Jack would let you direct if Rissa threatened to quit.'

'Jack has an arrangement with Leo.' Rissa would be terrified to make such a demand. 'Leo's had a lot of experience. He's twice as old as I am.'

'You're sweet to let Rissa play the big star,' Celia purred. 'Most men wouldn't be so understanding.'

'Celia, you ought to think about pictures,' Max tried to divert her, aware that she was offering herself to him. 'You'd do well.' Though she was American born, she'd never make it on Broadway.

'Max, I want to make a lot of money. I have expensive tastes.' She moved closer. Her breasts grazed his chest.

'Actresses will make more money in movies some day than they ever made in theater. Within five years,' he prophesied, 'they'll be making five thousand dollars a week. Try it for the summer,' he urged. 'Go up to Fourteenth Street and talk to the people at Biograph.'

'I will.' Celia surprised him with this sudden acquiescence. 'You're smart, Max. Whatever you tell me, I'll do.'

'Change your name,' he advised. Was she out of her mind? Putting her hand between his legs. Involuntarily his eyes swung to the door.

'Lock it, Max,' she told him. 'Jack won't be back for an hour.' Her hand fumbled with the buttons of his fly. 'Max, don't you want me?'

'The door,' he stammered and bolted to lock it.

When he turned around, Celia was out of her shirtwaist and pulling away her brassiere. What a pair she had! Already his hands were at his fly.

'Hurry, Max. We don't want to lose that.' Her eyes were focused on his erect penis.

'Honey, you don't have to worry about me losing it.' He grinned. He wasn't fifty-five and tired like Jack. 'Lie down.'

They didn't bother with foreplay. Celia hiked up

her skirt, revealing that she wore nothing beneath in the July heat. No corset, no petticoat, no chemise. With a grunt Jack lowered himself above her and thrust himself between her perspiration-moist thighs.

Celia clung to him, but that was the extent of her efforts. This was an anonymous body receiving his passion. In a few moments he grunted in release and lifted himself from her.

She wasn't even a good lay. Why had he bothered with Celia Kamenstein when he had better at home? Yet he felt an odd satisfaction that she had bothered to pursue him. It wasn't just his body Celia wanted. Celia was after him to do for her what he had done for Rissa. It was an affirmation of his skill as a director.

For Shirley's birthday Rissa and Max took her up to Luchow's on Fourteenth Street for dinner. Only Rissa and Shirley knew that tonight was a double celebration. Rissa was sure she was carrying Max's child. Tonight, after they took Shirley home, she would tell Max about the baby.

Max would be pleased, wouldn't he, that late in April he would be a father? At intervals she was anxious. But it was important that they have a child. Max and she were all that remained of their families.

Rissa knew that Max favored Luchow's because Mr Griffith was said to dine here often. Shirley was entranced to be taken to so sumptuous a restaurant. She whispered to Rissa that Lillian Russell came here regularly when she played at the Academy of Music down the street.

'I heard somebody say that "Diamond Jim" Brady proposed to Lillian Russell at Luchow's,' Max told them. 'But she turned him down.' He accepted a menu from the waiter. 'I don't know what you two are having, but I'm ordering the *sauerbraten*. And for desert the *apfelstrudel*.'

'No Southern fried chicken?' Rissa teased. 'No pecan pie?'

She hoped tonight's dinner party, and the news he would receive later, would lift Max's spirits, low because he wasn't directing those two-reelers. But he had pushed Jack into paying her even more than Leo would receive next season. At the end of this month they would move into a fine new apartment on Ninth Street, just off Fifth Avenue. Shouldn't he be pleased about that?

Rissa gradually relaxed over dinner. Max was enjoying the evening.

By the time they left Luchow's, a slight breeze appeared to alleviate the heat of the past few days. Max and she walked Shirley home to Essex Street. People sat out on the stoops and on the fire escapes. Despite the lateness of the hour small children cavorted in the streets. The interiors of the tenements were like caldrons, to be avoided until dawn.

Here in America, Rissa rejoiced, she could have a child and not worry that he might be tortured or killed in a pogrom. Blood of children might fill the streets of Kishinev and Bialystok but not those of New York City.

Rissa and Max walked north and west to Washington Square. As they walked Max talked about the plays to be presented in the new season. It upset him that the finer plays were still neglected for cheap melodramas. But the New York *Herald* had recently reported that the Tolstoy estate had given Jacob Adler rights to his play *The Living Corpse* which Adler would present at the Thalia in November. And next year Rachel Kaminska would appear again in New York.

Max talked with enthusiasm about Adler's presenting the first American appearance of *The Living Corpse*. If the play was a success, it would prove that good plays were acceptable. Yet Rissa sensed that Max's earlier dedication to educating a Yiddish audience was disappearing. The movies held him now.

Tonight even their apartment overlooking Washington Square was hot. Max pulled up a chair before a window and eagerly accepted the glass of iced tea Rissa brought to him. She left him to change from her shirtwaist and skirt into the dainty lace-trimmed nightgown she had worn on her wedding night. Each year she wore it on the anniversary of their marriage. It seemed right that she should wear it tonight.

'Come sit with me,' Max ordered when she stood before him, and pulled her across his knees.

'Max — ' Her voice tremulous. 'How much time will Jack need to bring in someone to replace me in the company?'

'Rissa, what do you mean?' Max was startled.

'I figure I can play straight through December, but after that — ' Rissa took a deep breath. 'Max, you'll be a father in April.'

He was motionless for a moment.

'Rissa,' he said gently. 'You want this baby?'

'Max, yes! Yes!' She threw her arms about him and pressed her face against his. 'You want him, don't you?'

His arms closed in about her slender form.

'It would have made mama so happy,' he said.

'I'll be away from the theater for just the last half of the season. We have plenty in the bank to live on until I can go back to work.'

'You know that wise woman in your *dorf*?' Max was striving for humor. 'She wasn't wise at all.'

'Oh, Max,' Rissa cradled his face between her hands. 'I'm so glad!'

21

For Rissa pregnancy was a time of joy. She felt loved, protected, indomitable. In partnership with destiny. Max was less tense, less restless, absorbed as she was in impending parenthood. Together they were part of the miracle of life.

Jack Fain groaned and carried on, cursed Max for carelessness. But Max was pleased, saying nothing could make Jack more conscious of Rissa's value than her withdrawal for the second half of the season.

Rissa and Max moved from the room and kitchenette on Washington Square to two lower floors in a brownstone on Ninth Street off Fifth Avenue. When Max told her what the rent would be, Rissa was at first wide-eyed with dismay. Then she realized her salary had grown enough to pay for it.

Max pretended not to be impressed by the grandeur of their new residence, though Rissa sensed his pride.

'So it's two floors,' he shrugged. 'Adler lives in a four-story brownstone with a fountain and an elevator.'

'Adler gets a thousand dollars a night on the road,' Rissa reminded.

'So will you in another five years.' Max was complacent. 'You'll be talented and beautiful *and* rich.'

With exquisite pleasure Rissa explained to Shirley that although they had a fireplace in the parlor, they would not have to depend on that for heat. A furnace sent steam up through the four floors of the house. The parlor, a dark-paneled dining room, and a kitchen were on the first floor. On the second floor were three bedrooms and a bathroom. The rear parlor led out into a tiny garden where the baby would be able to play. They would have a telephone, so that when she was at the theater, Shirley could always reach her.

Rissa shopped for furniture at Wanamaker's amid encouragement from Max to spend as much as she liked. They didn't buy on Grand Street, where the poor dickered over the price of each chair, each bed. They had passed beyond Avenue A, where the middle class shopped. When the furniture truck arrived, Rissa stood on the sidewalk clutching Shirley's arm in pleasure. The Wanamaker truck was a symbol that Rissa and Max Miller had moved up in the world.

Rissa took Shirley with her to buy the smaller items. Beautiful Haviland china. Damask drapes, fine lace curtains and linens for the bedrooms. But Shirley refused to allow Rissa to buy baby clothes. She would make every garment by hand.

Long ago the name for the baby had been chosen. As the mother, Rissa's choice prevailed for the first child.

'If it's a girl,' Rissa said with exquisite pleasure, 'we'll name her Clara. For mama. If it's a boy, he'll be Chaim.'

'Rissa, he'll be an American,' Max clucked.

'Charles. When he goes to school, let him have an American name.'

Rissa was small and slight. Since the middle of her third month Shirley had been putting inserts into her skirts. Max insisted that she be delivered by a doctor rather than a midwife. To Rissa's astonishment Shirley backed him up in this.

In April, three days after the tragic sinking of the *Titanic*, Rissa went into labor. She felt the dampness that was her water breaking. She said nothing to Max. Why should he worry sooner than was necessary? She knew he was afraid. She saw it in his eyes, felt it in the touch of his hand. Even when Shirley came up to the apartment for supper that night she said nothing.

They were having sponge cake and tea when she felt the first pain. She sat immobile. Waiting for the next pain.

'Rissa?' Shirley knew.

'I think so,' Rissa whispered and Max looked from Rissa to Shirley. All at once he was pale.

'Should I phone for the doctor?'

'Wait.' Shirley's smile was indulgent. She exchanged a glance of amusement with Rissa. Women understood these things. 'Rissa will tell you when to phone.'

The pains came quickly. Stronger than she expected. At her first involuntary outcry Max leaped to his feet.

'I'll phone for a doctor.'

'Not yet,' Shirley stopped him. 'Why should he sit around and wait?'

When the time came for Max to call the doctor, Shirley went with Rissa into the bedroom and helped her into a flannel nightgown.

'When mama had Hannah,' Rissa remembered, 'I took the children into the woods so they wouldn't hear.' She was beginning to perspire now. 'I didn't know it would hurt like this,' she admitted, clutching at her swollen belly.

'Afterwards you'll forget,' Shirley soothed. 'It'll be worth it.'

By the time the doctor arrived, she was in hard labor fighting to silence the shrieks that rose in her throat, tearing at the towel that Shirley had put in her hands. Pots of water were steaming out in the kitchen. Her body was a twisted mass of pain.

Max wanted to remain in the room. The doctor was shocked.

'This is my wife and my child,' Max shouted. 'I'll stay.'

At three minutes past four in the morning Shirley placed Rissa's daughter in the curve of her arm. Max hung over the bed, simultaneously haggard and radiant.

'Our daughter, Max.' Tears spilled over from Rissa's eyes. 'Our child.'

Max reached for one tiny flailing hand.

'Clara,' he welcomed her.

She would bear mama's name, Rissa thought with pleasure. If only mama could have been here to see her first grandchild.

* * *

Clara slept in a cradle beside her parents' bed. At the slightest sound Rissa left the bed to hover over the cradle. Already Rissa was convinced that Clara, whose tiny face was framed by an astonishing mass of dark hair, was the replica of her grandmother.

When the new theater season opened, Clara would move with her cradle into Shirley's bedroom. Rissa's life seemed complete. She had her daughter and she had her husband. Max spoke little of the movies these days. He was enchanted by his daughter.

At odd intervals Rissa was frightened by her happiness.

'Shirley,' she confided in a moment of doubt, 'I'm so happy I'm scared. How long can such a beautiful time endure?'

'Rissa, enjoy,' Shirley clucked, but Rissa knew she understood. 'Life's a patchwork quilt. Some times are bright and happy. Some are dull and sad. Enjoy,' she ordered.

The spring and early summer of 1912 was a period of euphoria for Rissa and Max. Shirley managed the household. Away from the theater Rissa and Max devoted themselves to tiny Clara.

For hours Max would sit beside Clara's crib alternating between looking at her and reading the day's newspapers. He was engrossed in the activities of the political conventions. The Republicans, meeting in Chicago, were split between President Taft and former President Roosevelt. Taft was nominated. Roosevelt split the party by assuming leadership of a third party. With the Republicans divided, the odds were in favor of the Democratic candidate, Woodrow Wilson.

Rissa's euphoria gave way to reality when she saw Max reading a story in the 13 July New York *Times* about an imported movie starring Sarah Bernhardt. She knew that Max's mind would turn to the movie industry.

'Rissa, look at this!' He churned with excitement. 'There was a special invitational matinee at the Lyceum yesterday of *Queen Elizabeth*. Bernhardt playing Elizabeth to Lou Tellegen's Essex! In a movie! Even in July famous people flocked back from their seashore and country houses to be there. It's the first time in history that a major legitimate theater has been used to present a film!'

'How could they make a movie of a whole play?' Momentarily Rissa was intrigued.

'It's four full reels,' Max explained. 'It runs an hour and a half.' Thus far a half-hour movie was considered long.

'But no voices,' Rissa pinpointed. 'How can Bernhardt in a movie compare to Bernhardt on the stage? How could so great an actress stoop to that?'

'Bernhardt is making history. She's leading the way for other great performers. Think of it, Rissa. Future generations will be able to see the great Bernhardt long after she's gone.' Max put down the newspaper. His mobile face showed his excitement. 'We'll go to see Bernhardt,' he promised. 'Someday we'll tell Clara how we saw Sarah Bernhardt playing Elizabeth.'

Max was immersed in the success of the Bernhardt

film, brought to the United States by a man named Zukor. He chortled with approval at the posters on display, showing large photographs of Bernhardt. They resembled stage posters rather than the usual gaudy movie bills. Tasteful ads filled the entertainment pages of the newspapers.

'Bernhardt is giving new status to the movies,' Max declared.

But when they sat in the Lyceum Theater watching the performance, Max was critical of the French-made film.

'What was the matter with the director?' Max whispered. 'Her gestures are fine for the stage. They're too exaggerated for the camera. Why didn't he point this out to her? But she's paved the way.' Max was reverent. 'The industry is indebted to Bernhardt. And the company will make a fortune on the film.'

Late in August Rissa went into rehearsal for the first production of the new season. This season Max would not be hovering in the wings. He relinquished his job as stage manager in order to devote himself to searching for new plays for Rissa.

Both Max and Rissa realized she felt secure enough now not to need him constantly in the theater. If there was a scene that troubled her, they would work together in the evenings.

'I've got to find good plays for you, Rissa,' Max said. 'Jack has to understand the time has come to put aside *shund*.'

Rissa was alternately mesmerized by Max's determination to see her in fine plays and alarmed that arguments over them would cause her to lose her job in the middle of the season. She wasn't a member of the union. If there was trouble, she couldn't go to them for help.

At last Jack relented. They would try a new play Max had brought to him. Leo was outraged. This was a play with a great role for Rissa. His role, in the hands of a Jacob Adler, could have been a show-stopper. But Leo insisted on directing as though the play was a melodrama.

Rissa performed with the quiet intensity of Rachel Kaminska. Everything Max had taught her had become part of her now. Max was ecstatic. With this production Rissa was reaching new heights. She was taking her place beside the stars.

The reaction to the production was mixed. The critics applauded Rissa's performance as restrained and superb. She was entrenched as the darling of Second Avenue. But the others in the company, under Leo's direction, flared into melodrama. What had been anticipated as one of the rare long runs on Second Avenue was aborted. Jack returned hastily to *shund*.

Rissa was disappointed, but Clara was now the focal point of her existence. She was too engrossed in the baby to be conscious of Max's returning restless-ness. He devoured the movie news in the trade papers and reported everything new to her. She listened with seeming attentiveness when he talked to her about the developing Famous Players Film Company, formed by Adolph Zukor following his success with *Queen Elizabeth*.

273

'Rissa, they're raising the level of motion pictures. They're hiring stage performers to work before the cameras,' Max said with evangelical zeal. 'Zukor is spending forty thousand dollars on a picture!' He paused dramatically. 'They're talking with Belasco about buying some of his plays. They're negotiating with John Barrymore, Mrs Fiske and Lily Langtry to work for them.'

Rissa's eyes widened.

'John Barrymore?' The Barrymore family was her idol. At every opportunity she went uptown with Max to see Ethel, John or Lionel onstage. 'Max, an actor like that would appear in movies?'

'Rissa, you're burying yourself down here. You don't allow yourself to see beyond Second Avenue. First Bernhardt, now Barrymore on film. Can you turn your back on that?'

Max's eloquence seeped through for the first time. Even on Second Avenue actors were growing conscious of the movies. It was 1913. Twenty million people a year, the newspapers proclaimed, were going to the picture houses. Stars like Mary Pickford and Tom Mix were making hundreds – some said thousands – of dollars a week.

'They won't like the way I photograph,' Rissa objected. But Max felt she was weakening. 'I talk with an accent.'

'You'll photograph magnificently,' he insisted, reaching for her hand. 'Besides you don't need to talk in movies. When sound comes, you'll be ready.'

'Max, I'm afraid.' She was wavering.

'I'll talk to the people up on Fourteenth Street,' he

promised. 'I'll bring them down to see you. Then you'll talk with them. Making movies won't take you away from the theater,' he soothed. 'It's something extra. Another few weeks or so and the theater will be closing for the season. We can't go on tour with the baby.'

For Rissa he would not have to chase after independents. The members of the Trust knew of Rissa Lindowska by now. The era of feature films was arriving. The new films, with length that demanded plot and character development, would require actors with real ability.

The independents struggled to survive. In order to succeed they had to be able to show their films in theaters licensed by the Trust. But if a Trust theater showed an independent film, it would be cut off from the Trust films that offered the familiar faces. They would be forced to close.

'When will you talk to the movie people, Max?' Rissa asked after a few moments.

'We'll see,' he hedged.

No need to make Rissa nervous. He would bring down an important producer from the Trust to watch her at the first chance. Afterwards they would go to the Café Royale and talk business. Rissa could do pictures and still be a star on the Yiddish Rialto.

On 4 March Woodrow Wilson was inaugurated as the twenty-eighth president of the United States. Max believed that business would improve with Wilson in the White House. The Yiddish theaters were encountering financial difficulties. Second Avenue still reeled from the suicide last year of Keni Liptzin's husband, Michael Mintz, who could not face his unpaid employees.

That same month the Woolworth Building in New York was completed. It was the tallest building in the world at sixty stories. Considered a 'wonder' by New Yorkers.

On a Friday evening late in March Max sat beside Roland Ackerman, a producer from a Trust company. At intervals his eyes left the stage to check the producer for reactions. The man seemed impressed.

Max sent word backstage to Rissa that she was to come to the Café Royale straight from the theater. He would be waiting there with Roland Ackerman. He could envision Rissa's astonishment. He had given her no warning.

Everything would be just right. He'd talk to Ackerman while they waited for Rissa to arrive at the café. He'd explain that he always worked with Rissa. She was marvelous to direct. She would understand that to play for the camera meant to cut down on gestures. On expressions. Rissa would walk into the Café Royale, and Roland Ackerman would realize she was a star. On Second Avenue, on Broadway, in movies, Rissa Lindowska would be a star.

He would make a deal, Max plotted, that would include himself as Rissa's director. They would want her badly enough to go along with this. Rissa would insist. God, he was twenty-nine years old. It was time people looked at him and saw somebody who was more than Rissa Lindowska's husband.

At the Café Royale, where Max was well known

now, they were seated at what the waiters had come to recognize as Rissa's favorite table. In truth it was his choice. Rissa always deferred to him. Only in this business of making movies had Rissa ever opposed him.

'Stage people are realizing the importance of movies,' Roland Ackerman said expansively. 'Every day I'm at the Lamb's Club talking to important actors.'

'Rissa has refused a dozen Broadway offers,' Max fabricated. 'She's waiting until her English is perfect. Though what accent she has is charming. More British than Polish.' His face brightened. 'Here she is.'

With her compulsively quick steps Rissa was walking toward their table. Smiling here and there in response to greetings. At a table close by, two men rose to their feet and applauded as she passed them.

Max introduced Rissa to Ackerman who offered perfunctory admiration for her performance. It would be bad business to show how eager he was to sign up Rissa.

Max summoned a waiter to the table. While Ackerman was Jewish, he was unfamiliar with the glory of Yiddish cooking. Amused by his uncertainty Rissa urged him to order her favorite *palatchinken* – Hungarian crêpes suzettes.

For a while the conversation dwelt on the new muscial *The Sunshine Girl*, starring Irene and Vernon Castle, which had been a tremendous hit in London before opening in New York. Max turned the table talk to politics. He was a great admirer of President Wilson.

'Wilson is a true liberal,' Max declared. 'The people will benefit with him in the White House.'

Not until their tea arrived did Roland Ackerman settle down to business.

'We've come together at the right time,' he told Rissa. 'We've bought a play that will be perfect for you.'

'Max makes all these decisions for me,' she said sweetly. 'He orchestrates my performances.' She had culled this phrase from Max. 'He knows what is right for me.'

Ackerman wavered for a moment. The man from the Trust understood that Rissa meant for *him* to direct. Max strived to conceal his excitement.

'Everything will be arranged to insure our finest performance,' Ackerman said gallantly. 'Our new picture plant in California will be ready within ten days – '

'California?' Rissa interrupted. Her eyes swung accusingly to Max.

'Los Angeles is perfect for making pictures.' Ackerman was unaware of the undercurrents that zigzagged between Rissa and Max. 'The climate is wonderful year round. The sunshine right for outdoor shots. We're opening our studio on Sunset Boulevard near Vine Street.' He radiated enthusiasm. 'It's not actually in Los Angeles. It's in a little suburb called Hollywood. On the northwestern side of the city.'

'Mr Ackerman, I thought we were talking about

278

making pictures in New York.' Rissa's face was composed, but Max felt her inner rejection. 'I couldn't possibly leave the city. I play in the Yiddish theater.'

'Rissa, the theater closes in a few weeks,' Max reminded, but he was uneasy.

'We could shoot during the summer months,' Ackerman compromised. 'And during the theater season you could arrange to take two months to come out to make additional films to fill in. We're out to build stars, Rissa. You'll have to be seen on a regular basis.'

'I can't go to California.' Rissa was firm. 'I couldn't take two months out of the theater season. Nor would I drag my baby all the way across the country twice a year. I thank you, Mr Ackerman. But for me to make pictures for you in California is out of the question.

'What about shooting in New York?' Max was devastated. 'Rissa would be available on a year-round basis here,' he pointed out to Ackerman. 'Except for matinee days.'

'We're moving our entire operation out to California. We don't have enough studio space here in the city. Too many months in New York there's not enough sun.' Ackerman pushed back his chair. He was irritated at wasting an evening on Second Avenue. 'If you change your mind, call me.'

Rissa watched in anguish while Max withdrew within himself. But she was unrelenting. How could they leave security in New York to go out to California? How could she know she would be a success in pictures? How could they run back and forth across the country with Clara like gypsies? They had responsibilities. A child. If she stayed away from Second Avenue for a year and then came back, how did she know she would find a place for herself again? *She wasn't even a member of the union.*

When the theater season closed, Rissa talked about their renting a cottage in the mountains for the summer.

'It'll be hot in the city for the baby.'

'I don't know that we should spend the money,' Max hedged.

Rissa stared at him in astonishment. She was always holding *him* back from fresh extravagance. Only last week he said they should make arrangements to order her costumes for the next season from Lucile, who was Lady Duff-Gordon.

'Max, with the money we earn?' Her laugh was indulgent. 'Each week we put so much money in the bank.' The fine bank run by Mr Mandel, who was himself in the bank every day. Max had wanted to put their money in the big National Bank. An American bank. This was an affront to Rissa's Jewishness, and Max had agreed to stay in the Mandel Bank.

'The money you earn,' Max corrected.

'It's our money we put in the bank,' Rissa insisted. 'We earn it together.'

'It won't go on forever,' he warned. She gaped in astonishment. 'We know that President Taft vetoed the immigration bill with the literacy-test provisions three weeks before he left the White House. But there'll be more efforts in Congress.'

'Wilson will veto it,' she shot back.

'Rissa, immigration will be cut back.' Max was insistent. 'The Yiddish theater will lose its audience. The day will come when the Yiddish theater will be dead.'

'Max, you've never understood the Yiddish theater!' She had never felt this kind of rage toward Max. 'Sometimes I'm not sure you're a Jew. When I was a little girl, I used to hear papa say, "In America Jews forget they are Jews. Maybe twice a year – on Rosh Hashanah and Yom Kippur – they remember they are Jews and go to *shul*. Maybe they remember." Max, you don't know the Jewish world that is mine. Sometimes I think we're a little strange to you.'

'Part of you still lives in that *dorf* back in Poland!' Max shot back. 'Wake up, Rissa. You're an American now. The children born in this country and growing up here will look to American theater. American movies,' he said in a surge of triumph. 'How long can the Yiddish theater go on? Five years? Ten years? Your talent isn't labeled "Yiddish." You're an actress. You can play anywhere. In English,' he emphasized. 'In movies where there's no sound yet. And when sound comes, you can play that, too.'

Rissa tried to envision the future Max saw. No! There would always be a Yiddish theater. Her home. Her refuge. She would not – could not – play in English. She was a greenhorn.

'Clara's crying.' Rissa grasped at this excuse to escape from Max. 'I must go to her.'

* * *

281

Max refused to rent a cottage in the mountains. Inwardly Rissa railed at his making these decisions. Why must the wife always submit to her husband's wishes? She worked; she earned money. Even if she didn't why shouldn't she have a voice in what they did with their money and their lives?

Under Rissa's calm but firm assault Max compromised. He decided they should rent a cottage at Brighton. Two days later he bought their first car. A Chevrolet. He learned to drive. In mid-June he drove Rissa, Shirley and the baby to the cottage with whatever necessary items would fit into the car.

Rissa loved the cottage. She felt isolated from the ever present hostilities at the theater. She could forget Max's infatuation for the movies. Here was peace and quiet and sunshine.

Every morning she took Clara, now running rather than walking, to the beach to play in the sand. In the afternoons while Clara napped, she sat with Shirley on the small porch.

Shirley had discovered Mary Roberts Rinehart. While Shirley read the latest Rinehart, Rissa pored over Strindberg, Shaw and Shakespeare.

The Chevrolet sat in front of the house. Max went into the city three or four days a week, but he preferred the long trolley ride through Brooklyn, over the bridge into Manhattan, to driving his new car.

Rissa asked Max to teach her to drive. Now that cars had electric starters — and skirts had climbed above the ankles — why should women not drive? Max was indignant.

'Driving is a man's job,' he blustered. 'How can

you take a chance? You have a child to raise! Suppose you had an accident?'

Rissa realized after a few attempts that it was futile to try to change Max's mind. Men were drivers; women were not. How could Max, who was so sympathetic to women's wish to vote, be so outraged that they might also wish to drive?

In the evenings Max and she walked along the beach. These evenings were almost like the early days of their marriage, Rissa thought with pleasant surges of sentimentality. For a little while, hand in hand with Max, gazing up at the star-splashed sky, listening to the sounds of the waves hitting against the shore, she could forget the questions that had been haunting her these past few weeks.

Was Max seeing another woman? She worried about Max and Celia Kamenstein. The way Celia made a point of brushing up against him at any opportunity. Max never talked about what he did in the city on those days he went into Manhattan. She suspected he was chasing after a job with one of the picture companies still operating in New York. And if he was seeing other women, it wasn't Celia Kamenstein. Celia had walked out on the company three weeks before the end of the season. Nobody knew where she had gone. Max suspected she was in California working in pictures.

Late in August Max moved his family back to the brownstone on Ninth Street. It was necessary that both Rissa and he be in the city. He was in wonderful spirits. At last he had acquired an assignment to

283

direct a two-reeler. Clark Mattox had fired his wife's nephew, left his wife and acquired a new backer. Encountering Max in the Automat he had hired him on the spot. He would be earning seventy-five dollars a week. Five times what Jack had paid him to stage manage.

He said nothing to Rissa. When the first movie was finished, then he would tell her. Meanwhile Rissa would be in rehearsal for the first play of the new season.

Soon Max was learning the difficulties involved in making a two-reeler in a secret loft on West Twenty-sixth Street. They needed more space; there was no room for an adequate laboratory. They had to be ready to pack up lights and equipment and run if Trust detectives moved in on them. They were engaged in an illegal operation. If the Trust detectives discovered their setup, they would bring in the police and confiscate their movie equipment.

Max was trying to persuade Clark to produce a four-reeler. The Bernhardt film was a huge success. Griffith, commuting between New York and California, had directed a two-reeler 'spectacular' called *Judith of Bethulia* with Blanche Street, Henry D. Walthall, Lillian Gish and Mae Marsh, though it had not yet been released. Cines Films in Italy had produced *Quo Vadis* in eight reels. It was to be shown at the Astor Theater at a dollar top.

'Max, we can't do a four-reeler in New York,' Clark protested when Max started in again at a break for lunch. 'We don't have the facilities.'

'Take space out in New Jersey,' Max urged. 'It's

cheaper, and you don't worry that much out there about the Trust.'

'Let me think about it,' Clark hedged. Max sensed a breakthrough. Clark knew he was right. The time for feature films had arrived. Fortunes were to be made. 'All right, everybody,' Clark called out. 'Let's get back to work.'

Max was engrossed in devising a special camera effect when the detectives broke into the loft. They were accompanied by the police.

'You're all under arrest!' a Trust detective yelled even before the police moved into action. 'Don't anybody touch a thing!'

Rissa was sitting in an overstuffed chair beside a parlor window with a script in her hand when the telephone rang. She was still startled when the sound of a phone ring intruded upon her stillness in the apartment.

She picked up the receiver. Waving with her other hand to Clara, who was playing in a sandpile in the tiny yard behind the house. Shirley sat in a chair, sewing a pinafore for Clara while she watched her. Shirley's fingers – like mama's when she was alive – were not idle for a minute, Rissa thought with recurrent affection.

'Hello.' She expected the caller to be Max or Jack. It was rare that anyone else phoned.

'Rissa, listen to me carefully – ' Max's voice was strained.

'Max, what's happened?' She was instantly conscious of trouble.

'You know about the Trust. How they've been raiding the "independents,"' he elucidated because she seemed incapable of speech.

'You told me.'

'I wanted it to be a surprise about the picture.' Max paused. Rissa heard voices in the background urging him to hurry his call. 'I've been directing a two-reeler. Rissa, don't be upset. I'm at the police station. We were raided.'

'What's going to happen, Max?' She fought down her panic.

'I'll get out,' he soothed. 'But I need a lawyer. Call Jack and – '

'I'll talk to Shirley.' Shirley's list of acquaintances was endless. 'Jack doesn't have to know.' To be arrested was the ultimate disgrace. 'Where shall the lawyer come?'

She listened attentively to Max's instructions, then hurried out into the yard to tell Shirley.

'I know a lawyer on Jefferson Street.' Shirley was immediately in charge. 'Don't worry, Rissa. This lawyer will get Max out. He's got connections. His wife's second cousin knows Henry Schimmel, who's running for the Assembly. Watch Clara. I'll take care of it right now.'

Rissa stayed with Clara in the yard till it was time to take her into the house for her nap. Her mind was assaulted by frightening visions of Max behind prison bars. She had known vaguely that those who were engaged in independent film-making were considered outlaws. Max talked in eloquent outrage about the constant lawsuits. Jail was something else.

286

With Clara asleep in the bedroom she shared with Shirley, Rissa came downstairs to make herself a cup of tea, her solace in moments of anxiety. She shifted from alarm for Max's welfare to anger that he had put himself into such a position.

If Max went to jail, she would carry on alone, she told herself. She would find the strength to manage. Clara would not suffer. She would even be able to handle Jack. Max had taught her.

Poor Max. After trying so hard to find himself a job directing a movie, *this* had to happen. He must feel terrible. Her own feelings were in turmoil. Would the lawyer be able to get Max out of jail?

She left the parlor and went down the hall to the door to the vestibule. From here she could hear Clara if she woke up. She kept her eyes on the street.

Shirley was back at the apartment within an hour. The lawyer had gone over to the police station.

'He'll get Max out. Soon we'll hear,' she soothed.

Four hours after Max phoned, he arrived home. Rissa opened her arms to him. This was not a time to remind him that he had disgraced the family.

'Honey, I didn't mean to scare you – ' He sounded unnaturally humble.

'Thank God, you're home, Max.' She clung to him.

Now this crazy business with the movies would be over. Max would take no more chances.

22

In the new Yiddish theater season Rissa fought together with Max to persuade Jack to try out plays by new playwrights. Others beside Max were warning that the younger generation would make demands for finer entertainment.

Kobrin, who had translated *The Living Corpse* for Adler, was expected to be represented soon on Second Avenue. Sholem Asch and David Pinsky were to have plays on the boards. Rissa prayed that these efforts toward *beser teyater* would revive Max's waning interest.

Jack saw only the huge success of the Thomashefsky plays based on newspaper headlines. With the trial and vindication of Mendel Beilis barely over, though the courts still proclaimed that the 'ritual murder had been committed by Jews unknown,' Thomashefsky was about to present his newest concoction, *Mendel Beilis*. A favorite joke around the lower East Side was, 'When does Thomashefsky find time to write plays? Between all the acting and all the women, he needs two heads and a dozen penises.'

'Max, that's the kind of play that makes money. Bring me another *Mendel Beilis*,' Jack exhorted.

But while Jews were rejoicing in the vindication of Mendel Beilis in November, news filtered up from Atlanta, Georgia, about the imprisonment of Leo

Frank on a charge of rape and murder, which thinking people labeled blatantly false. As a Georgian, Max was upset and cynical. What Jew, he proclaimed, would receive a fair trial in the state of Georgia when the victim was a thirteen-year-old white Protestant?

After the raid on Clark Mattox's studio, Max never talked to Rissa about the moving-picture business, although she knew it occupied much of his thoughts. Sometimes she talked to him and he didn't hear her. And then a new alarm took Rissa prisoner. What had been a suspicion appeared a reality. Leo and Sara were dropping blatant hints about Max's infidelity. She didn't dare confront him. She couldn't cope with the possibility that they might be right.

Was Max finding comfort in the arms of other women? Women had always chased after Max. When Max reached for her in the darkness of their bedroom, she responded with the passion that always pleased him. But afterwards she lay beside him and wondered from whose arms he came to her.

Then word circulated around Second Avenue that Keni Liptzin was appearing before the cameras for the Famous Players Film Company in the Chandler Building on Forty-second Street. Rissa knew that Max would see Keni's film, *The Great Mistake*, when it was released next month.

Max's sole concern appeared to be promoting her career and playing the devoted father. But Rissa saw the rebellion in his eyes. He had been in New York almost nine years. It was not enough for a man of

Max's vaulting ambitions to be his wife's personal manager.

Max made a pretext of being involved in politics. He talked with her about Wilson's demands for banking reform. About the trouble in Mexico. About the war clouds that hung over Europe. He repeated what was said in the heated discussions he shared in cafés in Greenwich Village, where the young and rebellious gathered.

With Shirley, who on every possible occasion attended lectures at Cooper Union and religiously devoured the newspapers, he discussed the lurid headlines of the day. They argued good-humoredly about the garment-workers' strikes and the silk-workers' strike in Paterson, New Jersey, that had dragged on for five months before it was abandoned.

To Shirley's blatant enjoyment Max told her about life uptown.

'Ladies are smoking in the public rooms of the Plaza and the St Regis,' he reported and Shirley clucked in disapproval. 'The Waldorf-Astoria is serving unaccompanied ladies in their restaurants at any time.' And the *thés dansants* were presented in the best hotels in the late afternoon. Here came pampered matrons to dance with the handsome young men provided by the hotels. Often tea was abandoned for cocktails.

How did Max know so much about what was happening away from the lower East Side? Was he in the bed of some beautiful uptown *shiksa*? He told Shirley about the people he met in the Village too; American writers and actors and artists. He talked about people she didn't know. Jack Reed, Fannie Hurst, Lincoln Steffens, Willa Cather. He was fascinated by the people he met in an apartment that belonged to a rich society woman named Mabel Dodge.

Fearful of losing Max, Rissa decided that it was time Clara was presented with a baby brother or sister. With a son Max would have a fresh interest in life. Away from his Village friends. By the last day of Hanukkah Rissa was sure she was pregnant. A week later she told Max. This time, she was sure, she would give him a son.

Rissa was able to play right to the end of the season. Max was attentive and solicitous. He was aware that in this second pregnancy she was suffering from a physical discomfort that had not attacked her when she was carrying Clara. Rissa was convinced he was not involved with another woman.

For weeks Max had been locked in a battle with Jack over Rissa's contract for the new season. Jack had howled like a wounded puppy when Max listed the terms he demanded for the new contract: Rissa's salary was to be doubled and she was to have approval of all plays in which she was to appear. Considering the fact that she was now the darling of Second Avenue – though still not a member of the union, Max considered it unlikely that Jack would reject the conditions.

'Max, you're a grade-A bastard!' Jack yelled toward the end of June when Max complained that Rissa was still waiting for the contract. 'For money you'd fuck a duck!'

'Jack, Rissa's waiting for the contract,' Max reiterated. 'You want me to go talk to somebody else?'

'You'll have it tomorrow.' Jack retreated into injured feelings. 'After what I've done for Rissa, you never stop screwing me.'

She had signed the contract. Max returned it to Jack for his signature. Smug in having the contract signed by Rissa, Jack was stalling on signing it himself. But it was just a matter of days. Jack knew Rissa wouldn't set foot on a rehearsal stage until the contract was in their hands.

On 28 June Archduke Francis Ferdinand was assassinated in Sarajevo. With Europe on the brink of war Max was disturbed for the future of the Yiddish theaters. If war was declared, the gates would be closed to immigration. Their audiences, Max warned gloomily, would shrink. But caught up in the final weeks of her pregnancy, Rissa thought little of such predictions.

In early July — three weeks earlier than anticipated — in a delivery that was prolonged and dangerous, Rissa gave birth to a second daughter, Rachel. Known almost from her first moments as Rae. A dark-haired, dark-eyed replica of her mother, Max declared. He swore he would never allow Rissa to endure another pregnancy.

On 1 August Germany declared war on Russia. In a speech to a huge crowd in Berlin the kaiser said: 'Envious peoples everywhere are compelling us to our just defense.' American tourists in Paris were in panic, fearing they wouldn't get ships home. Some of them were pressed for funds. Sobbing women besieged the American consulate.

The London Exchange closed its doors. London newspapers reported that in the financial crisis generated by the war, Queen Mother Alexandra, sister of the Dowager Empress of Prussia, might be forced to pledge gold plates for security for a loan. The Cotton Board closed in New York, along with the Coffee Exchange.

In New York City crowds gathered at Times and Herald Squares to read the war bulletins posted until after midnight. On the lower East Side, however, the war news was to take second place to news that was of more immediate impact.

In the Miller apartment Shirley was clucking because Max was not yet home and Saturday supper was waiting to be served.

'Special for Max I made cabbage borscht and where is he?'

When Max arrived, Rissa realized instantly that something of serious import had occurred. Shirley bustled out into the kitchen to prepare to serve supper. Rissa waited while Max went up to the bedroom to look in on Clara and Rae.

'Max?' Rissa hovered at the entrance to the dining room. 'Something's happened. Is it trouble with Jack and the contract?'

'No, we'll have the signed contract the first of the week. Now that you're going into rehearsal in two weeks Jack knows he can't stall.' Max walked to his place at the head of the table. 'We didn't read this morning's *Times* well enough. I heard the news on

Second Avenue. Last night depositors stormed the Deutsch Brothers Bank on East Houston Street. People living in the houses around the bank threw water on them. The police had to be called.'

'I don't understand.' Rissa was bewildered. 'Why should the depositors storm the bank?'

'A petition in bankruptcy was filed yesterday against the bank. They're in trouble, Rissa.'

Rissa paled.

'You mean people may not get their money?'

'It looks that way,' Max admitted.

Shirley had come into the dining room with the tureen of cabbage borscht.

'The Deutsch Brothers Bank?' she asked while she put down the tureen on the white damask tablecloth.

'Shirley, that's your bank!' For Rissa the news was suddenly personal.

'So we'll see what happens.' Shirley was shaken but unruffled. 'So how much have I got in the bank? A big sixty-five dollars and forty cents.' But that was Shirley's entire savings. 'I won't go hungry. I've got a place to live.'

Rissa worried for the depositors in the Deutsch Brothers Bank. To the handful of Jewish banks on the lower East Side the immigrants went with whatever money they managed to save. For the past year or so there had been 'runs.' But everything was straightened out; nobody lost money.

'We don't have to worry about the Mandel Bank,' Rissa said with confidence, though Max had talked more than once in the past year about moving their money into an American bank. To her that was a sign of disloyalty. 'Mr Mandel is such a gentleman.'

On 3 August Germany declared war on France. The next day German troops invaded Belgium, and Great Britain declared war on Germany.

On the morning of 5 August, Rissa sat in a slipper chair drawn close to the window in the kitchen, reluctant yet to face the headlines that screamed from the New York *Times*. A whisper of a breeze alleviated the heat of the night. She had drawn one delicately veined breast free of her shirtwaist so that Rae might nuzzle greedily after a night of uncomfortable humidity.

'Rissa, listen,' Shirley ordered, as she read from the *Times*. 'Mrs Otto Kahn caught the last boat from Dieppe with her four children, a dozen servants and sixty-five trunks. She had to leave behind in France her two automobiles. Otto Kahn is a Jew, yes?'

'Yes,' Rissa laughed. Shirley found supreme joy in learning that prominent people were Jewish. 'Max says that downtown the Jews are turning their backs on art, but uptown men like Kahn are leading the way.'

'Max is right.' Shirley was as complacent as though Otto Kahn was a blood relative. 'I read in the newspapers. Otto Kahn is a *macher* in the Metropolitan Opera. He brings over from Europe the most important people to work for him.'

Neither Rissa nor Shirley gave voice to their unease about the banking problems on the lower East Side. In their fine brownstone off Fifth Avenue the difficulties of the banks seemed remote. The newspapers reported that depositors were not disturbed about the new rulings. Yesterday several of the banks had posted notices that withdrawals were limited to a hundred dollars. In some banks it was a fifty-dollar limit. Under the new regulations sixty days' notice of withdrawal was now required.

Rissa suspected that Max had gone over to the Second Avenue café where he liked to talk with the other men gathered there about the war and the bank troubles. It was rare that he left the house before nine in the morning. Maybe it bothered him that Rae had cried so much last night. Only when she took the baby to breast was Rae quiet.

'That's a greedy baby,' Shirley laughed while Rae uttered tiny noises of satisfaction.

'She's going to be an actress,' Rissa decided. 'Already she's onstage.'

Max pulled out his watch as he walked down Second Avenue. It was earlier than he realized. Not yet nine o'clock. He'd told Jack yesterday, 'Sign Rissa's contract and give it to me tomorrow, or we'll go elsewhere.' He was impatient with these games Jack played.

For the first time in three years Max felt real excitement about the coming season. Rissa had control of the plays she would do. Jack knew, of course, that meant *he* would pick the plays. Leo didn't have the sensitivity – the technique – to direct a play that was above *shund*. Rissa would insist that *he* come in to direct.

He'd learned a lot about directing, both in theater

and in pictures, in these last four years. He'd given himself a real education, Max congratulated himself. Now he churned to put that education to use.

Max stopped by the theater with little expectation of finding Jack in his office. He went into a café for coffee. The volatile conversation here this morning made him uneasy. On Monday nobody appeared upset that the banks were having some problems. That withdrawals were limited. Now the whole mood seemed to have changed.

Fighting apprehension Max left the café and hurried in the early August heat toward the Mandel Bank. By the time he was a block from Rutgers Square he could hear the tumult. He quickened his pace. Anticipating trouble.

About two thousand people – many of them immigrants – were crowded together in Rutgers Square. Some of them clutched bankbooks in their hands as they listened to the excited soapbox orators that dotted the square. They were depositors of the Mandel, Jarmolowsky and Kobre banks. Their faces showed their fears of losing their life savings. More than ten million dollars was said to be on deposit in these banks.

The police captain was urging the people to disperse. Police moved uneasily about the perimeter of the crowd.

'I won't allow a parade!' the police captain shouted. 'Move along now!'

'Let's go over to the Jarmolowsky and make those thieves tell us when they'll give us our money!' a man on a soapbox yelled. 'It's ours! We worked for it!' Approval rent the air.

Max was carried along with the mob that started across East Broadway. They began to march. At the head of the parade men carried two banners in Yiddish. On them was written: 'The 60,000 unfortunate depositors of the three private banks demand their rights from the governor of New York State. We demand our money, and we will not keep quiet!'

Max was compelled by the momentum to become part of the march. He shared the alarm of the other marchers.

They marched toward the Jarmolowsky Bank. The police captain summoned police from other precincts to stop the march. A handful of policemen charged forward and ripped away the signs. Instantly a riot erupted. Clubs were swung. Fists struck out.

Within minutes the police had quelled the disturbance. Nine people, including two women, were arrested. The others were dispersed. But several hundred decided to proceed now to the Criminal Courts Building to make demands.

Max separated himself from the crowd. He hurried north to Second Avenue. Instinct told him that Rissa and he might never see a cent of the many thousands of dollars they had on deposit in the Mandel Bank – all they owned in the world except for the furnishings of the apartment and whatever cash they had on hand for daily expenses.

Jack arrived at his office in the theater as Max approached again.

'I hear the banks are in trouble,' he greeted Max.

'The State Banking Department is moving in on them for being unsound.' He pulled out a key to unlock the door that led to his office. 'You keep money downtown?'

'Everything we've got is in the Mandel Bank. Rissa went to them when she first came to New York. She didn't want to change.' The whole situation was unreal, Max thought. But hadn't Wilson warned that the whole banking system needed to be overhauled? 'It's unbelievable.'

'Hot as hell in here,' Jack complained, throwing open the door to the office. 'If I didn't have to see people today, I would have stayed at home in front of a fan.'

'That's where I'm going when I leave here,' Max said. His eyes were questioning.

'Max, I'll drop by your place with the contract early this afternoon,' Jack said casually. 'I have to pick it up from the lawyer.'

'What's this lawyer business?' All at once Max was wary. 'Rissa signed. You need a lawyer to witness your signature?'

'I'll be no later than two,' Jack soothed. 'And have a glass of iced tea ready. This heat knocks the hell out of me.'

Max went back to the apartment. Shirley was out in the backyard with the two children. Rissa was sitting by a kitchen window reading one of the scripts he meant to spring on Jack as soon as the contract was in hand. Rissa was quiet when he told her what had happened at Rutgers Square.

'The money is gone, Max?'

'I doubt that we'll see even ten percent of it.'

'You said we should put it in an American bank.' Her eyes were troubled. 'It's my fault.'

'It's nobody's fault,' he said quickly. 'Just rotten luck.'

'Can something like this happen in America?' Rissa questioned.

'It can happen, Rissa. Let's hope with the new regulations it will never happen again.'

At a few minutes past two Jack arrived at the apartment. He carried his flannel jacket over one arm and his panama hat in hand.

'When are tailors going to learn that men don't like sweating like pigs in the summer?' he complained, settling himself in an overstuffed chair by the parlor window and in direct range of the electric fan.

'Shirley's bringing us iced tea,' Rissa comforted.

Jack reached into the inside pocket of his jacket with a self-consciousness that put Rissa on alert. He fussed over the sheaf of envelopes, finally pulled one clear.

'This is the contract my lawyers drew up.' Jack was avoiding both Max's eyes and hers. 'You'll have to sign again, Rissa.'

'Why will Rissa have to sign again?' Max's tone was ominous.

'My lawyer says it's not in my best interest to hand over rights that belong to the producer. It's my responsibility to pick out the plays.' He handed the contract to Rissa. When she made no effort to take it, he deposited it on the table beside the sofa where she sat.

'Jack, we had an agreement.' Max's color was high. Rissa knew he was fighting to control his outrage. Battles with Jack were apt to become screaming matches.

Jack shrugged.

'What can I do? My lawyer tells me I can't do it. I pay him to advise me.' He forced himself to look at Max now. 'We all know we're in for bad times with a war in Europe. The price of everything is going sky high. Who'll be able to afford to come to the theaters? Coal's going to be so expensive this winter we'll all freeze our asses off. Banks are closing – ' He gestured eloquently.

That was what happened, Rissa realized. The banks had closed. Jack must know that all their money was gone. *Jack knew her salary was all they had now.* A swift glance at Max's stricken face told her he must have admitted to Jack that all their money was in the Mandel Bank.

'Rissa won't sign.' Max was deliberately low-keyed. 'We had an agreement. Your word.'

'This is an act of God, Max,' Jack protested. 'We have a war in Europe. Can I afford to gamble with my business? I know what brings in customers. All you think about is doing fancy plays. That won't pay my rent on the theater, Max.'

'Rissa won't be with the company when it opens next month,' Max told him. Rissa fought against panicking. It was too late in the year for her to join another company! They were all set. They couldn't

301

go to the bank for money to live on. That money was gone.

'So Tania will play Rissa's parts if you feel that way,' Jack shrugged.

'Who's Tania?' Had Jack already replaced her? But audiences expected Rissa LINDOWSKA. *She* brought them into the Fain Theater.

'This broad I brought in from Chicago. Young, good-looking. She's spent three years on the road. She went to the union and passed the *probe*.'

'Some broad from Chicago isn't Rissa Lindowska,' Max scoffed. 'Rissa brings in the customers.'

'Tania is tall and good-looking. And she's cheap.' Jack's eyes narrowed as he turned from Max to Rissa. 'So who's it gonna be? Tania or Rissa?'

Max's face tightened in rejection. Fear flooded Rissa. They couldn't afford to gamble now. She reached for the contract. Avoiding Max's eyes.

'This time, Jack,' she stipulated. 'But next year I won't sign unless Max and I choose the plays. That's definite.' Max was staring at her as though she had plunged a knife into his back.

While she signed the two copies of the contract, one of which would be hers, Max walked out of the parlor. This was only the second contract with Jack that she was able to sign herself. Before she was twenty-one, Max had to sign for her because otherwise the contract was not legal.

Max waited until he heard the door close behind Jack to come into the parlor.

'Rissa, how could you do this to me?' A vein pounded in his forehead. 'This was my chance to direct a decent play on Second Avenue! You let me down!'

'How could I *not* sign, Max? You said yourself. Our money in the bank is lost. Who will hire me this late in the season? The companies are all set! We can't go on the road with two babies.'

'Go on, say it!' Max towered threateningly above her. She felt his pain. His humiliation. 'I'm no good as a husband. My wife has to support the family! This was my chance, Rissa, and you threw it away!'

'Max, please. What else could I do?'

Max turned away from her with a grunt of frustration, picked up his jacket and hat and walked out of the parlor and down the hall to the front door. Rissa flinched as he slammed the door behind him.

Rissa lay sleepless beside Max. He clung to the edge of the bed, his back to her. She suspected that he, too, was awake. She couldn't bear this wall between Max and her. She wanted one man in her life. *Max*. Other actresses might marry two or three or more times; that was not for her.

'Max,' she whispered. Desperate to know that he still loved her. 'Max?'

He pretended to be asleep. He had never been so furious with her. She moved her small, slender body close to his. One arm crept about his. Tears filled her eyes. What would her life be without Max's love?

Determined to crumple the wall between them she lifted one leg across his. Emboldened by her alarm she allowed her hand to travel from his chest to fondle his firm, flat belly. Her hand moved lower.

He was awake and passionate. She had not lost Max.

'Rissa – '

He turned to her, lifted himself above her. Her arms enclosed him as he brought himself to her, moved within her. When they made love, Max had to be in command. That was how it should be.

23

The city was assaulted by EXTRA after EXTRA as Europe was embroiled in war. Already those fearing that the United States would become involved were mobilizing for peace. An armchair crusader, Shirley repeated the suspicions of many — that the United States would be drawn into the war to protect a handful of multimillionaires whose interests were in jeopardy.

For Max this was a time for soul-searching. Day after day he walked miles about the streets of New York. Trying to bring his life into focus.

Here he was, a man close to thirty, yet helpless to support his family. What real job had he ever held except to clerk in Izzy's delicatessen? What use would he be to his family if he took a job in a store? That wouldn't pay the rent on their fine apartment.

It wasn't enough to be his wife's personal manager. Rissa didn't need him anymore. What he had to teach, she had learned.

Who would give him a chance to direct? In the Yiddish theater directors were entrenched for life. The bank failure had robbed him of his one chance. Uptown was even worse than on Second Avenue. And in truth he'd lost his driving ambition to direct plays. It was movie directing that excited him. God, the possibilities for new developments!

Somehow he must become part of the movie world. It was young. There was room for a man with his imagination. His vision. Independent pictures were being made in New York despite the problems. 'Outlaw' pictures. So he'd take chances. Adolph Zukor had been an outlaw producer until the Trust licensed *The Prisoner of Zenda*. Other independents with commercial ideas would be licensed.

He'd change his name for picture work. If he had the bad luck to be arrested again, no one would know he was Max Miller. Rissa would not have to worry he'd disgrace the family. If, God forbid, he went to jail, his wife and children would survive. Rissa Lindowska was a star. He had to fight for his own career.

Max haunted the hangouts of the movie people. He read every word that appeared in *Motography*, *Motion Picture World* and *Motion Picture News*. Finally his aggressiveness won out. He was hired as a director by a fly-by-night company operating in Riverdale. His salary was paltry. He would direct one-reelers with the worst talent. But Max was happy. He was learning his craft.

Max followed every happening in the movie field with the dedication of a religious zealot. Some leading stage personalities were lured into filmmaking. Jane Cowl made *The Garden of Lies* for Sam Goldfish in 1915. Lillian Russell appeared in *Wildfire*. They were followed by Fanny Ward, Elsie Janis, Mrs Leslie Carter, Lenore Ulrich. Cecil B. DeMille filmed opera star Geraldine Farrar in *Carmen*.

Max suspected that the audiences who were willing

306

to pay two dollars to see Broadway stars or five dollars to hear the likes of Farrar at the Met were not numerous enough to keep the movie tills jingling. Besides, most of these ladies were past their prime, and the camera was cruel.

Max was sure that Mr Goldfish and Mr Zukor would have to change the fare they offered. Right now William Fox was coining money with a new actress named Theda Bara in a picture called *A Fool There Was*. The press releases said her father was an Arab and her mother a French woman. Over dinner at Luchow's Max was informed that Theda Bara was a nice Jewish girl from Cincinnati, whose real name was Theodosia Goodman.

Max was fascinated by the stories he had heard from the movie crew about the spectacular new film D. W. Griffith had just finished and which was to open at Clune's Auditorium in Los Angeles in February. Called *The Clansman*, it was based on a novel by Thomas Dixon.

Max listened avidly to news of the revolutionary ideas Griffith employed in this new film. The battle scenes were tinted red. Griffith utilized new ways of shooting action scenes. He employed music as never before. Each actor was assigned a special theme.

Busy grinding out one-reelers, Max spent every free moment in studying what was being done by Griffith. He was the master. Max was relieved that Rissa refrained from probing about his activities away from the Fain company. He talked vaguely about working with amateur theatrical groups that were springing up all over the city.

'For what I do they pay me well,' he fabricated. Each week they were putting money into an American bank now. He knew the importance of 'cash in the bank' to Rissa's sense of security. If Rissa suspected he was working on outlaw pictures again, she kept it to herself.

Max made a point of being at the theater for a time each evening, lest Jack believe he had relinquished his position as Rissa's personal manager. He still argued about ads, complained about the choice of plays. And he found himself covertly pursued by Celia's replacement, who had Celia's physical appeal plus a respectable amount of acting talent. She didn't have Rissa's sensitivity, Rissa's timing, Rissa's versatility; but Tania Finkel was an asset to the company.

Sometimes he suspected that Rissa knew he was in Tania's bed at regular intervals. It wasn't that he loved Rissa less, he admitted to himself. But with Rissa he often saw himself a failure. Tania made him feel like a man.

Rissa was unhappy about the breach she felt between Max and herself and placed the blame on her own head. Her fault that they had lost their money in the Mandel Bank. Her fault that Max was not directing the Fain company. Max had expected her to hold out. *Maybe* Jack would have relented. But that was the difference between Max and her. Max was a gambler; she wasn't.

After they made love now, she lay sleepless. Feeling herself no more than a woman with whom Max found physical relief. He reached for her in the night because she was convenient, she taunted herself. Where was the man who had shared his every thought with her?

Max awoke early every morning, played for a while with the children, then disappeared from their lives for long hours. Shirley was sure he was working for a picture company.

'*He won't get caught this time*,' Shirley soothed. 'All over New York people make pictures. Can they arrest them all?' But Rissa worried.

Shirley too was fascinated by the pictures now. She couldn't bear missing an episode of *Perils of Pauline*. She devoured the fan magazines. With awe she told Rissa about the article in the May issue of *McClure's Magazine* that said that Mary Pickford earned one hundred thousand dollars a year.

'Rissa, more than the president. It says here she plays to more people in one night than Maude Adams does in a whole year!'

'Shirley, I won't ever do pictures.' Rissa tensed. Was Max still waiting for her to relent?

Rissa and Shirley sewed for the Red Cross. Rissa joined other Yiddish performers in doing benefits. When the season drew close to the end, Rissa abandoned thoughts of asking Max to rent a cottage for them for the coming hot months. She was anxious to add to their savings.

The nation was dedicated to supplying food, clothing and medicine to the Allies. People howled about the escalating prices of the necessities of life.

On 7 May Americans were shaken by the sinking of the *Lusitania*.

'It'll drag us into war,' Max predicted. 'The most terrible war this world has ever seen.'

Three weeks later Rissa suspected she was pregnant again. She'd wait another two weeks to be sure before she told Max. She prayed for a boy. Let her give Max a son. He'd feel himself a man. Maybe then he would come back to her. It wasn't enough that in the darkness of their bedroom they were together.

When she told Max she was pregnant again, he was upset. He remembered her last pregnancy.

'Sssh,' she whispered. 'You want your son to hear?'

'Ah-ha. You're sure it'll be a boy? You had a special message from God?' This was the old Max, she rejoiced. 'Will we put it back if it's a girl?'

As always when she was pregnant, Rissa felt very close to Max. Together they grieved over the lynching of Leo Frank in Marietta, Georgia. They were upset that Griffith's spectacular new film, *The Birth of a Nation*, appeared sympathetic to the Ku Klux Klan.

Max admitted to deep respect for Griffith's innovations for the film, which Rissa and he saw shortly after its opening at the Liberty Theater. Running two hours, the film was shown twice a day at a two-dollar admission, when the top price for a movie was a quarter, and a nickel was the standard admission.

When the Ku Klux Klan was revived in Atlanta, Max was vitriolic. He yearned to direct a movie that would unmask the Klan. Only now did Max admit to Rissa that he was working in illegal films. He had been promoted to two-reelers and had some freedom to experiment with new ideas. But no one knew him as Max Miller. Even if he was part of another raid, no one would know that Rissa Lindowska's husband was involved.

In February Rissa gave birth with astonishingly little difficulty to their first son. Joseph. Named for Max's father. Max was beside himself with pleasure.

For the *bris* he invited half of Second Avenue, Shirley scolded. But for three days she baked. Endless loaves of *hallah*, honey cakes, sponge cakes came out of the oven. She shopped for herring with onions, sent Max to buy whiskey and wine.

Shirley shared Rissa and Max's happiness. Was not the birth of a son the most joyous moment in life?

Rissa gloried in Max's devotion to the children and her. Joseph, already a tiny replica of his father, had brought Max back to her. It seemed to her that their lovemaking had acquired a new depth.

But Rissa's happiness was clouded by the news of the war in Europe. In the last months the Germans had overrun Lithuania and most of Poland. Russian casualties had passed the four million mark. Russian companies went into battle with one gun for every three to five men. There was a shortage of big guns and shells, inadequate food both for the army and civilians. The Czar had taken command of the armies himself, leaving the evil Rasputin to become virtual ruler of the country.

The Germans had introduced the horror of poison gas in fighting the French troops. German bombs were raining on England. In the United States voices were raised in a cry for preparedness. With the world entering into its third year of war, how long could the United States remain neutral?

In the United States, factories were working around the clock. Civilian war programs abounded. Victory gardens appeared. Herbert Hoover, brought in by President Wilson to supervise the food situation, declared meatless and wheatless days. Americans were exhorted 'not to take the fourth meal.'

In July Rissa realized she was pregnant again. She was ambivalent about this new pregnancy. She would have to leave the theater in mid-December at the latest. In the heart of the season. While she felt herself entrenched with the audiences, she was aware that Tania Finkel was making a place for herself in the company. For the first time she felt a breath of competition.

Like herself Max was ambivalent about another child. But of course, they would both love the new baby. At the theater she told only Jack. Again he cursed Max for interfering with his theatrical season.

'Jesus Christ, Rissa, can't you two learn restraint or caution?' He grinned. 'Knowing Max, you'd better settle for caution. Is he trying to be another Adler?'

Rissa's smile was strained. She remembered that Adler was said to have fathered, in addition to those who bore his name, a string of illegitimate children.

A few days after they went into rehearsal, Tania came into her dressing room to borrow makeup.

'Are you all blown up again?' she asked and Rissa blushed. 'That Max,' she laughed. 'He wants to win the fucking award of the year!'

Max said Tania was the only actress he knew who could use dirty words and still look like a duchess. Rissa liked Tania. She could like her even more if she was sure Max hadn't slept with her.

Max prophesied that Tania would not be around Second Avenue too long. She was American-born with aspirations to be a Broadway star. But in one area Tania was unexpected support for Rissa. She hated films with a vengeance. Max said this was only because she knew she'd never photograph well.

Shorty before Hanukkah Rissa withdrew from the company. As in each pregnancy she spent long hours each day with books and newspapers. Like many of those on the lower East Side she was emotionally involved in the struggle of the Russian people.

Russian soldiers were deserting by the thousands. The country was besieged by strikes. At the approach of the New Year Rasputin was murdered. Revolution was in the air. On 8 March striking workers stormed the bakeries. The next day mobs roamed the streets. For the first time the cossacks refused to fire on the crowds. On 15 March Czar Nicholas abdicated.

When the news of the abdication reached New York there was jubilation among the Jews, long victims of the Russian pogroms. Rissa and Max sat at the breakfast table discussing the news of the abdication. All at once she stiffened in pain. She was going into labor. She had not shared even with Max or Shirley her anxiety about this latest pregnancy. The other babies had been small. The doctor warned that this time she carried a large child. She had kept her fears from Max and Shirley.

'Rissa?' Max put down his cup of coffee.

'We're off to the races again.' She tried to smile.

'Shirley!' Max yelled.

'Max, the baby won't be born for a while,' she laughed, then clenched her teeth because already a second pain racked her body.

Despite her protestations Max called the doctor while Shirley helped her into the bedroom. By the time the doctor arrived she was in hard labor, of a kind that was worse than she had ever experienced.

'Max, get the children out of the apartment,' she managed to say between the pains that were coming one on top of another now. 'They shouldn't have to hear.'

'I won't leave you now,' Max protested.

'Call somebody,' Shirley ordered. 'Mrs Gallagher upstairs will take them.'

Max took the children to their neighbor and rushed back to the apartment. The doctor was anxious. He wanted to move Rissa to the hospital where anesthesia would be available.

'No!' she gasped. 'No anesthesia. It might hurt the baby. I want to have my baby here!'

In mid-afternoon Rissa gave birth to a third daughter. Katie, named for her aunt who had died in the pogrom. The doctor told both Rissa and Max that she must never have another child.

Rissa's recovery was slow. She spent hours sitting in the garden with the newspapers across her lap, reading the daily fresh horrors of the war in Europe. Then on 6 April the United States declared war on Germany.

Patriotism gripped the nation. In New York and Hollywood, producers raced to make films about the war. On Second Avenue timely plays appeared. *Jewish War Brides, Yiddish Martyr in America, The World in Flames*. Rissa joined other Second Avenue stars selling Liberty Bonds and raising money for the Red Cross.

On 26 June the first American troops landed in France. Rissa thanked God that Max, with a wife and four children, was exempt from military service. Fleetingly she feared Max might enlist in a moment of impassioned rage at the atrocities that rocked Europe. But Max was a pacifist.

Max was excited now about the prospect of directing a feature film to be shot out in Fort Lee. A six-reeler! He hoped that Mattox, who had surfaced again and was pushing for a quality film, would be recognized by the Trust. Then his real name could appear on the film.

Though a poet named Vachel Lindsay, whom Max encountered at regular intervals in Greenwich Village cafés, protested loudly in the *Atlantic Monthly* and *New Republic* that the early one-reel movies were true American poems, the nickelodeons were being replaced with attractive and comfortable theaters showing features films. The Strand occupied a whole block on Broadway between Forty-seventh and Forty-eighth streets, and seated three thousand five hundred. Marcus Lowe was converting some of his vaudeville houses to feature films.

Movies were becoming big business. Adolph Zukor

and Jesse Lasky had taken over the Paramount releasing company. Sam Goldfish had withdrawn from the Lasky organization to open Goldwyn Pictures with Edgar Selwyn – and henceforward would be known as Samuel Goldwyn. Now stocks of the film companies were put on the market. Wall Street took notice of the important new industry. Even Rissa, Max told himself, would have to be impressed by the future of movies.

With Max's film all set to start shooting, Mattox announced that plans must be canceled. His backer had run out. He needed another six thousand to bring in the picture.

'Clark, wait,' Max urged. 'Let me talk with my wife. Maybe we can bring in the money.' If he brought in the money he would be a partner. They'd make a killing.

Rissa was aghast at the prospect of withdrawing almost their entire savings. Max's movie was a gamble. How could they gamble with four children to raise? They would soon need a larger apartment. Already she dreamed of college for the children. Suppose something happened to one of them, God forbid, and they had to pay big doctor bills?

'I'll talk to Jack about your directing this season.' Rissa was frightened by the desperation she saw in Max's eyes. 'I'll talk to him today.'

'You'll talk.' Max dismissed this with impatience. 'And Jack will say no.'

'I'll tell him I won't play,' she insisted. 'Even with

the new salary you negotiated.' Rissa's new salary was the gossip of Second Avenue.

'Talk, Rissa.' But Max was skeptical.

They were one week from the beginning of rehearsals. Jack was astounded when Rissa approached him.

'Rissa, you know. Leo directs.'

'Leo will ruin the new plays this season. He doesn't understand them.' Max had pushed Jack into doing three new plays by new playwrights that Rissa and he found thrilling. 'Jack, you have to do this for me.' Her eyes pleaded with him.

'Rissa, the theater is business. We try to make money.'

'The theater is made up of people, Jack. There has to be room for heart. I have to give this to Max.'

'All right,' he acquiesced. 'Max directs the *first* play. But if it looks bad, he goes out. I can't afford to lose money because Max is giving you a hard time.'

Max was disbelieving at first, then exhilarated. He had great belief in the play. It was a perfect vehicle for Rissa. He threw himself into the rehearsals with an enthusiasm that transmitted itself to most of the cast. Leo and Sara were difficult.

'Leo's nose is out of joint,' Tania told Rissa. 'He can't stand the boy genius.'

Rissa marveled at the freshness of Max's direction, his innovative ideas. But Leo complained bitterly to Jack. All of a sudden Jack was sitting in at rehearsals. Two days before they were to open, Jack asked Max and Rissa to join him in the office at their lunch break. Neither suspected what Jack had in mind. In short, clipped words Jack fired Max. Leo was to take over the direction.

'We don't need revolutionaries on Second Avenue,' Jack scoffed when Max protested. 'We'll give the audiences what they've always paid to see. Not fancy nonsense. Let somebody else gamble on new ideas.'

Max stared at Jack in disbelief. Jack turned his back and walked out of the theater.

'That goddamn bastard!' Max seethed. 'Tell him you'll walk out.'

'Max, how can I?' Rissa was stunned. 'I have a contract. If I walk out on Jack, who would ever hire me again?'

'You'd let him do this to me?' It was a stranger staring at her.

'Max, what can I do?'

'We're getting out of New York,' Max's face was set. 'Clark's out in California now. He has new financing. I'll talk to him about a job.'

'But I have a contract here,' she reminded.

'Fuck the contract,' he brushed this aside. 'We're leaving for California. We have money in the bank. It's time to gamble on my career.'

'Max, how long will that money last in California?' She yearned to do this for Max, but reality intruded. They had four children, here she had regular work, a fine salary. 'Max, after we paid for the train trip to California, we'd have only enough to live on for a year or so.'

'That's long enough.' Max was grim. 'We'll stretch it to two years if I need that long. Rissa, I'm the husband. The man makes the decisions!'

'I can't leave New York.' Rissa was trembling. 'We have security here. We talked about buying a house in another year or two. How can we give that up for a movie gamble? We have to think of the children – '

'I'm thinking of all of us! What kind of a family is it when the wife makes all the money? We should have gone out to California four years ago. Damn it, Rissa, let me be a *mentsh*!'

'I can't go, Max.' She clutched at reality. 'How do we know what'll be in California?'

'Rissa, I'm going,' Max said with a cold detachment that frightened her. 'With or without you. Here my wife is a star,' he said derisively, 'but I'm nobody.'

'Max, if you leave, our marriage will be over.' Max would be unfaithful to her. He was not a man to be without a woman. 'I'll never let you see the children again,' she threatened in panic. Her world in shambles. This couldn't happen to her. It was a scene in a play.

'Go back to rehearsal, Rissa,' Max said. 'I have to go up to Grand Central to see about a ticket to California.'

Rissa rushed back to the apartment as soon as rehearsals were over. Shirley was in the kitchen. Her stricken face told Rissa she knew.

'Shirley, where is he?' Rissa asked. *They had to talk.*

'He packed up a suitcase, he kissed the children and he left,' Shirley's voice broke. 'Rissa, how did this happen?'

319

'I told him he could never see the children again if he left.'

'He said his train was scheduled to leave in two hours.' Shirley seemed numb with shock.

'When was that?'

'About an hour and a half ago,' Shirley judged. 'Rissa, he won't stay. He'll come back.'

'He'll stay.' Rissa fought back tears. 'Shirley, I have to go to the station. I have to see him once more.'

Rissa took the subway up to Grand Central. It would be faster than trying to find a cab. She paused for a moment before the handsome classical structure that was Grand Central Station, opened to an admiring public on 2 February 1913. Her heart pounding, she walked into the awesome cavern of the grand concourse with its marble wainscoting, its curved ceiling with a mural that was a page from a medieval manuscript on astronomy.

She searched for someone to tell her where to find the train to Chicago, first stop on his journey west. She spied the information counter and hurried over.

Max's train was scheduled to depart in a few minutes. She hurried toward the gate where the Pullman awaited its passengers, knowing only that she must have one more glimpse of Max before he moved out of her life.

'Max!' The name slipped through her lips without sound as she froze at attention.

Max was striding toward her. His face stern yet sad. He hadn't seen her. *She didn't want him to see her*. But when he disappeared through the gate, she hurried forward. Several late arrivals, fearful of missing the train, pushed past her.

She hovered at the head of the ramp, searching for Max among the last boarding passengers. *There he was*. Max Miller. Her husband. Walking forever out of her life.

She saw Max disappear into a center car of the train. She stood there, watching while the train began the slow underground chug that would take it out of the station. Last night Max had held her in his arms and made love to her. How would she sleep tonight without Max beside her? How would she sleep in the frightening, empty years ahead?

Two nights later Rissa opened in the drama of a beautiful young deserted bride. Leo had redirected the cast with the heavy hand of melodrama he admired. But in her dressing room, laying out her first-act costume chosen by Max at the little shop on Fifth Avenue that specialized in Paris imports, Rissa knew she would play from her heart tonight. The way *Max* had directed her.

On her entrance she heard the usual admiring comments about her taupe silk frock, shown in a recent edition of *Harper's Bazaar*. But as the play progressed — as she threw herself into the role of the heartbroken young bride whose husband had just left her, she heard the sobs in the audience. And she knew.

With the speed in which gossip sped around the lower East Side, they had heard that Rissa Lindowska's husband had left her.

24

The Santa Fe's deluxe California Limited, which Max had boarded in Chicago, sped westward at ninety miles an hour. The massive coal-burning locomotive pulled the train across the plains of Kansas where corn shimmered over endless acres and sunflowers grew to staggering heights.

Still suffering from shock, Max sat staring out the window of his compartment without seeing. Only when the rumblings in his stomach told him that it was time to eat did he emerge from his compartment and go into the magnificent wood-paneled dining car, where waiters in immaculate white jackets served gourmet meals.

He upbraided himself for walking out on his wife and children. But each time another part of him answered that Rissa was walking out on him. A wife should go with her husband. Didn't she know that somehow he would manage to provide for them? A man could find a job in the factories if he had to. War had brought prosperity to the country. But that wouldn't have been necessary, he remembered with a new bitterness; they had money enough to last a year while he broke into the movie business. Rissa's money. She wasn't willing to gamble on her husband.

He had taken from their last joint account only sufficient money to pay for his transportation to

California plus enough to cover two months' modest expenses. Money that *he* had earned. In two months, he promised himself, he would have a job. What remained in the bank was Rissa's.

He reexamined his life in minute detail. He had come to New York with such confidence. Such ambition. *Where had he gone wrong?*

He never should have allowed himself to become involved in the Yiddish theater. He should have fought for a foothold on Broadway. Then he would have had the background to push his way into the movie Trust companies. Moviemakers had respect for Broadway. This time things would be different. He had always been an outsider in the Yiddish theater despite his Jewishness. Jack laughed and called him 'the *goy* from Georgia.' But in pictures he had come home. He belonged in the movie industry. He would become a power there. Before he was thirty-five.

With the realization that within another forty-eight hours he would be in Los Angeles, Max went into the dining car tonight with a new sense of destiny. It was late. Only a few people sat at the tables, draped in the pristine white cloths that reminded Max of Friday-night suppers in Belleville, Georgia. He focused on the menu. His funds were limited. Max chose a simple dinner.

When the waiter left, he stared out into the night. Now Rissa would be leaving the theater. Shirley would be home with the children. All of them asleep. Did Clara and Rae cry when they realized papa wouldn't be there to play with them in the morning? Joseph and Katie were too young to be aware.

323

'Do you mind if I sit at your table?' a feminine voice inquired, and Max turned from the window with a start.

'No,' he said quickly and then remembered that most of the tables were empty.

'I'm so tired of sitting in my compartment and just staring out the window.' She sat in the chair across from him. 'I haven't talked to anybody since I got on the train in Chicago.' She was a roly-poly but pretty girl in her early twenties, with light brown hair and appealing blue eyes. 'I'm Laura Ainsley.'

'Max Miller,' he introduced himself. He suspected her name was made up.

'Are you going out to work for one of the picture companies?' she probed. 'You look like a movie actor.' Her admiration was a balm to his shaken ego.

'I'm not an actor.' He hesitated. 'I've directed some films back in New York. Nothing good. Two-reelers.'

'The train's full of stage people going out to work in pictures,' she confided. 'Soon every movie will be made out there. The California sun is wonderful for film. The whites and blacks come out real sharp and firm. Only the business offices will stay in New York,' she predicted.

They paused while Laura made a swift decision from the menu and the waiter left them alone.

'How do you know so much about pictures?' Max was intrigued by her aura of self-confidence.

Laura giggled.

'Since *Photo Play* brought out its first magazine six years ago, I haven't missed an issue. When I was out living in Illinois, I read Louella Parsons' motion-picture gossip column for the Chicago *Record-Herald* every day and the big film supplement on Sundays. When I couldn't get a job on *Photo Play*, I moved to New York and got myself hired as a typist for *Movie Play*. I spent ten months there hoping to be a writer. They wouldn't let me, so I decided to go out to Hollywood to be a free-lance reporter. If I send them stories postmarked from Hollywood, they'll buy. I'm awfully good. Did you know that in Hollywood they're paying Broadway stars fifty thousand dollars to make a picture? My father hasn't made that much in his whole life.' Max recognized the glitter that came into her limpid blue eyes.

'Not everybody's making that much money,' Max warned.

'*We* will,' Laura decided and laughed. 'Where are you staying in Hollywood?'

'I don't know yet,' he admitted.

'I got the name of a rooming house. Somebody on *Movie Play* gave it to me. If you want to, you can come along with me,' she offered.

When they left the dining car, Laura invited him into her compartment. Half an hour later she invited him into her berth. Max told himself there was no reason to refuse. How better to spend the long hours before they arrived in Los Angeles?

Twelve hours later they were traveling across the desert. The heat was unbearable. Laura was sure it was hot only in her compartment. They moved to Max's. The tiny little fan provided by the railroad was useless. Max opened the window. They were assaulted by a minor sandstorm. Max hastily closed the window.

They found minor diversion when the train stopped at Albuquerque. Laura was fascinated by the Indians selling silver jewelry at the station. Then they moved on, beyond the desert into the cool mountain air of the Rockies. Between conversation they locked the compartment door and made love. Laura was explicit. She expected no commitments in return for her favors. She told Max without self-pity about the suffocating drabness of her life on an Illinois farm, how she had run away from home to Chicago to make a new life for herself.

'Until then I didn't really know what I was going to do with my life. Except that I was going to be rich.' She studied Max for a few moments. 'Now I know. I want to write about the movie stars. Look, I've got contacts out in Hollywood. We could help each other.'

'How?' He was amused. A typist at *Movie Play* had contacts?'

'I've got phone numbers to call. I snitched them from the files,' she admitted. 'But when I call and say I'm out visiting in Hollywood and I'm with *Movie Play* – ' She giggled. 'They don't have to know I was a typist, and I've quit. I'll get invited to parties. That's how you get to know the right people out there. And you're gorgeous-looking – it'd be good for me to walk in with somebody like you.'

'So let's go to the parties.' Max was ebullient. Back in New York his social life had been limited to late suppers at the Café Royale or lunch at Ratner's. The only party Rissa and he ever gave — after their wedding reception — was Joseph's *bris*. They had lived in the tight little world of Yiddish actors.

With comfortable camaraderie Max and Laura viewed the splendor of the Rockies. They shared a sense of anticipation when, at last, the scenery evolved into endless acres of orange and lemon groves, and they knew they were approaching their destination.

Together, as though they had known each other for years, they left the drab, dumpy, red brick building that was the Los Angeles railroad station and walked out into the burning heat of the day. Sunlight gave the streets an aura of gold that looked indeed as if the streets were paved with it.

Max and Laura traveled by trolley to the Los Angeles suburb of Hollywood. In the four years since a Scottish artist in Sir Henry Irving's company persuaded Jesse Lasky, Samuel Goldfish and Cecil B. DeMille to rent a barn on Sunset Boulevard and Vine Street for the purpose of making it into a film studio, Hollywood had become a boom town.

'The Jesse Lasky Company came out here three years ago with six thousand dollars,' Laura told Max while the trolley car carried them to their destination. 'Now it's a four-million-dollar concern.' Max winced, remembering when Rissa refused to invest six thousand in Clark Mattox's film.

They left the trolley at the proper stop and began to look for the rooming house where Laura was sure they could find accommodation. Max was shocked

327

when he saw signs on the lawns that read, 'No Jews, dogs or picture people allowed.'

'Three or four years ago it was like that all over Hollywood,' Laura reported. Grimacing in distaste though she herself fit none of the three categories. 'Folks out here didn't mind stage actors, but anybody who worked in the "flickers" was a bum to them.'

'What about the place we're supposed to stay?' Max's bile rose at such intolerance.

'No problem. The fellow who told me about the rooming house is the son of a rabbi. His name is Eric Wickersham. He plays English character roles. Did you know that Douglas Fairbanks is supposed to be half-Jewish?'

'No,' Max conceded. Involuntarily he thought how this would please Shirley.

'Of course, the *Movie Play* wouldn't run that,' Laura said. 'They have to go along with the studios if they expect to get cooperation.'

Laura and he found rooms — separate with an adjoining bath — at Mrs Madigan's rooming house on Western Avenue. Max was charmed by Hollywood with its oleander trees and towering palms, the flowers that blossomed everywhere. The winding country road lined with pepper trees that was called Sunset Boulevard.

Then he came face to face with another Hollywood — the boom town. Cowboys poured into town because they could earn seven dollars and fifty cents a day making movies. Ambitious mothers arrived on every train, hoping to make their daughters into another Mary Pickford. Stunt men were on hand to take any risk for a fast dollar.

Hollywood was an extension of the studio sets. Mack Sennett cops were filmed racing down Sunset Boulevard. Actors in full makeup and costume lunched in the small parks. The air crackled with the knowledge that this was a make-believe world that was unlike anything else on this earth.

Max sought out Clark Mattox on Poverty Row. Here were the tiny offices of the shoestring producers, the hopeful promoters, lined up one after another along Beachwood Drive and around the corner on Sunset Boulevard. Behind the offices were stages available for rent when a 'quickie' producer needed interior shots.

Max found Clark with his feet on the desk, trying to make a deal on the phone, full of big stories about what he was about to accomplish. But he admitted he wasn't shooting a film at the moment. He urged Max to keep in touch.

'If you're not doing anything tonight, I'll take you to a party over at Mack Sennett's place, booze and women like you've never seen!'

Max went to perpetual parties for almost a week. Then he came down to earth, wrote Rissa a long letter about the glories of Hollywood and considered how he would pay his rent and buy food when his meager bankroll evaporated.

Laura knocked on his door early on a bright sunny morning with a cup of coffee she'd made on her one-burner hot plate. When Max was sufficiently awake to comprehend, she informed him that in view of their financial necessity they would report for 'extra' work at a film company reputed to be hiring extras and bit players.

Within forty minutes they were lined up in the extras' compound, more popularly called the 'cattle yard,' waiting for an assistant director to pick them out for work. Laura whispered that some people waited there for months without getting picked. But if they worked, it was three dollars a day.

To Max's astonishment both Laura and he were picked. He suspected it was because the assistant director remembered Laura from an all-night party.

At the end of four days' work the picture was finished. Max and Laura were unemployed again. But Laura had hauled out her relic of a typewriter. She hammered away at an article about Mary Pickford based on what she'd picked up from other extras on the picture.

'Sweet as sugar,' Laura giggled. 'But movie fans all think she's this darling little girl who's never been touched. She's a married woman!'

'You're writing that?' Max was curious.

'Golly, no.' Laura was shocked. 'And spoil the dreams of all her fans? I can't say that any more than I can say she likes to hit the bottle. But they're bound to find out about the husband soon.'

'I've got to talk to Clark,' Max said with frustration. 'When the hell is he going to have backing for a picture?'

'Why don't you help him look?' Laura asked. Her

eyes crinkled in laughter. 'Max, you're a man who can always find a woman with money.'

Rissa dreaded walking alone into the apartment each night after a performance. Shirley made a point of waiting up for her.

During rehearsals and performances she was able to put out of her mind the ugly reality of her life. She was a deserted wife. But to walk into the apartment and know Max was not there was torment.

At the theater there was a pact not to talk about Max. She had told the others that Max had gone out to Hollywood to talk about making a film. But they knew. Jack had thrown him out as director, and Max had left her.

Was Max all right? But logic told her there could have been no train accident. She would have read about it in the newspapers. Why didn't he write? He knew she would worry about him. He went out with so little money. Into a strange new world. Even though he left in such a rage, he knew she would want to hear from him.

Words from the Talmud flashed through her mind: '*Husband and wife are like one flesh.*' Max had torn their flesh apart. '*A man must not make a woman weep, for God counts her tears.*' Her tears, in her solitary bed, would make a river.

She lay awake each night until she slept from exhaustion. From habit she slept on the left side of the bed, as though waiting for Max to come into the bedroom and slide into place. How could Max have expected her to walk out on the company? Who would ever hire her again? What else could she do but act in the Yiddish theater?

Suppose she had been willing to gamble on going to California. What would happen when their money ran out? Max had vowed never to work in a store again. But if she was there with the children, he'd have to take some job he hated – and then he would hate her and the children for making him do it.

Now she told herself that Max would tire of California. He would miss the excitement of the city. He would miss the children. He would miss her. He would come back home again and everything would be all right.

Two weeks after Max left, Rissa came home from a full day at the theater to be met at the door by Shirley.

'I saw you coming from the window.' Shirley's face was incandescent as she extended a letter. 'From Max.'

Rissa trembled as she held the letter in her hand. She was afraid to open it.

'Read it,' Shirley commanded.

Max wrote like a devoted husband reporting on his activities away from home – though there was no reference to his return.

'California is magnificent,' he wrote. 'I'm meeting fascinating people.' *Women*, Rissa translated.

He was convinced that he would make the right connections shortly. Optimism crackled from the three pages of tightly written script. And he missed the children and her.

'What does he say?' Shirley could not restrain her eagerness.

'Here.' Rissa handed over the letter. A coldness filtered through her despite the heat of the early September night. *He said nothing about coming home.*

Rissa waited three days before she answered Max's letter. Shirley hovered over her every moment that she was home, urging her to write. When she did, the letter was calm and impersonal.

At Shirley's prompting she reported on the children's activities. Clara was impatiently waiting to begin kindergarten. Joseph had his first haircut. Only when Shirley sat in the chair and held him in her lap would Joseph allow the barber to cut. Now he looked like a real boy instead of a beautiful little girl. Katie was teething. At Jack's urging she would allow Clara and Rae to appear in one of the new plays, though only on matinee days. They wanted to be with mama on the stage.

From birth the children heard both English and Yiddish. An unspoken pact existed between Rissa and Shirley; the children would speak both English and Yiddish.

Rissa refrained from writing Max that each night Clara asked plaintively, 'When will papa be home?' And each night she said, 'Soon.' After the first week Rae had stopped asking.

Rissa wrote Max, who kept insisting that the end of immigration would be the death knell of the Yiddish theater, that the theaters were packed. Audiences sought relief from the horror of the war in Europe. Many had family caught in the Old Country.

Most of the plays, she admitted, were *shund*. But already it was becoming obvious that those who were born in America or arrived as babies were demanding better theater. The kind of theater that Max used to talk about doing on Second Avenue.

Weeks blended into months with no indication that Max was about to return from Hollywood. He wrote brief, sporadic letters, which she steeled herself not to answer immediately. More by what Max didn't say than what he did she sensed he was making little progress.

Hanukkah had always been a special time for Max and her; he had delighted in bringing some small present on each of the eight nights. Last Hanukkah he had given her a gold-plated Kiddush cup for the Sabbath meal.

On this Hanukkah Rissa focused on the children. She told them about the Feast of Hanukkah, which celebrated the victory of the Jews over the Syrian tyrant Antiochus IV in about 165 B.C. She told them about the miracle of the oil lamp which had burned for eight days in the temple of Jerusalem.

Each night Rissa burned another candle, according to tradition, in the golden menorah she had bought in a fine downtown store. Instead of Hanukkah *gelt*, she gave the children gifts.

'They're from papa,' she said.

But Max didn't even remember that Hanukkah was here. He didn't remember his wife and family in New York.

25

As Max had done, Rissa fought now with Jack about the quality of their plays. Why couldn't they do plays by Asch, Pinski, Kobrin? The younger theatergoers made fresh demands. But Jack complained that they couldn't afford to take gambles. One bad week could set them back a month and a half.

'Let Thomashefsky bring over new playwrights and take gambles,' Jack brushed aside her entreaties.

An unexpected closeness developed between Rissa and Tania despite Rissa's suspicion that Max had been in her bed. Tania was almost abrasively honest, which Rissa found refreshing, and she shared her eagerness to do fine plays.

On impulse Rissa invited Tania to come to the apartment for the last night of the Hanukkah festivities. While the children played with their *dreidels* and munched nuts in the dining room, Rissa and Tania sat before the fire burning in the parlor grate.

'Sometimes I think I want success more than anything else,' Tania laughed, 'so I can have a flat with steam heat. Instead of a stove that burns my *tsitskes* and freezes my *toches*.'

'You're a very good actress, Tania,' Rissa said with respect. 'Jack would love to dump Sara and have you play her roles. If he does, you can have a flat with steam heat.'

'I stay on Second Avenue because I know I can eat,' Tania admitted. 'But I mean to go uptown. I mean to shine right along with Ethel Barrymore and Billie Burke and Laurette Taylor. Uptown I will be Terry French.' She paused. 'I know you don't like to talk about it, but what do you hear from Max?'

Rissa was disconcerted. At the theater nobody questioned her about Max. She had told them Max went to California. Her attitude made it clear she did not mean to expand on the subject.

'He writes that Hollywood is fascinating,' Rissa faltered. 'He's done some work as an extra. He hopes to find a directing job.'

Tania chuckled.

'God, he would have been out of his mind if he had been in the theater when D. W. Griffith came downtown to see us last week!'

'Max says Griffith is the master.' Rissa remembered Griffith rising from his seat to address the cast with his admiration. '*What a privilege it is to see your work.*' After the performance the cast had gone with him for supper at Moskowitz and Lupowitz. Why hadn't Max been here to enjoy this with her?

'Max doesn't talk about when he'll return?' Tania probed.

Rissa felt color rise in her cheeks.

'Max is busy trying to be a director.' Despite herself sarcasm crept into her voice.

'Rissa, I know it's none of my business – ' Tania leaned forward earnestly. 'But sometimes I think Max feels you're married more to your career than to him.'

'Because I refused to leave New York to go on a

wild-goose chase with him?' Defensiveness evoked defiance in her. 'He's a married man with four children. He should remember that.'

'So maybe having a wife who's a star made him feel less than a *mentsh*. The season closes in four months. You don't go on tour with the children. You say you'll never play vaudeville or musicals.'

'With my voice it would be an insult to the audience.' Rissa's smile was rueful.

'Why don't you take the children out to California for the summer?' Tania urged. 'Max would be so happy.'

Rissa stared at Tania. At unwary moments she had thought about this for the past few weeks. But wouldn't that look as though she were giving in?

'It would only be for the summer,' Rissa stipulated. 'I'll have a commitment for next season.' If she went out to California and saw Max, would she have the courage to leave and come back to New York? But she couldn't desert what she had built up in the Yiddish theater. She *would* come back.

Why couldn't Max come back and work in films in New York? The Trust was broken now. Everybody was making films without worrying about lawsuits or arrests. Max had gone out to California because of Clark Mattox, but he wrote nothing about working with him. *Let him come back to New York and look for a directing job here.* There were still as many films made in New York as in Hollywood, though the fan magazines made it seem otherwise. They didn't have to worry about Max's earning money. He could take all the time he needed.

'So write Max you'll be out when you close at the theater.' Tania dragged Rissa back to their conversation. 'Let him look for a house for you out there.'

Rissa waited for Max's next letter, perversely slow in coming because she was so eager to give him her news. How could she survive without Max? she would go to Hollywood with the children and Shirley and convince Max he must come back to New York with them.

She was impatient with the constant bickering at the theater. Leo was impossible. Jack was afraid of change. Her mind churned with the possibility of becoming a star-manager.

She was fearful of touching the money that she had built up in their bank account after the horror of the bank failure, yet instinct told her this was the time to move ahead. For weeks she had been conscious of the empty movie house on Irving Place that had shown German films for several years. With no foreign films coming into the country, the movie house had closed. The house was empty. It would be easy to change it over from a movie house to a theater again.

Max would come back to New York, and he would direct at the Lindowska-Miller theater.

In his small shabby room on Washington Street Max dressed in preparation for the lineup of Hollywood parties to which Laura had inveigled invitations for them, or which they were prepared to crash. On the threshold of New Year's Eve, 1918, he was assaulted by visions of Rissa.

338

By now Rissa knew she could manage well without him. But she missed him in her bed. Or *did* she? Men must be beating down the doors to Rissa Lindowska. Who remembered that she was Rissa Miller?

The homesickness that attacked him at regular intervals was a tidal wave tonight. He missed Rissa and the children. He missed the city and a winter that brought cool temperatures. He yearned for the sight of Washington Square blanketed in snow.

He had been in Hollywood over four months without making one of those great contacts Laura kept insisting would come along. All that he had seen were 'extra' jobs. For weeks Clark had been on a seesaw, and he with him. One day they were scheduled to start production. The next day the production was off.

What did it matter that Clark had picked up a name player between films and that the actor agreed to work on a quickie for a percentage and nothing else? That he himself had worked out a script line that would utilize a set they could rent from Paramount for a pittance? Without money from the banks or a releasing company, they couldn't shoot.

Tonight the future seemed a dreary dead end. The sole bright light that Max could see was the collapse of the Trust. An avalanche of sharp-minded entrepreneurs had invaded the film industry and forced recognition for themselves. Among them Carl Laemmle, Adolph Zukor, Jesse Lasky and Samuel Goldfish.

'Max?' Laura called from behind the door of their adjoining bathroom. 'You almost ready?'

'A couple of minutes,' Max said and reached into a drawer for a tie. He paused with a twinge of nostalgia. Rissa had bought most of his ties.

Was Rissa right? Was Hollywood an insane gamble? *Should he go back to New York?* He had just about enough cash to buy a ticket home. But what would he find in New York but more frustration? His wife and family were in New York, his mind taunted. What was he doing in this insane town, where make-believe was the norm and reality an oddity?

While Max swore over the task of knotting his tie, Laura knocked.

'Max!' Despite all her show of optimism, Laura was anxious. She had sold one article in four months to *Movie Play* in New York. She fumed that she couldn't break into the elite ranks of the *Photo Play* writers.

Max pulled the door open, inspected Laura with admiration. In the four months in Hollywood she had slimmed down. Also, she had borrowed a Hupmobile from an assistant casting director who'd taken a train home for two weeks.

'How do I look?'

'Take off another ten pounds and you'll be in pictures,' he predicted.

'That's not what I'm after,' Laura reminded. 'Let's move.'

They left their rooming house and drove up into the hills, where the successful of Hollywood – stars, producers, directors – lived in elaborate Spanish stucco haciendas. Laura was ever awed by the splendor of these mansions with their gardens, fountains, swimming pools and tennis courts, that were miraculously open to those with the *hutzpah* to crash.

They moved from one party to another. Max trusted Laura's instincts. He enjoyed the convivial spirits everywhere that for the moment blocked out reality. In truth Hollywood was as exciting at night – except for private parties – as Belleville, Georgia, Max thought in wry amusement. Where was there to go in the evening in Hollywood? The weekly dance at the Hollywood Hotel, for those who could afford this, or the Montmartre or the Ship Café on a pier above the Pacific. When Laura and he had the price of a few mugs of lager, they visited the Ship Café.

Max went through the screeching scene of midnight in a slight alcoholic haze. Laura disappeared with a Latin-type actor while a gorgeous seventeen-year-old, mistaking him for a Hollywood bigwig, dragged him into one of the endless upstairs bedrooms that made the home of his current host appear more like a hotel than a private house.

When the would-be starlet discovered Max was unemployed like herself, she left the bed, put on her clothes again and stalked from the room in irritation. When he emerged a few minutes later, he spied Laura at the foot of the stairs waiting for him.

'There's nobody here that can do us any good,' she reported. 'Let's go on.'

'To Sennett's place?' Max inquired with interest.

'We'll go to Sennett's party last,' Laura said. 'Anything goes there. His parties are bawdy as hell.'

341

'We haven't been going to church picnics,' Max reminded. The lack of inhibitions at Hollywood parties had been unnerving at first. He had been shocked at his own reservations. But everything that happened in this town was unreal.

Their next party was in an imposing colonial mansion set high on a hill. The ballroom-size parlor was furnished with priceless antiques. A trio of oriental rugs were islands of beauty on the yellow marble floors. The room was lighted as though a film were to be shot at any moment.

As usual Laura left him to circulate. He knew someone female and beautiful would approach him soon. This town was full of beautiful girls looking for a director or producer to make them a star. He had apparently acquired an air that put him in the line of fire.

Across the room a tall blonde spilling out of a black satin, coral-beaded dinner dress was casting avid glances in his direction over the head of a short balding man whose hand moved higher above her waist than decorum allowed. Max saw Laura pause in her stroll across the room to talk with them for a few moments. Who was the man? he wondered in curiosity. Laura reserved that faintly reverent look only for people who could do her some good.

Laura joined him as he detached himself from an overly pretty young man with obvious intent.

'Max, see the blonde by the potted palm?' Laura's eyes glittered.

'The one you were talking to just now?' Max focused on the girl.

Laura nodded.

'Go over and make a fuss over her. She's doing a picture for Klein-Meyers Films. I'll explain everything later. It's complicated. But make it look like you're mad about her.'

'What about the man with her?'

'He's leaving. She's Cleo Forbes. He's Arnie Cadman, the director.'

Max pushed his way through the partygoers to Cleo Forbes who wore as much makeup as she'd wear on camera. She was as tall as he was. Her green eyes said she was in perpetual heat.

Max and Cleo exchanged the usual party talk. Then Laura startled him by moving in close with the camera that accompanied her everywhere. As though on cue Cleo smiled dazzlingly and thrust her lush bosom against his chest. Remembering Laura's orders he dropped his arm about her waist a second before Laura snapped their picture. Cleo and he blinked for an instant from the blinding flash.

'You're taking me to the Ship Café tomorrow,' Cleo murmured. 'Pick me up at my place at seven.' She opened her small evening bag and pulled out a slip of paper with an address scrawled on it. 'Sweetie, I can't wait.'

All at once Arnie Cadman walked toward them. Laura reached for Max's arm and pulled him away.

'Are we leaving already?' Max was surprised.

'On to Mack Sennett's while I can still navigate,' Laura giggled. 'One more drink and I'll be seeing four of you.'

* * *

343

Max awoke at four in the afternoon. His head ached. His mouth felt as though the German army had marched through it. Despite the pounding of his head Max tried to restructure the events of the evening. What the hell was that business with Cleo Forbes? Laura had never got around to explaining.

Max groaned. Christ, he was supposed to take her to the Ship Café tonight. He doubted that he could abandon a horizontal position with any comfort. He flinched at a knock on the door of the connecting bathroom. It could only be Laura.

He struggled into a semisitting position.

Laura came in with a cup of black coffee. He grimaced at the aroma.

'You're seeing Cleo tonight,' she reminded and fished a bill out of her bra. 'It's on me.'

'What's this Cleo Forbes deal?' Max ignored the coffee.

'I have to get an item into Louella Parsons' column about Cleo and Arnie Cadman. Cleo has to be seen with somebody that looks like a sizzling new male star. I'll tack on a phony name – you don't have to worry. Nobody'll know it's you.' She paused with an air of drama. 'If I make Parsons' column, Arnie Cadman promises to get you into Klein-Meyers Films as his assistant director.'

Max gaped in astonishment. He'd heard stories about stars who kicked back a third of their fancy salaries to their producers, writers who paid off their directors. Now at last he was seeing on a personal basis some of the trade-offs in the movie business.

'I don't get it. Why didn't Cadman set it up with one of his actors? Why me?'

'Because Cadman is hot for Cleo.' Laura shoved the coffee cup into his hands. 'He doesn't trust his actors. He figures you want the job bad. You won't touch the merchandise. And Max, you fill the bill. If you weren't so dumb, you could be the next Milton Sills. Louella Parsons will *believe* Cleo is having a big romance with a new star.'

'I don't believe this.' Max slowly shook his head. Then he became alarmed. 'You're sending in the picture?'

'That'll cinch it.' Laura was triumphant.

'Laura, I have a wife in New York!'

'Parsons' column doesn't appear in New York,' she soothed. 'It's a Chicago newspaper and syndicated in eight or nine other cities. But not New York. And your name won't be used.'

'And for this I'll be able to get a job as assistant to Cadman?' Max was skeptical.

'Honey, that's the way Hollywood works,' Laura drawled. 'You scratch my back, and I'll scratch yours. I'm in this deal, too. If you're at the studio, you'll be able to get me in to do interviews with the Mort Klein stars. *Photo Play* will buy those.'

Max had infinite respect for Mort Klein, who had moved into the Hollywood scene just three years ago but already had brought in two hits for Klein-Meyers Films. He was reported to be a shrewd, conniving, belligerent son-of-a-bitch.

'Cadman's a rotten director,' Max said.

'What do you care?' Laura shrugged. 'You'll be

345

working for Klein-Meyers Films. You'll shove that asshole right out of his job when Klein sees how good you are.'

'How do I show him?' Max tried to appear cynical. Klein had been lucky with his two hits. They were straight out of the headlines and packed with drama. The direction had been shit.

'You'll know. Be nice to Cleo Forbes.'

Right on schedule Max appeared at Cleo Forbes' apartment door. He knew right away she wore neither corset nor brassiere.

'Want a drink?' she asked as she held the door wide for him to come into the small apartment she shared with another actress.

Max shuddered.

'After last night not even water.' He looked at Cleo with no sexual interest. By now she'd probably been laid by half of Hollywood.

'I was sorry you couldn't come home with me last night,' she pouted. 'I thought we were going to be close friends.'

'I was in no condition for anything last night,' he said bluntly. But other guests had been in condition, he recalled. When he went to the bathroom he walked into three male guests intent on satisfying a tall redhead. They hadn't even noticed him.

'We'll make up now.' Cleo walked toward him. Already she was unbuttoning the front of her crepe de Chine blouse.

Max hesitated. What about Arnie Cadman? Laura said, 'Don't touch the merchandise.'

'Your friend the director won't like this,' Max warned.

'Are you going to tell him?' Cleo laughed. 'Arnie's spending the day with his mother.'

Max hoped that he could perform.

He could.

Four nights after he had dinner with Cleo Forbes, Max received a call on the hall phone at the rooming house. It was a secretary at the Klein-Meyers studio. He was to report next morning to Arnold Cadman, who had just begun to shoot a new film.

Max had little respect for what he had seen of Cadman's work. But when he arrived on the lot the next morning, he knew he must conceal this. Cadman was a small man with massive shoulders and chest and a Napoleonic complex. Max hated him on sight.

It was Max's job to hire the extras and bit players, check out costumes and props, search for locations for shots away from the lot, arrange for the police permits that were necessary for shooting in the streets and public parks. He even had to order the box lunches and see that they were delivered. Max felt more like a stage manager than an assistant director. It was the Yiddish theater all over again.

But he saw his chance when Cadman came down with a violent stomach upset. While Cadman threw up all afternoon in the bathroom, Max assumed directing. He was conscious of a new respect from the cast as he belted out instructions. Even Cleo, whom he treated as though she was a small girl in his Sunday-school class, responded with a performance that surpassed anything he would have expected of her. He'd heard Mort Klein, who looked through assistant directors as though they were nonpresent, complain to Cadman that the pacing was too slow. Klein wouldn't say that tonight when he saw the rushes.

Max made the cast rehearse each scene several times until he had achieved exactly what he wished. Only then did he tell the cameraman to shoot. He shocked the company when he ordered one scene reshot. With film so expensive every scene was supposed to be shot only once. But he had suddenly become aware of new bits of business to give the actors. Mort Klein wouldn't bitch about the extra film, instinct told him.

Later Max was nervous as he sat beside Mort Klein in the darkroom. Cadman had gone home. Only Klein and the cutters were in the darkroom with him. He knew the scenes he had shot were excellent. *Was* Klein going to bitch about wasted film?

For several moments Klein sat motionless and silent. Then he turned to Max.

'Cadman's off the picture. You're taking over. But for Christ's sake, watch the extra shots or I'll break your balls.'

Early in January Tania invited Rissa to join her brother and his new law partner from Chicago for supper after the performance at the Café Royale. Rissa tried to make excuses. Tania refused to hear them.

348

'Rissa, you never go to the café with us anymore,' she scolded. 'Tonight, you go.'

After the performance Rissa and Tania were met by Georgie Finkel and his law partner, Lou Feinberg. Rissa's throat tightened as she walked into the Café Royale, bustling with patrons at this hour. Always before when she came here, Max was at her side.

Although she had not been at the café for over four months, a waiter took them to Rissa's favorite table. He remembered. Rissa was aware of admiring stares from some of the diners. People stopped by to comment on her performance. *'Rissa, you were wonderful!' 'Miss Lindowska, you made us cry.'*

Georgie was pleased at the attention Rissa attracted. Lou seemed faintly self-conscious. Georgie had Tania's flamboyant good looks. Lou was handsome in a quiet, aristocratic fashion. His voice was low and mellow.

'My mother won't believe it when I tell her I ate supper at the Café Royale with Rissa Lindowska,' he said. He was almost shy in his admiration, yet Rissa felt a maturity in him that far surpassed that of Tania's brother. They made an interesting pair of law partners. 'Will you back me up, Georgie?'

'It's a deal,' Georgie promised. 'You know, we have some good Yiddish theater in Chicago,' he boasted. 'Right, Tania?'

'For Chicago it was good,' Tania teased.

'Let me see,' Georgie mused. 'What's playing at the Pavilion now?' He reached into his coat pocket to pull out the Chicago *Record-Herald* he had brought along on the train.

'There used to be a wonderful old actor named Muni Weisenfreund with the company,' Lou said reflectively. 'People flocked to see him. Then after a while he wasn't there.'

'Georgie, be careful,' Tania scolded as her brother spread the paper open and flipped the pages in search of the theater section. 'Georgie, wait!'

Tania took the paper away from her brother and folded it back.

'Rissa, look!' Tania's voice was electric. 'Isn't that Max?'

'In a Chicago paper?' Rissa was dubious, but she leaned forward to inspect the segment to which Tania pointed.

'It's Louella Parsons' column,' Tania explained. 'She writes movie gossip – ' Tania's voice ebbed away. Her face paled.

Rissa fought hard to hold on to her composure as she gazed at the photograph and read the names beneath.

'That's Max,' she said. 'I don't know why he's using that phony name.' Max, with his arms around a Hollywood actress named Cleo Forbes. Underneath the columnist gushed about the 'new Milton Sills' who was smitten by Klein-Meyers Films' new starlet, Cleo Forbes.

'Maybe it isn't Max,' Tania tried.

'It's Max.' Rissa's voice was harsh with her effort not to fall apart.' The stickpin he's wearing. I gave it to him on our seventh wedding anniversary.'

'But Max acting?' Tania pretended skepticism. She

350

was upset. Rissa knew she was cursing herself for having called attention to the item.

'He wrote he was playing "extra" roles.' Max was always acting, Rissa tormented herself. Acting when he signed his letters, 'I love you, Max.'

Tania diverted the conversation away from Max. Lou Feinberg helped. Rissa was grateful for his compassion. Georgie pushed the newspaper back into his pocket with an air of disappointment.

The waiter arrived. Rissa went through the pretense of enjoying her supper. She talked with the others about President Wilson's idealistic 'fourteen points' message to Congress, aimed at laying the groundwork for permanent peace in the world, though Georgie was skeptical that it would ever succeed.

When she returned to the apartment, Shirley was waiting up for her with a pot of tea. She listened to what Rissa had to report.

'Rissa, write Max,' she pleaded. 'Ask him, who's this Cleo Forbes?'

'She's sleeping with Max.' *Her husband*. The man she had expected to be part of her life forever. She lay awake night after night crying inside because Max was not with her. And all the while there were other women in his bed. How many women had Max slept with since their marriage? Over and over again she had lied to herself. 'I know all I need to know. I don't want a man that I have to keep under lock and key. I'm divorcing him, Shirley. Tomorrow I'll call up and make an appointment with Lou Feinberg.'

'Why not Tania's brother?' Shirley asked.

'Lou is Georgie's partner. He handles the divorce cases.' She had deep respect for Lou, whose father was a professor at Columbia University and whose mother was active in Jewish charities. She'd feel comfortable with Lou. 'Shirley, it's not a disgrace anymore to divorce. It happens up and down Second Avenue.' But she had never suspected it could happen to Max and her.

'A divorce will make you stop loving Max?' Shirley challenged.

'I'll never stop loving Max. But I won't share him. Don't expect me to do that, Shirley.'

'Write Max,' Shirley pleaded again.

'I don't want him anymore!' Her voice was strident. 'Not now, when the whole world knows he's sleeping around. Before I could pretend. I can't anymore.'

'Rissa, the whole world doesn't read the Chicago *Record-Herald*. Besides, who's to say Louella Parsons didn't make it all up?'

'The photograph,' Rissa shot back. 'Sitting there with his arms around that woman. While he wears the stickpin I gave him for our seventh wedding anniversary.'

'Would it have been better if he had not worn the stickpin?' Shirley asked with bitter humor, and reached to pull Rissa into her arms as the storm within her broke.

Lou Feinberg tried to persuade Rissa to consult with Max before she took a divorce action. Rissa was adamant. The only consultation was to be between Max and Lou. She listened in distaste to Lou's explanation of New York State divorce laws.

'But these days you can get a fast divorce without complications by taking up legal residence in Nevada. All you have to do,' he pursued, holding up a hand to forestall Rissa's protests, 'is to live in Nevada for three months, presumably with the intention of becoming a bona fide resident of the state. Nobody pursues that aspect, of course. If we can persuade Max not to contest the divorce, you'll be free in three months.'

During the ensuing weeks Lou was in heavy correspondence with Max. Rissa refused to reply to Max's outraged letters. When a birthday present arrived for Joseph, Shirley was instructed to acknowledge its receipt. Rissa reiterated to Lou that she wanted no contact with her husband; *he* must make all the arrangements.

On the threshold of Purim, Lou reported that Max had angrily capitulated; he would not contest the divorce, which would be requested on the grounds of desertion. But he told Lou that he thought Rissa had lost her mind.

'Max wrote that if you're sure you want the divorce, then he won't fight it,' Lou told her on the eve of Purim.

'I want it,' Rissa confirmed. 'I'll be able to go to Nevada early in May.' By then the theater season would be over.

Her heart pounding with the enormity of the decision, Rissa listened while Lou explained that he would arrange with a Nevada lawyer to rent a house for Rissa. The children and Shirley would go with her to spend the required three months. Rissa would appear before the judge for only a few minutes since the divorce would not be contested.

When Rissa arrived home from her meeting with Lou, Shirley greeted her with the present that Max had sent for Katie's first birthday.

'Katie's going to know that papa sent her a present?' Bitterness crept into Rissa's voice. 'Why wasn't he here when she took her first steps last week?'

Later Rissa climbed the stairs in the synagogue with Shirley and the children. It irritated her that, in the Orthodox synagogue, the women must sit upstairs away from the men – or in a small *shul*, behind a curtain. An actor from the company who attended the same synagogue offered to take Joseph downstairs with the men. Even at two years old Joseph had to be apart from the women.

She was secretly pleased when Joseph insisted on being with her. He sat on her lap while Clara, Rae and baby Katie sat between Shirley and her. Shirley had made long dresses and gold paper crowns so that they were three miniature Queen Esthers. Even tiny Katie was aware of the importance of this occasion.

Together they listened to the story of the biblical Queen Esther, who persuaded her husband, the Persian King Ahasuerus, to cancel the decree issued by the wicked Haman to kill all the Jews in Persia in about 480 B.C.

Only Clara, poignantly sweet and earnest, was old enough to understand; but the other children along with her would be delighted with the *hamantashen* and *groggers* that would be dispersed later. At all other times the children would be expected to be quiet in the synagogue; Purim was an occasion for noisemaking.

As on every holiday Rissa's thoughts dwelt on her family who perished on the seventh eve of Passover. Would mama be upset that she was divorcing Max? Would mama think she was disgracing the family? But what else could she do? She was not like the women of Thomashefsky and Adler. She could not sit by and share her husband with other women.

But how was she to survive without Max?

26

The day was overcast and chilly, reflecting Rissa's own mood as she sat with the three little girls in the rear seat of the taxi. Shirley sat up front with Joseph on her lap.

The taxi pulled up before the Forty-second Street station. The driver hurried from behind the wheel to bring out the three suitcases that were to accompany Rissa, Shirley and the three children on the train. The trunks for the three-month stay in Nevada had been shipped ahead.

Rissa's heart pounded. The moment she set foot on the train, she would feel herself divorced from Max.

A redcap came forward to take their luggage. Rissa paid the driver and reached a hand out to Clara and Rae while she tried to juggle the maroon velour coat she held over one arm. She was conscious of the admiring glances of a man emerging from a car ahead of the taxi.

In a gesture of defiance she'd had her hair bobbed in the Irene Castle fashion. The tight gray satin toque emphasized her exquisite features. Her one-piece gray satin frock displayed her still-tiny waist, the curvaceous bosom and slender hips unmarred by carrying four children. At twenty-six years, Rissa appeared a girl.

Rissa was grateful that she had refused the offers of both Lou and Tania to see them off today. Her hold on composure was precarious. But she thanked God for friends like them.

'Rissa?' Shirley turned nervously at the entrance.

'We're coming,' Rissa soothed and Shirley moved aside, anxious to keep their redcap in sight.

Clara and Rae's faces glowed with anticipation. Joseph seemed wary. But all the children were excited at the prospect of spending five days aboard two trains. Shirley had made the long monotonous journey appear to be a grand adventure.

Rissa fought against an overwhelming suffocation as she walked through the cavernous Grand Central terminal. She remembered her anguish as she stood and watched Max hurry toward the gate that would take him to the train. She remembered the parade of nights when she had cried into her pillow because Max had left her.

For a while she had cherished a hope that Max, who continued to write that he desperately missed the children and her, would make the trip from California to Nevada to see them. She harbored a wild vision of Max swooping down upon them and refusing to allow her to divorce him. But Lou had cautioned both Max and her that he must not appear in Nevada lest the divorce appear to be an act of collusion.

The porter settled them in the large drawing room and left. Now Shirley told Rissa that Lou had insisted on arranging for a separate compartment for her.

'We know you love the children,' Shirley said

firmly, 'but there'll be hours when you'll welcome a little time away from them.'

'We'll take turns with the children,' Rissa compromised. She was aware that visitors were being exhorted to leave the train. In moments they would be on their first lap to Nevada. To the divorce that would separate her from Max forever.

What am I doing here? How can I divorce Max? A piece of paper handed down by the court won't make me stop loving him. How can I endure the rest of my life without Max?

Max and she had dreamed of a trip to Europe when the children were older. She'd hoped to show Max the theater where she had played in Warsaw. To introduce her fine husband to the Paulowski family. Perhaps she might even perform at the Kaminska Theater while they visited Warsaw. But now Poland was torn by war, and Max had abandoned the Yiddish theater.

The train began to inch through the murky underground tunnel. When the lights blinked for an instant, the children squealed in mock terror. At last they emerged into daylight.

Shirley was fascinated by the opulence of the Pullman car and by the associations her lively mind conjured up.

'Rissa,' she whispered, as though someone eavesdropped at the door, 'do you suppose Mary Pickford sat in this drawing room when she came to New York to start on the Liberty Loan tour?' Shirley was radiant. 'Maybe all of them sat here to play cards together. Mary, Douglas Fairbanks, Charlie Chaplin and William S. Hart!'

'Shirley, they're just people,' Rissa teased. But Shirley was devoted to the fan magazines. She was sure that Shirley prayed every night and asked God to send her – Rissa – into films.

In Chicago they changed for the luxurious California Limited, which offered its passengers an observation car with a library, a barber shop, a beauty shop, and wire services that provided the latest stock market reports. The dining room served the same lavish meals available in the finest New York restaurants. En route such delicacies as fresh mountain trout were brought aboard to lessen the monotony of the trip.

Still, to Rissa, the days and nights on the train seemed endless. Rissa thanked God for Shirley's presence. She could not love Shirley more if she were her sister by blood. To the children Aunt Shirley was as much a part of their lives as mama. At intervals Clara asked about papa. Soon she would forget; papa had been gone from their lives for almost nine months.

At last they were in Nevada and en route to the Spanish-style house rented for their stay. The children were tired and querulous from traveling. Rissa was painfully conscious that they were almost on the Nevada–California border. Max was so close and yet so far from her.

If the children missed New York, they gave no indication. Rissa devoted herself to arranging diversions for them while Shirley cared for the rented house and prepared their meals. To Shirley this strange new landscape was a never-ending source of pleasure.

'Rissa, did you ever see such country? Such mountains? And even in the desert, plants grow!'

'I could do without the heat,' Rissa said. 'But the land is beautiful. And it never seems to rain.'

Still she harbored an illogical hate for the state of Nevada. She was here to cut Max out of her life. Perversely she was angry that he did not ignore the lawyer's instructions to stay away from his family while they were in residence in Nevada. If Max came here, would she have the strength to divorce him? Rissa knew she would not.

Rissa and Shirley learned to drive. Rissa rented a car so that they might explore some of the vastness of the state. They drove to Carson City, Reno, Lake Tahoe. Max would be livid if he knew she had the temerity to drive. That was the man's prerogative.

But no three months in Rissa's life offered such torment. Each day pushed her further away from Max. At last she sat in the courtroom.

'When did your husband desert you?' her lawyer asked gently.

'On August twenty-eight of last year.' Rissa's heart pounded. *What am I doing here? I don't want to divorce Max! I want him to come home!*

'And he refuses to return to your four children and you?'

'Yes.' *He's running around with Hollywood starlets. How dare he write how much he misses me!*

360

Rissa walked out of the courtroom with a shattering sense of loss. In the eyes of the law she was no longer Max's wife. But Max and she had been married by a rabbi. Until a divorce was granted by the rabbi, she was his wife. She would not ask for a religious divorce.

Involuntarily her fingers moved to touch the slender gold band she still wore. The ring that Max's mother had worn from wedding till death. She would wear it until she, too, was dead. In the eyes of God she was still Max's wife.

Immediately upon their return to New York Rissa went into rehearsals. Maurice Schwartz had left the Kessler Theater and, with Max Wilner, took over the Irving Place Theater, which Rissa had hoped to make the Lindowska-Miller Theater.

Rissa discovered that the New York Yiddish theater had undergone a summer of chaos. The producers were fighting amongst themselves, snatching theaters away from one another. Jack had taken over another theater for the new season.

'He wrapped the lease around your neck,' Tania confided in distaste. Rissa stared without comprehension. 'He got the lease on the understanding that you would play out the full season. With Max and you separated he was sure you wouldn't be pregnant again this season. Four babies in five years,' Tania clucked humorously.

'How could Jack make that commitment for me?' Rissa was indignant.

'You signed for the season.' Tania was unruffled.

'The only out you'd have would be to get pregnant. He knows that won't happen.'

'So I was Jack's bargaining point?'

'You were, darling. He couldn't get the theater without you.'

Tania was talking about trying for a part in a Broadway play. It didn't concern her that she had a union contract for the season. On Broadway there was no union.

'Let me find a job,' she said bluntly. 'You'll see how fast I'll leave Jack Fain. Rissa, in five years only old actors and actresses will be on Second Avenue. The young – like you and me and Adler's children – will be uptown on Broadway.'

'Not me,' Rissa vowed. 'I'll never desert Second Avenue.'

Clara started school. Rissa was enchanted that she had a daughter attending a fine private school.

Not long after the opening of the school a new sickness appeared. Spanish influenza. New York City was hit by rising numbers of cases each day. Word came from such faraway places as Denmark, Tahiti and China that the disease was spreading in alarming numbers.

On 4 October the New York City Board of Health issued orders governing opening and closing time for places of business and entertainment, in order to reduce crowding on the transportation lines. In cities and towns across the nation, schools and theaters were being closed. The National Association of Motion Picture Industry announced they would discontinue all releases after the fifteenth of the month until the epidemic was halted. But new theater productions in New York continued to open.

The Globe at Broadway and Forty-sixth Street was offering a new edition of *Ziegfeld Follies* for three weeks only. At the Lexington Theater at Fifty-first and Lexington, Klaw and Erlanger were presenting *Ben Hur* with three hundred and fifty people on the stage and twenty horses in a chariot race.

Rissa had looked forward to seeing John Barrymore in his new play *Redemption*. But caution urged her to remain away from as many public gatherings as possible. She was astonished, when she read the reviews in the *Times*, to discover that Barrymore's *Redemption*, was, in reality, Jacob Adler's *The Living Corpse*.

Rissa worried about the theaters and schools in New York remaining open. Lou confided that Dr Copeland, the head of the Board of Health, had told those close to him that seven hundred and fifty thousand of the one million school children in the city were from unsanitary and overcrowded tenement homes. He believed it was safer to keep the children in school under supervision of teachers and with doctors and nurses on call.

But Rissa decided to keep Clara home when she read that the death rate was so high many bodies lay unburied in the cemeteries. In some cities there was a serious shortage of coffins.

'Why don't they close the theaters?' Shirley worried. 'All those people every night carrying germs!'

Rissa and Shirley knew that the theaters were

regularly inspected. Only very small storefront-type movie houses with inadequate ventilation, however, had been closed. In both movie houses and theaters announcements were made before each performance to explain the danger of infection from coughing and sneezing.

For a while, at least, the war in Europe took second place to more personal concerns.

Tania came to the theater, her eyes red from crying. 'My mother heard from the war department,' she told Rissa. 'My youngest brother – the one who went over with the Rainbow Division last November – he was killed in action. Rissa, he was eighteen months younger than me!'

'Oh, Tania.' Rissa was cold with shock. Only when something like this happened did they feel the real impact of the war.

'He never even lived. He never kissed a girl. He never made love. He was going to be a lawyer like Georgie. Now he's buried in a hole in the ground in France.' Tania's face tightened. 'I'll make sure I don't miss anything in this world, Rissa. I won't be cheated like my baby brother!'

Rissa remembered the letter that waited for her when she returned from Nevada. Izzy had written to tell them about his older son in the marines. He had been wounded in Belleau Wood, on the road to Paris. He would spend months in a hospital in England before he was brought home. He had lost both legs.

'How do I tell Ida her son is coming home without

his legs?' Izzy asked. 'You know she has a bad heart. How do I bring her such *tsores*?'

That evening at supper Rissa noticed that Joseph's eyes were red. Always an exuberant child, tonight he was lethargic.

'I'll get a handkerchief for Joseph. His nose is running.' Shirley fought a losing battle to conceal her alarm.

'I'll take him upstairs,' Rissa said swiftly. The doctor kept saying that an influenza victim must be isolated from the others in the family. 'I'll call Dr Held.'

'First finish your supper,' Shirley ordered. 'In an hour you have to leave for the theater.'

'I'm not hungry,' Rissa scooped up Joseph in her arms. 'Shirley, he's so hot!'

While Shirley stayed downstairs with the three little girls, Rissa went upstairs to the bedroom. She undressed Joseph and put him to bed, then tried to reach Dr Held. His wife reported that he was out on calls. She didn't know when he'd be back.

'Sometimes he's out all night with so much flu in the city,' Mrs Held explained compassionately. 'But when he comes home, I'll tell him you need him.'

Rissa sponged Joseph down with cool water, sat by his bed waiting for him to fall asleep. When she was sure he slept, she phoned Lou. If anyone knew how to get a doctor for Joseph, it would be Lou, she told herself.

'Let me come over with the car,' Lou said gently, 'and we'll take him to the hospital.'

'No!' Rissa's voice was shrill with fear. 'He'll stay here with us. Shirley and I will take care of him.'

'I'll find a doctor,' Lou promised. 'I'll be in touch as soon as I have word.'

Rissa went back into Joseph's room. She was sure he was running a temperature. How had he caught the flu? Only Clara went to school; the other children played in the yard behind the house. Rissa was terrified.

She took her purse from her bedroom and went downstairs. Shirley was waiting for her at the foot of the steps.

'Lou is trying to get a doctor. Dr Held is out on calls — his wife doesn't know when he'll be home.' She fought to keep her voice even.

'You're going to the theater tonight?' Shirley was somber.

'I must go,' Rissa said defensively. Attendance was low but still a performance was demanded of her. 'I'll phone between acts.' She hesitated. 'Shirley, keep the children downstairs tonight. They'll sleep in the parlor. I'll tell Jack he'll have to replace me tomorrow night. Until Joseph is well, my place is here.'

Jack was indignant that Rissa was withdrawing until Joseph was over the flu.

'Three hours a night, Rissa! You owe that to the theater. It's going to help Joseph that you're standing by his bed? Better you should hire a nurse!'

'His mother will nurse him.' Rissa left Jack and hurried into the dressing room. How was she to give a performance tonight?

At intermission Rissa telephoned the apartment.

Lou answered. Dr Comstock, a friend of his family, was with Joseph. Despite the extreme shortage of beds in the hospital, Dr Comstock offered to find a place for Joseph. Again Rissa refused. She would nurse Joseph. Shirley would watch over the other children on the floor below.

'Lou, is Joseph asking for me?' Rissa's heart pounded in anguish.

'He's sleeping most of the time. Shirley says you're not to worry,' Lou soothed. He paused. 'Joseph is a very sick little boy, but Dr Comstock is one of the finest doctors in the country. Trust in God.'

In every crisis Shirley said, 'Trust in God.' But where was God, Rissa tormented herself, when the peasants came into their *dorf* in Poland and murdered her family?

Rissa hurried home from the theater. Lou sat at the dining-room table with Shirley. The three little girls were asleep in the parlor. Shirley brought out a pot of tea while Lou tried to comfort Rissa.

'He's going to be all right,' Lou insisted. 'You'll see.'

Rissa sent Lou home lest he become infected. She would remain upstairs with Joseph. Shirley was to bring food trays halfway up the stairs. Rissa would come down and pick them up. The important thing now was to isolate Joseph and herself from the others.

By the third night Joseph's condition was critical. Dr Comstock remained at the bedside through the night. Pale and exhausted from lack of sleep and anxiety, Rissa hovered over Joseph.

'We can only wait and pray,' Dr Comstock told Rissa as daylight arrived. 'I must go to the hospital now. I'll be back in three hours.'

Shirley came up to the second floor when Dr Comstock left, brushing aside Rissa's warning that she must not contaminate herself.

'Rissa, you have to eat,' she scolded. 'You'll waste away to nothing.' Her eyes asked urgent questions while she talked. 'I'll fix you some eggs.'

'Dr Comstock says we can only wait and pray,' Rissa told her. *Max ought to be here.*

'Max doesn't know Joseph is sick,' Shirley scolded.

'He knows about the flu epidemic. He hasn't written in three weeks.' All at once fresh alarm invaded Rissa. 'Shirley, do you think he's sick?'

'He's directing a picture.' Shirley refused to be concerned. 'When Max is doing a picture, he knows from nothing else. When he's finished, he'll write.'

'He ought to be here with Joseph!' Rissa vacillated between anger at Max's absence and fear for Max's health.

'I'll send him a telegram.'

'Why alarm him? You know how long it would take for him to come here from California.'

Within hours they would know if Joseph would be all right. Involuntarily she remembered Max's grief over the death of his parents and his frustration that the train could not even get him there in time for their funeral.

'I'll try to phone Max.' He had written that he had moved out of his rooming house into a bungalow with a telephone on Western Avenue. Since 1915 it

368

had been possible to telephone California from New York.

'How can you phone him at this hour?' Shirley protested. 'It's three o'clock in the morning in California.'

'*He should know about Joseph.*' All at once it was imperative to talk to Max. She had not spoken to him since the day he walked out of the theater when she refused to go with him to California. But with Joseph so sick the past fourteen months seemed nonexistent. She longed to hear Max's voice. To have Max reassure her that Joseph would be all right. '*We can only wait and pray.*' Dr Comstock's diagnosis ricocheted in her brain.

At last the operator connected Rissa with Max's California number. But Max did not answer.

'Please try again,' Rissa pleaded. 'This is an emergency.'

She waited, the nails of one hand digging into her palm.

Apologetically the operator told Rissa there was no reply at the other end. She suggested that Rissa try later in the day.

'Thank you.' Her face taut with reproach Rissa put down the phone. 'It's three o'clock in the morning in California. Why isn't Max home?'

In whose bed was Max lying while his baby fought for life?

Max lay sleepless in a tiny plaster-peeling rooming-house in the small town of Tucson, Arizona. With a hastily assembled Hollywood company he had

369

arrived in Tucson early yesterday. Once the cast and crew had been settled in their lodging, he had taken off with a cameraman to scout for locations in the nearby desert. He had been pleased with the potential shooting in the desert. And Mort was right; Tucson itself had the appearance of a real frontier town, even to the dirt streets.

Cast and crew ate supper in the rooming-house dining room, where extra tables had been set up to accommodate them. After supper they'd sat around and sang songs while their landlady pounded the keys of the old upright piano.

By ten o'clock Max banished the company to their bedrooms. Tomorrow at sunup they would begin to shoot the scenes they'd come out here to do.

In the darkness of his bedroom Max leaned over to look at his watch, on the table beside his hard narrow bed. A glimmer of light that came in through the spider web shade allowed him to note the time. It was 3:00 A.M.

He hated the Western films Mort was assigning to him, though he knew Westerns were making money. He'd have to do something special to make this one stand out. He'd talk to Clint, his cameraman, about trying out some different shots. Make the audience stand on its head in suspense.

Tired and tense Max lay on his back and pulled the thin flannel blanket over his shoulders.

He'd been having trouble sleeping these last few weeks. Ever since the lawyer sent him the papers that said Rissa was no longer his wife. He'd never dreamed that Rissa would take such a step.

Rissa would come to California, he'd told himself, when he was a success and could support the family. He'd never doubted this. But now he knew that to Rissa, her own career came first.

He stared up at the ceiling until the first pink streaks of dawn invaded the room, and he heard the clatter of pots in the kitchen downstairs.

Rissa sat beside Joseph's bed. Her eyes clung to his small face. He was so still. She leaned forward to reassure herself that he was breathing. Dr Comstock would be back soon. She felt more confident with Dr Comstock at Joseph's side. *They wouldn't let Joseph die.*

Max should be here with them. Not running around to Hollywood parties. Not sleeping with strange women. Couldn't he see the future that lay ahead for them?

Already Clara and Rae were in love with the theater. They couldn't wait for the times they were allowed to play onstage with mama. Katie, too, would be an actress. Uptown there were the Barrymores. Downtown the Adlers – and one day there would be the Lindowska-Millers.

But Joseph would grow up to be a doctor. Dr Joseph Lindowska-Miller. Sitting beside her son's bed she made a pact with God. Let Joseph live and I promise he'll be a doctor. A man to go out and save lives.

'Please God,' Rissa prayed, 'let Joseph live.'

27

'Mama – ' Joseph's plaintive summons punctured Rissa's introspection.

'Yes, darling?' She leaned forward to caress his small face. He seemed less hot.

'I'm hungry.'

'Dr Comstock will be here soon,' she soothed. 'He'll tell us what I should make for you.'

'Dr Comstock is here,' a warm voice announced from the doorway. From the doctor's smile Rissa sensed that Joseph was past the crisis. *He was going to be all right.*

Rissa wanted to throw her arms about Dr Comstock's neck and swear eternal gratitude. Instead she hovered at one side of the bed while he examined his small patient.

'He'll be fine,' Dr Comstock reassured her. 'Let him have a soft-boiled egg now. But keep him in bed for a few days. We don't want him to have a relapse.'

Joy reigned in the house. Rissa promised herself that she would send money to the day nursery on Montgomery Street and to the just-forming Fund for Jewish War Sufferers, in gratitude for Joseph's recovery. Shirley was exhorted not to write Max about Joseph's near-tragic case of the flu.

By early November the newspapers noted that the epidemic was petering out. But this news was lost in the excitement that ricocheted around the world. On 7 November the World War ended. Business stopped in every city and town and hamlet.

In New York people poured into the streets. Blowing horns, snake-dancing, singing. Fifth Avenue was closed to traffic. Broadway was so mobbed it was impossible to walk. Ticker tape deluged the celebrants in the streets. On the Hudson and East rivers, ships and tugboats blasted their horns without ceasing. Then suddenly horror descended. The reports of an armistice had been premature. The world was still at war.

Four days later – before dawn – Rissa awoke, like millions of other New Yorkers, to the shrill sounds of sirens, of factory whistles and church bells. This time there was no mistake. The most horrible war the world had ever seen had come to an end.

By early 1919 the war seemed far behind. War heroes were job hunting and the National Prohibition Act was passed by Congress over the veto of President Wilson. In Hollywood the prospect of having to disguise cocktails as tea or coffee seemed hilarious.

The woman suffrage amendment had passed both houses of Congress and, hopefully, would soon be ratified by the necessary thirty-six states. Women's skirts climbed to eight inches above the floor, and worse was expected. The whole social and moral climate of the nation was changing with dizzying speed.

Hollywood was acquiring a reputation for riotous living. A wave of agitation had started among the clergy and various women's groups, who complained that movies were a bad influence on the population, that they contributed to the corruption of public morals. There was a loud demand for censorship of films. The clergy called for the closing of theaters on Sundays.

At first it was only the fly-by-night companies that produced salacious films. But now some of the important companies were following suit. The public was fed up with war movies. The younger generation was out for fun. The more responsible producers were concerned that censorship might be imposed.

Max was struggling to convince Mort Klein that this was a time to produce better films. Mort was dubious. They had to give the customers what they wanted – and he had his own definition of that.

'Max, you're a bright boy. You think these new flappers and their boyfriends want to see great theater?' He was amused and skeptical. 'They want to kick up their heels in new freedom. They want to drink and screw.'

Max grimly continued to turn out Grade-B movies, waiting for a chance to move up into class productions. He wasn't a director, he complained to Laura. He was a goddamn nurse-maid to his actors.

He had to fight to begin shooting at the scheduled 9:00 A.M. time. Sometimes hours were required in makeup and wardrobe before actors were ready for the cameras. Max made frenzied phone calls, sent studio cars to bring hungover actors to the lot. He pleaded with them to get a decent night's sleep, to guard their health.

'Listen to me, you son-of-a-bitch!' he yelled at one would-be great lover, 'you can't spend all night drinking and whoring and expect it not to show up on the cameras! You want to do pictures, you take care of your health! The camera tells everything.'

At regular intervals Laura called on him to be her escort at some affair at the Cocoanut Grove at the Ambassador Hotel. Laura was now svelte and chic and selling regularly to *Photo Play*. Tonight Max was slated to take her to a banquet at the Cocoanut Grove.

Max loathed the Cocoanut Grove with its papier-mâché palm trees strewn with stuffed monkeys. The music was unpredictable — sometimes poignant, sometimes noisy. But here gathered the famous of Hollywood. Here those ambitious to climb upward made important contacts.

Driving to the Ambassador Hotel in the Rolls-Royce Laura had borrowed for the night, Max was touched by nostalgia. In New York spring was arriving in bursts of balmy air. The flower boxes that Rissa had him install in the windows of the apartment would be erupting with tulips and hyacinths. Clumps of daffodils would be in bloom in the yard behind the house. In Hollywood the scenery never changed.

What would Rissa and the children do this summer? If he had enough cash put aside, he'd ask Rissa to come out here with the children. When he left New York, Katie wasn't sitting up alone yet. Now Shirley wrote that Katie ran like the wind. Clara was in the second grade. He missed them all!

'You're quiet tonight,' Laura chided. 'Is Mort being nasty to you?'

'Mort's never civil to anyone,' he admitted. 'I can't get it through his head we have to start doing better pictures.'

'He's supposed to be spending a fortune on a new picture,' Laura had that special tenseness in her voice that told him she was out for gossip.

'The most expensive the studio ever made,' Max admitted with some frustration that he was not involved.

'As much as Fox spent on *Salome*?' Laura pursued. Max smiled.

'Not quite. Fox threw over a million into that. They had Theda Bara and a cast of three thousand. But Mort expects this one to make more than Chaplin's *Shoulder Arms*.'

'Because Mort has the hots for his beautiful new star?' Laura tried to be casual.

'He's screwing her between every take,' Max said bitterly.

'That'll be a real item,' Laura said with a lilt in her voice.

Max's eyes left the road for an instant.

'You're using that for a *Photo Play* column?'

'I'm using it for my new newspaper column.' Her smile was triumphant. She leaned forward to squeeze Max's arm. 'I just got the deal set!'

'You can't use that item about Mort,' he protested. 'You know how he is about keeping his private life under wraps.' Mort was addicted to quiet parties at his magnificent home on fashionable Franklin

376

Avenue, where only the elite of Hollywood appeared. Mort lived in a thirty-four-room house with his wife, his mother-in-law and a dozen servants. At intervals his daughter Rita, a student at Vassar, came home for brief visits.

'Why can't I use it?' Laura countered. 'Everybody on the set must know. Mort can't pin it on you. Keep me posted, Max. I need lots of items.' Laura giggled. 'Mort's wife won't see it. The only things she reads are the letters from her daughter.'

'Why are we going to this thing at the Cocoanut Grove?' Max was curious. Wherever Laura went, she had an ulterior motive.

'It's a shindig for some new writer who's just come from New York. I don't meet too many writers. Just this one poor little guy who's complaining that he's tired of writing about love. He's dying to do a realistic scenario with an unhappy ending.'

It wouldn't do any harm for him to meet new writers, Max considered. If he found a sensational scenario, maybe Mort would let him direct it.

Money was running like water in Hollywood. For those at the top. He wanted to move into one of those fancy new houses high in the hills. He wanted to go back to New York and throw his success at Rissa's feet. She'd see he'd been right in coming out here.

Rissa and he would marry again, he dreamed. He'd bring her out here and make her a star. With one picture she'd be as important as Clara Kimball Young or Anita Stewart.

When Laura and he walked into the Cocoanut

Grove, the orchestra was playing a slow fox-trot. Max was pleased to note that a sprinkling of rising young actresses were among the dancers. He spied, among other young beauties, gorgeous Doris Kenyon, Mary Miles Minter, dark-eyed Alma Rubens. If he didn't move ahead soon at Klein-Meyers Films, he'd pursue one of these gorgeously gowned young guests; they were in a position to make demands of their producers. In Hollywood it was who you knew that counted.

Laura darted off to a table where a small, balding young man beckoned to her in delight. He hadn't been sure Laura would show up. He didn't know that Laura had told Max she might be going home with her new contact. Max could take the Rolls home with him tonight. She'd pick it up tomorrow. Laura lived now in a bungalow shared with a would-be starlet. It was a scant five minutes' walk from Max's.

'Max!' a strangely familiar voice called to him from across the room. 'I don't believe it!'

A statuesque redhead in a silver brocade evening gown cut daringly low to display her magnificent bosom pushed her way through the dancers toward him.

'Celia!' He held out his arms in welcome.

'Carla,' she whispered in his ear. 'I'm Carla Kendell now.'

'Shall we dance?' He was amused by the new image.

'Why not?'

Celia moved into his arms. She'd acquired a new sophistication, Max noticed. She was sure of herself.

'How long have you been out here?' Max asked.

'Almost a year,' Celia told him. 'I'm staying at the Alexandria in Los Angeles.' Celia was well connected, Max's mind tabulated, if she was staying at the Alexandria Hotel. She was being kept by a Hollywood character who meant to keep the relationship away from prying eyes. 'For a while back East I was working in pictures out in New Jersey.' She grimaced. 'They were awful, but I was learning. But I told you once – I have expensive tastes. The money's out here.'

'Are you working?' Max probed and felt an unexpected sense of guilt. At times the constant race for contacts in Hollywood irritated him. But to make it in this town he had to play the game.

'I'm hoping for a small part in a new movie. Not a quickie,' she said. 'Something that'll show me off.' But Max caught the edge of desperation in her voice.

'Marvelous.' Max made a show of approval. Even with her limited talent Celia could make a place for herself in films. If she found a place for herself in the right bed.

'What are you doing, Max?' She hesitated. 'Is Rissa making a picture?'

'Rissa and I are divorced.' For a moment his eyes were opaque. 'I wanted to come to California. She wanted to stay in New York. I'm a director at Klein-Meyers Films. Doing Westerns,' he said quickly, lest she thought he was in a position to cast her in a film. Celia – Carla, he corrected himself – wouldn't see herself in a Western. 'For now.'

The orchestra finished the number. Celia was already glancing about the room.

'Remember, I'm Carla Kendell,' she murmured. 'I'll see you around.'

Celia hurried off to a table at the other side of the room. Max followed her with his eyes. He recognized the producer who pulled Celia into the chair beside his without interrupting his conversation with another director. Celia was traveling in high company.

Tonight Max was restless. Celia had been a touch of home. She reminded him how much he missed Rissa and the children, and how long he'd been away from New York. God, how little he had accomplished!

If Mort would let him get away from the garbage detail, he'd make real money. A hell of a lot of pictures were coming out of Hollywood. With the war and the flu epidemic past, people were flocking to the movies. With Prohibition there'd be even more people running to the movies.

One solid picture would establish him. One hit movie and they'd all be chasing after him. He could move into an apartment at Garden Court on Hollywood Boulevard and try to persuade Rissa to come out with the children. How much longer would the Yiddish theater provide a living for her? He brushed away his guilt at having sent no money for the children's support. Rissa made ten times what he earned.

If Rissa came out here with the children, they'd send Clara – and Rae and Katie when they were older – to the Hollywood School for Girls on Franklin near

380

La Brea. Cecil B. DeMille's daughter went there, and Louis Mayer's girls.

Driving home Max allowed his mind to dwell on his prospects. Should he stay with Klein-Meyers Films or try to move on? He knew Mort liked him. But Mort kept him on a string. When the hell would Mort give him a chance at something besides Westerns?

Mort complained about the insane salaries the stars demanded.

All the producers had contempt for actors, Max conceded. All of the bigwigs bitched about the split demanded by the distribution companies. And now Hollywood was rampant with rumors that the four top stars and a top director – Mary Pickford, Douglas Fairbanks, William S. Hart, Charlie Chaplin and D. W. Griffith – were secretly negotiating to form their own company.

Mort would have fierce competition. Right now he was able to sell the dogs he was producing on the strength of his one big star. The theaters had to take all Mort's films to get him. Max thought about Celia. A meager talent but *he* could make her look like a star. If he brought Mort a potential new star, he could push the son-of-a-bitch into letting him direct her.

Max felt a surge of optimism. You couldn't wait for luck; you had to go out and make things happen. He'd wait a couple of weeks, then see what Celia was doing. Carla, he corrected himself with a grin. She'd been in Hollywood almost a year. She was getting edgy.

* * *

When Max tried to reach Carla Kendell née Celia Kamenstein at the Alexandria, he learned she had checked out. Her producer friend had moved on to somebody new. It was a familiar story. But he was able to acquire Carla's forwarding address. He found her living in a ramshackle house at the edge of Hollywood with four girls, all of them subsisting on what extra work they could pick up at the studios.

He took her out to dinner at the Hollywood Hotel, though this would make a dent in his budget, because he had arranged for Laura to meet them there later. It was important to Laura to be seen at the hotel dining room with what she referred to as 'gorgeous picture people.' It could also be important for Carla. With no frills he laid out the facts for her. This could be a partnership that would be advantageous to both of them. But he'd only go ahead if she played exactly as he called it.

'Max, you're smart.' The fresh optimism that radiated from her was honest. 'I'll do whatever you say. I went into pictures back East because you told me to try them.'

'Laura Ainsley will be joining us in a few minutes,' Max continued. 'Laura owes me favors.' And in Hollywood favors were usually collected.

'The one who writes the movie column?' Carla was impressed.

'Do you read her stuff?' Max was pleased. Sometimes it astonished him to realize how far Laura had moved ahead.

'Doesn't everybody?'

'Laura is setting up some items for you in her

column. You'll be dating some actors the studios are trying to promote. Don't question anything she wants you to do,' Max warned. 'She's sharp. She'll do you a hell of a lot of good.'

'Whatever you say, Max.' Carla, as Max forced himself to think of her now, was docile.

Max saw Laura coming into the dining room with a tall muscular Adonis who looked like a road-company Francis X. Bushman. He saw Laura's eyes dart about the room. She'd tablehop before she joined them.

This was going to work out, Max promised himself. He would bring Carla to Mort, and show Mort how to build himself a new star. And he – Max Miller – would direct a Class-A film at last.

28

Rissa was amazed by the endless procession of men in pursuit of her. The only angry words that ever passed between Shirley and her were because of her insistence on continuing to wear her wedding band despite the divorce.

'Rissa, enough already,' Shirley complained in frustration. 'It's time to go on living. You want to spend the rest of your life sleeping alone?'

'You do,' Rissa shouted back.

'For me it's different,' Shirley said stubbornly. 'What man will want to marry me when I tell him I can't give him a child?'

'You might be surprised,' Rissa tried.

'I've had enough surprises,' Shirley brushed this aside. A cloud passed briefly across her face. 'But you,' she said, brightening, 'you need a man in your bed.'

'Lou's taking me tonight to see Tania's new play,' Rissa evaded. Her first play had closed in a week. The new one, with a small but showy part for Tania, was a hit. Now she was Terry French.

'Lou's crazy about you,' Shirley said.

'Lou's a good friend,' Rissa said. He advised her on investing money, aghast at the huge sums she had been allowing to remain idle in a savings account. She didn't want to acknowledge the fact that he was in love with her. 'He understands how I feel about Max.'

'The lawyer who arranged for your divorce,' Shirley jibed. 'He knows you're not married.'

Almost in self-defense Rissa began to see Lou frequently. Lou took her to the opera, to the Broadway theater, to Carnegie Hall. She could relax in the knowledge that Lou had too much sensitivity to push himself on her.

With Lou she heard Rachmaninoff at Carnegie Hall. He took her to the Metropolitan to hear Caruso and Geraldine Farrar. It still astonished her that the great Farrar had gone to Hollywood four years ago to play *Carmen* in a film for Cecil B. DeMille and had followed that with DeMille's *Maria Rosa* and *Joan the Woman*. Shirley, an avid movie fan, was entranced by Farrar's leading man, handsome Wallace Reid.

On every possible occasion Lou took her up to Broadway to see whichever of the Barrymores was performing. Rissa knew that Lou hoped she'd move uptown herself one day.

In April Max sent a belated birthday present for Katie and one for Clara that arrived on her birthday. As always when a communication from Max arrived, Rissa was overwrought for days.

'Rissa, why are you eating yourself up this way?' Shirley scolded when they sat alone in the parlor after Rissa had returned from the evening's performance. 'Lou's mad about you. His family has all kinds of money. He's a catch. And he's such a fine man,' she added softly. 'He'd be good to you.'

'You know I'll never marry again!' Rissa shot back.

'You're waiting for some miracle to come and bring Max and you together again. You act like a young girl in a movie. Life's not like that. You want Max back, do something about it. Take the children and go out to California this summer. Let Max see his family. Let him see you.'

'No.' Rissa's pride rejected this. Max had walked out on his family. 'If Max wants to see the children, let him come to New York.' But even the prospect of seeing Max started her heart pounding.

As the end of the season on Second Avenue approached, Jack tried to persuade Rissa to sign for a European summer tour. They'd make a fortune, he promised. He'd give her a percentage.

'Rissa, don't you want to see Europe again? London, Paris, Warsaw, Carlsbad – you can play them all!' He cajoled.

Rissa refused to drag the children on tour. They were too young, she argued. Nor would she leave them behind with Shirley, though she knew Shirley was a second mother to them.

'Jack, it's out of the question,' she told him for the fortieth time on the eve of their closing. It was bad enough that a continent separated Max and her. She would not add an ocean to the distance. By law they were divorced, but in her heart she was Max's wife. 'You'll have to find someone else.'

Jack was surly with the company. Rissa knew it was because she refused to go on the European tour. She realized that without her Jack wouldn't be able to sell the company. Even Leo was not the draw he had been the first season. But in Europe they'd heard about Rissa Lindoswka. She wasn't surprised when Jack conceded he was abandoning the European tour.

Rissa feared she would have problems with Jack in negotiating her contract for the next season. He complained that audiences were demanding operettas. Replicas of the Broadway musical comedies. She refused to sing.

This was the time when she should rise to new heights, Rissa told herself. The long-established stars were growing old. Keni Liptzin had died. Adler was a shadow of himself. Now was the time for the young performers like herself to take over the Yiddish theater and give it new life.

The nation as a whole appeared prosperous. Families had put aside savings during the booming war years. Wilson was fighting for a League of Nations that would forever prevent another world war. While millions were running regularly to the movies, Rissa was convinced that the Yiddish theater had yet to reach its heights.

Rissa was uneasy when Jack stalled about discussing terms for next year's contract. In late June she confronted him in his office at the theater.

'Times are bad, Rissa,' Jack whined, fiddling with a pen on his desk. 'I'm asking everybody to take a twenty percent cut.'

Rissa tensed. She didn't believe that. He thought that without Max he could handle her.

'I won't sign,' she said quietly. Refusing to allow him to see her rage.

'You think about it a few days, Rissa.' Jack avoided meeting her eyes.

Outside the theater she encountered the young comic of the company. He was en route with two friends to Moskowitz and Lupowitz for sponge cake and tea.

'Come along with us,' Murray invited. 'So we can all complain about what's happening on Second Avenue. But not him,' Murray pointed to one of his companions. 'He'll be with Maurice Schwartz at the Irving Place when it opens with *Tevya, the Dairyman* the end of August. Art theater,' he derided good-humoredly, but they all knew Murray's immense respect for the company that was to present Sholom Aleichem.

Over sponge cake and tea they dissected the problems of the Yiddish theater.

'Since Peretz Hirschbein's play *Farvorfen Vinkel* succeeded, everybody is becoming literary,' Murray explained. 'The great Yiddish actors castrate Ibsen, Strindberg, Tolstoy. Even Dumas and Shakespeare. But a new theater is coming,' Murray predicted. 'We – the young actors, the new stars – are rebelling!'

Talking about what Yiddish theater should be, Rissa knew what she must do. She would not argue with Jack about a contract for next season. She, Rissa Lindowska, would become an actress-manager.

It was a terrifying step to endanger everything that she had saved since the 1914 bank failure, yet instinct told her she would succeed. She was a star; she brought audiences into the theater. She had been aware for weeks of an available house.

It would be a race to bring a company together in time to open the season. But already her mind focused on the actors and actresses she wished to bring together. She would have to find a good director. Not another Leo Gunsburg. *Why wasn't Max here?* This would be the company he had dreamed about! But Max had moved beyond the Yiddish theater. Their timing was out of kilter.

The parlor of the apartment became Rissa's office. Shirley, who displayed an astonishing aptitude for figures, became her assistant; and a woman was hired to clean the apartment and watch over the children when Shirley was occupied with theater business. Everything that Rissa had learned came into focus. Shirley encouraged her when she saw her bank account balance evaporate with unnerving swiftness.

'Rissa, you can do it,' Shirley was a staunch believer. 'Rissa Lindowska, star-manager. That's the way it should be.'

Rissa was happy with the company, though there was the customary backstage bickering. She chose to have a Shaw play translated into Yiddish. A play with a challenging role for herself. *Candida.* Rissa had learned that Arnold Daly's production of *Candida* at the Prince Theater in 1903 had been a sensation.

Rissa opened her first production on a Wednesday night so that little time would be lost until the reviews came in on Friday. On opening night Rissa arrived at the theater with Shirley at her side.

Her heart pounding in anticipation of what she was about to see, Rissa stepped out of the taxi and paused at the curb. Her eyes swept upward to the electric sign that hung at right angles to the front of the theater, the sign lighted for the first time tonight. *Lindowska Theater.*

Tears filled her eyes and spilled over. Shirley squeezed her arm in a gesture that offered at once comfort, congratulations and sadness that Rissa's family could not be here to share this time of glory. For a few moments Rissa was back in the *dorf*, leaning over mama. She was stumbling to the door of the next room of the cottage to discover her murdered family, grandpa, still wrapped in his *tallith*, clinging to Katie's tiny hand. Papa holding Joseph in his arms. Hannah and Chaim clutching each other in death.

'Rissa – ' Shirley tugged at her arm. 'They're with you tonight. They're here.'

'Mama, this is for you,' Rissa whispered. 'For you and the whole family.'

To outward appearances on opening night Rissa's company was an outstanding success. But when the reviews came in, they were mixed. The dean of the Yiddish theater critics, Abraham Cahan, was lavish in his praise for the acting, particularly for that of the star. But reading Cahan's review Rissa understood what had bothered her during the frenzied weeks of rehearsal. Shaw's Candida was not a woman who could be translated into Yiddish with success.

Rissa berated herself for making such a foolish choice for their opening production. It was not enough that she herself had been highly praised by Cahan. The Lindowska Theater must be financially

390

successful. All of her funds were invested in the company.

'Darling,' Shirley consoled when Rissa seemed disconsolate, 'even Mary Pickford has movies the people don't like. Who had anything good to say about *Less Than the Dust* or *The Pride of the Clan?*'

While the company continued to present *Candida*, Rissa scheduled a new play to move speedily into their repertory. She gritted her teeth and rejected the *schund* that her director suggested. While they would not join Maurice Schwartz in presenting 'art theater,' at least they would offer a play that didn't make her cringe.

By Hanukkah, Rissa had a repertory of five plays, all of which were well received. Soon, she promised herself with new confidence, they would have a play that would be a real hit. The Lindowska Theater had made a place for itself on the Yiddish Rialto. Again Rissa was making weekly trips to deposit money in the bank. She was astonished by the profits that rolled in now. Being a star paid well. Being a star-manager paid far better.

Max approached New Year's Eve, 1920, with a new zest for living. Mort envisioned himself a star maker in the Cecil B. DeMille style, and Carla was working out well. Also, Carla spent much time on her dressing-room couch with her producer. Mort had launched Carla as an exotic. The new Theda Bara. As Max himself had set her up via Laura's column, now syndicated in a dozen large cities.

Max was not proud of the film they made with

Carla from an artistic standpoint, but it was a money-maker. His own status had zoomed upward with the film's success. His new deal with Mort was gratifying. Meyers, of Klein-Meyers Films, wired from New York that Max's salary on the next picture was to be tripled. While most of the filming was done in Hollywood, the money end of the business remained in New York.

While he dressed for the New Year's Eve dinner at Mort's house on Franklin Avenue, he plotted how he would manipulate the schedule of Carla's next film to allow him a month in New York. It was time he went back to see his children. With luck he would persuade Rissa to remarry him. The women he slept with in Hollywood were a physical necessity. But he wanted his wife – his family – back with him.

Shirley wrote how hard Rissa was working to keep the theater running. It was time she moved away from Second Avenue. In Hollywood, too, she'd be a star. Rissa had a quality that the cameras would bring out as the stage could never do.

He'd talk to Mort right after the first of the year, Max decided. He'd go to New York, see the children, talk to Rissa. Just show up one day. Without warning.

Jubilant with this decision, Max left the bungalow and drove in his recently acquired Pierce-Arrow to Mort Klein's house. It was the first time Mort had invited him into the family home.

The tall white colonial with six Doric columns looked as though it belonged on a movie set. Already two Rolls-Royces, a Cadillac and a Stutz were lined up at the curb. It appeared that every light in the house had been switched on for tonight's festivities.

Mort had made it clear that the invitation was for dinner only. Mort always expected his guests to leave by ten. Nor would any liquor be served though other Hollywood hosts managed to circumvent the law.

At home Mort was as moral as the Pope. He had even confided to Max that he had not slept with his wife in sixteen years. Bertha had given him one child after four miscarriages. Mort decided not to try for more.

Max hurried up to the house with the knowledge that tonight could be important to his career. When Mort brought anybody into his home, it was a signal. A butler admitted him and led him into the fifty-foot parlor furnished in baroque Louis XIV. The chairs and sofas were covered in velvet and tapestry. The woods of the cabinets and tables were adorned with ivory, mother-of-pearl and tortoiseshell marquetry. Magnificent damask drapes hung at the tall narrow windows.

Max had expected Mort's wife to be a portly graying woman with little style. Instead she was slender, taller than Mort by two inches and smartly gowned. Max concentrated on being charming to Bertha Klein, and sensed that she knew he was making this effort. The other wives huddled together discussing children and houses.

The talk among the guests, as at most Hollywood parties, centered on business. Here were the moguls who made the industry hum. Mort Klein reported that Myron Selznick was preparing to produce a picture called *The Flapper*, with Olive Thomas. Someone else gossiped about Mary Pickford – would she divorce Owen Moore to marry the now divorced Douglas Fairbanks? Didn't Pickford and Fairbanks realize they would ruin their careers?

Max was conscious of being by far the youngest guest in the house.

Bertha kept looking toward the door with increasing nervousness. The butler, too, appeared in the doorway at regular intervals for some covert exchange with their hostess.

'We should go into dinner,' Bertha told Max. 'I don't know what's taking Rita so long this evening.'

'Oh, she's back from Europe?' Max had never met Rita, but Mort's conversation often focused on his only child.

'I thought it was insane for Mort to let her go alone with those three girls. Traipsing all over Europe by themselves for over half a year. But he promised her if she graduated from college she could have the trip.'

'It must have been exciting for her,' Max consoled.

For a moment Bertha's face lost its aura of serenity.

'Wherever Rita happens to be is exciting.'

Max was suddenly wary. He had jumped to the conclusion that Mort had invited him tonight because he was being brought into the inner circle. Now he suspected Mort had invited him to be Rita's dinner partner.

Max knew when he saw Bertha's face brighten that Rita was coming into the ballroom-size parlor. He made a point not to turn. Instinct told him Rita meant to make an entrance.

'Rita, darling,' her mother called tenderly.

'Am I late?' a girlish voice asked and Max swung about to face the newcomer.

'You're holding up dinner,' her mother scolded. 'This is Max Miller, one of papa's directors,' Bertha introduced, drawing her daughter into their circle. The other guests were inspecting Mort's daughter with admiration. 'My daughter, Rita.'

'Hello, Max.' Rita's voice might be girlish but the rest of her was all woman. Dark hair worn unfashionably long. A body that might be too voluptuous for the cameras but that, Max guessed, made every man among them want to throw her into bed.

'Your father didn't tell me you were as beautiful as one of his stars,' Max said.

'What did my father tell you?' Rita challenged. Her mother signaled to the butler that they were ready to go into dinner, and she slid her arm through his. 'That I'm going to give him a nervous breakdown? That's what he always tells me.'

'He said you were very bright. That you graduated college last May with honors.'

All at once Max knew how to climb over the heads of all the other directors fighting to be Mort Klein's right-hand man. All he had to do was climb into Rita Klein's bed. Her eyes told him she couldn't wait. So the trip to New York would have to wait.

29

On a snowy morning Rissa waited in her tiny office at the Lindowska Theater for her new director to arrive for a conference. Business was so heavy she wished she had a larger theater to accommodate the customers. All of Second Avenue talked about the success of the Lindowska company after a somewhat shaky beginning. But now in February, with weeks to go before the end of the season and two new plays to join their repertory, their director had resigned to go out to Hollywood. *Why wasn't Max here?*

The new director, Ben Lowenstein, was Murray's friend. Murray and he had both worked for three years with an amateur-theater club presenting Yiddish one-act plays. On an off night Murray had persuaded her to go down to see a play directed by Ben. She had been impressed. But opening the first season as a star-manager she had been wary of hiring so inexperienced a director. Now she would have to take that chance.

Ben's directing reminded her of Max's. From Max she had learned to see how a play could be pulled together by a director. Ben Lowenstein had a special touch, like Max. He invented wonderful bits of business that an audience might not recognize as direction, but which, as an actress, she saw and respected. He had Max's enthusiasm for Yiddish theater before he defected to movies.

Rissa tensed as she thought of Max. For a month she had been contemplating a deal to play two weeks during the summer at a Yiddish theater in Philadelphia and another two weeks in Chicago. She dreaded the idleness of summer. Absorbed in roles she could forget the nights when she lay alone in the bed she had shared with Max.

Sometimes it frightened her to realize how much she missed their lovemaking. Tania said some women could spend their lives without a man and not care. For women like Tania and herself making love was a necessary part of their lives. All she had now was a ghost lover. The memory of lying in Max's arms. The memory of her body filled with Max. Even now, remembering how it could be with them, she was aroused.

Perhaps she ought to accept the Philadelphia and Chicago offers. The money they were willing to pay was enticing. Shirley and the children could go along with her. Perhaps Max might come to Chicago to see the children.

Max corresponded regularly with Shirley. When Max's first important movie with Carla Kendell played at the beautiful new fifty-three-hundred-seat Capitol Theater, she had allowed Shirley to persuade her to go along. It had been a shock to discover that Carla Kendell was Celia Kamenstein. Max and Celia together in Hollywood. Disturbing visions haunted her for weeks.

But it worried Rissa that the children were growing up without their father. How could she tell them that their father preferred working in California to being with them in New York? Only Clara remembered him. But how clear was the memory after almost three years? Yet they were so proud about the presents Max sent them from California – she'd seen Clara hold up her pretty round muff and say with such joy, 'Papa sent it to me from Hollywood.' From Shirley, who took Clara and Rae to the movies sometimes, they knew that 'papa works in pictures.'

When they were old enough to understand, she would tell them that their father had a wonderful talent and couldn't be tied down to a family. *But how can I tell them Max wanted us to go with him to California, but I was afraid?*

Rissa started at the knock on the door.

'Come in,' she called.

The door opened. Ben Lowenstein walked into the office. His cocky air of confidence, his insouciant smile reminded her of Max. Even physically he was like Max.

'Am I late?' he asked with mock apology.

'A few minutes. It doesn't matter.' She reached into the top desk drawer to bring out a script. 'I'd like to talk to you about a new play. It's a little different from what we've been doing all season – '

'Experimental?' She heard the excitement in his voice.

'It's a modern play,' she pointed out, handing him the script. With nice little parts for Clara and Rae, who would appear only for weekend performances. Nothing must interfere with school. But already Clara and Rae were being prepared for a future in the theater. They took dancing lessons and singing lessons. Clara had just begun piano lessons. 'Not like what Schwartz is doing at the Irving Place but a good play,' Rissa emphasized. Max would like it, she thought. Five years ago Max would have liked it. Why did she keep thinking of Max? It was because Ben Lowenstein sat across the desk, flipping through the script. His resemblance to Max was unnerving. Why had she never noticed until now?

'You know who would be wonderful as Peter?' Ben's face acquired a zealous glow. 'Muni Weisenfreund. But of course, he's tied up with Schwartz.'

'Murray will play Peter.' Rissa made a point of being firm. She had learned to let every member of the company know that although she was a woman, this was her theater. She made the decisions. That was her responsibility. The future of this theater was her children's future.

'Rissa, it's going to be wonderful to be working with you.'

All at once she was aware of an amorous glow in Ben Lowenstein's eyes. Color edged her high cheekbones. As soon as a woman was divorced, she was fair game for any man.

'We work hard here, Ben. This is a professional company. Not an amateur theatrical club.' She frowned. She had not meant to sound condescending. 'I'm sure you'll fit in well.' But not in her bed. Let Ben Lowenstein get that straight right now.

But, in spite of her convictions, Rissa found it was difficult to be impersonal with Ben. He was warm, like Max. He was enthusiastic about Yiddish theater, as Max once was. If she allowed herself, she could become emotionally involved with him. She strengthened her resolve.

Unlike the other theaters on Second Avenue that played eight or nine performances a week, Rissa had laid down the rule in the beginning that the Lindowska Theater, like those uptown, would be dark one night each week. The union couldn't complain; she paid full salaries. But actors deserved one night a week away from the theater. These were the nights when Lou escorted her to a Broadway play or an opera or concert.

Occasionally Lou took her to dinner at the home of his family in their fine house on Fifth Avenue. Rissa knew Lou's parents were anxious for him to marry. She saw the questions in their eyes each time she visited their house, and was uncomfortable.

Tonight he took her for dinner at Luchow's. Lou's hands moved across the white tablecloth to cover one of hers.

'Rissa, I hadn't meant to talk about something so serious over dinner.' His eyes were anxious. 'I thought we'd talk after the performance.'

'Lou, is something wrong?'

'No. Not wrong,' he emphasized. 'But I have to know. You've been divorced for almost two years. I love you. I've loved you since that first night in the Café Royale. Rissa, will there ever be room in your life for me? Not as a friend. As a husband.'

'Lou, I – ' Rissa fumbled for words. 'I love you the way I love Shirley.' She hurt at the sight of his wince.

'You're one of my dearest friends. I depend on you. I lean on you,' she admitted. 'But in my heart I'm still Max's wife.'

Lou withdrew his hand from hers. Rissa watched as he pulled his thoughts together. She didn't want to hurt him. Why had she let this friendship between them continue so long without letting him know that she'd never marry him? She had clung to Lou because she needed him.

'I was afraid you'd say that,' Lou confessed. 'I hoped, but I was afraid.' His smile was rueful. 'I can't see myself going through life without a wife and a family.'

'Lou, I wish the best for you.' Already she felt a void in her life.

'It'll be a second-best,' he said.

'You have so much to give, Lou. Find someone worthy. Be happy with her.'

'You'll let me continue to be your friend and your attorney?'

'Always, Lou.'

But Rissa understood. Lou and she would have dinner tonight and see the play together. But Lou was looking for a wife. He was thirty-one years old and his family was pressing him to marry. He would have no time to be Rissa Lindowska's companion.

She was glad she had written the Philadelphia and Chicago managers that she would accept their offers to play two weeks in each city.

En route by taxi to a party at Tania's elegant new apartment at the Ansonia, Rissa felt a certain strangeness in appearing alone. But she would have to adjust to this. Already Lou was seeing a girl; she suspected he would marry her. For a tentative moment she had considered inviting Ben to be her escort. Instinct told her he would accept this as an invitation to pursue her. She'd had problems enough these last three months in discouraging this.

The taxi pulled up before the monumental Ansonia on Broadway between Seventy-third and Seventy-fourth streets. Emerging from the taxi Rissa remembered that Tania had been lyrical about the unheard of luxury of shops in the cellar, about the two swimming pools and the roof garden. Caruso and Ziegfeld and DeWolf Hopper lived here. She hurried into the Ansonia and upstairs to Tania's apartment. Conscious of the quiet in the building. Then Tania opened the door to admit her, and the sounds of a party broke the silence.

'Darling, how wonderful to see you!' Tania pulled her into a warm embrace. 'So many exciting people here,' she whispered. 'John Barrymore promised to show up later.'

Rissa admired the large, high-ceilinged parlor. In reckless abandon Tania had furnished the apartment in Art Nouveau. At least thirty people gathered about the room in animated clusters.

Despite her self-consciousness at appearing alone, Rissa realized she was enjoying the party. She was astonished to discover that some of the Broadway actors and actresses knew of Rissa Lindowska. Max always insisted nobody above Fourteenth Street ever heard of the Second Avenue theaters. But Jews were living all over Manhattan – in Harlem, on the upper

West Side. Lou's parents lived in a Fifth Avenue mansion, and Jacob Adler, in the East Seventies. In America Jews did not live in a ghetto.

'Why do you stay in the downtown theater?' a big-time producer demanded of Rissa. 'You're young and beautiful and talented. You belong on Broadway!'

While Rissa tried to explain her dedication to the Yiddish theater to the producer and two other men who joined them, the subject of films was introduced. Rissa was astonished at the respect she heard in their voices.

'I'm not sure that Paramount-Cosmopolitan is smart in making a film of Fannie Hurst's novel, *Humoresque*,' one of the men said. Rissa remembered that Shirley had loved the book. Any book that made her cry, Shirley said, was wonderful. 'They're using a fine actress from Second Avenue.' He turned to Rissa with a smile. 'Vera Gordon.'

'Yes, I know Vera. She's marvelous.' It had shocked her to hear that Vera was going into a picture. But Vera would be wonderful in the role of the Jewish mother.

'Do you realize that thirty-five million people a week are going to the movies?' a man, whom Rissa recognized as the prestigious director of Tania's play, asked the circle. 'Already film company issues can be bought on the New York Stock Exchange. Movies have become big business!'

'Hollywood is a wild place to live,' an actress who had joined them contributed. 'The capital of drink, dope and sex. Fascinating,' she conceded, 'but kind of scary.'

* * *

When Tania's director, drinking too heavily, insisted he would see Rissa home, Tania arranged for an older character actor, the epitome of gentility, to put her in a taxi.

Rissa decided that when they returned from the two-city summer tour, she would buy a car and hire a chauffeur. The man could take her back and forth to the theater and drive Clara and Rae to school.

Lying sleepless in bed Rissa understood that Tania had hoped to tempt her into going into a play uptown. She realized the absurdity of her fears. But still she refused to appear on Broadway or in films. In the Yiddish theater she was *safe* – loved, admired, secure. How did she know what would happen if she tried a Broadway play?

She had four children to raise. She must know the money was there for them in any emergency. To see them through college. After college the girls would come into the theater with her. Joseph would go to medical school. Her face softened as she envisioned the nameplate on his office door: Joseph Lindowska-Miller, M.D.

With the theater closed Rissa devoted her time to making arrangements for the four-week engagement in Philadelphia and Chicago. Shirley would write to Max and mention that they would all be in Chicago. *Would Max make the trip to Chicago to see them?*

It was a long trip even to Chicago, she reminded herself. But if Max wished to see them, he would come. It would be almost three years since she saw Max. Even now she trembled at the prospect of coming face to face with him.

Tomorrow Shirley must write to Max. She couldn't wait to hear what he had to say. She wouldn't allow herself to think about the women who'd filled these three years in Max's life. Max was not a man to be celibate.

Rissa and Shirley sat together in the dining room to compose this important letter to Max. In the parlor Clara was practising her scales at the fine new Steinway piano.

'Shirley, don't make it sound as though I'm *asking* Max to come to Chicago,' Rissa exhorted while Clara roamed from scales to her favorite new popular song, 'Whispering.' Today she didn't even scold Clara for playing by ear. 'Just tell him we'll be there.'

After three versions of the letter had been drafted, Rissa was content. Max would know his family would be in Chicago for the first two weeks of August.

30

Drained from a twelve-hour day on the set plus another two hours seeing the rushes, Max left his Pierce-Arrow and walked across the lawn to his expensive new apartment on Hollywood Boulevard. Carla's second movie was in the can. Tonight, viewing the rushes of the final scenes, he knew he and Mort had another money-maker on their hands.

He'd tackle Mort in a few days about doing a quality film. He'd come across a book last week that would make a tremendous movie. They'd bring in a big stage name for the lead. Do some heavy promotion. It was time Klein-Meyers came up with a prestige film.

Max unlocked the door to the apartment and shoved it open, reaching for the wall switch on the left before he closed the door.

'What took you so long?' Rita's voice was petulant. She stood at the bedroom entrance in her flannel bathrobe, tied carelessly at the waist. She was just out of the tub, he guessed. Rita had a mania for taking baths. Sometimes three a day. 'I've been waiting here for hours.'

'Blame your father,' Max apologized with an appeasing smile. He was never entirely comfortable when Rita was here, though Mort would never believe his darling Rita would go to a man's apartment. She'd had a key to the apartment since he moved in two months ago. She was still an innocent little virgin to her father.

'I want you to take me to dinner,' Rita sulked.

'Dressed like that?' Max grinned.

'Dressed like this.' Rita dropped the bathrobe to the floor. 'After dinner I want you to take me to a new place I heard about. Everybody sits in a circle in silk kimonos and they drink and smoke.'

'Rita, no.' Max was firm. Rita had a rotten habit of dragging him to places where opium and marijuana were brought out to patrons in tea carts. The whole situation made him nervous. It was bad enough without the drugs to get some of the stars to the set in condition to photograph. 'I can't go running around Hollywood when I have to be at the studio again in seven hours.'

'I'll make us scrambled eggs and coffee,' Rita decided. This was her entire culinary repertoire. 'And what will you do for me?' she challenged, moving toward him.

'I'm too tired to do anything but collapse,' he warned. But already the provocative thrust of her huge-nippled breasts was arousing him. Damn little bitch, she knew what she could do to him.

'Let's get you undressed and into bed,' she crooned. 'We'll have our eggs and coffee there. Afterwards.'

'Don't you ever get tired of screwing?' Max laughed.

'Do you?' she demanded, dropping a hand to his crotch.

Rita filled a void in his life. Still, he knew it was a

dangerous game to be screwing Mort's only child. Dangerous, and useful. Rita was his friend in court.

Swinging her generous-sized rump Rita preceded him into the bedroom. He undressed as he walked.

'Leave the lights on,' he ordered when Rita made a move to turn them off.

'Lie down,' she told him. 'Let me do the work.'

He lay along the length of the bed and waited. Knowing each bit of business that Rita would employ. Knowing for a while he'd forget the whole world while Rita devoted herself to bringing him pleasures. He grunted in reproach when she bit him. 'Are you crazy? You want to put me out of commission – forever?'

'What a way to go!' she laughed and raised herself above him.

He closed his eyes and moved with her. God, how could he have thought he was tired?

Afterwards – still nude – Max lounged against the pair of pillows while Rita moved about his tiny kitchen preparing scrambled eggs, toast and coffee. Only now did he notice the letter lying on his dresser. When Rita was here, she always brought in the mail.

He left the bed and crossed to the dresser to pick up the letter. It was from Shirley. Was Rissa surprised when he started sending child-support checks? It made him feel like a man to send money to his children.

He ripped open the envelope and read Shirley's chatty letter. Shirley was his lifeline to the family. Then he stiffened in an excitement that bore no relation to passion. Rissa would be playing in Chicago! She'd bring the children with her!

He reread the letter, savoring every nuance. Rissa must know that Shirley had written about the Chicago performances. He'd work out a schedule that would allow him to be in Chicago the first two weeks in August. He'd see the children. He'd see Rissa.

Those were the good years, when Rissa and he fought together to make a place for her in the Yiddish theater. For a while it had been enough. A fresh optimism welled in him. He'd see Rissa in Chicago, and he'd make her understand this time that she could be a star in films, too. He could make her as big a star as Pickford. He'd choose her films. Direct her. Make her Klein-Meyers' biggest box-office attraction.

'Max — ' Rita's voice brought him back to the moment. Rita and Rissa. Their names so close — their personalities so different.

'Are the eggs nice and dry?' he asked.

'Perfect,' she boasted, bringing in the tray and putting it across his lap before she joined him. 'After we eat, will you take a bath with me?'

'After we eat, you get the hell home,' he said. 'I can't do a picture on two hours' sleep.'

'What's that?' Rita's eyes were skimming the letter on the bed beside him. He saw her face tighten in irritation.

'A letter from a friend in New York.' He hastily picked up the letter and put it behind the pillow. 'She keeps me posted on what the kids are doing.'

He had to be careful around Rita. She was jealous of any woman he looked at.

Mort and Bertha never knew that Rita was in his bed regularly, and in other beds as well. By now Rita had rejected a young attorney handpicked by Bertha and a young doctor sponsored by Mort. While they might not know that Rita bedhopped, they were nervous that their flapper daughter might appear a 'loose woman' to serious suitors.

Rissa and Shirley were busy with preparations for the trip. Rissa's wardrobe, as always, was Shirley's cherished responsibility. Shirley checked for loose hooks and buttons, laundered, pressed. They would travel with two steamer trunks of costumes.

Today Clara had been invited to a birthday party at a classmate's house. Rissa sat in the parlor with Rae while her second oldest rehearsed the scene in which she would appear. Joseph and Katie pretended to be the audience.

'There's Aunt Shirley with Clara.' Rissa heard sounds in the hall.

'Mama, you didn't let me finish.' Rae's dark eyes were aggrieved.

'Darling, I'm sorry. Let's do the whole scene for Aunt Shirley and Clara.

Rissa sensed that Clara was upset, though she dutifully sat on the sofa beside Joseph and Katie to watch the scene from the play. Only afterwards, when Shirley took the other children out to the kitchen for milk, did Clara reveal what troubled her.

'Mama, I was so mad,' she blurted out. 'At the

party one of the girls from my class asked me if you speak English.'

Rissa's eyes widened in dismay.

'I bragged about how you are an actress in the Yiddish theater. With your own theater. But she thought that meant you speak only Yiddish.' Tears of humiliation spilled over. In America to speak only Yiddish was a disgrace.

'Darling, she didn't understand that American actresses play in Yiddish. Your Aunt Tania played in the Yiddish theater before she went uptown to Broadway.' Rissa pulled her small daughter into her arms. Would she dare to play a role on Broadway? *For the sake of the children.* But panic moved in. No! She couldn't. Not even for the children. She forced an encouraging smile. 'When we come back from the tour, we'll have a party. You'll invite all your friends. They'll see that your mother speaks English.'

Rissa waited impatiently for the tour to begin. How could she bear the two weeks in Philadelphia before they moved on to Chicago? Why hadn't she insisted that they play Chicago first?

Shirley handled the mechanical requirements of their traveling. She bought all the necessary tickets. She made their hotel reservations in Philadelphia and Chicago, arranged for the shipment of trunks.

Before they left for Philadelphia, Rissa spoke with Lou on the telephone about certain investments he had recommended. He was engaged, Lou told her. Leah and he would marry after Yom Kippur. A date

411

had not yet been set. His future bride and her mother were checking on places to hold the reception.

A week before Rissa was to leave for Philadelphia, a letter arrived from Max. This time he wrote directly to her. Her hands trembled as she ripped open the envelope. He began with trivia about Hollywood, which she skimmed impatiently. Then he was more serious.

'Rissa, you must face the problems that are coming up for the Yiddish theater. The young are going to Broadway plays and to pictures. Now immigrants won't be coming to replace them, even though the war is over. Everybody is convinced that in less than a year a strong restrictive immigration act will be enforced. Second Avenue will lose its audience.'

Rissa frowned. Max was always seeing doom ahead for the Yiddish theater. But she found pleasure in his concern for her. She turned over the sheet of writing paper, and her face grew luminous. Max was coming to Chicago to see them. Shirley was right. She eagerly scanned the next few lines. Max was making reservations at the Blackstone. The same hotel where they were to stay.

'Shirley!' she called exuberantly. 'Come read Max's letter! He'll be with us in Chicago.'

She'd make Max understand that it was time to come home. He could be a film director in New York. Despite all the talk in the fan magazines about Hollywood, lots of pictures were being made right here. By Paramount-Cosmopolitan in Manhattan – with all that Hearst money behind them. By all the studios in Brooklyn and Astoria.

If Max wanted to buy into a new film company, they could even manage that. She'd sell some stocks if need be. She couldn't believe Max's foreboding about Yiddish theater. She was a star. She'd go on making money for years. She'd replace the stocks she sold.

Now was the time for Max to grow important in films. In New York.

Max said nothing to Mort until early June about taking time off to go out to Chicago to see his children. He explained that Rissa had the children with her in Philadelphia, and would take them along to Chicago in two weeks. Mort was indulgent.

'Sure, Max. Go see the kids. Enjoy yourself. You deserve a couple of weeks off.'

Max was sure he'd encounter trouble when Rita learned about his trip to Chicago. While she tripped through an avenue of beds, she liked to believe only she occupied his.

A few nights before he was scheduled to leave, Max told Rita about the Chicago trip. He chose a time when he was having dinner with the family, hoping Rita wouldn't make a scene before her parents. He drew a sigh of relief when she gave no indication of hostility.

He was conscious only within the last few weeks that Bertha was making an effort to throw Rita and him together within the family circle. While he knew that Bertha was frantic to see Rita married, he had not expected her to accept anything other than a doctor or lawyer. Certainly not a divorced man with

413

four children. But he wouldn't worry about that now. Nobody could be upset if he remarried Rissa. Except Rita.

He came home from the studio the day before he was to board the California Limited for Chicago to find the lighted apartment in shambles. Rita had smashed the lamps, slashed his mattress, broken the china. He found her soaking in the bathtub while she drank champagne from a water glass.

'Rita, what the hell!' He hung over the tub in fury.

'You're going back to your wife,' she accused.

'We're divorced,' he reminded. 'I have no wife.'

'You'll sleep with her,' Rita wailed.

'I'm going to Chicago to see my chidren,' Max insisted. 'Now get out of that tub and go home. Do you know what time it is?'

'Who cares?'

'I care.' Max was firm. 'Your folks are nervous already about you.'

'Oh, Max – ' She pulled herself to her feet and flung her wet arms about him. 'I'm so miserable. Make love to me.'

'Then you'll go home?'

'I'll go home.' She was suddenly demure. 'After all, I won't see you again for two weeks.'

They made love on a cluster of pillows on the floor because the mattress was unusable. Afterwards Max helped her dress and put her into her car. In a dozen hours, he told himself, he'd be aboard the California Limited.

* * *

414

At nine sharp the telephone jarred him into wakefulness. It was Mort's secretary. Mort had to talk to him right away. At the studio.

'Goldie, I'm taking a train to Chicago,' he reminded.

'Mort told me to send a studio car for you. Bring your luggage. He said not to worry about the train.'

'I'll be right there,' Max said tiredly.

He dressed in a hurry. He had packed a valise before he went to bed. He was swigging down a cup of coffee when the studio car arrived.

Fifteen minutes later he sat in Mort's office sputtering in rage. So Mort had rented a yacht for two weeks and was taking a cruise along the California coast. How did Mort have the nerve to shanghai him?

'Mort, you can't do this to me!' he protested. 'You know I'm going to Chicago to see my kids. I haven't seen them in three years.'

'You'll go to New York next month,' Mort soothed. 'Stay *four* weeks. I need you on the yacht. We've grabbed that new Austrian broad who's such a hit in the German picture. You know who I mean — ' Mort had a colossal difficulty in remembering names.

'Elizabeth Mahler.' Max struggled to control his anger.

'She'll be the biggest thing that ever hit the industry. I persuaded her to come on the cruise. It's a cruise for *her*, Max. I'll lose my mind if I can't sign her up for three pictures. She's tough to handle, everybody knows. You know how to deal with these women. Max, if we sign up Mahler, you'll direct,' he tempted. Knowing this was an offer Max could not refuse.

'Four weeks in New York in September,' Max stipulated. He'd have to wire Rissa at the Blackstone and tell her he'd be in New York for four weeks. So they'd have to wait another month. After three years that wasn't so bad.

But Max knew that in some fashion Rita had contrived for him to be part of the two-week cruise along the California coast. Maybe Bertha had some romantic notion that two weeks with Rita might push him into proposing. He'd have to do something about that.

No two weeks of performances ever seemed so long to Rissa as those two weeks in Philadelphia. The children plied Shirley and her with constant questions about their father. Clara assumed fresh importance in the eyes of the others because she had some vague remembrance of him.

'Show me the pictures,' Katie demanded imperiously over and over again, referring to half a dozen group photographs clipped from fan magazines, in which Max appeared among party guests.

Already baby Katie was demanding to know why their father didn't live with them. Why he never came to visit. But that would be all over, Rissa told herself. Max was coming home.

Rissa was exhilarated by the success of the Philadelphia engagement, even while she was impatient for it to be over. The morning after they closed in Philadelphia, they left for Chicago.

Now the train was pulling into the Chicago railroad station. Was Max already at the hotel? Rissa's heart pounded with anticipation.

They embarked from the train. Redcaps came forward to help with the luggage. They were helped into a taxi and driven to the fine Blackstone Hotel.

The children were tired and querulous from the trip. Shirley was alternately solicitous and stern with them. Rissa went through the routine of registering at the desk as speedily as possible. Her trunks had arrived, the clerk told her. They were waiting in her suite.

She hesitated. Should she ask if Max had arrived? No. She'd call downstairs later, she stalled. She looked a mess after the train trip. Let her make herself presentable. She turned to Shirley and the children, indicating that they were to follow the bellhop who was to escort them to their rooms.

'Did you ask if Max was here yet?' Shirley whispered while they waited for the elevator.

'No,' Rissa admitted. 'I'll phone down to the desk when the children are settled.' The possibility that Max might already be here in the hotel was simultaneously exhilarating and terrifying.

In their suite the children were all at once lively again. Katie was hungry. Joseph and Rae were thirsty. Clara tugged at her mother's sleeve.

'Mama, when will we see papa?'

'Soon,' she soothed. A knock on the door sounded abnormally loud in her anticipation. Her heart pounded. Max? 'Who is it?' She darted to the door and pulled it open without waiting for a reply.

A bellhop stood there.

'A telegram just arrived, ma'am.'

Rissa stared in trepidation at the small yellow envelope. Even now telegrams terrified her.

'Thank you.' She reached out a hand for the telegram and turned mutely to Shirley, who was digging change from her purse for the bellhop.

'Rissa, open it,' Shirley urged. But her eyes were anxious.

Rissa opened the envelope and pulled out the small yellow sheet of paper. She glanced first at the signature. The telegram was from Max. He wasn't at the hotel.

UNAVOIDABLY DETAINED IN HOLLYWOOD ON BUSINESS STOP DEVASTATED STOP WILL BE IN NEW YORK FOR WHOLE MONTH OF SEPTEMBER STOP ALL MY LOVE, MAX

'He can't make it.' Rissa handed the telegram to Shirley. Clara looked ready to cry.

'Darling, he'll see you in another four weeks,' Shirley consoled as her eyes swept over the message. 'Some emergency came up. You'll see him in September.'

31

The *Contessa* had dropped anchor in the San Diego harbor two days ago so that the crew would have ample time to put the quarters in perfect order for the cruise guests. All except Elizabeth Mahler, expected later in the morning, had arrived in time for dinner last evening.

Conditioned to rising before 6:00 A.M., Max stood alone at the railing of the deserted deck and admired the splendor of the pink-streaked sunrise. Rissa would have received his telegram, he reasoned. She'd understand that their reconciliation was merely postponed for four weeks. She knew the demands of the entertainment world.

Max relished the luxury of the *Contessa*, at the disposal of Mort and his wife, Rita, Carl Meyers from the New York office, Elizabeth Mahler and himself for two weeks away from civilization. Only now did he realize how tense and tired he was from the long grind at the studio. Mort expected a cast to work until everybody collapsed. Actors swore they'd never work for him again, but of course they did.

The three-hundred-foot yacht had eight guest cabins and an apartment for the host on its top deck. Below was an ornate lounge with old masterpieces hanging on the walls. He recognized a Gauguin and an El Greco. A Rembrandt hung in the crystal-chandeliered dining room. Bertha was in awe of the paintings. Mort was more interested in movie posters.

Mort had confided on the drive to San Diego that the yacht's music room had been converted for the cruise to a projection room. He meant to impress Elizabeth Mahler with their output. Max suspected Carl Meyers was here to assess the value of Mort's coveted new star, and to hold him down if Mahler's demands were too high.

So far Rita was behaving herself. He was apprehensive about how long she could maintain this aura of demure innocence. He couldn't afford to have Mort discover Rita in his bed. The only way to salvage his position in that kind of situation would be to marry her. He had no such plans.

'Would you care for coffee, sir?'

Max turned about with a start to face a crew member carrying a tray with a carafe of coffee and the necessary essentials.

Max smiled brilliantly. 'An unexpected pleasure at this hour.'

Max sat at a small table on the deck and consumed three cups of perfectly brewed coffee before the sea air soothed him into drowsiness. He left the table and stretched out on one of the deck chairs. Despite his anger at being shanghaied this way when he meant to be in Chicago with Rissa and the children, Max felt some of his tension retreating. In moments he was asleep.

Max awoke to the sounds of exuberant greetings further down the deck. He pulled out his watch. He'd been sleeping for four hours.

'Max!' Mort's raucous voice was jarring in these serene surroundings. 'Come meet Elizabeth.'

Max hauled himself from the depths of the deck chair and approached the cluster around the newcomer, who appeared to have arrived with at least a dozen valises. She was small, fair-haired and exquisitely fashioned. Drawing closer he was impressed with the perfect oval of her face, her delicate features, her jade green eyes, focused now on him.

'Elizabeth, this is Max Miller. Already they're calling him the Boy Genius.' Mort was effusive. 'He's directing all our top pictures now.'

'Welcome aboard,' Max said with plotted casualness. Mort was right. This could be Hollywood's new reigning star. She'd photograph like a dream. Instinct told him that first highly successful Berlin-made picture had not been a fluke.

'It was so hot driving down here.' All at once she was wistful, pleading to be cuddled. Her accent was charming, but of course, nobody would hear that in pictures. 'So tiring.'

Max beckoned to a steward.

'Please bring Miss Mahler a glass of orange juice. Bank it in ice.' Other stewards were taking her luggage to her cabin.

He pulled her small, slender hand over his arm and headed toward a shaded area of deck chairs. He saw the pleased exchange between Mort and Carl Meyers. Rita looked stormy. Her mother was trying to draw her into conversation.

Max made a point of being attentive to Elizabeth, though he explained to Rita that this was at her father's orders. They had to sign up the Austrian import before the other vultures enticed her away with higher offers. Rita sulked. Her mother looked unhappy. Max was nervous.

Elizabeth came from a well-placed Austrian family. She had gone to school for a while in London, hence her command of English. She had left the German studio after a battle with her director. Besides, she told Max, she was eager to see America. She had heard that American men were fascinating.

Max warned Mort and Carl not to talk business with Elizabeth until she was relaxed. She had fired her European agent and declared she would handle her own business affairs. Carl considered this a strong advantage. Outside of Pickford and Chaplin, what movie star had a head for business? Mort hated all agents. A bunch of bastards out to screw the producers.

Rumors had it that she was difficult to handle. Laura had passed on some choice tidbits. But the results would be worth the effort.

On their third night aboard Mort showed Elizabeth their latest film with Carla. Max sat beside her, whispering comments. Carla was not a quality actress. Carla had none of her sensitivity, her mobility of face. Max was excited about working with Elizabeth. No actress had excited him this way since Rissa.

'Max,' Mort demanded impatiently when they met for an arranged early breakfast on the fourth morning, 'what do you think? Can we sit down and talk business with her tonight?'

'I don't think it's time,' Max said.

'So how long do we have to wait? You screwed our new star already?' Mort's eyes were avid.

'That would be a big mistake,' Max warned. 'At this point.' Elizabeth was sending out hints that she would not repulse his advances. 'She's not our star yet.'

'I see it coming.' Mort nodded in confidence. 'She wants you to be her director. Bertha was smart in telling me to bring you along. My wife has a smart *yidishe kop*.'

His wife had a conniving daughter. Rita had put her mother up to inviting him on the cruise. But mama was keeping a sharp eye on Rita. Bertha Klein might already be shopping for Rita's trousseau in her mind, but she was determined that Mort see his daughter as the sweet little virgin from Vassar. Next to the studio she was the pride of his life.

The days passed by in leisurely procession. The men waited for the psychological moment to discuss a contract. Mort's patience was growing short.

'Max, she knows we didn't invite her on the cruise because Carl and I like to play pinochle with her every night,' he argued.

'Talk to her tomorrow,' Max advised. 'Just Carl and you and Elizabeth. Don't let her see me on your side. I've got to direct her. I've got to be her friend.'

Mort nudged him and grinned.

'She's got the hots for you already. You're cutting me out.' He pretended to be annoyed. But Mort was intrigued by the possibility of having a star that could take her place beside DeMille's Gloria Swanson.

Elizabeth charmed everybody on board, with the

exception of Rita. Though Rita was not overtly hostile, it was clear to the others that Elizabeth was not one of her favorite people. Elizabeth seemed eager to win Rita's approval. Yet at each overture of warmth, Rita flinched.

By their sixth day on board Max began to sweat. While Rita sat next to him in the improvised projection room, where Mort insisted on showing another Klein-Meyers film each night, Rita whispered that she'd come to his room later. On the other side of him Elizabeth gently rubbed her thigh against his.

Max knew that Mort and Carl planned to corral Elizabeth into the lounge after the film to talk contract. Both Rita and her mother had been warned to absent themselves from the scene. As soon as the showing was over, he went directly to his cabin.

He opened the door and flipped on the wall switch. Rita lay across the bed with her dress hiked above her hips, one black-stockinged leg flexed in invitation. As usual she wore nothing underneath.

'Rita, what the hell are you doing here?' Max fumed.

'I feel like a goddamn virgin again,' she sulked. 'You haven't been near me since we came on board.'

'All hell will break loose if your mother finds you here.' Max was apprehensive.

'Mama is in bed reading *Photo Play*. She won't stir until she's read every page. Max, lock the door.' She sat up to pull the dress above her head. 'I swear, Max, if you don't come over here and screw me this minute I'll yell rape.' Her face was triumphant. 'And papa will believe me.'

* * *

Max left the bed and went into the bathroom. Normally it didn't bother him that Rita was a noisy lay. In truth it aroused him. But tonight he was sweating. He could see mama throwing rice at the wedding already. He would have to do something fast to get Rita off his neck.

Rita returned to her cabin. Max waited a few minutes and then went on deck. He could hear laughter in the lounge. Business must be going well. Then Elizabeth left the lounge to go to her cabin. Carl, ever the gentleman, was walking her to the door.

Max strode toward the lounge. Mort was at the bar pouring himself a drink of Scotch.

'How did it go?' Max asked.

'Like a dream.' Mort was ecstatic. 'We talked. I just happened to have the contract handy. She signed. Three pictures, Max; and I didn't have to raise the ante one cent!'

'Great, Mort. You pulled it off again.' It was politic to make Mort believe this deal was one of his making.

'I'm sending word to Laura Ainsley to join us the last days. Let her get a head start with Elizabeth. I want a feature story in *Photo Play*. I want items in the gossip columns.'

'The sooner we start building her, the better,' Max agreed.

Laura would be delighted to spend two days on the yacht. She was smart; she'd built up, in a startlingly short time, the strongest of loyalties in Hollywood. Both producers and important stars were in her debt.

'Max, I've been thinking.' Mort's tone put him on

guard. 'Maybe you shouldn't get too thick with Elizabeth. How can you handle a star on the set when she's been in your bed the night before. Be friendly, but no screwing.' Max interpreted it as an order. 'I look to your future, Max.' He laid a hand on Max's shoulder. 'You're like my own son now.'

What Mort had in mind, Max understood, was son-in-law. His mind jumped into action.

'Mort, I have to be honest with you.' He was deceptively gentle. 'I've kept it pretty much to myself. I haven't said a word to Rita yet. On my honor,' he swore. 'But Rita is about the sweetest, loveliest girl I've ever known. It'd make me sick to mess around with Elizabeth, feeling the way I do about Rita.'

'Max, why didn't you tell me?' Mort glowed.

'There's a problem,' Max apologized. 'I thought it only right, when we're so close, to tell you. I had something going with one of the bit players. God, she was marvelous — ' Max whistled in appreciation.

'So the wives have to know?' Mort clucked. 'What they don't know won't hurt 'em.'

'I picked up a dose of clap,' Max confided and Mort grimaced in sympathy. 'I went to a good doctor, and he cleared it up for me. But Mort — ' He leaned forward as though in deepest confidence. Knowing Mort's yearning for a grandchild. Knowing Rita was his only means of fulfilling this wish. 'I'm sterile now. Not impotent,' he stressed, 'but no children.'

Mort paled. His hand shook as he lifted his glass.

'Max, I told you, I feel toward you like I would toward a son. But not a son-in-law.' He shook his head. 'A son-in-law I expect to give me grand-children. But you'll get over Rita,' he soothed. 'Bertha's been talking about taking her to New York for some shopping. Then maybe they'll go to Paris. And for you, Max, I'll do what I never did for anybody. Not only will you direct Elizabeth Mahler. You'll be coproducer with me on her pictures!'

32

Rissa returned from Chicago and went immediately into rehearsal for the new season. Because she was so involved with production details at the theater, she commissioned Shirley to go up to Altman's and Best's and Bonwit Teller's to shop for exquisite, shockingly expensive chiffon negligees and nightgowns. An enormous bottle of Houbigant of Paris *Quelques Fleurs*.

New drapes must be hung in the parlor. A new counterpane bought for their bedroom. Red roses must fill the house on the day of Max's arrival.

Rissa searched her reflection in the mirror. Had she been wrong to bob her hair? Would Max hate it? Would he think she had grown too slim?

Max, of course, would stay at the apartment. He would share her bed. The court might say they were not husband and wife. In the eyes of the rabbi they were still married.

She marked the calendar on the day that Max was to leave California. Each succeeding day she made a mental note of where he was. He was traveling across Kansas. He was changing from the California Limited to Chicago to the Twentieth Century Limited. By the time she knew that Max's train was racing along the shore of Lake Erie Rissa felt as though the years had melted away. *Max was coming home to her*. This was the way wives must feel whose husbands had been away at war.

Max would arrive tomorrow. The night the theater would be dark, she rejoiced. She would be at Grand Central Station when the elegant Twentieth Century Limited arrived. Tomorrow night they would all sit down to dinner together.

Shirley had been cooking for three days. She refused to allow anyone except herself to prepare dinner on such an occasion. But Rissa insisted that Fanny, their good-natured buxom maid, be persuaded to remain past her normal time to serve the meal. Shirley was part of this family. She would not leave the table.

Yesterday she talked with Lou, busy now with preparations for his wedding.

'Leah was upset when the rabbi told us the date we settled will be *tishah b'Ab*. The *mishnah* says this is not a day for marriage – it's a fast day,' he pointed out humorously. 'The day commemorating the fall of the temple in Jerusalem. But everything is working out. You'll receive your invitation any day. Rissa, you will come?'

'Lou, of course. You're a very special person to this family.'

Then she told him about Max's coming to New York and her hopes for their future. Lou had checked on her stocks and decided which she should first consider selling in the event Max needed financing to buy into a film company. He was respectful of the booming film indusry, and in view of Max's knowledge and contacts considered this change of investment promising. When she had gotten off the phone with Lou, she felt that life was, indeed, promising.

'Shirley, I'm so happy I'm scared,' she admitted. 'I'm afraid that it's too good to last. Just think, Max will be home by tomorrow at this hour!'

'Rissa, Max will be here for a month.' Shirley was anxious. 'He's a movie director in Hollywood – '

'He'll be a movie director in New York,' Rissa vowed. 'It'll be wonderful. With Max maybe I'll even make a film. Shirley, do you realize he hasn't seen the children in three years? Only Clara remembers him!'

'The girls are home.' Shirley rose to her feet. 'I'll go let them in.'

Rissa stood at the window watching while Fanny intervened in a small battle waging between tempestuous young Katie and Joseph.

Shirley was talking with Thomas at the door. He was taking the car to the garage to be washed. It must be shining when they drove to Grand Central to pick up Max tomorrow. Had Shirley written him about the black limousine she had bought, and that they had Thomas to drive for them now?

Rae walked into the parlor first. Unfamiliarly somber. Behind her came Clara, eyes red from crying. Shirley trailed behind them.

'Clara, baby, what happened?' Rissa stretched out her arms to her eldest with loving solicitude. Sweet, sensitive Clara. 'Did the dancing teacher scold you?'

'It wasn't Miss Dozier,' Rae said ominously. 'It was Eleanor. She said bad things about papa.'

Rissa tensed. The children were so excited about Max's arriving tomorrow. They must have been bragging again about their father, the movie director.

430

Rissa tried to appear calm. 'Darling, what did Eleanor say about papa?'

'She said her mother said that papa was no good. She said papa's always running around with Hollywood actresses. She brought this to the class and showed it to everybody!' Clara sobbed, pulling a newspaper clipping from the pocket of her pinafore. She handed the clipping to her mother as though the paper was scorching her small hand. Shirley darted to Rissa's side.

'It's Laura Ainsley's column.' Rissa's eyes were fastened to the gossip tidbit about Max, circled in pencil. She knew that Laura Ainsley was Max's friend. Shirley reveled in Max's friendship with name personalities like Laura Ainsley. 'The item says that everybody in Hollywood is sure Max was secretly married to Elizabeth Mahler when they spent two weeks together on a yacht cruise last month.' *When Max was supposed to have come to Chicago to be with his family.* How could he do this to her? To the children? 'Shirley – ' She fought to keep her voice even. 'Who is Elizabeth Mahler?'

'An Austrian actress who's come to America.' Shirley was pale. 'But a newspaper item, Rissa. What does that mean?' She tried to dismiss this with a shrug.

'You told me yourself that Laura Ainsley is a close friend of Max.' Despite Rissa's efforts her voice was shrill with pain. She wouldn't say that if it wasn't true!'

'Rissa, in Hollywood they say all kinds of things. If Max was married, would he be rushing to New

431

York to see you?' But Shirley's reasoning had no effect on Rissa.

'It says here that Max and Elizabeth spent the last two weeks on a yacht off the coast of California. That's why he couldn't come to Chicago. He was – ' Rissa broke off because Clara and Rae were avidly absorbing every word. 'Shirley, Lou offered me his family cottage up at Pine Hill for a few days if I wanted to go up with Max. I'm calling him to say I'd like to borrow it right now. I want you to take the children and go up there. Thomas will drive you up and stay until it's time to come back to New York.'

'Rissa, talk to Max,' Shirley pleaded.

'I'll talk to him,' Rissa promised. Her eyes indicated they mustn't talk in front of Clara and Rae. Both little girls were disturbed without fully comprehending what was happening.

'Mama, how can we go away when papa's coming?' Clara was troubled.

'We can't go away,' Rae insisted. 'We have to go to school.'

'You'll have to miss a few days.' Rissa was resolute. 'Papa isn't coming. He's busy with his new wife. You'll return from the cottage in a few days,' she promised. She wouldn't allow Max to see the children. Not when he'd hurt them this way.

Shirley hurried Clara and Rae out to the kitchen before they could question their mother further. Rissa was already at the phone calling Lou. *How could Max do this to them?*

* * *

Rissa sat in a chair by the parlor window and stared into the garden without seeing. The children had been put to bed. Clothes to care for their needs for three or four days were packed. Thomas knew that they would leave early in the morning for the cottage at Pine Hill.

'Rissa, talk to Max,' Shirley urged again. 'What's in gossip columns isn't always the truth.'

'Maybe Max isn't married to her,' Rissa conceded. 'But he spent two weeks on a yacht with her when he was supposed to be in Chicago with me. I want no more lies from Max. I can't put up with Max's women. And I won't let him see the children. You saw how upset Clara and Rae were when they came home from dancing class.'

'That nasty little girl!' Shirley churned with rage. 'How could she behave that way?'

'She heard her parents talking about it.' Rissa recoiled from being involved in Hollywood gossip. But Max's children were her children; she was part of it. 'I can imagine what they said. But I won't allow Max to hurt the children this way again. I won't give him the opportunity.'

'Rissa, they're looking forward to seeing Max. That's all they've talked about for days,' Shirley protested.

'They're children. They'll forget fast.'

'Rissa, Max made mistakes in your marriage,' Shirley conceded. 'But he was hurt. You were a star and he was nobody. When he wanted to take the family to California, you wouldn't go – '

'Shirley, how could I? How could I have gambled

with the children's security?' Her eyes searched Shirley's. In anguished moments she asked herself if she had been wrong to refuse to go to California. 'You think I should have gone?' she accused, trembling now.

'Rissa, I could have done no differently,' Shirley admitted. 'You'd worked so hard to get where you were. Who would have hired you again on Second Avenue if you walked out in the middle of the season? But Max didn't see this. Max and you can start all over again. Both of you have to compromise. Life is made up of compromises.'

'I don't trust Max anymore,' Rissa said slowly. 'When I saw that column about Max and Elizabeth Mahler, I knew I'd never trust him again. Every time he'd be away from me, I'd wonder in whose bed he was lying.'

'Sometimes it's better to close your eyes, darling.' Shirley's face was tender with compassion. 'You still love Max. *Compromise.* Enjoy what you can have together.'

'I can't. In other things I can compromise. But not in my marriage.' She knew the legend on Second Avenue that men like Adler and Thomashefsky – and Max had their magnetic charm – could not be faithful to one woman. Nobody expected them to be. Not even their wives. But she, Rissa Lindowska, expected her husband to be faithful.

Rissa started at the intrusion of the doorbell.

'Is Lou coming over?' Shirley asked, rising to go to the door.

'No. We talked over the phone,' Rissa reminded. He had been disturbed by her news.

She sipped the strong hot tea, unmindful of the humidity of the early September evening. She had been afraid something would happen to disrupt her happiness. Why must life always be like that? Little patches of pleasure, grabbed with such eagerness and hope.

Shirley came back into the parlor with a small yellow envelope in her hand.

'A telegram from Max,' Rissa guessed. 'Telling us he can't make it.'

'It's for Max.' Shirley was surprised. 'Some business from Hollywood, I suppose.'

'I'll give it to him when he arrives here tomorrow,' Rissa said. 'Put it on the breakfront.' She rose in decision. 'Max is old enough to find his way to the apartment, I won't be at the station to meet him.'

The Twentieth Century Limited had passed the Spuyten Duyvil Station. In twenty-two minutes it would be pulling into Grand Central Terminal. Max sat in the smoking car because he was too restless to remain in his own compartment.

He had tired of playing cards with the cluster of movie people en route to New York whom he had encountered in the dining car on the first night aboard the California Limited. He'd ignored the attractive young starlet who'd been eager to while away the journey in bed with him.

Mort told him the five days on the train would be a rest cure. He needed one after the last two weeks.

First the stormy scenes with Rita, who fought against traveling to New York and then to Paris with her mother. Somehow, she suspected he was responsible. Then the problem of getting to know his new star. Elizabeth vacillated between dramatic bouts of self-doubt and nights of demanding proof of her sexual appeal. He'd never slept with a woman of such voracious appetite.

Elizabeth would be marvelous on the screen. He had been sure of that the moment he met her. But she made every temperamental actress he ever encountered look like a pussycat.

She accepted direction the way Rissa did. She was capable, like Rissa, of the most subtle nuances. All he had to do was suggest and her face reflected the emotions he asked of her. But she lacked Rissa's stability. Rissa's sharp mind. When he got back in October to start the picture, he could count on months of hell, but Elizabeth Mahler would be electrifying on the screen. And he'd be her producer-director. He had waited a long time for an opportunity like this.

Max's eyes fastened on the smoking-car window at his left. He was beginning to recognize the Manhattan skyline. He reached into his pockets to pull out the envelope of snapshots that he had brought along to brighten the trip. Bless Shirley for sending him so many pictures of the children. Katie had been a few months old when he left. Now she was three and a half, and Joseph a year older. Clara and Rae both went to school.

He'd have to make Rissa understand that to stay

with the Yiddish theater was suicide. So right now it seemed a new golden era. It would disappear fast. Besides, why should Rissa limit herself? She had such enormous talent. It was time she pushed aside the childish fears. She was twenty-eight years old. Her career as an actress was just beginning.

Max was impatient with the final, slow pull into the station. At last they were on the platform, the famous red carpet laid in place. A redcap came forward to take his luggage. He gazed among the crowd for Rissa. She wasn't there. He was disappointed.

'A taxi, please,' he told the redcap.

In the taxi en route to the apartment Max remembered his despair, his humiliation when he had left New York. But nothing had been right for him here. It took him a while; but once he broke the ice in Hollywood he moved ahead with the pace he appreciated. Meeting Laura on the train going out had been a lucky break. They had been good for each other.

His eyes skimmed the streets as the taxi moved down Park Avenue, then turned west to Fifth and south again. He was aware of changes, even in three years. But then Hollywood, too, had changed in that short time.

By the time the taxi pulled up before the brownstone, Max was envisioning Rissa in his arms. For the first time in three years he'd make love to his wife. Not one woman ever satisfied him like Rissa.

Stepping out of the taxi his eyes went to the window boxes across the lower floor apartment. Pink and red geraniums and coleus bloomed healthily. Rissa always had to have pots or boxes of flowers.

Rissa started at the sound of the doorbell.

'Fanny,' she called, but Fanny was already hurrying down the hall to answer the summons.

Fanny knew what was happening to this family, Rissa thought bitterly. In a dozen ways today she had shown her sympathy. All Fanny had been told was that the children's father was coming today. Rissa said nothing about his staying. She had not even told Fanny whether Max would be here for dinner. She saw no reason that he would be.

Her heart pounded at the sound of Max's voice in the hall. Why had he done this to them? Why hadn't he come to Chicago when he was supposed to come instead of going on that yacht with Elizabeth Mahler? Max always said that if timing was not right in a play, then the play wasn't right. In life it was the same.

'Miss Lindowska's in the parlor,' Rissa heard Fanny say, and then Max was bounding into the room.

'Rissa!' He came toward her with outstretched arms. She stood motionless, fighting to appear impersonal. 'Oh, Rissa — '

She managed to move her face so that his mouth brushed her cheek. She felt him stiffen in astonishment.

'You're looking well, Max.' She avoided his eyes. 'Fanny, will you bring us tea, please.'

'Where are the children?' All at once he was wary.

'Max, there was a telegram for you.' She turned away and walked to the breakfront across the room to retrieve the yellow envelope. 'It came yesterday.'

Max took the envelope, ripped it open and pulled out the small sheet. He scowled and swore under his breath.

'Damn it, can't they leave me alone even for a week?'

'You have to return to Hollywood,' she guessed.

'I may have to go back sooner than I planned,' he admitted. Puzzled by her coldness. Rissa knew that Shirley had led him to believe she would welcome him with warmth.

'To your bride?' Rissa couldn't prevent the sarcasm that crept into her voice.

'Rissa, I'm not married.' Max stared at her in shock. 'Who gave you that idea?'

'Your friend Laura Ainsley.' Rissa picked up the neatly clipped segment of newspaper and handed it to Max. 'A little girl in Clara and Rae's dancing class gave it to Clara. She was terribly upset.'

'Rissa, it means nothing,' Max protested. 'Publicity for a new star the studio's building. You know how the public eats up that stuff. But Laura should have checked this one with me.' His face was grim.

'Did you enjoy the cruise with your new star?'

'Rissa, Elizabeth Mahler means nothing to me. Every day that we've been apart I've thought of you. You don't know the nights I lay awake wanting you beside me. I stopped fighting the divorce because your lawyer was so insistent – and what did I have to offer you then? But everything is changed now. Rissa,

439

there's no limit to where I can go in the movie industry.'

'But not with your family,' Rissa threw at him. 'I won't have the children hurt this way again. I won't be hurt again. Stay out of our lives, Max.'

Max's eyes searched hers. She battled to hold herself aloof. Inside she was a shambles. She longed to be in Max's arms. She yearned for him to convince her that they could have a life together again. But she knew she could never believe him again.

'I'd like to see the children, Rissa,' he said after a moment.

'I've sent them to the country. After what happened yesterday, it would be bad for Clara and Rae to see you.'

'Then let Shirley bring them to me in Hollywood for a visit,' Max said. 'During the long school holiday.'

'That would be absurd. They'd have ten days of traveling. There'd be no time for visiting.'

'Have Shirley bring them out to me next summer.' Max was fighting against anger.

'I won't allow them to visit Hollywood. The whole world knows what that town has become.'

'That's a crock of shit,' Max brushed this aside. 'A bunch of nervous clergymen and hysterical women making noises. Despite all the ridiculous publicity, Hollywood is a small town. People work like dogs at the studio, go home and sleep at night. The town closes up by nine o'clock.'

'Max, don't expect me to believe that!' Rissa's color was high. 'Everybody hears about the wild

Hollywood parties. And I doubt that you're sitting them out. When Joseph was so sick with the flu two years ago, I called you at three o'clock in the morning – California time. You weren't at home.'

Max was ashen. 'Joseph was very sick and you didn't let me know?'

'I called and you were not at home. You never once thought to ask if we were all right.' All Rissa's pent-up hurt was welling up in her. 'All you thought about were the damn pictures you were making!'

'The flu epidemic was in the autumn,' Max searched his memory. 'That's when I was on location with the company. That's right, we were in Tucson shooting scenes for a Western.'

'When Joseph was so sick we were afraid he'd die, I couldn't reach you, Max. Didn't you worry about the children when the whole world was terrified of the flu? There's no room in your life for anything but pictures. It's been that way a long time.'

'I didn't know you hated me so much,' Max said.

Rissa turned her face away lest he read her anguish. Hate him? She'd never love another man.

'There's no need for you to stay in New York. You can go back to your studio as they've asked.'

'I want you to send the children out to spend time with me next summer,' Max said. 'I want summer custody of my three daughters and my son.'

'I won't let them go out there. I won't let them see you here.' Rissa was in control of herself now. She would be father and mother to her children. As she had been for the past three years.

441

'I'll go to court and ask for summer custody,' he warned. 'They're my children, too.'

'I'll fight you. I'll declare you an unfit father!'

Rissa saw Max wince. He couldn't afford the ugly publicity that would come out of a custody fight. He wouldn't fight her for the children. He wouldn't take that chance.

Even if the gossip column was wrong, how could she expose her children to a father who made a mockery of marriage? Every time something went wrong between Max and her, he would run to another bed. She couldn't expose *herself* to that.

Tonight she'd lie alone again. The exquisite new nightgowns and negligees would hang in the closet. Her beautiful dream was shattered. Nothing had changed.

33

Max sat with Carl Meyers and his wife of thirty-five years in a smart speakeasy situated in the basement of a midtown brownstone house and tried to appear attentive to Carl's tale of troubles. He had phoned Carl, according to Mort's instructions, and been invited to stay at the Meyers' town house overnight. Nobody was concerned about the emergency in his life. Carl and his wife thought he was here on a vacation.

'Look, Max, you know how excited Mort gets sometimes. Now he's convinced he had a heart attack yesterday. Bertha says it's indigestion. Mort never knows when to stop eating. But the fact is – he can't cope with Elizabeth.'

'But, Carl, we don't start shooting until next month.' Max was still unnerved by the confrontation with Rissa. He had expected to be received as the conquering hero. Damn it, he meant to reconcile with her. He wanted his wife and his children more because he still loved her. He was sick to death of living the way he did in Hollywood. 'How much trouble can Elizabeth be causing?'

'She refused to go to the studio for her fittings. She won't come in for photographs. She refuses interviews.' He looked at his wife for a moment in mute apology. 'Right now no fifteen-year-old messenger boy is safe around her. Mort is scared to death somebody'll complain to the vice squad! Max, you know the trouble we're having with these rotten women's clubs and the churches. A scandal would kill Elizabeth before she makes her first picture in America.'

'I'll be on the Twentieth Century when it leaves tomorrow afternoon,' Max promised. Rissa had heard all the gossip about Hollywood. No wonder she didn't want the children to visit. But she really didn't understand what Hollywood was like. It thrived on gossip. Why couldn't she give him a chance to explain? She was sure he spent every night in another woman's bed. Hell, he didn't have that kind of energy after twelve to fourteen hours a day at the studio. 'I'll phone Mort in the morning,' he said.

'Phone Elizabeth, too,' Carl urged. 'Make her come to her senses. Max, you know how to handle women.'

'Carl, enough shoptalk,' his wife objected as the waiter arrived with impressive-looking steaks. Earlier Carl had boasted that this was a speakeasy where the food and liquor were superb. 'Max, it's a shame to spoil your vacation,' she soothed. 'But that's this crazy business. Thank God, we're in New York. The stories Bertha tells me!' She clucked in distaste.

'But Bertha doesn't mind spending the money Mort makes in this crazy business,' Carl said drily.

Max was relieved when Carl suggested they leave at an early hour. He needed the privacy of the Meyers' guest room to sort out his feelings about what had happened in Rissa's apartment. The apartment *he* had found for them with such joy in his heart.

He slept little in the large, high-ceilinged guest room. Rissa had become a vindictive, unforgiving woman. But she was even more beautiful than when she had been a girl. Lying here alone in the darkness he remembered what it was like to make love to her.

But he wouldn't let her keep the children from him. His children, too. He remembered the agony of their birth — and then, after Katie, when the doctor told them there must be no more children.

Rissa would not keep the children from him, he vowed. His children would come to know their father.

Max cursed the slowness of travel across the continent. Five days wasted. Maybe they could push the picture schedule ahead, he plotted on the second day, and ordered a porter to bring him writing paper. He'd use these days to work out details on Elizabeth Mahler's first American film. He couldn't sit here on the train and stare out the window till they arrived in Los Angeles.

Wrapped up in the projected movie, Max found relief. He didn't love Rissa any less, but there was less time to think. He was more than a director now, he reminded himself in satisfaction. He was a coproducer on Klein-Meyers' most ambitious production.

When the train pulled into Los Angeles at last, Max felt a little less lonely. He was part of this town now. He thought about buying a house. Maybe on

Hollywood Boulevard. A house large enough so that each of the children could have a bedroom on visits to California.

New buildings were rising everywhere. The pepper trees which he had admired on first arriving were being chopped down so that the new stores and cafés, in the shape of enormous wieners, windmills, dogs, were more visible. The orange groves were being chopped down, depriving the town of the scent of orange blossoms. Even the yucca was disappearing. Bulldozers were digging into the hills to clear sites for new houses.

Back in Hollywood Max settled down into the role of producer-director. At Mort's prodding he took over Elizabeth Mahler as his personal project. Laura was enlisted to help in promoting the side of their new star that Klein-Meyers wished to present to the public.

On the set Elizabeth vacillated between passivity and bitchiness. But after a difficult day Elizabeth would appear with presents for everybody and charming, abject apologies.

There were nights when Max worked alone with her to bring out an element that the next day the cameras would perpetuate for future generations. And there were nights when Elizabeth sobbed in his arms because she distrusted her talents and was afraid. Those were the nights when Max stayed in Elizabeth's bed. Mort was blunt. Better him than some fourteen-year-old kid she might drag home with her.

* * *

Despite Shirley's exhortations Rissa limited her life to the theater, the children and lunches uptown with Tania. She vowed to devote every possible moment to the children. She would fill their lives with love. They would not miss their father. She brought the three girls, even little Katie, into the new theater season. All three were ecstatic at sharing in this side of mama's life.

Yet sometimes the poignance of Clara's small face worried her. Clara more than the others had been upset that they had not seen Max. Rissa discovered that Clara had become an obsessive reader of the fan magazines that Shirley kept on a chair in the kitchen.

Shirley took the children to see Elizabeth Mahler's film, produced and directed by Max. Shirley said Elizabeth was wonderful. She told Rissa about the various actors with whom Elizabeth was reported to be having romances. But the situation had not changed, Rissa told herself unhappily. If Max wasn't sleeping with Elizabeth Mahler, then it would be another woman. Max couldn't be faithful. She, Rissa Lindowska, could not accept less.

Rissa enjoyed having Clara, Rae and now Katie appear at some of the performances. Joseph showed little interest in the theater. The three little girls darted back and forth backstage as though this was a second home.

Rissa sat in the dressing room with her door slightly ajar. Two of the actresses in the company were talking about the children.

'Rae and Katie are such beautiful children,' the

older actress said. 'Isn't it a pity that Clara is so plain?'

Rissa stiffened. Clara was *not* plain. She was pretty in a delicate fashion that would blossom into real beauty in a few years. Dear, sweet, vulnerable Clara. How could anyone call her plain?

'Mama – ' Clara appeared in the doorway with a brown bag from the delicatessen. *She had heard.* Rissa saw the hurt in her eyes. 'Mr Levy said he was sure you'd like the apple strudel. He said it was a present.'

'Thank you, darling.' She held out her arms to Clara. How could she make Clara understand how blind those women were?

Now Rissa began to search seriously for a house. The apartment Max had found for them held too many memories. With Shirley she traveled all over Manhattan. When she saw the graystone house on Riverside Drive in the Seventies, she knew she'd found their new home.

They spent the summer getting settled in the four-story graystone with magnificent views of the Hudson. The four small bedrooms on the top floor were assigned to the children. On the floor below, Rissa and Shirley each had a large bedroom. The parlor and a room Rissa set aside as her office occupied the floor below. At street level was the kitchen, the dining room overlooking what Rissa meant to be a beautiful garden, plus a spare bedroom.

Rissa was busy shopping for furniture, for material for the drapes and curtains that Shirley would make on her new sewing machine. Fanny took the children down to play at the edge of the river every day. On hot nights Thomas drove them far up along the Hudson, all the way to Riverdale.

In the fall Joseph went into kindergarten. Katie fumed at being left behind, though Rissa allowed her to appear in more performances at the theater than Clara and Rae, who had to be up early on weekdays to go to school.

Rissa followed the activities of Maurice Schwartz, who took over the Garden Theater when Jacob Ben Ami left him for Broadway. Rumors were circulating around Second Avenue that he was bringing the fine German-Yiddish actor Rudolph Schildkraut into the company.

She yearned to follow Schwartz in presenting 'art theater,' but each effort brought reverses. Again Tania, in the midst of an affair with a highly placed producer, begged her to consider a lead on Broadway. Tania was impatient with her devotion to Second Avenue.

Shirley continued corresponding with Max, who sent lavish birthday gifts to the children. The child-support checks went regularly into the bank. When the children were grown, Rissa promised herself, she would give the money to them.

Max had bought himself a house on Hollywood Boulevard. He sent photographs to Shirley. He still tried to persuade Rissa – through Shirley – to allow the children to come to him for the summer months, when there was no school. Rissa ignored the requests.

Shirley made a point of telling Rissa in detail about Elizabeth Mahler's latest romances, as though to vindicate Max. Mahler's pictures were huge box-office successes.

When Max's name appeared in the column now, it was not linked with romance. He was the dashing, handsome genius of Klein-Meyers Films. The man who had created Hollywood's latest star. Laura Ainsley lauded him as a 'young DeMille.'

'Rissa, you could be as fine a film actress as Elizabeth Mahler,' Shirley scolded.

'I want no part of Hollywood,' Rissa snapped at her.

'You could make pictures in New York.'

'I'd look awful,' Rissa declared. 'You don't see Tania rushing out to do pictures.'

'Tania would look awful,' Shirley said. 'She says that herself. She's a beauty on stage, but the movie cameras would kill her.'

'Shirley, please. No more about pictures.'

Rissa felt justified in her attitude toward Hollywood when early in February of 1922 the newspapers headlined the murder of movie director William Desmond Taylor. His bullet-ridden body had been found on the floor of his study.

Mabel Normand, the Mack Sennett comedy star, was known to have been with him for cocktails just before his death. Mary Miles Minter was said to have been romanced by him. Newspapers hinted that fans would be shocked at the stars – both male and female – who would be drawn into the case. Lurid details were spewed out daily.

Hollywood moguls knew the time had arrived to

protect themselves against charges of immorality. In addition to the Taylor murder they worried about the headlines on Wallace Reid's drug problems and the suicide of Jack Pickford's wife, actress Olive Thomas. Hollywood must battle against censorship. Acquire an aura of respectability.

Exactly one week after the discovery of William Desmond Taylor's body, Max received an urgent call to leave the set and come to Mort's office. He knew that only some disaster would motivate Mort to pull him off the set.

Ten minutes later he sat in a chair on one side of Mort's desk. Laura sat in a chair on the other side. Mort was pale with shock.

'Laura, what are you talking about? You can't run a story like that about Elizabeth. We've got over a million invested in the picture Max is doing with her!'

'Mort, I won't run it,' Laura soothed. 'You know I wouldn't do that to you. But somebody else is going to run it. Don't ask me who,' she put up a hand to stop him. 'I have my spies, but I can't get them in trouble. Elizabeth has been seeing this young girl. She – '

'Laura, you know Elizabeth,' Mort protested. 'What could happen with Elizabeth and a girl?'

'The same thing that happens with Elizabeth and a man,' Laura told him.

'This girl grew a penis?' Mort scoffed.

'Mort, they're lovers,' Laura insisted. 'A columnist – whose name I can't mention,' she said pointedly, 'has photographs of them. Naked and making love.'

'Oh, my God,' Mort dropped his head into his

451

hands. 'Can you imagine what the women's clubs and the churchmen will make of that? Do you know what this will cost us? We'll have to junk the picture! And there's the one that we just released! I don't feel so good,' he said weakly. 'Maybe I'm having a heart attack – '

'We don't have the time,' Max said brusquely. 'We've got to jump the gun on that whole situation. Is the girl an actress?' he turned to Laura.

'She hopes to be.'

'Okay. Give me her name. I'll have her black-balled at every studio in Hollywood. She'll get out of town fast enough.'

'That won't stop the column,' Laura warned.

'I have something in mind that will stop it.' Max was grim.

'What?' Mort was alert.

'I'm marrying Elizabeth Mahler. Laura, I want you to share the exclusive with the columnist you can't mention. Let her know if she dares to print that story about Elizabeth and the girl, we'll see to it that she's barred from every studio in Hollywood. And who'd believe it when *Photo Play* runs your story of the Mahler-Miller wedding? Elizabeth will give the performance of her life – I promise you.'

'Max, suppose Elizabeth turns you down?' Laura was ambivalent.

'She won't turn me down. I'm what holds her together.' Later they'd arrange a divorce. Right now the important thing was to stop a scandal. 'Call me tonight, Laura. At the house. You can come over and interview the happy bride and groom. Bring a photographer. I want the story on the front pages tomorrow. A "special" from Hollywood.'

Rissa knew when Shirley came into the apartment after going out as usual for the morning newspapers that something terrible had happened.

'Shirley, what is it?' Her heart pounded as Shirley walked to the dining table and sat beside her. 'Is Max all right?'

'Max is fine.' Her face was grim. She unfolded a newspaper and showed Rissa the photograph of Max and Elizabeth Mahler on the front page. 'They were married yesterday. By a judge.' Shirley grunted in distaste. '*He married a* shiksa.'

Rissa took the newspaper and placed it on the table before her. She didn't read beyond the heading: '*Hollywood Star Elizabeth Mahler Marries Producer-Director Max Miller.*' She focused her eyes on Max's photograph. It was as though the calendar had fluttered backwards fourteen and a half years and she was seeing Phillip's face on the page of a London newspaper.

'Max knew when he came here in September that he would marry her!' Rissa's voice broke. 'He only came because he wanted to see the children!'

'Rissa, darling, you made it plain you'd have no part of him,' Shirley reminded.

'He might have said something to you. He writes every month. Why did I have to see it in this way? On the front page of a newspaper!'

Max and she were divorced. In the face of his infidelities she had refused to reconcile. But deep

453

within her she had cherished a hope that someday they would come together again. Some miracle would occur, and she could bring herself to take him back. But now he was married to somebody else.

'Max should have written.' For the first time since he walked out of their lives, Shirley displayed overt hostility toward Max. 'That much he should have done.' Shirley pushed back her chair and rose to her feet. Dismissing Max from their lives with this gesture. 'I'll put up fresh tea for us. Then you'll try on the new dress from that fancy French dressmaker on Madison Avenue. I think two hooks should be moved over a quarter of an inch before you take it to the theater.'

Rissa knew that everybody at the theater had read the headlined story about Max's marriage. She was relieved that no one brought up the subject.

Within an hour after learning of Max's remarriage, she had removed his mother's wedding band from her finger and placed it on a cotton bed in the small, shell-shaped, enameled box that Max had given her for their third wedding anniversary. She prayed Max would not ask for its return.

Tania was out of town with her new play, but the following morning she phoned from Philadelphia.

'Maybe now you'll come out of the convent,' Tania said bluntly. 'How can a young, beautiful woman live like a nun? Don't tell me you don't need a man in your life. Rissa, I know you.'

'Tania, my life is too busy to worry about such

things,' Rissa lied. 'The children, the theater, the house – '

'And when you go to bed, you go alone,' Tania pounced. 'For some women that's all right. For you and me it's wrong.'

34

On an early March morning Rissa received a phone call from Lou. As always she was pleased to hear from him. He asked about the children. She inquired about his wife.

'Leah went down to Florida with her mother last week,' he reported. 'She'll be home the end of the month. I had dinner last night with my friend David Rossman and his family. He'd like to bring his grandmother down to see you play tonight. It's her seventy-sixth birthday.'

'How many seats would you like, Lou? The tickets will be waiting in your name at the box office.'

'Three would be fine, Rissa. I'd like to tag along.'

'Be sure to come backstage and see me after the performance,' Rissa said with pleasure. She had talked with Lou over the phone two weeks ago; she had not seen him since his wedding.

'David's grandmother would love that,' he said instantly. 'She said at dinner last night that she had not been down to the Yiddish theater in a dozen years.' Irony seeped into his voice. 'The family lives now on Fifth Avenue. The children prefer to take her to Broadway. But at dinner the talk turned to the Yiddish theater – ' Lou chuckled. 'I brought it up. I knew Mrs Rossman would be excited to hear that Rissa Lindowska is my friend.'

'After the performance,' Rissa decided impulsively, 'I'll take you all to the Café Royale.' Lou must know about Max's remarriage. He was too sensitive to question her. 'It'll be a small birthday party for Mrs Rossman. But don't tell her,' Rissa instructed. 'Let it be a surprise.'

When Shirley came home from shopping Rissa told her about the impromptu party.

'Ask Fanny if she can stay with the children,' Rissa added. 'If she can, then go with us to the Café Royale.'

'I'll tell her it's an important occasion.' Shirley glowed. Pleased, Rissa understood, that *she* would have a social evening. 'And after the Royale, we'll come home for tea and cake. I'll make a birthday cake,' she promised effervescently, 'that even Ratner's can't beat.'

After the performance Lou brought Mrs Rossman and her grandson back to Rissa's dressing room. Rissa loved the high-spirited old lady on sight. She had been brought to America as a little girl and lived in Charleston, South Carolina, until she married Elihu Rossman at fifteen, two months before the outbreak of the war between the states. They moved to New York, where a distant childless cousin had promised to take him into his store.

'We had no Yiddish theater in New York in the old days. There was no Yiddish theater anywhere.' Mrs Rossman nodded knowingly. 'I remember when my husband, may he rest in peace, first took me to the Bowery Garden. That must have been forty years

457

ago. And every week he took me to the Bowery Garden until we moved uptown eighteen years ago. All of a sudden my children had to see only Broadway plays,' she laughed. 'They don't know what they miss downtown.'

Rissa nodded, enjoying Mrs Rossman's enthusiasm. While she complained with others, like Adler and Schwartz and Ben Ami, about the prevalence of *schund*, there was much in the Yiddish theater of which she was proud. John Drew, Jack Barrymore, Ruth Chatterton, came downtown from Broadway to see what was happening on the Yiddish stage. Critics like George Jean Nathan and Stark Young were fascinated by the repertory system that was the lifeblood of Yiddish theater.

'Shirley, take everybody over to the Royale while I change,' Rissa ordered. 'Ask Hymie to put us at my regular table.'

The dressing room cleared, Rissa rushed to remove her makeup and change into one of her new dresses by Lucile, with the fashionable waistline that dropped to the hips. Looking at quietly handsome David Rossman, who was about her age, she understood why Lou had offered so quickly to get tickets for tonight's performance.

But how could she be angry with Lou's matchmaking? He meant well. Lou would always be her very dear friend, though she suspected that the bride was not appreciative of this friendship.

By the time Rissa arrived at the Café Royale, the evening was in full swing. She had appeared so infrequently these last five years that her arrival always created a furor. Mrs Rossman was entranced.

458

'I haven't enjoyed an evening like this since my golden wedding anniversary eleven years ago.' For a moment sadness brushed her face. 'Only a year later I was alone.'

'Grandma, only happy thoughts tonight,' David scolded.

Rissa was aware of David's shy admiration. She was pleased by his love and attentiveness to his grandmother, who shamelessly admitted that, of her seventeen grandchildren, David was her favorite.

'He's so smart,' Mrs Rossman effervesced when the ordering was completed and they were free to talk again. 'Young as he is, already he's vice-president of the stores.' Only now did Rissa realize that Mrs Rossman and her grandson were part of the wealthy Rossman mercantile family.

Rissa was conscious that David's eyes lingered regularly on her while Mrs Rossman reminisced aloud.

'I remember,' she said with an air of imparting a great secret, 'when many Orthodox Jews wanted to run the Yiddish theater out of business. They said it was shameful. But that didn't stop the actors. I remember Boris Thomashefsky playing when he was no more than sixteen.' She reached to cover Rissa's hand with hers. 'And when – I think it was 1884 – the Russian-Jewish Opera Company arrived, I was in heaven.'

After everyone had finished off the Royale's superb chicken *paprikash* and glasses of tea, Rissa announced they would go to the house for dessert. It pleased her that Mrs Rossman found such delight in the evening.

The birthday cake was a huge success. Tears filled Mrs Rossman's eyes. 'Rissa, you are a beautiful lady,' she declared. 'Inside and out.'

When her guests left, Rissa was conscious of an emptiness in the house. For a while she had been able to put aside the recurrent pain that had become part of her life since she learned of Max's remarriage.

She went out into the kitchen to help Shirley with the dishes. Fanny had gone home. The children were asleep upstairs.

'He liked you,' Shirley said smugly. 'He couldn't keep his eyes off you.'

'Shirley,' Rissa reproached. 'I'm a divorced woman with four children. He was just fascinated by the actress. Tomorrow he'll forget he ever saw me.'

But at eleven the next morning David Rossman called her. He asked to take her out to supper after the performance.

'I must thank you in person for making last night such a wonderful evening for my grandmother.' He paused. 'And for me. May I pick you up after the theater tonight?'

'All right,' she said after a moment. She slept so badly these nights. Maybe having supper with David would relax her.

All at once Rissa was seeing David every night. He was warm and intelligent and wonderful company. She was astonished when she realized how she looked

460

forward to their evenings together. David made her laugh. How long it had been since she had laughed.

He filched days away from his office to drive her up into the country, careful always to bring her back to the city in time for the night's performance. She remembered day trips into the English countryside with Phillip, and later the trips with Max. She had been a girl then. Now she was a woman.

Then she became aware of a new urgency in David. She was conscious of her own response. She told herself that she must stop seeing David. Already he was hinting at marriage. But in the eyes of the rabbi, Max and she were still married.

She spent endless hours of torment, exhorting herself to stop seeing David. Yet the thought of not seeing him was unbearable. She knew the time was coming when soft good-night kisses in the shadowed hall of the apartment would not be sufficient for them. David was a passionate man.

She tried not to think about Max and his new wife. But Hollywood was constantly in the news. An evil, depraved city, according to many angry voices. With the William Desmond Taylor murder still unsolved, fresh scandal hit the headlines. After a drunken brawl in San Francisco, where a young actress named Virginia Rappe died, Fatty Arbuckle was arrested and charged with rape and murder.

Max resumed writing to Shirley at regular intervals. She was his lifeline to the children. He mentioned his marriage briefly. 'A marriage for business reason,' he wrote. He pleaded – futilely – with Shirley to persuade Rissa to allow her to bring the children out to spend the summer with him.

'I know Rissa thinks Hollywood is a terrible place. That's untrue. Terrible things happen in New York, too; but New York doesn't exist in a constant spotlight like Hollywood. I promise you, the children will have two wonderful months out here, *in your care*. How could anything bad happen to them?'

It surprised Rissa when David condemned those who labeled Hollywood immoral. Who insisted films were immoral. Clear-headed and impartial he pointed out the fine comics who brightened the movies with clean fun. Charlie Chaplin, Harold Lloyd, Charles Ray, Buster Keaton. Rissa recalled that Joseph and Katie clamored to see every movie with these comedians. Katie brought laughter in the house with her imitations of Chaplin and Keaton.

At Shirley's insistence she invited David to the apartment for a festive dinner with the chidren. She was touched by his tender attentions to her family. Katie did her imitations for him. Clara played the piano while the other three sang 'Raisins and Almonds.'

She remembered how Max said he had learned to be a Jew on the lower East side. In Belleville, Georgia, he knew he was a Jew when he stayed out of school on Yom Kippur and Rosh Hashanah, when his mother lighted candles on Friday nights, and when they celebrated Purim and Hanukkah. The rest of the days of the year he was a Georgian.

She suspected that David's Jewishness was similar to Max's before he came to New York. David's

462

parents stressed that they were Americans first of all. They took their children to Temple Emanu-El on the high holidays. They contributed heavily to both Jewish and Christian charities, and took covert pride in the number of illustrious Jews in history.

It was Grandma Rossman who made David aware of being a Jew. She took personal pride in the statement by President Taft, when he was in office, that philanthropist Nathan Straus was 'a great Jew and the greatest Christian of us all.' Rissa watched David's face when the children sang the Yiddish folk songs Shirley and she had taught them. He had the look of a man who had come home.

On a late May morning of her day away from the theater, David appeared unexpectedly at the house and suggested that they drive out to the family house in Southampton.

'The house won't be opened up until sometime in June, but we could have a magnificent day out there. It's directly on the beach. This time of year nobody will be there but the gulls and us.' David's face was alight with anticipation. 'We'll take along a picnic basket and dine on the porch. Blue sky, blue ocean, white beach.'

Rissa hesitated. She loved the ocean. But her mind would not let her forget the nights when Max and she had walked along the beach at Brighton. When she had been so sure they would be together forever.

'What about your office?' Rissa hedged. 'Don't you have to be there?'

'I'm presumably away on business all day.' His

smile was warm. 'One of the privileges of being a boss.'

'Is it a long drive?' she hedged. It was absurd to feel self-conscious at spending a day at a house in Southampton alone with David. She wasn't a young girl who must be chaperoned. 'Will we get back to the city awfully late?'

'Does it matter?' David challenged. 'You don't have to be at the theater tonight.' He reached for her hand and brought it to his lips. 'I promise you, my intentions are honorable,' he teased. 'At the first sign that you won't run, I mean to ask you to marry me.'

'David – ' All at once her heart was pounding.

'I know,' he said swiftly. 'You're not ready yet. But I wanted you to know.'

'I'd love to go with you to Southampton,' she capitulated. 'What shall I ask Shirley to prepare for us?'

'Everything is on the back seat of the car,' he admitted. 'Packed in ice. Bring a warm coat. It might be cold along the beach.'

Five hours later they sat on the porch of the rambling white frame house and ate the gourmet picnic meal David had assembled. Rissa was entranced by the seascape that sprawled before them. Beneath a perfect blue sky the water glistened in the sunlight, moving toward the shore in mesmerizing surges. The only sounds were the pounding of the waves against the sand and the occasional caw of a gull.

Rissa's eyes swept up and down the beach. David was right. The beach was deserted this time of the year except for the gulls. David broke up chunks of bread and tossed the bits onto the steps that led to the porch. The first brave gulls were already approaching.

'I always bring along a loaf of bread to feed them. Watch!' he ordered and tossed a wedge of bread into the air. A gull lifted himself with magical grace to catch the treat.

'Let me,' Rissa coaxed, feeling very young and carefree. Such beautiful quietness here. Such peace. The day was so warm that in a few moments she discarded the jacket of her casual suit.

The gulls swooped in like an invading army. Rissa and David devoted themselves to tearing the bread into pieces small enough to be devoured by their appreciative guests. Making sure the timid were not cheated of their share.

'Let's walk,' David said. He rose to his feet and extended a hand to Rissa. She picked up her jacket and draped it about her shoulders.

They strolled over the sun-warmed sand, caught up in the splendor of sea and sky and beach. At intervals Rissa paused to collect a few special shells, stuffed them into her jacket pocket to take home to the children.

David halted and pointed to indentations in the sand. 'See those marks?' He inspected the tracks of the gulls that crisscrossed the beach. 'Don't they look like strange hieroglyphics?'

'They're sending out a message,' Rissa said exuberantly. 'Southampton is wonderful! Southampton is wonderful!'

David scrutinized the sky. All at once the sun had scampered behind deepening clusters of gray.

'Look at those clouds. It's going to pour any minute. Let's head back.'

Lightning darted across the grayness above. Clutching hands they raced toward the house. By the time they reached the porch, rain was pelting the beach.

Rissa lifted her face to David's while they stood arm in arm on the porch.

'Oh, it's beautiful. I've never seen a storm over the ocean.' She washed from her mind truant memories of a downpour she had watched with Max on the porch of the rented cottage at Brighton.

'Come sit down.' David drew her beside him on the wicker swing.

They sat in cozy silence while Nature presented her dramatic show in the sky. A chill wind swept in from the ocean now. Rissa reached to pull on her jacket. David dropped an arm about her shoulders. Then all at once the rain slanted onto the porch, driving a salt spray against their faces.

'Oooh!' Rissa laughed in reproach.

'We'd better go into the house. I don't want you catching cold.' David's voice was a caress.

Rissa and David went into the high-ceilinged parlor, which was almost the width of the house. Cut-up sections of white birch logs were piled high at one side of the marble-faced fireplace. David drew old newspapers from a box at the other side, reached for a match from a holder above the mantel. Rissa watched while he focused on building a fire in the grate.

In minutes a crackling blaze created a toasty warmth in the parlor. The pungent scent of birch permeated the room. Outside the storm raged in mock fury. David collected brightly colored pillows from about the room and improvised a couch before the fireplace.

Rissa dropped to the pile of pillows and held her hands toward the burning logs.

'David, this is wonderful.'

He reached to pull her close.

'You're wonderful.'

'David – ' For a moment she was uncertain. Then his mouth claimed hers, and the world ebbed away.

While the rain lashed at the windows of the house and the logs crackled in the fireplace, David made love to her. It had been so long since she had been held this way, touched this way. Her body responded in the familiar manner that she once had feared was wanton.

All at once she was here alone in a beach house with Max. It was Max holding her. Max making love to her. She closed her eyes in joy. Her body welcoming the weight of him above her. Eager to receive him.

She responded with a passion that matched David's. With an abandon that startled yet delighted her. They touched and kissed and touched again. And soon David – *Max* – was filling the emptiness of her yet again.

'Rissa,' he whispered while they clung together, 'I knew it would be like this for us.'

467

35

David's courtship grew in intensity. Rissa waited for the nights when they could be alone together in the privacy of the little room beyond the parlor. In David's arms she could forget that Max had married Elizabeth Mahler and was forever out of her life. She enjoyed David's companionship, his eagerness to bring a smile to her face.

The first night that David came to take her to dinner with his family, Rissa was nervous. She was conscious of the significance of this meeting. Her hand in David's, she approached the house in trepidation.

The exterior of the cream brick structure was deceptively unpretentious. But the moment a uniformed maid ushered them into the wide foyer, illuminated by a chandelier from Louis Comfort Tiffany, its marble floor covered by a priceless oriental rug, Rissa recognized that she was in the presence of great wealth.

David's mother and father were gracious, though Rissa sensed that they were not entirely at ease. Were they disturbed that David was about to marry 'beneath him'? His two unmarried sisters were polite but curious. She was conscious of their covert admiration for her Lanvin dinner dress. To David's sisters, Rissa thought with a touch of humor, an actress from Second Avenue was something of an exotic.

Sitting in the elegant family dining room at a perfectly appointed table, Rissa was grateful for the warmth of the elder Mrs Rossman. Here was a demonstrative love for family that was an echo of Rissa's childhood. But with David's mother and sisters she felt faintly uneasy. They spent their days engaged in charitable affairs, their evenings in social functions that hinted at culture. They talked about the performances at the Metropolitan Opera, the latest paintings acquired by the Metropolitan Museum, the decorating decrees of Elsie deWolfe.

David's mother talked about the imminent departure of the Rossman women for the Southampton house. From the questioning glances the younger Mrs Rossman cast at David, Rissa suspected she was trying to decide whether it would be appropriate to invite Rissa to visit the Southampton house during the summer. She didn't know Rissa had already been a guest in their beach house. She decided against extending an invitation tonight.

Three days later David reported that his mother, grandmother and unmarried sisters had gone off to Southampton where they would remain until mid-September. Mr Rossman was scheduled to spend alternate long weekends at the beach house.

So that his father would feel less alone, David decided that Rissa and he would take Friday night dinners with him on those weekends when he remained in the city. This was a signal, too, that the family must consider his courtship of Rissa seriously.

Tonight David called for Rissa to take her for their first dinner alone with his father.

'We'll go out to spend a week with the family in August,' David said when they were in the car en route to the Fifth Avenue house.

'A whole week?' Rissa stammered, though the prospect of seven days at Southampton was enticing. 'David, I don't know that I should leave the children alone that long!'

David laughed. 'Rissa, they won't be alone. They'll be with Shirley.' His hand left the wheel to cover hers for a moment. 'Maybe at Southampton we can tell the family when we mean to be married. They're bursting with impatience.' David laughed. 'Like me.'

'We'll tell them at Southampton in August,' Rissa agreed, and David squeezed her hand before returning his to the wheel.

Mr Rossman, David and Rissa sat down to dinner in the dining room, where a recently installed ceiling fan alleviated the summer heat. A slight breeze drifted in from Central Park through the tall narrow windows. The servants moved noiselessly in and out of the room, serving a gourmet meal.

Rissa spoke little. She knew that Mr Rossman suspected David and she would soon announce their marriage date. The message shone from David. Tonight Mr Rossman seemed elated at the prospect – even though David was about to marry an actress from the Yiddish theater.

When dessert was served and the maid had left the dining room, Mr Rossman looked from David to Rissa with the air of a man about to make a momentous pronouncement.

'I've given serious thought for a long time to a new

470

business move,' he confided. 'A big store – like the one here in New York – for Cleveland. The possibilities in Cleveland are tremendous.' His eyes rested with pride and affection on David. 'And you'll be president of the Cleveland store, David. It'll be your baby.'

'Have you talked to the real estate people in Cleveland?' David asked. Rissa felt his inner excitement. 'Location is important.'

While David and his father talked avidly about the new store, Rissa fought against panic. *Mr Rossman meant the Cleveland store to be a wedding present. He meant for David and her to live in Cleveland.*

Didn't David realize that was impossible for her? She had her theater here in New York. What would she do in Cleveland? That was a place where actors went who could not yet join the union. A star might appear there for a performance or two.

Rissa sat in silence, her throat constricted, when they retired to the parlor. Her mind in chaos, she listened to Mr Rossman and David discuss plans for the new store. *No one asked her if she wished to live in Cleveland.*

She had taken it for granted that they would live in New York. David would move into the house on Riverside Drive. Shirley was already dropping hints about moving into the spare bedroom on the street-level floor so that the third floor could be for David and her.

As soon as it was polite to leave, David told his father that he would drive Rissa home. The atmosphere was electric with Rissa's acceptance into the Rossman family.

In the car Rissa listened while David reminisced about the founding of the Rossman stores. The first store that Elihu Rossman owned was opened in 1883. Eleven years later he bought into a store in Brooklyn, which he eventually took over. Now Rossman, Inc., owned six stores across the country, each in the hands of a Rossman brother or son.

Merchandising was in David's blood, the way theater was in hers. But David thought nothing of asking her to give up the theater so that he might open a new store in Cleveland. The way Max had meant for her to give up everything she had achieved to go out to Hollywood with him on a gamble.

How could she give up the Lindowska Theater? A living memorial to mama and papa. To grandpa and the children. Someday Clara and Rae and Katie would star in the Lindowska Theater, carrying on the Lindowska name to another generation. The theater must be there for them. For their children.

David parked before the Riverside Drive house. Rissa and he went inside and upstairs to the parlor. Rissa knew David's ritual by now. He liked a glass of wine with her before they went into their little sanctuary. But tonight David and she must talk.

While Rissa poured wine into two long-stemmed glasses, David settled himself on the sofa. He talked about Lou and his wife, who were expecting their first child. Lou was ecstatic at the prospect of becoming a parent.

'Lou even worried about Leah taking the long train trip to Florida,' he chuckled. 'The baby isn't due until January.' He took a glass from Rissa and pulled her down beside him. 'I don't suppose I'll be much different from Lou.'

David meant for them to have children. How could she have expected anything else? But the doctor told her she must never have another child. With four other children to raise, how could she gamble her life on a fifth? What kind of insane dream world had she been living in all these weeks?

'David, I – there's something I have to tell you – ' All at once she was trembling.

David put down his glass of wine.

'Rissa, why are you so upset?'

'David, I should have told you before – ' She struggled to keep her voice even. 'I won't ever be able to give you a child. The doctor warned me after Katie was born. No more children.'

David was silent for a moment. This was a blow.

'We have four children.' He was trying to be philosophical, but Rissa knew this was not easy for him to accept. 'A ready-made family. Why should we be greedy?'

'And I can't move to Cleveland.' Her hands were perspiring now. 'I have my theater here – '

'We'll find a manager who'll be happy to take over,' he soothed. 'It's a gold mine.'

'David, you don't understand – ' For a little while she had behaved like sixteen. She had allowed David to sweep her along with him into a play world. Now reality intruded.

'We won't stay in Cleveland for more than three or four years,' he promised. 'Just long enough for me to put the new store on a firm foundation. Train a responsible staff. I'll go out to Cleveland three or four times a year then, to check everything out. We'll come back to New York. Find a house of our own near the family.'

'David, I'm an actress.' Why must a wife's needs always take second place? 'For half of my life I've been an actress.'

'Rissa, you won't miss the theater. I promise you. Mama will bring you into all of her charities. There'll be dinner parties, balls, nights at the opera and the theater. If you like, we'll build a house for ourselves and the children out at Southampton for the summer. You'll find yourself just as busy as you were in the theater.' He reached to draw her into his arms. Oblivious of her inner turmoil.

'David, I can't marry you.' She pulled away from him and rose to her feet. 'I can't be the wife you expect me to be. I can't fit into the mold.'

'Rissa –' He leaped to his feet in shock.

'David, the life you plan for us would never work for me. I'll always be Rissa Lindowska, actress. The theater is my life. I can't give you children. I can't play the part of a society wife. I'd loathe it. David, we don't fit together.'

'We'll talk tomorrow,' David said. 'You're tired now. We threw too much at you at one time.'

'I'll miss you,' she admitted. 'I'll miss you desperately. But I can't make myself over into a Rossman wife. I don't *wish* to do that. You'll find someone else, David.'

'I don't believe this is happening.' David was distraught. 'Rissa –'

'Better now than later,' she stopped him. 'David, let's be honest with each other. We had something beautiful for a little while. But we don't want the same things. I can't live your way of life. You can't live mine. We'll both hurt for a while. But believe me, this is right.'

'We'll talk tomorrow,' he tried again.

'No,' Rissa said with finality. 'We've said all that needs to be said.' She reached up to kiss him on the cheek. 'Good-bye, David.'

Rissa waited until she heard the front door close behind David. Now she climbed the stairs to her room. Knowing she would not sleep tonight. No light showed beneath Shirley's door. She was relieved that Shirley had gone to bed early. Tomorrow they would talk.

She lay in the darkness remembering these last weeks with David. She had been running from Max. From images of Max and his new wife that taunted her awake and sleeping. She had known when she stood under the *hupah* with Max that she would never love another man.

But she would survive. She had the children and the theater. They would be her life. Someday, she promised herself with fierce pride, she would play on the stage of the Lindowska Theater with her grandchildren.

At last Rissa fell into nightmare-filled sleep. She awoke to a sultry morning. Her head pounded. The sheet beneath her felt dank from perspiration. She had kicked off the top sheet during the night. No breeze from the Hudson relieved the heat wave that engulfed the city.

Her eyes sought the clock. It was early. She had slept hardly three hours. The house was quiet. But Shirley would be downstairs in the kitchen. Even now Shirley awoke religiously at 6:00 A.M.

Rissa rose from the bed, slid her feet into her slippers and reached for the kimono at the foot of the bed. Shirley would be so upset that she wasn't marrying David.

Outside her door she listened for sounds from the floor above. The children all slept. In this heat they would sleep late. Shirley would have a pot of tea brewing by now. Joseph always teased her about drinking hot tea even when everybody complained about the hot weather.

'Why are you up so early?' Shirley scolded, going for another cup and saucer.

'I couldn't sleep.'

Rissa geared herself for what must be said. Shirley listened in troubled silence.

'Rissa, darling – ' Tears filled Shirley's eyes.

'Shirley, I'm all right,' she insisted. 'But I'd like you to take the children for a picnic for the day. Ask Thomas to drive you. I need to be alone.'

'I'll take them to the beach,' Shirley decided. 'They love the water.'

'Perhaps we can rent a house at Long Branch for August,' Rissa said. 'I know it's late, but we'll try to find something. The children will like that.'

'Rissa, you're sure about David?'

'I'm sure.'

476

Rissa forced a smile. Even if everything else had been right, it would have been wrong to marry David when she still loved Max.

Rissa roamed about the empty house. Max had never been in this house, yet his presence was everywhere. She went up to her bedroom. In the top drawer of her dresser lay the enamel box that held her wedding ring. She brought out the box, lifted the lid and picked up the simple gold band. She slipped it onto her finger again. Visualizing Max performing this act.

Max was married to Elizabeth Mahler in the eyes of the world. Before God he was still married to her. The wedding band would not leave her finger again. As Max would never leave her heart.

The day grew hot and sultry. Rissa was restless. Today the house was a prison. She would go for a walk. A long walk. She remembered Max's passion for walking about the city when he was troubled.

She left the house and headed uptown. Walking with compulsive swiftness despite the heat. Walking without direction. Seeing no one. Hearing nothing.

A car screeching to a stop that brought expletives from pedestrians pulled Rissa back to the moment. She was on Broadway. In front of the impressive new Capitol Theater. Her eyes moved to the marquee. The Capitol was showing Elizabeth Mahler's latest picture. A line of people waited to buy tickets.

Almost involuntarily Rissa joined the line. Sure that no one in the ticket line at the Capitol Theater would recognize her. But the middle-aged woman before her, restless at the wait, turned around to talk to Rissa.

'I hope you don't mind me saying it,' she said after a casual exchange about the weather, 'but you look a lot like Rissa Lindowska.' Rissa froze. 'You wouldn't know her,' the woman smiled. 'She's a star down on Second Avenue. A wonderful actress. Older than you,' she surmised. 'But you could pass for her sister.'

The line was moving now. Rissa reached into her purse for money. But with the ticket in her hand at last she felt a touch of panic. Why was she going into the Capitol Theater to see a picture starring Max's wife?

As though sleepwalking Rissa moved with the others into the lush darkness of the huge picture palace. She walked down a carpeted aisle and took an end seat, as though prepared to run if this experience became more than she could endure. Her heart was pounding. She was oblivious of the others crowding into the seats around her. Unaware of the air of anticipation that pervaded the theater.

The theater went black. The film credits appeared on the screen:

A Klein-Meyers Production

Rissa leaned forward in her seat as though this movement brought her closer to Max.

Produced by Morton Klein and Max Miller

Max had been right about the future of films. But how could she have known? How could she have

478

gambled on the children's security. How could she have abandoned what she was building up in the Yiddish theater? Her memorial to mama and the family.

Directed by Max Miller

A deep excitement took root in her as the film was flashed on the screen. She watched Elizabeth Mahler, but it was the Max Miller touches that claimed her attention. The performers were voiceless, yet their faces, their gestures, conveyed their emotions with consummate artistry.

She could hear Max complaining about the direction of Sarah Bernhardt in the movie of *Queen Elizabeth* after they'd seen the film at the Lyceum Theater. '*What was the matter with the director? Her gestures are fine for the stage. They're too exaggerated for the camera.*

Max worked with Elizabeth Mahler as he had worked with her. Max was proving himself one of the great directors.

Rissa felt herself alone with Max in this magnificent new temple to moving pictures. Unconsciously the fingers of her right hand sought the wedding band on her left hand.

When at last the film was over, she waited in the darkness until most of the appreciative audience had filed out. Her mind was clear and sharp now. She had lost Max, but she would survive. She had the children, and she had her theater. She was fulfilling the promise she had made to herself over mama's body. The world would continue to know and respect the Lindowska name. Her life would be full.

But Rissa knew that, through the years ahead, there would be private intervals in the darkness of a movie palace when she would live again with the Max she used to know. For a precious parcel of time she would feel again that she was Max's wife. In the eyes of God, she told herself as she rose from her seat to join the dwindling audience, she was Max's wife. In her heart she would always be Max's wife.